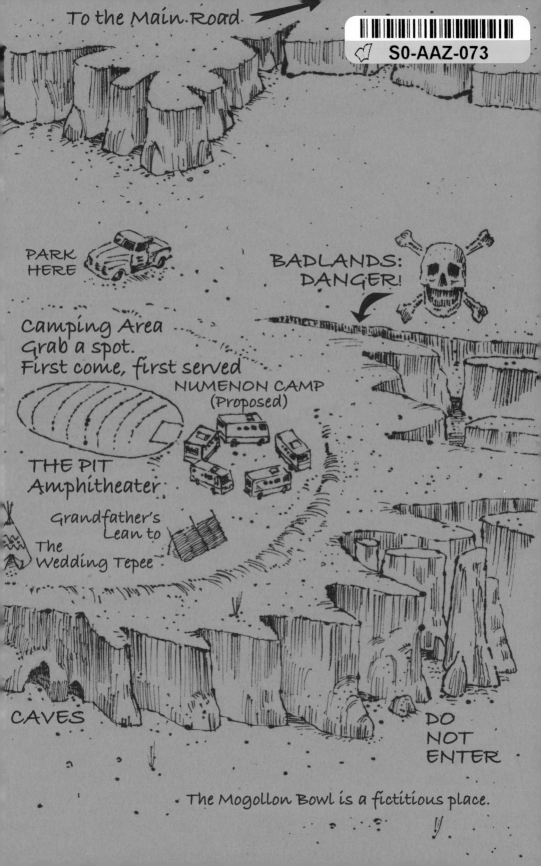

NATIONAL AWARD WINNER!

NUMENON won:

THE INDIE EXCELLENCE AWARD for RELIGIOUS FICTION
THE BEST BOOKS AWARD for VISIONARY FICTION (USA Book News)

NUMENON

ALSO BY SANDY NATHAN:

Stepping Off the Edge: Learning & Living Spiritual Practice

A TALE OF MYSTICISM & MONEY

NUMENON

Sandy Nathan
6/1/08

THE BLOODSONG SERIES I

SANDY NATHAN

VILASA
PRESS

SANTA YNEZ, CA

Publisher's Cataloguing-in-Publication information

Nathan, Sandy.

    Numenon / Sandy Nathan. —Santa Ynez, CA : Vilasa Press, 2008.

       p. ; cm.
       (Bloodsong series ; 1)

       ISBN: 978-0-9762809-2-7 (cloth) ; 978-0-9762809-4-1 (pbk.)
       "A tale of mysticism & money."—Cover.

         1. Spiritual life—Fiction. 2. Technology—Social aspects—Fiction.
     3. Indians of North America—Fiction. 4. Shamanism—Fiction.
     5. New Mexico—Fiction. I. Title.

PS3614.A843 N86 2008   2007922652
813.6—dc22   0804

Book consultant: Ellen Reid
Editor: Leonard Tourney, PhD
Cover design: Patricia Bacall
Interior design: Ghislain Viau
Numenon logo, author photo, galley cover design: Zoë Nathan

Peace ... comes within the souls of people
when they realize
their relationship,
their oneness,
with the universe and all its powers,
and when they realize that
at the center of the Universe
dwells Wakan-tanka,
and that this center is everywhere,
it is within each of us.
This is the real peace ...

Black Elk, Oglala Lakota

To the Great One that pervades all creation—
I offer this work as a prayer.

AUTHOR'S NOTE

This is the first book of The Bloodsong Series. This series emerged from one of the most challenging periods of my life. After two years that demanded that I use all my spiritual, emotional, and intellectual skills to survive, I went on a meditation retreat in 1995. I worked and prayed and studied, doing everything I could to imbibe the essence of the retreat. It worked. I left feeling renewed and ready to begin again.

A few days after getting home, I had a miraculous experience in which the plot of *something* was injected in my brain. Zap! It was like a lightning bolt hit me on the right temple and continued through my skull. Nothing like that had happened to me before; I didn't know such a thing *could* happen.

I dashed to my computer and began to write down what that Zap! contained. Two hundred and seventy-five pages later, I realized I had a book. As I continued, I realized it was a series. Writing more, I found it was two series. I wrote for nine years, completing drafts for nine books. This is the first book of the Bloodsong Series. I hope you like it—the series unfolds like a roller coaster. *Numenon* is the initial climb and plunge.

Please be aware of this: My first book, *Stepping Off the Edge: Learning & Living Spiritual Practice,* is an intensely spiritual book. It packs a wallop. I'd give it a G rating if it were a movie. *Numenon* is an intensely spiritual book that would probably get an R. It contains strong language, sexual content, and other stuff you can see on daytime TV. If you liked *Stepping Off the Edge*, be aware that *Numenon* is *different*.

Having said that, let's get on to the confessional/gratitudinal/ let's-get-it-straight portion of this note. *Numenon* is a novel. A novel is *fiction* by definition. The word *fiction* has many meanings, all of them hinging on the unreal, untrue, and imaginary quality of whatever's been labeled fiction.

You may read the description of the caravan moving across the desert in New Mexico and think, that's more like Arizona's Painted Desert. Doesn't she know that? Yes, I do. And I know that the Mogollon Rim in is in Arizona. That's not the Rim to which I refer in the novel. Also, you may envision the Numenon party going east from Tucson into New Mexico and think, where's Lordsburg? And Silver City? Are they going to stay at the terrific bed and breakfast in Mogollon, the ghost town those folks are revitalizing? Why does she make the desert *flat*? The Mogollon Mountains are *mountains*; they're in the middle of a major *mountainous* wilderness. And there isn't any Mogollon Bowl. Plus, where's the rock band, *Mogollon*? Is she going to ignore it?

Readers—I have taken liberties with the State of New Mexico, carving and sculpting, moving masses of rock and dirt to suit my whim. That's the glory of fiction. I also ignore certain of the state's cities, ghost towns, and residents. Though there is a Mogollon Bowl. They're building it in Las Cruces. It will have ninety-five lanes. A whopper.

No. That's a *lie*, which is loosely related to fiction.

Messing with states and even universes is my prerogative as an author. I do apologize to you, New Mexicans, for any hurt feelings. If you're mad at me, wait until you see what I do to California and Oregon in the sequels to *Numenon*.

There's more: The character *Grandfather* is a fictitious character. I made him up. He does not represent or portray any living or historical Native shaman or holy man or woman of any tradition. What he says and teaches, his people and their practices, what happens at the Meeting, and the Meeting itself—all of it is made up.

This must be clearly understood. American Indians have had their religion stolen from them, their spiritual beliefs and experiences misinterpreted, and their spiritual leaders killed and discredited by European-based society from the minute we came in contact with them.

I didn't want to make the situation worse, so I set a few rules for myself. I don't write about American Indian ceremonies unless they're something that *everyone* has heard about, like the sweat lodge. You've heard of this, yes? With the exception of the quote from Black Elk earlier and use of the word *Cherokee*, I don't mention the Sovereign Nations to which Native characters belong. This immediately brands my work as fiction, since the People always refer to themselves by Nation or Band.

Omitting tribal names obscures the multifaceted nature of Indian cultures. I think it's a necessary omission when non-Natives write about Native life. We blithely name sports teams and products after American Indians' tribal identities. Why don't we do this to other ethnicities? Why don't we sell a nifty SUV called the WASP? Why not a cool off road vehicle named the Polack?

When I started reading about American Indians as I researched this book, I smacked myself on the forehead and said, "Holy macaroni! It will take the rest of my life to get this right." Indigenous cultures are that deep and beautiful; a lifetime would be required to adequately portray them. But these books were banging around inside my skull, demanding to get out. I had to write them. So I adopted the rules above.

Part of it is that I'm sixty-two years old. I feel the pressure of time and the reality of death. Life does that to you if you stay awake at the wheel. The pressure to write these stories was so strong that I felt that I would die if I didn't write them. So I wrote, trying to portray my characters' humanity as accurately as I could.

There's more. Although Grandfather is fictitious, I owe my meditation masters, Swami Muktananda and Swami Chidvilasananda, a debt of gratitude for their inspiration. The experiences I have had with them and their path of spiritual study (or discipline) and meditation, the Siddha Yoga Path, continue to be invaluable.

Nevertheless, this book is my creation, springing from my experiences, spiritual life and imagination. Some of the scenes in this book that seem fantastic are, in fact, write-ups of my spiritual and meditation experiences.

While this story emerged from my heart and brain and I claim responsibility for it, I hope that my readers will feel the unseen power that imparted it to me.

And finally, what about Numenon, the corporate leviathan whose name adorns this tome? Is it the same as the Noumenon Corporation? No. For one thing, they're spelled differently. Also, *which* Noumenon Corporation? I found a bunch. One's Web site shows it registered in Decatur, Georgia; another (manufacturing fuel oils) is located in Morgantown, West Virginia; and still another is a software developer in Alameda, California. And then there's Noumenon Records, Noumenon Press, and a CD called *Noumenon* by the rock group, Absurd Minds.

The word *noumenon* is a concept from philosophy. As such, it is nonproprietary. I used a lesser-known spelling and created my Numenon Corporation. If a corporation with that name exists, it's not the one written about here. My Numenon would be headquartered in Palo Alto, California, the heart of the technological gold rush. I'd slap the international headquarters on a fictitious hunk of land in the heights of Page Mill Road.

And Will Duane, Doug, and the rest of the Numenon crew (or any of Grandfather's people)—what if you're *sure* that I'm writing about you as I describe their nasty bits?

The corporate side of *Numenon* is just as fictitious as the Native side. A corporation like Numenon has never existed, and a CEO like Will Duane has never walked the earth. And, in all probability, I don't know you. So you can relax. I'm not writing about you.

The thing about humans is: While our angels sing with myriad voices, our dirty socks smell the same. If this book cuts close to the core, that's because we're all the same inside. In my view, the differences between people revolve around which parts of ourselves we use most and the targets we aim to hit.

This author's note is about viveka. Viveka is a Sanskrit world meaning "discrimination." Not discrimination in the nasty sense of racial discrimination, but discrimination meaning you can tell what's good for you from what's not, and what's real from what's fictitious. Viveka is about learning to distinguish reality from the delusion that we create in our minds. "Why don't they clean up the mess that's inside?" said Professor Higgins in *My Fair Lady*. Cleaning up the mess inside is what I'm doing here.

Happy trails,

SN

1

He darted across the lawn, fleeing along the lake's shore. Treetops lashed the sky and leaves tumbled past him. Looking over his shoulder, he saw the towers of his home stark against the thunderheads. Something was after him. He couldn't see it, but knew it wanted to destroy him.

He felt the wind blowing off the lake the way it did when he was a child. The piercing cold left him shivering and weak. He heard his father's voice, bellowing from within their stone mansion.

Then he was inside, moving through the great hall. Gothic arches admitted slashes of light. People and things seemed to pop into existence out of the shadows. "Hello, Master Will," a servant fawned. "Good show on winning the championship!" Win more! Win more!

He ran along the lakefront, his soul tossed like the treetops. Something was trying to get him. He dodged this way and that, searching for a way out. Tears stung his eyes and his legs ached.

Will sat up in bed, heart pounding, sweat running down his cheeks. He looked around frantically, before realizing it had been one of his ... Had

anyone seen him like that? His eyes searched the room until he was satisfied that he was alone.

He didn't try to go back to sleep. Will got up and put on his jogging
clothes. He would run in the gym until he was so exhausted that the nightmare couldn't return. As he left his room, he glanced at the book by his bed.
He seldom read psychology. He thought it was self-indulgent twaddle. But
someone had written a book supported by decent research, a book that gave
him answers.

People called him a genius. The label didn't matter to him, but he knew
it was true. Only a genius could do what he had done. That book explained
the rest of it: The flashes of insight, the vision of what life could be, and the
drive to create it formed the sunny side of his brilliance. The nightmares and
horrors were its other side, the negative perks that came with his gifts.

Will snorted bitterly. His dark side was as big as the light. He made his
way to the gym on the lower level of his home. The house was shuttered for
the night. Bulletproof metal shades covered every window. He placed his
palm on the sensor by the elevator. The door opened.

"Is that you, Mr. Duane?" A voice came from a speaker. An operative.

"Yes. The sun will rise again." He carefully enunciated that night's
passwords for the voice recognition system. He knew he had been moni-
tored from the moment he stepped outside his bedroom. "No surveillance
while I'm running," he ordered.

Lights went on when he entered the gym, rippling across the equip-
ment-filled expanse like the surf rolling across a rocky beach. The house's
lower level was dug into the hillside to allow it a larger footprint than the
fifteen thousand square foot residence above. Every conceivable training
device found its place on the floor. An indoor track circled the workout
area. Handball courts were beyond the far wall; outside, past steel-clad windows, the pool awaited.

Will was a runner. He didn't warm up; simply launched himself onto
the track. He'd run until the sound of rough breathing, the smell of his
father's cigars, his gravely voice, and the revulsion at what happened disappeared. He'd run until his chest ached and he couldn't think. If he were
lucky, the joy that came from running would set him free. His legs moved

easily as he began. His breathing expanded and became rhythmic. He'd hit a groove in a few minutes. Until then, his mind roamed.

He'd had the nightmares as long as he could remember. He thought of them as spells. He had no idea what anyone else would call them. Once past childhood, he'd never told anyone about them. They were deeper than dreams. Sometimes he'd come out of one to find that the world seemed dangerous and unreal. He had a hard time shaking the feeling.

They all began the same way. The world became silent and empty, a colorless, foreign landscape. He could feel the malice behind everything. And then he was running along the North Shore of Lake Michigan where he had been raised. His father bought a mansion built by one of the old robber barons the moment he could afford it. He manufactured a family tree to go with his new wealth. Will scowled. They were not American royalty. They did not have a fancy pedigree. Will hated pretense. He'd seen enough.

He could recall the whiskey-roughened voices in the library when his father and his friends played poker. Cigar smoke penetrated the walls. They joked about fancy women and what they'd do with them later. His mother was in the house, awake. How could his father talk about that with her there? They spoke of Micks and WOPs and kikes. These were good Christians who praised Jesus on Christmas Day and screwed anyone they could the rest of the time. They got country clubs, while their workers got union busters and substandard wages.

During the day, he was the perfect son. But in his sleep, he found himself running along the lake. As a child, the nightmare came almost every night. A river of darkness sucked him down. The evil in that darkness was so absolute that no terror could express it. He fought the murk and filth as something toyed with him, a malignant something that hid behind the opacity of daytime life. If he made a mistake, it would capture him. He would have to crawl for it forever, doing its will.

He'd awaken, screaming and sobbing. His mother would come.

"Will, Will—what's the matter, darling?" He'd rave about something terrible that was going to get him. She'd sit up stiffly and pull the bell cord for his nanny. "Will, I don't know where you get these stories. I simply don't understand you." She'd finger an amulet she had, a jade piece, as she left the room. Her quick steps and averted eyes told him that his mother was afraid of him.

What happened next depended on his nanny. They changed all the time. A few held him and petted him until he went back to sleep. Most caned him for his wild imagination and refusal to shut up. That was at his father's orders: "Make a man of him."

The beatings taught him to bury his screams in his pillows and never tell a soul about the night visions. With good reason—they took him to realms that separated him from everything good.

They say I'm the Prince of Darkness, Will thought, pausing to tie his shoelace. I am. You can't be a good person and know what I know. He had seen things about human nature that revolted him in his spells, but he knew what he saw was true. His reality wasn't for ordinary people; it was his special gift. Will's mouth tightened.

All his life, his father had told him what he thought of him: "You'll never be the man I am." He bellowed the words when he was drunk, and said them silently when he was sober. No matter what Will won, or what team he captained, or how good his grades were, they were never good enough.

His nightmares ended the same way: A vortex dragged him toward the malevolence at the core. The stalker. He clawed against the whirlpool. His father appeared above him, grabbing his arms and hauling him to safety. Will looked into his father's eyes with sobbing gratitude, and saw the stalker's hatred blasting back. His father was the demon, as evil as hell.

The old man bent to Will's ear, drawing in a breath to say something.

And the dream ended. Wherever he was sleeping—at school as a youngster, or later, in some woman's bed or his own—he woke up, sweating and gasping. If he wasn't alone, he'd hide his panic, jumping out of bed and throwing on his clothes.

"Is there anything wrong?" the woman he was with would say, confused.

"No, no. No problem." He'd leave no matter what time it was. He couldn't let any of them see his terror. They'd be afraid of him if they knew what he saw. They'd leave him.

Of course, he would never go back to any of them anyway. They'd seen him like that. He stopped bringing women home, and never took them anyplace he couldn't make a fast exit.

Will took off, flying along the track. Unaware of the pounding of his feet on the gym floor, the sweat flying from him, or how long he'd run.

He would forget. He would forget.

He couldn't forget.

The funny part was, even if he wanted to tell someone how much he suffered, who would care? His father had been a millionaire, and he was the richest man in the world. No one cared about the rich kid. Will knew that better than anything.

He knew what his father was going to say when the dream stopped:

"It will get you in the end, no matter how hard you run."

Will ran faster. His torso was erect and his mind clear. His breath moved in and out without effort. His legs fired away like steel shafts. He could go forever. He was so strong, he would go on forever. He tore around the track.

When he ran, nothing but his power existed. Will didn't feel the ache in his heart that whispered on quiet nights. He had no longing for a childhood that didn't happen or anger over the one that did. He never noticed the little boy inside him that still hoped everything would turn out fine. When Will ran, only running existed.

Tonight he wanted more than relief from pain. Will pushed his limits, hoping that it would happen.

It did. When he ran himself close to oblivion, the light burst from the base of his spine and traveled upward. His back arched and his chest expanded. The force moving through his body was so powerful that he couldn't run. He stopped abruptly, bouncing along the track. He slammed into the side of the gym, sliding for a yard or two. He stayed on his feet and swung to face the wall, pressing his chest against it. The column of light rose up his back. Groans escaped him. He put his arms out, palms hugging the wooden surface. His head twisted to the right, as though he were trying to face the center of the room. His face contorted as the energy moved upward. He couldn't stop what was happening, and didn't want to.

The pillar of light rose up his back. When it climbed above his head, it exploded into a brilliant golden fountain, brighter than the sun. He rose onto his toes. The energy unfurled around him, spreading and spreading, moving everywhere. It felt like it reached the edges of the universe. Will was its center. He knew things when the light surrounded him; he could see relationships between ideas, organizations, and people who were hidden from him before. The worst business problems became simple.

The bliss that came with the light was hard to believe. He felt so much pleasure that it shocked him. He had chased pleasure all his life, but this was beyond that. Sex paled in comparison. He pushed off the wall and walked down the track, his hands reaching up, enraptured. He talked to it, the Light.

"I love you. I love you. Oh, stay with me. I love you." On and on like that, words he'd never spoken to anyone. The Light could understand what he said, he knew that. It heard his dreams and desires, his sadness and pain. And it fixed him. It healed him, at least for a while. With it, he could keep going. The Light was the most precious thing in his life.

Will had no idea what it was. The closest he could come to an explanation was that column was his soul. Or maybe God. He thought it might be God, except that he didn't believe in God.

The bliss played with him, flowing upward in a torrent. He moaned in delight, walking around the track, face alight. He held his hands high, reaching for something unseen. "I love you!" he shouted. "Oh, I love you so much." He danced, filled with joy. Tears of gratitude splattered the floor. The gym was magic, enchanted. He skipped and laughed like a child.

The Light had come to him years before. After being whipped because he had had a nightmare, Will crawled into his bed and pulled his quilt over his head. He shook with a child's shuddering sobs—and the Light came to him. Delight traveled up his spine, erasing his pain. Will found himself lifted to a place as wonderful as his nightmares were horrible.

The Light showed him a world he never dreamed existed. In it, he found creatures, people and animals and things he'd never seen, moving between luminous hangings across a mythical landscape inside him. Every touch was ecstasy; every sound, a chorus.

The dazzling column had no physical characteristics, but he felt it was a person. It could understand like a person. It had different parts. One was female. She was like a mother or angel. Her presence suffused the good place, and she enfolded him, making everything that happened all right. He called her Beloved. She and the Light kept him alive.

If the dark torrent yanked him down, the ones who lived in the bright place brought him back. They brought him back, regardless of what he did in the ordinary world or the dark dreams. They loved him no matter what he did.

One day, they showed him a world where people cooperated, where commerce served everyone, and the good that everyone said they wanted came to be. They told him that his job was to make it real. It was real; he had touched it. Reality, the numenon. The thing as it exists. He named his corporation after it.

The world of Light was his deepest secret. He couldn't explain the beauty of that realm. Words would defile it.

Besides, if they thought he was crazy because of his nightmares, what would they say if he told them about a Light that gave him answers and protected him? Or an angel called Beloved?

Will didn't trust his experiences. He thought he was crazy.

He'd never heard of anyone who had such encounters. They didn't talk about them at Stanford or its Graduate School of Business, from which he had graduated. No one talked about such things at meetings of the Numenon board or any other corporate venue. He wished he could ask someone, "Does a brilliant light surge up from your ass and give you unbelievable pleasure—then tell you how to solve that merger problem?"

He knew how that one would go over, so kept his mouth shut.

Will felt the rapture drifting away. "Don't go!" he cried. It always left. He knew it would come back—when he needed it. Running as hard as he could was a good way of getting it to return, but he couldn't make it do anything. It came tonight because he needed it. After Marina kicked him out, after everything else, he needed it.

When the light had gone, Will threw a towel around his shoulders. His legs shook as he walked to the elevator. He was so exhausted that he could barely place his palm against the sensor. "The sun will rise again."

He got into the elevator and became aware of something. He punched a button on the wall and spoke into a microphone.

Rick Bromberg took off his headset and handed it to the guy on the next shift, still shocked by what he'd seen. He resisted the desire to tell his replacement about it. Pretty good for my first night at the freak house, he thought.

He had been thrilled to get the job, even it if was the night shift. It paid better than any job he'd ever had and offered perks you couldn't get anywhere else. Passing the test to get into the place took everything he'd learned getting his MA in computer science and what the Marines taught him about surveillance. But he passed.

And he signed the inch-thick contract that granted him the privilege of coming to work. He knew all about the noncompetitive agreements that were standard in Silicon Valley employment contracts. But this one, shit. If he breathed one word about what he saw in this house, they'd have his first-born child.

He hadn't meant to do it. It was just so boring, sitting in that cubicle alone. There were five of them on duty. He didn't realize they'd be manning separate stations. True, it was better professional practice to have five people in separate rooms monitoring the screens than all of them together. The urge to talk came up when guys were together—it was a natural thing. Rick had even given in to the urge to drink beer once in a while on other jobs. He never brought the stuff, but if it was there, hey … Yeah, guys in the same room could miss things.

Before showing him to his security booth that night, his supervisor had told him that they meant it here. His name was Dunkirk. He was a fucking stiff. A Brit who acted like the empire hadn't fallen. He was one of the commandos Duane had all over. "We are here to facilitate Mr. Duane's security. We do that, and nothing else. Have you read your contract?"

Yeah, he had.

"Any breach of contract will be taken very seriously. Mr. Duane gives the orders. If he tells you to do something, or not to do something, you will do whatever he wants. If you don't, you're fired, that's it. No appeal." Dunkirk had looked at him with those frost-blue British eyes. "Or, if you must appeal, you will appeal to Hannah Hehrmann. You will never forget that experience, and you will lose. Now, it's time to begin the shift."

Everybody was scared stiff of Hannah Hehrmann. He hadn't seen her. Hadn't seen Will Duane either until the monitor showed him walking out of his bedroom in the middle of the night. Looked just like all the magazine covers: white hair, tall even on a screen. Good looking for an old guy. Duane was in his mid-sixties. Rick couldn't imagine being that old.

He heard him say, "No surveillance while I'm running." Yeah, Rick heard it. But as the time went by, he began to get worried. Duane's old, he thought. How could he run that long? What if he had heart attack and they didn't find him until the next day? So, he flipped a couple of switches and fired up one of the screens.

Rick knew that Will Duane couldn't tell he was watching. He knew his stuff. He had an advanced degree in stealth. Besides, Dunkirk gave him his introductory walk around that afternoon. They stood in the gym, and he said, "Mr. Duane does not like to be aware that he is being observed. The house's surveillance system is designed so that none of the monitors or sensors can be seen or detected in any way. For instance, do you see any cameras in this room?"

He looked around and shook his head. "No. Nothing." Yet when Dunkirk took him to his cubicle and replayed the videos, Rick could see himself on five cameras and hear every word they said. The gym was loaded. That's what he called smooth.

He wasn't worried that his boss would know he was taking a peek. When he first saw the old man on the screen, he couldn't believe how hard he ran. He must have been an Olympic runner when he was young. Now, for Pete's sake, Mr. Duane was tearing up the track, and he'd been out there a long time.

He almost punched a button for help when his boss suddenly stopped and bounced into the gym wall. A heart attack, Rick was sure. That's what he gets for being so built at his age. He couldn't help but compare his paunch to Will Duane's nonexistent belly. But then, Duane put his hands out straight and started moaning and arching his back like he was humping the wall. He turned his head to the right like a corkscrew. Rick's eyes widened. Jesus, was he possessed, or something?

He'd heard a lot of stories about Will Duane being a warlock or the fucking devil, even. Lots of stories about his new boss were out there. When he started doing that shit, Rick stared into the monitor, mouth open. His new boss started dancing around, waving his arms and screaming, "I love you." This was certifiable, Rick thought. Real nut case stuff. Which he'd also heard—that Will Duane was crazy.

But then his shift was over and he came back to earth. What Duane did was his own business. If you're the richest man on earth, you can do what you want. If he wanted to hump the wall or dance around his gym all night, who cared?

Rick went to the checkout point where they patted them down before letting them go home. As he was being searched, he thought, Why all the need for security? What else does Duane do in here? It was only his first night and the place was starting to get to him.

Dunkirk burst in, looking at Rick like he'd run over his dog. "Bromberg, in my office."

His office was a cement-walled cell with monitors ringing every wall. They hadn't been watching him, had they?

"I need your identification badge, your code book, and your keys." Dunkirk looked as scary as a skinny Brit could. He handed them over. "I need you to sign here, showing that you understand the reason you are being terminated and you will ..."

"What? I'm being fired? For what?"

"You were spying on Mr. Duane as he ran, Bromberg, against his orders."

The expression on Dunkirk's face and the cement walls, plus all the monitors and steel doors got to him. He told the truth. "OK. I did watch him for a while, but I won't tell anyone what I saw."

"Definitely not, Bromberg. You'll never mention it again, nor will you mention your reason for relocating."

"Relocating? I'm not ..."

"Yes, you are. And you'll be no more trouble to us. You are banned from employment at Numenon or any Numenon partner."

"That's practically the whole world!"

"Yes, it is, Bromberg. So you'll be happy that we secured employment for you at your new location."

"Where is it?"

"I'm not at liberty to say. A car is waiting for you."

"But how did you know?" Rick sputtered.

"Mr. Duane told me."

"How did he know?" Rick's voice rose in a wail.

"Mr. Duane knows, Bromberg. He knows without all this," he waved his hand at the banks of monitors. "I don't know why he keeps us on, really."

Will stood swaying in his bedroom. Traces of light seeped from behind the metal clad windows. The silk draperies didn't hide the fact that the new day had arrived. Should he get dressed for work? Will wore a robe embroidered with the Numenon logo that he'd put on after showering. His face felt like a leaden mask. His eyes kept blinking as though they were filled with grit.

He couldn't think of his schedule for the day, didn't notice the lovely furnishings of his vast room. Not the Turner over the bureau or the little Monet he loved. The bed beckoned. A minute won't hurt, he thought.

Will laid down and pulled the quilt over his head.

He ran through the gray-green world, the thing he feared behind him, roaring for his blood. He turned his head, and something overran him. He was tossed without mercy, slammed into the ground. He rolled and tumbled, landing on his feet, battered but alive. He watched the juggernaut's howling progress.

It destroyed everything. He watched everyone die, smashed and bent, torn to pieces. The maelstrom killed those he loved first, then the rest. Everyone died; all humanity. Billions of bloody, ruined bodies piled up around him. He was the only one left.

He stood in the void, surrounded by nothing.

He had to live when everyone he loved was dead. Everyone he hated too. Nothing was left, not even hatred. He had to go on living and living and living. Realizing that caused his jaw to drop, and pulled his hands to his mouth. Made him curl into a ball.

He lay there, dazed. His chest rose and fell. The movement of his ribs was the only thing he could grab on to to tell him he was alive.

Was it a prophecy? Was that going to happen? Nothing could tell him. Everything was gone. He felt a rumbling below the earth and heard the sound of rocks grinding together. His stomach roiled at the noise.

He realized what it meant: The stalker was coming for him.

His Beloved appeared from nowhere, speaking softly. "Yes, my darling, it is true. The fate you have fought for so long will come to be very soon—

in days. You have one chance to save yourself and all you love." Whispering, she told him the way out.

Will did as she directed. It was already shaping up. He had a call in to the Indian shaman. He'd made it in hopes that what Marina said was true. He'd heard from her once since she threw him out. She wrote. "He's a great holy man who has helped many people. If Grandfather tells me I should see you again, I will. But only then, Will. You and I are done."

She included a phone number where he could reach the shaman.

He originally called the old man hoping he could get her back, but then he had that dream. He had to go now. The world of light required it.

The sucker didn't return his call. He kept *him* waiting.

When the shaman finally called him back, Will was ready to detonate. He forced himself to be civil and agreed to everything. "I'll go wherever you want. I'll do whatever you want. I'll go on your retreat, just tell me how to get there."

The old man didn't sound surprised. It was as though he knew what Will would say.

"Bring your best warriors," the shaman said. "As many as you want, as long as they're your best." And then he laughed.

Will's stomach clenched. The joy in the old man's laughter hit him like a fist.

And then he gave orders that would make it come to pass. "I want you to go, too, Betty, and a few others from the headquarters." They looked at him in disbelief. He convinced them. "We have to go. This is the most important thing we'll ever do."

But he would never tell them the real reason for their pilgrimage.

2

The boy felt his legs trembling and cramping, moving purely by the force of his will. He heard the breath enter his lungs, rage, burn there, then exit, only to re-enter, burn again. The child couldn't run any longer; he was run out. He shouted at his little brother, "Go there! Into the canyon! Hide!"

The younger child veered off, going in the direction the older boys had taken. He turned, running at the horsemen, trying to provide some cover for his brother. The two horses headed straight at him. He heard the hard staccato of the gallop on rock. A lasso's whir filled his ears as one rider swung his loop overhead. He charged the men, waving his arms.

The horses ran past him. He stopped, bewildered. Before he could turn, something grabbed him around the waist and jerked him backward. He was dragged, popping over ruts like a twig. One bounce flipped him onto his belly. His face hit a rock. His arms were pinned to his sides. He couldn't protect himself. The impact was so hard that he didn't know his tooth had chipped. He didn't know what happened until everything stopped and he found himself lying in the path.

The lariat's loop bound his body. Like a tight fishing line, it ran straight to the stranger's saddle. At the end of the rope, the horse loomed above the boy, larger than any horse he had seen. It stared at him, ears pointed like spears. Loud blasts of air came from its nostrils. It moved the thing in its mouth, and streams of white foam splattered its chest. When the beast's hooves hit the rocks, sparks flew. It danced around and the foreigner yelled at it.

"Whoa, Buddy. *Whoa*. I know he smells like shit. It won't kill you! *Whoa*, you …"

Eventually, the horse settled and stood stiffly, arching its neck, and backing to keep the rope taut. The man looked directly at the child. The boy had seen such men before, but never had been close enough to one to see his pale blue eyes. He became stiff, shaking.

"Y're in a hell of a fix, ain't you?"

He couldn't understand the stranger's words, but the man smiled in a way that told the boy what he already knew. This man would enjoy killing him. His father had warned of these people, and kept their band out of their way. The warnings had not been strong enough.

His breath came in fast pants, and his heart felt like it would jump out. He shook all over. The man began reeling him in, hand over hand, looping the lariat on his saddle, dragging him across the rough ground. Rocks struck him, bloodying his face, bruising his flesh. The smashing impacts dazed him, and as they did, he realized that a monster was ahead of him. It was a two-headed demon, both horse and man. A skinwalker, a giant of the mountains, come to eat his flesh. His body moved like he had the falling sickness, shaking out of control.

Windborne streams of sweat and saliva lashed him as he groveled. Rowels of spurs that were as big across as his face spun and flashed. The interloper's stench assailed him. The closer he got, the more terrifying the monster became. The giant horse began tossing its head. Its feet started moving up and down so fast that sparks flew without stopping. When he finally was dragged next to the animal, he felt nothing, no pain, no injury—only terror. His body went limp. The horse spun away from him and tried to run.

"Knock it off. It's just a kid. A fucking digger kid."

The rider reined hard and finally, the animal stood still. When that happened, the cowboy yanked him up, dangling him in front of his face like a fish on a line. They looked into each other's eyes. The man was opening his mouth to speak when suddenly the boy's paralysis lifted. In that instant of freedom, the child lunged, tearing into the flesh of his captor's chest.

"God damn it to hell!"

The man shouted, and then struck him. A blow made his ears ring. Another blow, and everything went blank. When he could remember again, he was tied facedown on the saddle in front of his captor. Something was stuffed in his mouth, and something else was tied around his head.

"Try that again, you little bastard!"

The other rider returned with the smaller boy over his saddle. "The big ones got away," he said to the first.

"This little fucker bit me, damn it to hell!" He rubbed his chest. "Damn waste of effort. You can't do nuthin' with this bunch. They're never gonna educate 'em fit for nuthin'."

"It's a job, Roy. It pays good."

A third rider came up behind them and halted his horse. "Slim pickin's," he said, eyeing the two little boys.

"The rest of 'em hightailed it up that draw."

"Why, hell, that's a blind draw, I bet," the third one said, grinning. "It'd be easy as shootin' fish in a barrel." The other two grinned back. "Throw me them runts, an' you go get the rest. We'll save the taxpayers some money." The boy was thrown across the front of the third man's saddle. It wasn't hard to do. He was small, even for his People. His younger brother was tossed on top of him. When they ended up back at the band's camp, the boys were dumped into a mule-drawn wagon, along with some girls their age and some older kids who were too slow making their escape.

Dazed and exhausted, the boy saw his father standing in the open space before their shelters. His face was bruised and bloody, and men with guns surrounded him. The agent waved a paper in his face.

"I do, too have the right. My right is here. They gotta go to school— it's the law. We'll make 'em civilized Christians. We'll make 'em good Americans, every one." The children sat in the wagon, crying silently, looking at their parents who stared back with hopeless tears. The mothers' faces beseeched the agent and his hired hands. The boy sat looking at his father. Why didn't he do something? He looked for his mother, and then remembered she ran away with his baby brother and sister when the scouts came back saying that the white men brought a wagon. The band knew what that meant. The boy's father had protected his clan as long as he could, moving far into the wilderness. They couldn't go any farther.

His father was a man of peace. Surely he could reason with these white men. Then the group waited, silently, until the two riders returned.

"Couldn't find any of 'em! That's the last of the bunch I reckon we'll get. The rest got clean away." One rider chuckled. He'd have to clean his guns when he got home.

As the wagon pulled out, the boy's father came to life. He remembered the words in English, though he knew his father spoke in their language. Try as he might, he couldn't remember a word of his tribe's tongue.

His father shouted, "I will come for you!"

He called his son's name, but when he recalled the incident, his mind went blank. He couldn't remember his own name, the name his father had given him in their language. He couldn't remember it at all.

"I will come for you! I must move the camp. I must find the boys who ran. Then I will come for you!" The wagon pulled out and his father ran beside it, looking in the boy's eyes, "You are the leader, my son! You will be chief one day. You will be great. I will come for you, my son. I will come for you, or the sun will cease to shine."

His father couldn't keep up. The boy watched him recede into the distance. That was the last time he saw his father. It was 1918.

The old man lay back on his bed, gasping at what he had remembered. Starlight illuminated the interior of the lean-to, but all he could see was his father's form, hands grabbing the wagon as he ran alongside so many years before. The sun was going down, and it outlined his father's head, the bright light surrounding him like a halo. He turned to the wall, pinching back tears.

Even with his eyes closed, his mind showed him the canyon where it happened as clearly as if he stood in the path. A brilliant blue sky arched overhead. Canyon walls topped by spiky pine trees loomed on each side. The cheerful sound of water played down the streambed, dancing past rocks and trees with fluttering leaves. He and his brother ran through the scene, a beautiful place where something ugly occurred. He had lived perhaps eight summers when he was stolen.

The old man's mind was an open corridor. That morning, he could see everything he had ever done and feel each event as though it were happening. Bud Creeman had told him about amusement parks. The shaman had never been to one. He told him about a ride where you got in a little boat that floated in a darkened indoor stream. Without warning, the channel would widen and—wham!—a scene would appear. This morning, the boat took the direction it had been commanded, going back in his life. He would watch whatever it presented, knowing the Great One willed it, knowing he would need what was revealed in the week to come.

He reflected upon what would soon unfold. Thousands were coming to be with him and learn what he had to teach. The coming week was the last Meeting—the retreat had grown beyond anything he imagined. It was the last chance that many of his People would have to meet him and imbibe wisdom of their ancestors.

Preparations had been made to assure the Meeting's success. The campgrounds were groomed and facilities repaired. The Founders had studied everything touching the Meeting, making sure they were ready. Paul Running Bird's report, tabulating the data he'd gleaned, was part of the preparations.

Grandfather knew all this, just as he knew that those questions Paul had presented to him last night were the reason he felt the pain of remembering his past. He wanted to hate Paul's report, but he knew that everything that happened was the work of the Great One.

3

For thirty-five years, Will had stood where he was at some point during the night. The wide balcony that formed the entrance to his home gave him a perfect view of the living room below. Ordinarily, his nocturnal prowls occurred because of his insomnia or the nightmares. This night, he was clean-shaven and wore a business suit. His wakefulness was intentional.

He looked down, noticing the things that he noticed every night, waiting for the beauty of the place to soothe him. He glanced at his hands, resting on the rail. They surprised him, the way that seeing his white hair in a mirror surprised him. His hands were still long and bony, but their skin seemed to have grown. It covered the backs of his hands in puckered triangles. The rest of his runner's form could pass for what it had been when he and Kathryn built the house, but he wasn't the same man. It wasn't the same house, either. The original furniture was long gone, along with his wife. He'd been alone for so many years, he couldn't imagine living any other way.

Will's eyes continued exploring his living room. They followed the path carved by splashes of light coming from pinpoints in the ceiling. Furniture groupings and all the paintings and sculpture were illuminated, leaving the rest dark. The highlighted colors glowed: burgundy, deep green, and ivory—the colors of the mid 1990s.

The textures of glass and metal, suede and chenille led him to the fireplace centered on the far wall. One of his Rothkos hung on its left side, and on the right, a new painting, something his curator had picked up by a young artist ... What was her name? Will couldn't remember it. He shook his head. He would remember it. Couldn't. Panic rose inside him. What was her name? Her name? He ran a hand through his hair. What was it?

Let it go, he commanded himself. Look at the room. You won't see it for a while. He studied the intricate tableau. This had been his haven, his one safe place. He kept waiting for the internal "click" that came from experiencing perfection. It didn't come.

Something else did, something that happened when he was under fire. His perception sharpened and deepened. He could see the room's interior as if the designers' presentation boards were laid out before him. He saw the pattern, the skeleton of a living thing. Will had always been able to find the structure in whatever he was observing, whether it was a dysfunctional corporation, a jammed negotiation, or an intricately designed room.

His vision enlarged again, zooming outward like a high-tech camera's lens. He could see the house's floor plan as though he were hovering over the building. He could see the building's electrical, plumbing, and heating systems. He could see every opening in the house's shell, and location of each of the security systems. He felt the sensors and alarms, and knew the lasers' coverage. The house was impenetrable.

How did they bug it? How did they destroy his perfect world?

He stepped back as though he'd been punched. They'd found bugs in the living room, a meeting room, and one of the guest rooms, the largest one, which they might have thought was his bedroom. Horror shot through him. Not only that, but the devices also were from an unknown manufacturer. That was impossible. He knew all the surveillance hardware and who made it. He made the best. Will felt hollow. His world was not secure.

He swung around. Where was Hannah? He looked toward her office at the end of the balcony. She was supposed to meet him before he left. He looked at his watch. Three minutes to one. He was early. She'd be out in three minutes.

Turning toward the center of the broad mezzanine, a powerful fragrance struck him. A mass of lilies four feet across sat on the round table in the middle of the balcony. Stargazers. They hadn't been there when he went to bed. Will smiled; he loved lilies.

"I thought they'd please you, Mr. Duane." Hannah's heels clicked on the pale stone floor, announcing her arrival before her heavily accented voice did. "A fresh arrangement will be waiting when you return. And the house will be secure." She smiled, as tough and no-nonsense a woman as existed. She was tall and muscular, looking like the martial artist she was. Her dark hair was cut straight across all around. She swung the briefcase she carried onto the table and opened it. The top held a computer screen and the bottom was jammed with electronic devices.

"With the *Ashley's* satellite dish, you can see every room in the house on the screen wherever you are. You can also hear what the mikes are picking up, and lock down the house if you need to. You can reach me at all times with this," she pointed to a device. "I'll be living here while you're gone, with my team. We'll find the perpetrators, I assure you." Her eyes did assure him. "It happens to everyone with your influence, Mr. Duane. But you're safe now, you will be safe on your journey, and you will be 100 percent secure when you get back."

He felt weak with emotion, momentarily wanting to hug her. He didn't. No one hugged Hannah Hehrmann. And he didn't hug people, anyway. "Thank you, Hannah. I appreciate what you're doing."

"It's my job, Mr. Duane. Have fun on your camping trip." She shook his hand formally, then cracked the tiniest smile. "If there's any trouble, I'll call my brother. He'll be here with the Israeli army," she snapped her fingers, "like that!"

"If you pick up that new red phone in your office, you'll have the United States Army faster than that!"

"Two armies should be enough." They laughed, but without mirth. The bugs had been placed when Hannah was on duty. She was as disturbed as he was. "Have a good trip, Mr. Duane."

He walked away from the table with the lilies, past the entrance balcony's commodious furnishings. Thirty feet deep, the balcony ran the width of his living room and was decorated as elaborately as the salon below. Its stone floor flowed outside to an equally grand entrance under a wide overhang. Will walked toward the entrance doors. Tall sheets of glass swung outward.

The front of his house, three stories high and two hundred feet long, was an unbroken expanse of glass. He wanted to have it shielded by metal shutters like the rest of the house, but his architect said he'd quit and never work for him again. "That would be a crime against aesthetics," he'd said. Will backed down.

The view made him pause. The hills of Menlo Park spread before him with a sprinkle of lights. His eye moved past them to Palo Alto's tighter clusters of illumination. A black expanse signaled the San Francisco Bay, and on the other side of the Bay, a jumble of neon announced East Bay cities.

Will grimaced, annoyed every time he stood there. This hill had the best view on the Peninsula, and they built a freeway in front of it. The noise was worse every year. He tried to get them to put it one hill over when they built it in the 1960s, but he couldn't stop Caltrans back then. At least you could only see one corner of the house from I-280. Any more and he'd have to move. Will didn't want to move, and he didn't want to leave that night.

He forced himself down the path. He had to go. They'd invaded his home. And ... Marina's face flashed before him. And what happened with her ... He had to leave, he was in danger. The dream said they were in danger. The briefcase he carried felt as if it held the weight of the world.

Voices spoke from hidden speakers as he walked along the path: "431," "571," "893." They were operatives in various sectors of the estate reporting in as they saw him pass their monitors. They changed the codes daily, sometimes more than that. The final checkpoint: "274. We are secure, Mr. Duane." The voice said the words crisply, completing a ritual.

Will nodded, standing as erect and striding as firmly as ever, knowing he was being filmed. Knowing he'd walk to his grave the same way. If they were going to kill him, he would go like a man.

Hannah wanted him to take operatives with him. "That medicine man said you could bring warriors. I can give you warriors, Mr. Duane. You can fill the motor homes with my people. You will be safe."

"He didn't mean that kind of warrior, Hannah. He meant spiritual warriors."

"A warrior is a warrior."

He had dissuaded her, he hoped. The last thing he needed was a troop of Hannah's commandos wrecking this. The car was waiting for him at the end of the walk, one of the small limousines, unmarked, with the driver standing by the open rear door. It was a new driver. He didn't like new drivers. He had complained to Betty about it when they went over the plans. "Why can't I have Mark?"

"Will, all your favorite drivers are on their way to Tucson with the motor homes. Mark is driving the *Ashley*." He'd forgotten.

This was Robert Frye. His personnel file unfolded in Will's mind's eye exactly as it looked on his office's computer screen when he looked him up. "Robert Frye. 167 Palmyra Ct. Campbell. Married. Two children." Some references, all excellent. Will nodded at him and got in the car. Betty was inside, looking exhausted.

"You couldn't sleep either?"

She shook her head. "No. I picked up the briefs at the office on the way up here. They're in the trunk. We can put them in the jet with our luggage."

Her drawn face told him she'd worked at the office until eleven before giving the briefs to publications for binding. The sadness on her face told him that John was waiting when she got home. He was angry, and said something like, "Why didn't that asshole give you more than three days to get ready? You wrote a book for him." Which was true, he gave them just three days to prepare, but that's all he'd had. Her trembling hands said they'd fought and she couldn't sleep in the hour she had before the car picked her up. He didn't ask what else happened, and she didn't tell him.

"I put the summary you wanted in the back of each brief," she said. "If people can't remember names or whatever, they're listed there."

"Good." He thought he would faint as they pulled away from the house. He used to travel. He'd been all over the world. Now, he went back and forth between his home and Numenon's international headquarters, less than ten minutes away. Why didn't he go anywhere? Why didn't he entertain? He had entertained thousands at his estate. What happened?

He knew that perfectly well.

"Are we secure, Robert?" he said to the driver, who was flipping levers in the driver's seat.

"We are secure, Mr. Duane."

As secure as people can be on a moving time bomb.

Betty's head lolled forward before they got to the bottom of the drive. He pulled a pillow and blanket out of a cabinet. Giving them to her, he said, "Get some sleep, Betty. I'll be the lookout." She was asleep in seconds. He watched her, feeling odd observing his secretary when she was so vulnerable. Fine lines around her eyes, a few at the corners of her lips. A little gray in her hair. We're getting old, he thought. She was still as beautiful to him as she had been when they began. She had stayed while Kathryn had left. What did they have, he and Betty? They had never been lovers, and never would. Maybe she's the only woman in the world who will put up with me, he thought. His heart ached, a physical pain. He might have been alarmed, but his doctor had pronounced him fit the day before when the same thing happened.

"It's stress, Will. You need to work less. This camping trip will be good for you. I can prescribe something for tension ..." Will cut him off. He would never take any of that shit. He knew all about prescription drugs. "You may have chest pains again. Just know it's stress, most likely."

No, it's heartache. His heart ached seeing his secretary sleeping in his car. He ached, knowing the fragility of everything he loved.

Fear hit him like a wall. Were the others safe? He whispered into the microphone on the door. "Robert. The others going on the trip—where are they now?"

Robert hit a button on the screen on his dash. A divided screen appeared showing road maps and flashing lights. "They're almost at the airport, all but us and Gil Canao. He's still home."

"Get a hold of Gil. See that he's OK."

Robert tapped his screen and spoke into a hidden microphone. A few minutes later, he reported, "Gil's on his way. The baby was crying and he didn't want to leave his wife like that. He'll be there before we are."

Will grabbed his heart with both hands and lay back against the seat. Oh, God, what had been done?

The pains drifted away and so did he. By the time they reached the Numenon terminal next to the San Jose airport, he was dozing. Dark dreams. A face searching for him. Blue eyes, blond hair. Dark eyes, dark hair. Shifting over centuries, chasing him. Will hovered in the world between sleep and wakefulness. "You invited them to keep them safe," her voice said. "That's why you picked them. They're the dearest to you in the world." Yes, that's why he chose them.

Then images came, one after the other. Images and facts. This was where he learned things, and knew the truth. This state was where all his innovations originated, what they called his genius.

He woke up abruptly. The artist's name was Biff Hycoff. She was twenty-three and got her MFA at the Rhode Island School of Design after graduating from Yale. His curator made a good call buying her work. She would become very successful. He would order him to buy more. And he needed to do some trading. He tapped a button on his door and spoke softly into the mike. His broker in New York answered sleepily. "As soon as the exchange opens, I want you to sell ..."

By the time they disembarked at the Numenon terminal, Will felt good. He'd made a little more than a million dollars on the way to the airport, vastly more when you counted the lifetime appreciation of Biff Hycoff's work. When people asked him how he made his fortune, he always said, "I do it in my sleep ..."

4

Grandfather lay still for some time. The question that had prompted his reliving of those horrible hours when he was torn from his family was: Why doesn't Grandfather talk about his past? He's lived our history; why doesn't he tell us what happened to him?

This was a question a tourist would ask. A tourist visiting Indian Country, looking for an authentic tale to tell his friends, a tale to repeat with teary eyes and a heart that didn't bleed. Grandfather didn't speak of his past because he couldn't bear the pain.

Looking out of the front of his lean-to, he thought the night sky looked like a blue velvet shirt with tiny buttons sewn all over it. He was in his lean-to in the Mogollon Bowl, on reservation land in southwestern New Mexico. It was within minutes of four a.m. on Sunday, March 23, 1997. Palm Sunday, the Sunday before Easter.

For the previous ten years, he had awakened in the still darkness on this spot and waited for the Great One to send him the directions to the Meeting that would begin the next day. The One always came to tell him what to do and say, day by day, hour by hour, for the retreat's seven days. All he had to do was wait.

Not this year. He sat up, shaken from remembering and driven to complete his task, a task he neither asked for nor anticipated. He scowled. This was a very strange Meeting, marked long before it began.

When he arrived at the Bowl the night before, he was tired. He could admit that. He was an old man, and he'd driven five hours across rocks and dirt in an old truck with no springs that he could discern. Bud and Bert Creeman had picked him up at his hogan and carried him to this sacred place, as they did every year. He was tired. He was also worried about Bert. As pregnant as she was, all that bouncing couldn't be good.

But she said, "I'll be fine. You and Elizabeth will be there. The baby's not due for two weeks, anyway."

"We'll have seven more doctors at the Meeting this year," he added.

"See, I'll be fine. I'd rather have any of you deliver our baby than that idiot where we live. Nothing will make me miss the last Meeting!"

That's how Bert was. That's how all the spirit warriors were. That's why hundreds of them slept in the Bowl beneath his lean-to. None of them would miss the last Meeting.

Did he get to eat his meal in peace last night, or visit with those who came early to talk to him? Did he get to heal anyone before the Meeting began, as he did every year? No. Paul Running Bird dashed up to Bud's truck before they could climb out.

"We've got your place all set up, Grandfather." He beamed, pointing to the shaman's lean-to, a short distance from the truck. It sat on the rim of the Bowl so that he could see his People camped inside and look out the other side to the vastness of the desert. "The best seat in the house, like always!"

"Thank you, Paul." His spirit soared the moment he set foot on the Bowl's holy ground. Bliss rose inside him like the dust puffing around his feet. He turned in a circle, noticing that the amphitheater where they held the Meeting was ready for the crowds. Its benches were repaired, and the long stage across the back where he sat looked presentable. All this effort because of the special guests. His teeth ground together as he lay in his bed, the way they had the night before. He had continued to survey the Bowl, ignoring Paul's impatience. It looked the same. A shallow crater three miles across, with only slightly fewer cacti and rocks than the surrounding desert. Ecstasy poured from every stick and pebble. The Bowl was alive. People didn't believe that until they saw what it did. Only fools thought its power came from a meteor striking there eons ago. No, the Bowl was alive.

As he appreciated his surroundings, drums began to pound in his heart and the songs of the ancestors rang in his ears. He felt light, like he could float to the cooking area and see his old friends, like he could glide around the camp headquarters, the dingy cement buildings left by the scientists, and greet everyone. He was surprised when others said they couldn't hear the drums and singing, but he knew almost all of them would hear the beautiful sounds by week's end. Did he get to visit with his old friends? Or chat with the warriors who'd worked so hard to prepare for the Meeting? No.

"Grandfather, I have some really important things to discuss with you." Paul ushered him toward his lean-to. A table and chairs had been set up outside—plastic. He hated plastic. Paul pulled out a chair for him. "Sit here. We have a lot to cover and it's getting dark." Yes, the sun was setting. He turned toward it and closed his eyes, thanking the great sun for the day. Praying to Creator for renewed light.

Paul turned to Bud. "Put his things in his lean-to, Bud. And could you bring us some dinner? We have to work." Paul was his old self: imperious, oblivious, and dressed like the fanciest Indian in the world. He laid his new Stetson hat on the table, probably to admire it. Grandfather had seen one like it years ago. Hoss Cartwright wore one on the television program *Bonanza*. It had a high crown that peaked higher in back than in front. He wondered how Paul had found such a new-looking old hat.

Paul noticed him looking at the hat. "Do you like it, Grandfather? Everyone's wearing them where I take riding lessons. It's the latest style."

Nothing was new, not even hats. Everything came around again. He frowned. "Paul, I need to put my medicines away and bless my lean-to. I need to visit with the People."

"Well, just let me show you this." He put a small suitcase on the table. Grandfather knew what it was—a briefcase. The tribe's finance chief had one. "Remember my Web site?" How could he forget it? The thing had turned his life upside down. "Well, I put in a forum, that's where people can log on and write a message. There was so much interest in the Meeting, I can't tell you." Grandfather sat impassively in the face of Paul's enthusiasm. He had told him that the Meeting was not to be discussed on his Web site, or any other. "Well, people got wind of it, and what could I do? Not respond to their questions?"

"Yes, Paul. That is what you could do. That is what I told you to do."

"I know, but look how well everything turned out. Four thousand people are coming because of it, Grandfather. Not even Rising Wolf has such a big turnout. And think of our special visitors! Nobody's had Will Duane..."

"Be quiet, Paul! Do not speak." Grandfather had not been upset in a long time. The last time he was upset was when Paul came to his hogan last fall and told him what was going on. He had called upon the Great One, the ancestors, and his teacher, Great-grandfather, to calm him. They did. Last night, as Paul's jaw kept moving and his words spilled out, he prayed again, Oh, Great One! Oh, my ancestors! Oh, Great-grandfather! Be with me so that I can hear whatever Paul says. Be with me so that I do not direct my rage at one of my People. Make me calm, I beg you. The prayer worked.

"Show me what you have, Paul."

"It's really simple." He pulled a very large yellowish envelope out of the briefcase. It was stuffed with papers. "When I was at Wharton, we used feedback forms all the time. People on my forum had so many questions, I tabulated them." He handed over a precisely formatted table. "They're arranged according to the number of people asking the basic kind of question. The frequency is shown right here..." He pointed to a number beside one. "Five hundred eighty-six people asked that question alone, and look at the others. This is really good response rate."

His eyes scanned the list. Sighing, he pulled his spectacles from one of the pouches at his waist and put them on. He had gotten them in 1954. He could read very well with them and saw no need to "upgrade," a word Paul had taught him.

"Oh, wow, Grandfather! Where did you get those glasses? Fifties-retro— They're so hip!"

"Hip?" He turned his attention to the questions Paul had presented him, hoping to hear a chorus from the unseen ancestors. "Kill him!" Or at least, "Throw him out of the Meeting." He'd been wanting to do that for years, but Great-grandfather and the Great One wouldn't let him. "He has work to do, let him do it," they'd tell him as he sat quietly, listening to the voices inside and outside him. Paul did all the organizing for the Meeting and saw that the camp was ready and everyone's needs were met. Everything was repaired and shipshape for this last great Meeting due to Paul's organizing. He had to give Paul credit. He was the person who came up with the idea of the Meeting. It wouldn't exist without him. And soon it wouldn't exist again. This was the last Meeting. The disaster would soon be over.

He waited, feeling the spirits clamoring around him, feeling the Great One surge up from the ground, and feeling his beloved teacher looking out from his own eyes. A smile came to his lips. Now they would chastise Paul for his disobedience, for daring to mention him on this Internet! Now Paul would see the source of his powers, which was what another question asked—Where do you get your Powers? He waited for the Great One's command to attack.

"I've also got feedback on how you come across at the Meeting, Grandfather. They're on these performance evaluation forms. We use these at work—I'm still an executive at Microsoft, though I hope to change jobs soon. The major business schools use the same technique. You get rated for how well you do in different aspects of your job, so there's an objective measure ..." Seeing Grandfather's face, Paul looked down. "You can look at those later ... Hey! What's happening?"

The papers on the table rose in the air like a tornado, swirling as though they might reach the heavens. Grandfather stood up, ready to curse Paul as soon as he got permission. Then he sat down. He could see spirits reading the sheets as they flew through the air. A familiar inner voice said to him, "This is very interesting, my dear Joseph. This tells us how the People think. It's easier than reading their minds." Which were very hard to penetrate, even for spirits with supernatural powers. The voice continued, "You need to read these papers, and answer the questions. You must begin now. There are many questions."

The ancestors, Great One, and Great-grandfather approved of what Paul had done. He sat, stunned, as the papers spiraled back down to the table and arranged themselves as they had been.

"Wow, Grandfather! What you can do is amazing!" Paul's delight was transparent. His faith in his teacher had been renewed by a bit of hocus-pocus that he didn't even do. Bud arrived with a tray of food. "Oh, just put it here, Bud. We'll eat while we go over the schedule for the Meeting." He turned to face his teacher, apparently unaware that what he'd said was heresy. "I also put together a daily schedule and list of discussion topics. Some of the feedback indicated that people felt the Meeting was kind of unorg— …" Paul fell silent as Grandfather rose to his feet. Although he was a tiny man, just over five feet tall, the power Grandfather manifested when expressing his displeasure—or anything—made him a giant. Both Bud and Paul pulled back when he rose.

Grandfather spoke to Bud, his voice tense, "Please put the tray in my lean-to and go back to Bert." Bud did what he was asked, and quickly. He turned to Paul, his rage mounting. "Schedule? You made a schedule? You know the Great One gives me the directions for the Meeting on Sunday morning, every year. I only do what the Great One tells me to do. I will never follow your schedule." He was so appalled that he couldn't speak further.

The momentary look of guilt on Paul's face indicated he knew he'd made a mistake. "I just wanted to make things more organized. I mean, look at the feedback sheets … They say the Meeting's too … Uh, just look at them. We can talk tomorrow." He closed his briefcase and started to leave. Grandfather took the heavy envelope.

"Get rid of these," he indicated the plastic table and chairs.

"Sure, Grandfather, right away." Paul stacked the chairs and waddled off with them. "I'll send someone for the table."

When he was finally alone in his lean-to, the first thing he set up was his altar. He took out the ritual objects, the feathers and stones, and arranged them with the other things that were so holy that they remained in pouches. He set his picture of Great-grandfather next to his bed. He dropped to his knees before the shrine, feeling tears welling inside. His soul cried. Why must I live in such a time? He couldn't imagine soliciting a performance review or feedback for Great-grandfather, or proposing a schedule for something so holy as what would happen in the coming week. He couldn't imagine having a follower as dense as Paul, but he knew that many others were like him. The old man's heart surged and ached. He addressed the Great One, "Why must I live now?"

"Because you do, my son. It is your time on this earth. Complete your job. Look at the papers, and answer the questions." As always, the familiar voice of the One comforted him.

He had to do it. It was a direct order. He wanted to finish putting away his things, to arrange his medicines and herbs properly, to put the rest of the sacred objects and amulets where they belonged. He longed to eat the stew that Bud had delivered. Avalina Cocina was a very good cook. She had made this stew, he could tell by the smell of the herbs. But no, he couldn't eat until he satisfied the Great One. He took out the questions and read them. He began to think about the answers, framing them in his mind so he could tell the People later.

"No. You must write the answers down. People only understand what they read these days. They don't listen, and they don't hear. Write the answers. The visitors can copy them on their machines and give them to everyone." The Great One spoke in his mind. "Use that..." A clipboard was stuffed in the envelope, and a bunch of pens. Ballpoint pens. He preferred the kind he used when he was in school. You dipped them in ink. He had been told they weren't made anymore. That was a great loss. This ballpoint pen slid across the paper too quickly. He couldn't feel the paper beneath his hand properly. The paper was lined as it should be, but it was yellow, and a pad rather than a small book. Oh, he was too old for this world. He longed to leave.

When the Power got him, he couldn't stop writing. His penmanship was unchanged from what they taught him in the Indian schools: pointed, tiny, elegant, an antique hand from a bygone age. He read Paul's questions.

"1. I've been to [Grandfather—the average response was three Meetings. A total of 798 people answered the question. They ranged from people who'd just been to one Meeting, to people like me who've been to them all. PRB]"

The report went on like that for pages. Paul had added notes throughout. Grandfather knew he was trying to be helpful, but it made his account a swamp. The old man studied the sheets and deciphered the questions they contained. They were the same questions he always heard: I saw Grandfather do some marvelous thing—marvelous only to a beginner. How does he do it? Where does his power come from? Why doesn't he talk about his life? Is it true that he's psychic and can see into the future? Can he blow things up with his mind? There were more questions about different things. Did lots of people really get married at the Meeting? Why do the marriages last? What's a soul mate? And "Is a soul mate a Native American concept?" Is he really a revolutionary? And, as always, when will I get powers like Grandfather? How many Meetings does it take?

And then came the performance review. The Meeting was too unorganized, too this, too that. If he made all these people happy, they wouldn't have a Meeting. Every part of it offended someone. He raised his eyes to the Great One and begged for protection. Sitting cross-legged on his bed, he took comfort in the buffalo robe beneath him. His followers had fixed him up a fancy bed. A new mattress, sheets, and handmade quilts, all covered with a buffalo robe—he had to have that, or he wouldn't sleep there. The old man felt the rough wool between his thumb and forefinger. The robe was thick, with matted hair on one side and hide on the other. As long as he had that, he could face anything.

He wrote late into the night, turning on his kerosene lamp. Neatly stacked pages covered with his diminutive writing lay on his bed. He didn't know how long he wrote, but Bud Creeman came out with his lamp and said, "Grandfather, are you all right? It's pretty late."

"What?" He looked up, disorientated. "Oh, certainly, Bud. I'm fine. I'll just finish this page and go to sleep." And he did, but the questions had done their damage, as he found when he dreamed of the day he was stolen.

5

I'll be right down, give me a second." Gil Canao stood in the doorway of his Cupertino townhouse, speaking to a uniformed chauffer outside. A baby's howls poured from the open door. The driver nodded, retreating to the limousine parked on the curb. He leaned against the car and lit a cigarette. The streetlight illuminated him as if he were on stage.

Gil stood in the entry, looking out to the car, and then back into the house. The baby's screams reverberated from a hallway upstairs, filling the house, leaking out onto the street. He was surprised the neighbors hadn't called the cops this last week. Gil closed the front door and stood unmoving. He knew if he saw his wife's face, he wouldn't go. He couldn't stand her swollen, teary eyes, or seeing her lying there, passively not accusing him of getting them into this. He couldn't stand hearing her voice say, "Do whatever you want, Gil. I'll be fine." He couldn't stand *her*.

The nurse Will had hired to help Gabriela while he was gone tiptoed past him holding a hot water bottle wrapped in a towel. "It's all right, Mr. Canao," she said. "Some babies are like this. It's just colic. She'll be OK. We'll take her to the doctor tomorrow if we need to, but don't worry. Your wife and baby will be fine. They are fine. You can go."

The woman's blue eyes and Caucasian competence assured him on one level, but all the other levels were screaming. Why should a baby cry like that if there wasn't something wrong with her? Why did she keep crying? Why did Gabriela sob along with her? The parenting class they'd taken didn't say anything about this. They didn't tell you that you could do everything right and the baby would still shriek. In school and everywhere else he'd been, there was a formula. You got the formula down, and everything was cool. Gil had never seen anything like this; neither had Gabriela.

When Will asked him to go on this Indian spiritual retreat thing three days ago, he told him no. For once, he said it without squirming or hedging. "I'm sorry, Will. I'd like to go with you, but Gabriela just got home from the hospital. The baby cries a lot. I need to stay home."

Without missing a beat, Will replied, "That's fine, Gil. You stay home with your wife and baby. I'll get Dick Chao to come." He knew Gil would die before he'd let Chao take his place. Chao was his archrival at Numenon. He was from Hong Kong, while Gil's family lived outside Manila. Dick Chao was born to an upper-class family. He was smooth and classy, with manners like royalty. He was bred for Numenon, the Asian version of Will Duane.

When he went to California to school, Gil's family could barely pay his expenses, even after his scholarship and the grant. After school, he didn't go back home until he got a job with Numenon because there was no money for his plane ticket. He'd worked his brains out to get where he was. No way he'd let Chao take his place.

"OK, I'll go with you. I just don't know what to do about the baby. She cries all the time. Gabriela can't handle it."

They problem-solved. Will came up with the idea that Numenon would hire twenty-four-hour nurses to stay with his wife and baby, people from a top agency, so he could go on the trip. He agreed. He knew what this trip would mean to his career. This wasn't some management-training course. Whatever this was, Will was going along with them. That had never happened on all the stupid shit he sent them to, hoping to make them as good managers as he was. The people he selected were his favorites. Going on this trip meant he was the top of the top rung. Let Dick Chao go in his place? He'd kill him first.

Telling Gabriela was hard. He said that it would only be for a week. He could tell she knew better; they'd been married for eight years, to each other and to Numenon. They moved into the townhouse right after their honeymoon. Gabriela knew he'd be away a week this time, two weeks next time, then a month. She was going to leave him, he was sure of it.

He wavered in the entrance hall, his bags by the front door. Stay or go? Gabriela had said one thing that got to him in this week from hell: "My mother would know what to do." She would. So would his mother, all their collective aunts, great-aunts, cousins, and the whole extended clan. Those women would know what to do. That baby would be sleeping happily now. Gil wouldn't have to listen to the promises of some white nurse with a big resume. The baby's squalls hadn't slowed since she got there.

The problem was, his mother, Gabriela's, and all their other relatives were back in the Philippines where he and his wife had been born and raised. They were on the other side of the world. He'd left home to go to college, but went back to marry Gabriela after he got his MBA at Stanford. Gil couldn't remember a time when he hadn't been in love with Gabriela. They'd known each other all their lives. Their parents grew up with each other, and their grandparents were best friends. He'd been so in love with her when they married, and now … he was mad at her all the time. She would go back to the Philippines without him if he went on this trip.

Gil looked around, at his wit's end. An image appeared in his mind, an old photo of his grandfather. He was a teenager, standing in a jungle with a heavy rifle in his hands. Ammo belts crossed his chest. He was wearing rags and looked starved, but a light flamed in his black eyes. When the United States left the Philippines and the Japanese overran her thousands of islands, his grandfather refused to surrender. He retreated into the island's mountainous core and waged war from there. Hundreds of thousands of Filipinos did the same. Standing in his entry hall in the middle of the night, Gil could feel his grandfather looking down at him, the fiercest warrior he'd ever seen. That was his blood! That was who he was!

His grandfather fought until there was nothing left to fight, then came out of the mountains at the end of the war to claim a village that no longer existed. He walked past corpses and filth, past stench and disease. He reclaimed their land, the Canao family's land, and rebuilt their home. He grabbed a piece of the U.S. aid that managed to trickle down to their level, and started the shipping business that supported the family to this day. He married the one girl from his village who was still alive. "The prettiest one of all," he joked. And he worked for the rest of his life the way he had attacked the enemy from Japan.

"Good business is seeing what's in front of you," his grandfather had said. "If you live in a country made of thousands of islands, people will need to move things from island to island." So he started a shipping business that they'd had to fight to defend just like they were at war. His father had fought since he took over the business. Gil could feel his breathing lengthening and his rage rising.

Life was a war. He'd seen his father fawn and scrape, trying to fill the fat palms stretched out to him. He couldn't stand jokes about Imelda Marcos and her shoes. He and his family paid for those shoes. And paid for the champagne and caviar of a flock of vultures, politicians. He knew all about competition, and survival of the fittest.

The Spanish had screwed his country for hundreds of years, using their second-string conquistadores. The first team went to the New World and "civilized" Latin America. The Philippines got the dregs of Spain's administrators and the lessons in corruption they had to teach. Americans didn't know that. They weren't quite the liberators they thought themselves to be, either. Gil knew what his countrymen knew: American actions abroad served American interests.

One vulture after another had controlled his country and they'd learned their lesson well: screw or be screwed. So now they screwed anyone they could, mostly each other. His family had almost lost their business many times due to the hands reaching down from above, demanding tribute.

His family would be as rich as Dick Chao's except for what they had to pay to survive.

He was the pride of his entire clan. His parents and sisters and brothers, his aunts, uncles, all of them idolized him. He was the smart one, smartest kid in the province. The first to go to college, always studying practical things—business and how to make money. When the chance came to go to California, to the great business school at Stanford, did Gil Canao take it? He was gone before anyone could ask twice.

Was he going to lose everything because some woman couldn't hack it? No. He'd go. He'd fight the battle. Whatever Mr. Duane wanted, he'd do.

He didn't have a fancy house like the other MBAs on this trip. He had a plain townhouse. The rest of his money went home to his family. He was a Canao, he was a Filipino, and he would fight for what was his. That's what his grandfather was trying to tell him.

Gil picked up his suitcases and walked out on the porch, closing the front door a little too hard. The driver vaulted up the steps and grabbed his bags. He opened the car door for Gil and then put the bags in the trunk. "Do you need anything, Mr. Canao?" he said from his seat before they started.

"No." They took off as smoothly as an eel swimming in one of the rivers at home. The car smelled of new leather. A fresh *New York Times* sat on the seat next to him. A Thermos of coffee was tucked in a cabinet. Even a rose in a vase. Was he going to lose this for a woman?

Why couldn't Gabriela adjust? They'd been here eight years. Half of Cupertino was Asian. He'd taken her to community events, to Filipino events all over the Peninsula. Why didn't she settle in? Why did he have to be home to baby-sit her? Why had he married her?

They were driving down one of the peripheral streets, heading to I-280. Gil stopped his internal raving as they passed a housing project. Chain link fence surrounded the abandoned and half-finished development. Some of the windows were broken. Kids had written graffiti all over it. Gil had seen it before, but never like this. Something clicked. His eyes narrowed. He smelled blood.

"Driver, could you go back? Drive past those buildings again."

They stopped in front of the development. They were condos, maybe fifteen of them, abandoned before completion. That was easy to explain; somebody ran out of money, or a partnership blew up, or the bank called its loan. The development had been that way for a while, from the extent of the damage. Why hadn't some other guy grabbed them? Was a lawsuit hanging them up? Some environmental thing? This was a research project.

Gil took down all the information on the for-sale sign in front, and got back in the car, intrigued. This was exactly what he was looking for. If he could grab these, he could finish and sell them for a million each, minimum. The cheaper he got them, the more he would make. He pulled out his laptop and plugged into the Numenon database. It was the best database in the world, very proprietary, and not something you asked too much about.

Like, how did the managers of the database get access to the info they posted? "Don't ask, don't tell" had always existed at Numenon. The numbers were good; that's all anyone cared about. Where an ordinary person would see a blight on the urban landscape, Gil saw money waiting to be made.

By the time they got to the San Jose airport, Gil knew that a nasty divorce and lawsuit from a partner were behind the project's collapse. The bank wanted to dump it, but the wife's family was bailing her out. How could he get them to sell it to him? How could he bail them all out? There had to be a solution. He stewed for a while, then it came to him. He shot off a few e-mails. Numenon execs had the only wireless technology available in 1997—a little perk that went with the territory. It happened to be classified, military technology, but Numenon developed it. So where was the problem?

They pulled up to the Numenon terminal right behind Will's car. Will swept out of the limo like it was eight in the morning and he'd been sleeping for ten hours. He was beaming and bright, with his white head shining. He waved at Gil and helped Betty climb out. She headed through the terminal at top speed while Will waited for him, the gracious host, just as he was at Numenon.

Gil was impressed every time he saw his boss, even after working for him all these years. He was always so cool and unflappable, always knowing what to do. He'd seen him in action so many times. Not to mention hearing about him at Stanford. He was practically worshiped as a god there, the most successful graduate the Biz School had ever had. And look what he gave back. Will's parents had endowed chairs in their names. A new wing of the school was named for his daughter. He gave a dozen scholarships a year. Will even accepted a few little awards, like the grand prize, the Arbuckle Award. He could have won it every year, except it wasn't allowed.

"How much did you make, Gil?" Will looked like an excited kid, asking him the question Gil knew was coming. Numenon had many rituals, almost all instituted by Will. The competition to make the most money on the way to the airport—or anywhere—was one of them. Will's smile was the prize, and they fought for that. Fought everywhere. The most impressive winner was Doug Saunders, who made nine hundred thousand dollars while sitting on the can in Singapore. "It doesn't have to be legal, does it, Will?" Saunders quipped as he announced his coup.

"Jesus, Doug. How'd you do that on the crapper?" Will asked, ignoring the issue of legality. Doug whispered the secret to him, and the two walked off laughing, Will's arm around Doug's shoulder.

That's what he wanted. Will to care about him that much. Will to tell him he was doing a good job. To share in-jokes with him. So he dropped his plum: "When it all shakes out, maybe six million." Will's eyes went wide.

"Nice. What's the drive from your place? Twenty minutes?"

"Fifteen." Will smiled at him the way his mother did if he won something. They walked through the terminal with Will's arm around his shoulder and all the airport employees saying, "Good morning, Mr. Duane!" All bright and shiny, as if it was a normal hour instead of the middle of the night. They were happy just because Will Duane was there and was kind enough to own the terminal in which they worked, the fabulous terminal that had been in three design magazines and had won an industrial architecture award.

Gil thought his heart would explode. He did it! All he had to come up with was a million dollars to get the ball rolling. He didn't have it, and didn't tell Will. Who cared if it wasn't quite in the bag? You never knew what could happen in a week with Will. He attracted money like shit attracted flies.

Gil didn't notice how he changed in Will's presence, but he did notice his rivals at the bottom of the jet's stairs.

"How much did you make, Melissa?" Will said to the one female MBA on the trip.

Drawing herself up to her full five feet two inches and straightening her padded shoulders, Melissa Weir answered, "Nothing, Will. I meditated. I meditate every morning." She ascended the stairs with the air of a dowager empress.

Will poked him, laughing at her silently.

Melissa turned and glared at him, acting as though she had overheard them making fun of her. With an imperious toss of her head, she disappeared into the jet.

Will turned to Doug Saunders, the man everyone thought of as Will's true son, which is why they nicknamed him that. "Hey, guy! How much did you make?" Gil expected him to say fifty million dollars, way more than he could ever make.

Doug glared at his boss. "Nothing. I slept." He kept glaring, like he'd deck Will if he said any more. Will stepped back, surprised.

"You're not going soft on me, are you?" he asked in a conciliatory tone.

"I *never* go soft, Will. You know that." It was like a curse, the way he said it. Doug climbed into the plane, leaving them standing at the bottom of the stairs.

Gil was shocked. Will and Doug were supposed to be closer than father and son. They had partied together for years. In Numenon, partying meant … Gil never went with them. He was true to his marriage vows. He always had been. He wanted to ask Will what Doug meant, why he was so hostile. He looked at Will, who was staring at Doug's back, expressionless, but radiating pain.

"Well, let's get on board," he said. "Looks like it's going to be a long trip."

6

Dawn was nowhere in evidence. Grandfather lit his lamp and read what he had written the night before, crossing out a word here and there. Maybe this was good. Maybe if people had what he said in black and white, the gossip wouldn't be so bad. Maybe what people said about him would be more accurate. The question of supernatural powers always came up. He wrote:

1. My dear students, most people already have powers, but they cover them up with alcohol and drugs, with bad thoughts and nasty feelings. Powers happen along the spiritual path, but they aren't the end of it. The end of the path is joining with the Great One, merging into the love and grace that brought you here. That is what you should aim for, only that.

If you want more powers than you have naturally, almost anyone can get them. Charlatans who call themselves holy men will teach you tricks for money. They'll show you how to make smoke and ashes appear and do other things that mean nothing. These are like the mirrors and trinkets the outsiders used to fool our ancestors into giving up their land, into giving up the most valuable thing they had. But you can get such fake powers if you want. I won't teach you such magic, but others will. Once you've gotten these false powers, you have to please

Creator to keep them. You have to live like Great-grandfather demanded that his apprentices and I live—like warriors. When you want real power, true Power, you will come to me. I will tell you the truth. There are no shortcuts. To attain real Power, you must give up your old life. You must give everything you have, and love Creator with all your mind and heart.

When he was writing, he wondered if he should tell them all the truth. Would they understand it? Of all the thousands coming, how many would really understand what he did and said and take it into their souls? The Power nudged him inside and he realized he had no choice; this was the last Meeting. It was time to tell it all.

My only power is being able to open my heart to the Great One. I act like a lens for the Great One's will—that is all. Over the years the One has worked on my heart, shaping it and moving it. Sometimes breaking it open so I cried and sobbed in pain. In opening my heart, I received a great gift. I began to listen to the One, and then I could see the One. I was able to see the ancestors, and feel my dear Great-grandfather, the greatest holy man ever born.

Tears filled his eyes when he read of Great-grandfather, as they had when he wrote the words. He would never stop mourning his teacher. Could those coming to the Meeting comprehend a teacher whose sole purpose was to lead others to God? Someone so holy he burned away what wasn't divine in everyone he touched? Or would they only know lesser teachers who gave lessons in accounting or taught them how to play piano? A true teacher was God's jewel, a gift given to a very few. Meeting such a teacher required a lifetime's inner work, and yet was the starting point of real life. A faint smile touched his lips.

After I gave my heart to the Unseen, the inner world opened to me. So when I ask that a prayer be heard, that a healing take place, that a soul be saved, most of the time, the Great One says, "Yes!" and my prayers are answered. But the Power that heals and works miracles isn't my power.

People look all over for power, trying to buy it, trying to own it. All the time, the source hides very close. The Great One lives within each of us, a mighty river of love flowing in all directions, always there. All anyone has to do is go into his heart to find all the power in the universe. That's what I do.

That was a great teaching, he knew. But would anyone hear his words? Or would they hear echoes of words spoken through centuries, and discount them? Others had said such words. Others had flamed like pillars of fire, knowing the truth. And what happened to them? What happened to their wonderful knowledge after they died? People distorted it for their own ends. Dare he write more? This was so important, but his feedback sheets had said he was "boring" and "went on too long." "Show me, don't tell me," they said. The insult! His blood rose in fury. No! He was the teacher, not the taught. He would write what he needed to say.

My followers call my apprentices "spirit warriors"—but they are simply the ones who are most committed to my teachings and those of Great-grandfather. They are committed to the ways the Great One gave our lineage and keeps giving it. The Teachings are living, just like us. They change as we need to change. The Rules we use at the Meeting are easy compared with the old days. The ancestors know that we are weaker than they were, so they make it easy for us because they love us. They have done much of our work.

The Rules are: No nuthin. That's true. No drinking, no drugs, no laziness, no lies, no cheating, no sex at the Meeting, unless you've just found your soul mate and married. And sex only with your spouse, ever. Many more Rules exist, created by the Great One to see that you get the Powers that are meant for you.

I have the Powers you have seen because of the Rules. They are the reason that the spirit warriors can do what they do. Any of you can be a spirit warrior. If you live like me, and think like me, and worship like me, you will be able to do what I do. I follow the Rules. The warriors follow the Rules. You've heard of them, I'm sure. This year, they will be posted all over the Bowl. The warriors will take care of that.

That was enough, he thought. They needn't know all about his Powers. He seldom showed his real powers at the Meeting, they weren't for the uninitiated. How many powers did he have? He had no idea. Powers and more powers flocked to him, drawn like moths by the torch of his heart. He had to knock them out of the way so that he could work. He had no idea how many powers he had to use, not to own. Could he move mountains? Was he mightier than an atom bomb? He would find out this week. And so would they.

7

P eople! People! We need to get to work!" Will's voice filled the jet's cabin. Confident. Powerful. "Mark Kenna will meet us with the motor homes when we land. We face a long, tough drive. I have something I need to tell you first."

Betty Fogarty snapped awake, instantly focused on the man sitting across from her in the cabin. Dread found her just as fast. Her stomach clenched and a fine tremble invaded her hands. Her eyes sought Will's form. Her ears strained to hear his words. Make me believe, Will. Make it all right. His form grabbed her, as erect and striking as ever. His white hair made him more attractive than when he was young.

He had stood before her for almost thirty years, calling to her, leading her, making her believe in a possibility she couldn't see. She remembered the first time she heard him speak. It was at a Numenon recruiting rally in 1968. They held it in the corporate gym. He dazzled them, all of them. They competed to get jobs, fought to get in. He was so commanding, telling what he saw.

"Numenon is the world of the future, a world where technology and science, art and commerce will flower together." And Numenon was that. Its headquarters was an architectural masterpiece, as all the critics and textbooks said. Numenon was the best, from the design of its products to its corporate strategy to its employees. Will kept marching forward, dragging the world behind him.

Now, they held their annual rally in the Oakland Coliseum. It could barely hold the management and executives from around the world. Will stood on the stage, pacing and gesturing, with cameras broadcasting his tall, angular form to huge screens. Subtitles in a dozen languages ran below them. He spoke about a future so bright, so wonderful.

"I see a world where equality reigns, not just in concept, but in reality. Where the divisions between people break down and we see our common humanity, our common purpose. I see a world of greater prosperity than we can imagine. I see a world of hope and love... And in all of that—Numenon leads the way!"

He could see this world, and because he did, others could too. Spotlights roamed the crowds. Cheers erupted at every pause, every time he lifted his hand. Flags waved. Confetti flew. Political conventions were tame next to Numenon rallies. Will stood in the center. He had delivered on his promises.

Ice shot through her. Make it real, Will. Make me believe.

The others began to stir as his voice penetrated their slumber. Seating in the jet's main cabin was arranged in a circle so they could discuss things while flying. The three MBAs had settled as close to Will as they could get. They looked like sleepy children. They were children. Melissa was the oldest, just thirty-one. They were the Dream Team, the heirs to Will's kingdom.

Sandy Sydney dozed next to her. Betty jiggled her young assistant's arm. She didn't have to do more; her helper was awake and alert. Jon Walker was as far from everyone as he could get, wrapped in blankets and looking asleep despite Will's voice. Betty glanced at her watch. Four thirty in the morning. It was pitch black outside. They were heading for Tucson, Arizona. Will's voice cut through the darkness.

"I need to talk about the purpose of this mission. We're on a corporate mission this week, as well as a voyage of personal growth."

As she stared, a tendril of nougat-colored hair brushed her chin. Her rosy cheek was rosier from being pressed against the soft leather seat as she slept. Betty was the sort of aging woman that people noticed and said, "She must have been beautiful when she was young." "She's still a good-looking woman." At fifty-five, Betty was entering a state of nonexistence. She was already invisible to the carryout boy at the grocery store. Soon, she would vanish as a woman except as, "She must have been ..." Betty fought her demise.

Will's voice filled the cabin, masterful. In control. "You know I have a deep and abiding interest in Native American culture."

Her brow crinkled. She didn't understand this. Betty knew Will better than anyone on earth. She'd never heard him utter a word about Native Americans before this week. The trip seemed ill-timed. They were already overworked with the merger coming up, and the takeover rumors. But that was nothing new. Someone was always gunning for Will. He'd survived one coup attempt after another since he started Numenon in the late fifties.

"This is a delicate mission. That's why I picked you. You're my best and brightest. My most trusted command force."

She kept blinking. His voice wasn't having the effect it usually had. She didn't feel energized and alive, or inspired.

"We're going to study with the greatest Native American shaman ever born. That's what he is, isn't he, Betty?"

Betty nodded. She'd done the research for most of the brief. She tried to say, "Yes, but don't call him that. He hates it. He says it's an insult to his ancestors ..." Will was off and talking before she could open her mouth.

"It's an unprecedented opportunity. He's never allowed non-Natives to come to his little powwow. So we have to use our party manners." Betty looked at him. That grin, the charm. The man was irresistible. He wore a suit. They'd decided that wearing their ordinary business clothes would establish corporate presence. They all wore suits.

"I'm a student of cultures that work. I want us to take in everything about this man. He's supposedly got a great organization behind him. I want us to pick it apart. I want us to find out what makes it tick. And take it home."

When Betty started working for Numenon, it took her three years to claw through the secretarial ranks and demonstrate she was good enough to head Will's personal secretarial staff. Three years of busting her butt only to learn that it was just the warm-up. She'd worked harder since she became top dog. In the beginning, Betty was like everyone else. She saw Will, heard Will, and fell in love. For years, she lived in awe of him, half in love with him. His voice reverberated in her bones, in her flesh. She'd heard it so often.

"This is a historic journey, and an important one," Will was in fine form. They were all awake and listening. Believing. He raised his voice, "We're going to play as the Numenon team. These Indians will see who's in charge! Who they can trust ..."

The magic kicked in. Betty believed. The Indians could trust them, and the Indians could trust Will. He was a good man. Her jaw tightened along with her resolve. Those who criticized Will Duane were jealous little people. They couldn't stand someone that good looking and charismatic having *all* that money. He was a genius. Little people couldn't stand that, anymore than they could stand what he had created. Numenon wasn't just a huge corporation; it was a way of life. When you were with Numenon, your life meant something. Will Duane and his team did that! She felt like cheering. They were going to make a difference to those poor Indians! Yes!

"We must do our best this week! This is a mission!" Will was talking faster, making eye contact. Working the crowd. His fans. His devotees. His voice grew louder, and more commanding. It had a hysterical edge.

Betty became alarmed. She'd seen this before, when he was stressed. She covered for him when it happened at work. This is what his critics saw. Yes, if you'd seen him blow up and have one of his tantrums, it could frighten you. It was just because he cared so much about every little thing. He was so involved. She knew the real Will. She knew about his acts of charity and how he helped employees who'd had disasters. He gave more than anyone needed to give. Betty knew this very well. She wrote the checks. And she knew how sweet he could be, like a vulnerable little boy.

His voice rose and fell, cadenced, faster, and insistent. The purpose of their trip ... There was more to it than met the eye. He would tell them when they understood the importance of—Betty saw Will starring at Jon Walker.

She looked at the chef. He'd struggled awake, still wrapped in blankets, gazing around the cabin like an owl. Jon had dyed his hair a bright, true red. That must give Will fits, with the dress code. But she knew what Jon was going through. 'Rique Maldonado had been a wonderful man. The Latin Ralph Lauren, everyone called him.

Jon looked like he might cry. What was that poor boy doing with them? It was far too soon. 'Rique died in Jon's arms, Betty had heard. Couldn't Will get one of his other chefs for the trip? But Jon was "the best chef in the world." That's what they all were, "Beyond the Best, That's Numenon." The corporate slogan.

Seeing Jon so vulnerable, Betty felt something rupture inside. Her eyes stung. She had to hold back sobs. No. Will was going to tell them why they were here. It would be a good reason, a compelling reason. She had never regretted giving her life to Will Duane.

Why were they were going on a retreat in the desert with Indians? Tears spilled down her cheeks. Why was he in hyperdrive? What was this all about? She knew what happened to Will two months ago. Why wasn't he home with some shrink? And then he got to it and told them why they were there.

Betty listened, recoiling. Receding into her chair. Will's words stood out, like the air in the cabin had been cleansed so sound traveled better. She heard each word, aware that she was sitting there, Betty Fogarty, one of the most powerful women in the corporate world, listening to an important message. At the same time, she could feel something draining from her, like sand drifting away. Like whatever held her up was disintegrating. She looked at Will, but she saw someone else in her mind's eye.

He was fifty-six, broad-shouldered and square. Ruggedly handsome, he'd been faithful to her for thirty-two years. Betty had given up her husband, John Fogarty, to come on this dreadful misadventure.

John had told her the previous night, "I've had it, Betty. I'm sick of you leaving whenever he snaps his fingers. If you go, I won't be here when you get back." He meant it. John had slept in the guest room and didn't come out when she left.

She'd given up her husband for Will's latest greedy, immoral scheme, foisted on them as a spiritual retreat. He'd lied to her one time too many. It came crashing in on her, all of it. Years and years of things she knew that wouldn't stay hidden. They called her boss a genius. They also called him "The Prince of Darkness."

Betty hated Will Duane more than she knew she could hate.

8

Grandfather wanted to think about his special guests from the corporate world and what would happen with them at the Meeting. His mind ranged over the desert. He could feel them struggling toward him, which is how it should be. Coming home was difficult. But he wasn't allowed to think of them, or what their coming meant. The Great One grabbed his attention and focused it on the questions. He had to finish answering them before he could think of anything else. Picking up where he stopped the night before, he addressed the next question.

"I'm confused. I read about Grandfather, Great-grandfather, and Joseph on the Internet. Who are all these people? Are these different names for the shaman who leads the Meeting? Why does he have so many names? And who is Joseph Bishop?"

He couldn't imagine his People being so ignorant about names, but he picked up his pen and began.

Our traditions regarding naming vary. It's not unusual for Indians to have many names, though the way it works varies by Nation. In the old days, a father gave his son a name when he was born. He'd keep that name until he became a man—he would get a new name as the result of a ceremony or having a vision. A holy man might name him. If he did something remarkable in his life, or changed in his soul, he could change his name later in life. The rules were similar for girls and women. Some names were known only within a family or a tribe. Some were only between a man or woman and the Great One, or their holy man.

The majority culture gives a person one official name that doesn't change. It's easy to see how a new person could be confused by the names people call me.

He stretched and sighed. Answering the questions was hard. The Meeting was a spiritual trial for everyone who attended, but it had never been terribly strenuous for him. Before he died, Great-grandfather had done his work, drilling and pummeling him until he thought *he'd* die, removing his impurities and finally giving him his Power and blessing as the new head of the lineage. He hadn't expected another trial, but this Meeting was shaping up like that. We're never finished, not as long as we're alive, he thought.

The hard part came inside, with the things he didn't write. His father gave him a name. He couldn't remember it—no matter how many years pass or how much he learned, he couldn't remember the name his father gave him, or the language of his band. He couldn't remember his real tongue. The knowledge seared his being. He went back to writing.

When I was a young man, Great-grandfather was my teacher. We didn't call him Great-grandfather then. Everyone called him Grandfather, except us. We apprentices—and he didn't have so many, just a few—called him another name, which we kept secret. And he had secret names for us, which just the two of us knew. Each of us had many names. Joseph is what my friends called me in public when I was Great-grandfather's student. Some people who've known me a long time call me that now.

So, I am called all those names, and I am the person who leads the Meeting. If you are confused about names, be happy. You would be much more confused if it was the old days.

You'd have many more names to remember right now if you were a spirit warrior, he thought, because we use the old ways. You'll only become a spirit warrior if I see your passion and commitment to the One, and to our lineage, and ask you to join us.

Most of you will never be spirit warriors, but you'll hear of their power and want to be one. You'll run around the Meeting trying to impress me: "Pick me. Pick me. See how spiritual I am!" When that doesn't work, you'll examine everyone you see with narrowed eyes, trying to guess who is a warrior and who isn't. We won't tell you, though anyone with eyes can see who we are.

You'll be jealous of the warriors and angry with me because I didn't choose you. Then you'll gossip about the Meeting and me, and it will come back to me after you go home … He sighed. And all of this because I can see you aren't ready. Irritation grew inside him. What trouble this Meeting was! Thank the Great One this was the last.

Still, people had to be taught. He turned back to the pages he'd written.

When Great-grandfather was dying, he called his most advanced students to him. He talked to us, and he told everyone that I was his successor. I spent some time with him alone and he told me secret things. I felt his Power enter me, and then he died. After that, I was called Grandfather and he became known as Great-grandfather. That was logical. How could we call him Grandfather and call me Grandfather too? That would be confusing. So I am Grandfather and he is Great-grandfather. That's simple.

But it's not that simple, because in some of our People's traditions, the word Grandfather is used the way I say the Great One, to mean God. Other traditions call the Great One the Grandfathers, plural. So, those people wouldn't understand how we use Grandfather, except that they'd understand that with our People, names are based on tradition, tribal affiliation, and lineage. We have lineages of holy men and women whose Power is passed from generation to generation. You can be happy now. I've explained names.

He wanted to laugh, imagining the consternation his reply would cause. But the rest of the question wouldn't let him laugh. Who is Joseph Bishop? Joseph Bishop. The words swam in his mind, banging around inside him. Who is Joseph Bishop?

He found himself falling through time, spinning, and turning. He ended up on that little boat in the river of darkness, reliving the past. Earlier, his mind had shown him how he met white men. Now it would show him the other time, when he found out the truth. The boat cast off, bobbing merrily. Its channel widened, and a scene appeared. It wasn't what Grandfather expected. Rather than go straight to the heart, the little boat trolled slowly in shallower waters.

He could see the place where he and the children of his band were taken in 1918. They were dragged off the wagons and stripped of their clothes. Bathed. They had their hair cut and deloused, and were stuffed back into new, scratchy clothes, all alike: stiff suits for boys, stiffer dresses for girls. Each was given a new name, which no one understood. After that, they were loaded onto a train bound for the New Hope Indian School, along with children from other bands. It seemed like no time passed between these things, but it must have, in real life.

Grandfather could see the scene as though he was there. The children were silent as they stood in the dust awaiting their train. Shocked dull, every one. As the children of his band got on the train, a matron separated out the boy newly named Joseph Bishop. That was him. Also his little brother, now known as Raymond Bishop, and a girl they now called Sally Waters. Such beautiful children should go to a better school than the rest. They went into a different car. That was the first trick of fate that both doomed and saved the chief's son.

Six months later, when he had thawed enough to respond to the teachers and learned some English, Joseph Bishop's teachers discovered that he was smart. Very, very smart. Much brighter than the other children. By that time, he was also willing and pliant. He would take orders. Joseph Bishop was what the school administrators sought, an indigenous child who could and would reach the heights. And show the world what their programs could do.

From there, the old man's mind lurched forward. Nineteen years passed in a barefoot stagger. Grandfather went to ten boarding schools before graduating from high school. The best schools fought for him, the brilliant Indian boy who would prove they were right. He heard a succession of teachers and headmasters talk about him as if he weren't there.

'Joseph learns so fast."

"He's the only one who tries."

"Joseph Bishop is a good boy. He'll make a success of himself."

Grandfather could see himself copying his teachers. Aping anyone who promised to love him. He acted how they acted, moved how they moved, and spoke how they spoke. Why not? To his fellow Indian students, Joseph Bishop was a runty little suck-up. He could still feel the blows of the bigger boys who didn't know he was the chief's son. Who didn't know that the holy man had marked him for greatness.

The holy man's visit to his village was one of the few things Joseph remembered of his earlier life. He was five summers old when the great holy man came, searching for something, drawn by someone. The shaman examined the band, staring into everyone's eyes. He quickly returned to the boy who was to become Joseph Bishop, grasping his shoulders with bony, arthritic hands. The holy man looked at him. And—to the boy this was true— eagle claws flew from the shaman's eyes straight into his own. They pierced his eyes, moving deeper into him until they reached his heart and shredded it. The boy couldn't move or cry out. The holy man patted his head and stroked his hair.

"This one will save the People!"

He said it in their language, but whenever Grandfather remembered, he always heard it in English.

Joseph Bishop's path was set. After he was stolen, no one knew he was supposed to be the savior of his People. The other children saw him as a goody-goody. Outcast, the boy did what he had done at home. He always had given his father more than he expected, so Joseph Bishop did the same to his captors. He became the best student in the school. Some might say it was the holy man's prophecy that made him excel. Others might point out that it was his early conditioning, the high regard and good treatment of his family and band that brought out his best. Still others might say it was his innate ability. The boy had a high IQ; his not excelling would be harder to explain. For whatever reason, being the best was as much a part of this boy as breathing. In a very short time, Joseph became a perfect little white boy whose only flaw was the color of his skin.

Though he looked tame on the outside and felt it, the wild one in Joseph's soul did not die. Every night as he drifted to sleep, year after year after year, the wild boy heard his father's voice saying, "I will come for you, or the sun will cease to shine."

He heard this even when he could remember nothing of his earlier life. The wild boy could see the dark outline of his father's head as he ran beside the wagon. The sun made a halo around him. His father was a god. The boy never doubted that his father would come … He would come.

Tears ran down Grandfather's cheeks as he remembered. He chanted a few short syllables, *"Be with me! Be with me! Oh, Great One! Give me the strength to walk on."*

When he could, he wrote, *Joseph Bishop is the name the white man gave me. I use it when I sign legal papers.*

9

Will Duane stood at the top of the jet's ramp. Sloppy cones of light illumined the blacktop. It was pitch black. He looked at his watch. Four forty-five, Sunday morning. His melancholy had fled, driven out by a variety of feelings, as they grew closer to their target. Disgust choked him, rising in his throat. Of all the stupid places to be, the Tucson, Arizona, airport. He couldn't get that old man to come to him—and now he had to go to a revival meeting in the middle of the desert.

He waved at Mark Kenna, who was sprinting across the blacktop from the terminal with a luggage dolly. The other four drivers followed in military precision. Will's heart jumped, seeing their eagerness. Will walked down the ramp, the others behind him. He stopped at the bottom. Something arose inside him. He hated her so much that he could have blown up the whole place. He felt like those burning oil wells he'd seen at the end of the Gulf War. He liked the violence of the flaming columns. Now he shimmered in rage, glistened with it, as he stood at the bottom of the ramp. She had coerced him into this. He wanted to kill her.

"Will?" Betty was right behind him.

"Oh, sorry, Betty." He was blocking the ramp. "I have to go back in the plane. I forgot something." He had to discharge this fury.

Will moved aside to let the others pass. Betty Fogarty, the best secretary in the world. Sandy Sydney, her Wellesley graduate protégée. As angry as he was, Will couldn't help thrill at the next three, the Dream Team. That old Indian told him to bring his best. Here they were: Melissa Weir. Melissa's MBA was from Harvard. Gil Canao and Doug Saunders got theirs from Stanford. All three were top of their class. Will loved MBAs. His degree was from Stanford too. Last out of the plane was Jon Walker, the cook. Even he was world class. Will had stolen Jon from Ao Punto, the best restaurant in San Francisco, three years before.

"Get settled into the motor homes. I'll be right there." He marched back into the jet, running the last few steps. Rage fueled him.

"I need a secure line," he barked at the pilot.

He jumped into the cockpit and did something on an instrument panel. "You got it, Mr. Duane."

Will charged through the main cabin in three strides, throwing open the door to the smaller compartment that served as his private office and bedroom. He shut the door before crossing the room and reaching for the phone, which was mounted on a wall of floor-to-ceiling cabinetry. His lips were slightly parted, teeth glinting. His hand stopped an inch from the receiver. He stood, unable to pick up the phone, unable to move.

He had intended to call Jim Billinghorst in Palo Alto and put eight thousand people out of work. Billinghorst was handling the largest merger Numenon had ever attempted. It probably should be an antitrust case, but if the U.S. Department of Justice wasn't calling it a Sherman Act violation, who cared? If Will had his way, Recomtex Inc. would be a profit center as soon as Numenon took it over. Deadwood and waste would be eliminated. Eight thousand people would be without work as soon as they could do the paperwork. He was going to order Billinghorst to do it his way. No more discussion.

He tried to move his hand closer to the receiver. It wouldn't move.

If he made the call, Billinghorst would quit. His dainty liberal sensibilities couldn't tolerate making a tough business decision. The way he's been carrying on, you'd think we were putting his mother out of work, thought Will. He didn't have the balls to work at Numenon. This was the perfect solution; all he had to do was make the call. Billinghorst wouldn't be able to stand up to him. He would quit before Will got back, leaving Will with no legal problems, no wrongful discharge suit, no golden parachute payment. Just one call and he'd have one less thorn in his side.

His hand wouldn't move. Why? He could hear Jim whimpering in meetings, "Give them some time... Soften the blow. Attrition..." His hand hovered. Will stared at it as if it belonged to someone else. What was wrong with him?

Why don't you call her? A soft voice said inside his head. Call her.

Will jumped back, hand falling to his side. He stood in the middle of the room, swaying on his feet.

She won't answer me. She'll never answer me. Will's lips were dry. He moistened them with the tip of his tongue. He stood there, incredulous. What was happening? Why couldn't he pick up the phone? His legs seemed to melt. He was on his knees, and then fell forward onto his hands. What was happening? Pain filled his chest. Was he having a heart attack?

He saw a face looking at him from inside his own head. He'd never seen the man, but he knew who it was. That old Indian. Ever since speaking to him on the phone, Will had felt like something was pulling him somewhere he didn't want to go. He couldn't even make a business call.

Are you sure that's what you want to do? the quiet voice inside him asked.

Will moaned. The Indian was a sorcerer. He'd put some kind of spell on him. He'd have to get the others and go back home. They couldn't go to this Meeting, this Indian retreat in the desert. It was too dangerous. And they couldn't *not* go—he remembered his cataclysmic vision and the bugs in his home. It was too dangerous at home. They were all in danger until they got there. They had to go. He remembered what he'd told them in the plane. His cheeks flamed.

Why did I tell them that? Because it's true, part of him thought. "The best way to lie is tell the truth. Just don't tell *all* the truth." One of his famous maxims. Why couldn't he tell them the complete truth? He couldn't bring the words to his lips, or pull the images to his mind. He couldn't talk about his visions and the darkness that plagued him. He couldn't tell them what he really felt, or what losing her did to him. He was Will Duane, the richest man in the world.

What do you really want? the quiet voice asked.

Will knew what would happen if he didn't go, but what did he really want? He hadn't asked himself that in years. "I don't know," he whispered. "I don't know what I want. I don't know what to do." At that admission, he rolled back on his heels, cradling his head with his forearms. He had to know what to do! He was the commander of an empire. He didn't just move mountains; he owned them. He decided whether they existed or not. He had to know what to do.

Will crouched on the floor, surrounded by walls bearing his kingdom's logo, by leather and raw silk, granite and wool, the trappings of the most powerful man in the world. He could barely breathe. He became very still, almost dazed. He felt as if he was in an empty space, in nothingness. No motion, no people, barely a breath. I've got to get out of here, and call the others back. I've got to go home. Can't. Even thought stopped.

Will felt himself at a crossroads, a turning point. Something opened in the nothingness, a door. Will looked through and saw that there was only one choice. He could take the path before him and finish what he'd put in motion, or perish. He stepped through the door.

Life began again. Will pulled himself to his feet and stood for a moment, adjusting his suit. He blinked, feeling like a different person than the man who walked in the door, and totally the same. He walked out into the main cabin. He saw the pilot standing by the cockpit, staring at him. Will walked to the pilot. "Stuart ..." He took a hundred-dollar bill out of his wallet. "It's Emily's birthday tomorrow. Give this to her from me, will you? A girl doesn't turn eight every day. Say hi to Bev and Stanley for me, too."

The pilot gaped at the bill in his hand, then looked at Will, stammering, "Thank you, Mr. Duane. I will."

Will walked out the jet's door feeling both composed and disjointed.

"Thanks again, Mr. Duane!" the pilot called after him.

Will smiled. All he had to do was cough up a few details, and they thought he knew everything. They thought he was God. Of course, he did remember pretty near everything he read, and he could determine their fates with a word. He felt his equilibrium and his power return.

Will savored the view from the ramp. Surprisingly, he hadn't been gone that long. The others hadn't made it to the terminal. The three MBAs had shot ahead of the secretaries, speed walking across the blacktop. They were so competitive that they'd race each other to hell. Melissa split off at the terminal, saying something to an airport worker and disappearing into the building. Doug and Gil continued into the building and out of sight. Betty and Sandy walked together, heads almost touching as they chatted.

Will's nostrils flared watching Sandy Sydney. He could feel his body responding to her. The secretary was totally covered up and classy, but every inch was a come-on. The airport lights bleached the color out of her suit, but he'd seen its pale rose in the plane. The jacket was fitted. From the back, Will could see her tiny waist and the curve of her hips. The light, billowy silk of the skirt came almost to the young woman's ankles, accentuating their fineness. Sandy's blond hair wafted around her shoulders. Even from the back, even in the middle of the night in the shitty Tucson airport, she was enchanting. Will watched her, eyes narrowed, jaws clenched. This was the week, wasn't it, Sydney? You and I.

Shouting from the rear of the plane diverted Will's attention. Mark Kenna was down by the cargo bay arguing with Jon Walker. Mark wore the Numenon driver's uniform like the rest of the crew: black slacks, white shirt, and burgundy blazer with the Numenon logo in gold. The corporate colors. With his short dark hair combed precisely, he looked slick and professional, another company trademark. Mark was a medium-tall man about thirty, tanned and fit from surfing every hour he had off. He had a broad face with strong white teeth, a ready smile and boundless enthusiasm. He was Will's favorite driver. Mark looked up when he saw Will's white head move.

"I'm sorry, Mr. Duane," he said. He and Jon had been yelling at each other.

Will waved his hand to say, "No problem." He understood Mark's peevishness. He'd never felt as irritable as he had since they started this stupid mission. But things seemed better once they got under way. He liked the way the professional staff took what he said to them in the plane. No bleeding heart crap, not even from Melissa. Jon didn't even seem to notice. Still, everyone was on edge. Will could see Jon's bright red dyed hair even in the dim light. It violated the dress code, but he understood why he'd done it. When you lose someone you love, you do idiotic things, such as going on this trip.

He bounded down the ramp, heading for the motor homes. If someone had asked him what happened in the jet's cabin, he wouldn't have been able to recall.

10

Time doesn't exist. He wanted to tell the People things that were important, not answer their stupid questions. A fool thinks that time is like a string wrapped tightly between two sticks and marked off in equal segments. One year, two years, on and on, every segment the same size, every year something you could count with pebbles.

No, time didn't exist. Everything happened now—the past, present, and future—all happened now. He knew that we create our present and our future just as we created our past. Reality swarmed and swooped, each separate universe existing at once. That was easy for him to understand. He could see it. But he had had the advantage of living with Great-grandfather for all those years. He made the truth obvious. The slowest of his apprentices understood how it all happened at once, how we made a choice and moved from one universe to another, and how everything was intertwined.

Were he and his fellow students smarter than those who sought spirit today? He didn't think so. Certainly his best students—Wesley and Elizabeth, Leroy and Carl—were as quick as any of them. But the rest …

If he could explain the nature of the mind and how it wove time, that would be enough. Time wasn't like a string between sticks—it was like a weaver. Say a weaver sat at her loom, passing the shuttle in and out, in and out. Using different colors, following an ancient pattern or one she made up, she sat weaving. Something happened—her mind wandered, or she fell asleep, anything—and she made a mistake. Picked the wrong color, or made a line too short. The pattern became different from what it was supposed to be.

"Well," she said, "that's OK. I'll just make this be the pattern." She was too lazy to rip it out and fix her mistake, so she changed the design to incorporate it.

And on she went, weaving back and forth, back and forth. Except the design was all counted out to go the right way. All the other colors were set up so the rug would turn out the way it was supposed to be before she made the mistake. They weren't right now. So the rug got funny looking, out of shape. She tried to correct it by changing more threads, and colors, and the pattern changed again. Finally, she ended up with a catawampus thing, not straight or patterned right. A mess. In the real world, she could sell it to tourists, who would say, "It's so authentic" and "You can tell it's handmade by the mistakes!"

But what if she was making her soul? What if she made a mistake and wove it in, and kept the lie of the mistake running year after year, pretending that the warped shape she was taking on was what was meant to be? What if that mistake kept screaming every minute, "Fix me! Really fix me! Go back and tear out all the confusion and snarls around me. Set me straight." That's what the mistake wanted, to be fixed.

And what if what happened was more than just her mind wandered or she fell asleep? What if something awful happened? An earthquake? Or a fire? Or her husband came home and beat her unconscious because he was drunk? What if her children came down with terrible diseases and died? What if her land was stolen from her, and her loom moved to a strange place where people she didn't know came in and looked at her and said, "There's a real Indian. Look at her weave. Isn't she cute?"

What if the quality of the mistake was a tearing in the fabric of the universe? A rent in the soul of creation? What if time got all balled up in that moment's disaster and the threads—all the threads, all the threads of creation—snarled and turned back upon themselves, and then she said, "Well, I'm just going to keep going and weave around it. What else can I do?"

Because that's what we do, keep going no matter what. That's what we're made to do—survive.

What about that weaving? Would the person want to go back and fix that mess? Who would want to go back there? Yet there it sat in the middle of the distorted rug—all its threads screaming, yowling like a coyote, stinking worse than a polecat—every minute of the day and night. The weaver would try to ignore it, running around to bars, dancing with everyone, doing all that. But it couldn't be ignored, because it was too big and awful.

That's what he wanted to tell people. Time wasn't like a ruler so that things got better as more time passed. That instant of horror, that snarl in the threads of existence, that abomination, warped the whole design until the weaver stopped running and decided to clean it up. The only way to clean it up was to tear out the bad threads, to go all the way back to the rat's nest and tear it out. Then time could start flowing freely again, when the mistake had been examined and cleansed.

That was why people didn't get better as the years passed—his People and others who suffered great wrong. The roots of their wounds hadn't been cleaned. Only one who had such wounds could know how hard the task was. Facing the monster was a terrifying thing. Most people would have to face it again and again before being totally healed. That was the path of Spirit, the path of freedom.

Once a person woke up, getting the courage to go back and face the past wasn't hard. That's because it was happening every minute, repeating every second of the fiction that people called time. It colored everything the person saw, heard, or did, with no respite, no relief. Its pain would continue until the weaver untangled it and healed the wound. That's what he was. He was an untangler, nothing more. Well, maybe a little more.

That was how the mind worked. It saw the same thing all the time, all over the place. Anything that reminded it of what happened, bingo! The person was back there. The mind made the present the past until it was cleaned and bathed, and new yarn worked in, until the rug was rewoven. The mind also made the future the past, warping all the person saw so she created what happened again and again.

Many times, he had seen the weaver tear out the mess and weave in a new scene where it had been. A new design of new yarn so that you could see where the disaster had been, but it looked new and clean. The weaver did this to say, "This happened. This happened to me." And then she could go on making a life, making a work of art that the most discriminating of the People would know was real. Not something for tourists.

He told the rabbi who came and stayed with him about time and the weaver. The rabbi understood perfectly and said, "You're a Freudian."

"No. Freud was trying to be one of us. He was trying to understand what you and I know." He had smiled at his fellow man of spirit.

The past was tugging on him. He thought that Great-grandfather had helped him through all of it. He'd remembered what happened so many times, and thought he was over those years. Then something would happen … and he was back there.

He could hear them talking about him as he finished high school, always right in front of him as if he didn't exist.

"The boy is brilliant!"

"When he talks about scripture, it's like the Lord is standing right next to him."

Joseph Bishop ended up at a mission school run by a Protestant denomination. That's what decided his future. Grandfather smiled. His future had been decided long before.

Grandfather couldn't remember a time when he didn't have visions. They came to him just fine in the white man's Christian schools. Jesus was there for Joseph Bishop right from the start. He came to him and protected him at night. Then He saw that a nice matron took a liking to him and kept him safe from the things that happened to pretty brown boys in schools like his. Jesus made sure that someone was there for him all those long years.

Several of the children at the schools were mystics, a fact that they hid from the authorities. The teachers said the children were miserable sinners bound for hell, while their visions contradicted everything they were taught. They saw Jesus and Christian saints in their visions, along with wondrous beings that no one in the school told them existed. These creatures said they were wonderful and deserved great lives. They showed them beautiful things. The young mystics learned never to mention the truth they experienced directly. They learned to act as if the world of visions didn't exist, despite the fact that it was more real than the outer world in which they were trapped.

Joseph's spiritual life unfolded differently. He so identified with his captors and their world that without knowing he did it, he purged himself of experiences not in keeping with what they taught. Their theology became his theology. He forgot that he had known any other.

After high school, he worked for the mission a couple of years. He had such success at converting his brethren that the authorities could not ignore his calling. Joseph Bishop was a born minister. They took him to the reservations, preaching the Gospel—reservation after reservation. He saw his People for the first time, broken down, impoverished drunks waiting for the white man to feed them. The light in Joseph's heart grew hotter. The fire in his eyes became incendiary. He had finally realized that his father, the god, never came. Looking around the reservations, Joseph knew why. His father probably lay on his face like all the drunks, incapable of doing anything except rage and fornicate. Hatred fueled Joseph's passion to save souls.

"You should hear Joseph preach, Richard," his supervisor said to his own superior. "He makes hell real to me."

Joseph Bishop had to go as far as he could go. When he left for college, his teachers hailed him as a perfect product of the Indian school system—and he was. The young man spoke only English. He had almost no knowledge of Native American history. He didn't remember a single word of his own language. He knew nothing of his tribe, not even its name. He didn't know the state in which he was born.

They sent him to the All Faiths Theological Seminary in Oakland, California. His superiors at the mission disputed the wisdom of allowing him to wander so far from their conservative presence and so close to the libertine swamp that bordered Oakland, the notorious city of Berkeley. Yet good arguments existed for taking the offer. It was a full scholarship, all the way through doctor of divinity, should Joseph prove himself capable of earning the degree. Also, a director of the charity that would pay his way was the president of the seminary. He would "keep an eye on the lad" every day. Joseph would be protected from the temptations of Berkeley and its cesspool of liberalism, the University of California. The final argument was compelling. The scholarship was not only a full scholarship, it was the only scholarship offered to their star Indian and the only one likely to appear. They took it.

The old man laughed, remembering his first days in California. He worked at the seminary dutifully, doing everything expected of him for several weeks. When his watchers' vigilance slackened, he headed straight for Berkeley. The wild one in him knew there had to be a reason for them wanting to keep him away from the place. He walked around Berkeley in his black missionary school suit, gawking, a Native American boy from a Midwestern boarding school for Indians. Everything shocked him. The bohemians on campus and in town, the liberal attitudes of the faculty members, the communism and free love discussed and *practiced* by people his age. Berkeley shocked him from one end to the other. It was wonderful.

He quickly found what the seminary wanted to keep from him: communism, atheism, Asian philosophy, and other modes of thought that they condemned. He found places he could study outside the seminary's reach, and drank deeply, if secretly, from their wells. The wild parts of his soul, barely known to him, were awakening.

Just as he had survived everything else, Joseph Bishop adapted to his new life. Within months, he took the seminary by storm, getting his usual high grades, entering discussion groups and clubs when he was permitted. He still was an Indian, after all. Although he seemed perfectly content and happy, a thunderstorm brewed inside.

He chuckled as he lay on the buffalo hide. "Oh, Berkeley! I loved Berkeley." He was glad he'd seen Berkeley in the 1930s. He'd heard it was revolutionary in the 1960s, but he was sure nothing could match it in those earlier days.

His mind ground to a halt at the scene he had expected from the start. How he discovered what had happened. He was about twenty-seven, as near as anyone knew. A few months from ordination, his supervisors at the seminary gave him the task of counseling a condemned man in his final days. Frankly, the convict scared the older ministers. Frankly, they thought he was hopeless. Still, Joseph Bishop was such a promising young man— why not let him try? The condemned man was one of his own People, the People Joseph had been carefully nurtured to save.

The old shaman watched the scene in his mind's eye. The soon-to-be-Rev. Joseph Bishop found himself sitting in a wretched puke-green visiting cell in San Quentin prison, the infamous home of the incorrigibly bad. His client was one of the few "real" Indians the young seminarian had known outside his sheltered, model-school upbringing.

His name was Andrew Waters. The miserable wreck had killed an honest white merchant on Oakland's waterfront. He had six weeks to live. The time bomb in Joseph's heart was set at their first meeting. It would go off in that cell, four weeks to the day.

The killer Indian wasn't much to look at. He was small, like Joseph, and scrawny. He could have been forty-five. Where the divinity student's face radiated intensity and hope, his client's visage growled. The convict's hands were permanently grimy; his teeth, yellow stubs. Nicotine-stained hands shook. Alcoholism had made hamburger of his nose and cheeks. Despite his degeneration, the prisoner remained vicious and unrepentant.

The young almost-minister tried his hardest, pressing for a conversion. Pressing to save the reprobate's soul. Everything he did was met with silence.

Joseph Bishop finally stopped trying and began attending to his charge's needs, bringing him cigarettes and snacks, asking him if he wanted to talk about anything—not about God, just about anything. This worked better. After weeks of silence, the convict said,

"I wanna write my sister. She's a maid. In Kansas."

Joseph Bishop peered into the man's face.

"Go ahead, write to her. I'll mail it for you," he said, handing over some paper and a pencil.

The condemned man snorted. "I can't write. Been to school six years. Can't write a word."

Joseph looked at him. How could this be? He'd received a good education. The young pastor looked into the other man's eyes, trying to see his soul. What he saw shocked him. The eyes might have been his own. They had the same shape, size, and color. For an instant, Joseph wondered if this was his brother, but quickly realized the inmate was much older than Raymond. And he knew the man's name, Andrew Waters, from the paperwork. Still, were they related somehow? After a few questions, Joseph found the convict was Andrew, brother of Sally Waters, the little girl who had been separated with Joseph and Raymond for a better life. He and this killer were from the same band.

The dam broke as Andrew told his story. He was sent to the New Hope Indian School. From there, he was also sent from school to school but, unlike Joseph, Andrew Waters didn't take to captivity. He fought the authorities and was sent to schools for more and more incorrigible youths. He ran away from the last after a beating. Andrew was fifteen then. He could neither read nor write. He started drinking the minute he got out of sight of the reformatory. From there, it was a series of easy steps into San Quentin's death row. He barely remembered killing the merchant, barely remembered the last fourteen years. The only times he'd been sober were when he was in jail. Andrew Waters was closer to twenty-nine than forty-five.

After that, they spent their time together trying to reassemble their past. Like Joseph, Andrew couldn't remember his language, his tribe's name, his own name, or where they were from.

"It was in the mountains where New Mexico and Colorado meet. I think it was there." Andrew had figured it out from a picture book and memories of the trees and cliffs. If that was true, they could be from any of a half-dozen tribes. Still, it was a start. They could go home. No—Joseph Bishop could go home.

The minute he realized who Joseph was, Andrew changed. He seemed short-tempered and evasive. Joseph knew Andrew had something to say and didn't want to say it. He was equally ambivalent about knowing the secret. They both knew what it was about.

Grandfather moved in his bed, fingering the buffalo robe beneath him, gaining the strength to go on. After each session with Andrew, it was harder for him to go back to his studies and professors, harder to act the lackey he had become.

On what proved to be their last visit, Andrew Waters told Joseph what happened to their tribe and why his father never rescued him. "It was 1918 when they caught us. A while later—the leaves was turnin' and it was gettin' cold—your daddy rides into the school on a horse. He's like a chief from the olden days, sittin' up proud. Our men were with him, an' some more from other bands. They had a wagon. They were takin' us home!"

Andrew looked momentarily animated. The scene he painted hovered in the air between them. The dusty schoolyard with rows of buildings. Joseph's father meeting with the school authorities and the men with him telling the kids in the yard what was happening. The children were screaming with excitement inside—and utterly quiet outside. Andrew explained that Joseph's father had taken a few months to come because he had moved their camp to a place where the white man would never find it.

"They killed five boys in the canyon. Your daddy made a'official complaint, and that took time, too. But then he come to the school to get you an' the rest of us. You an' your brother an' my sister weren't there. The school lost your papers. They said sorry, they didn't know where you were. Your daddy said he would stay until they told him, forever if he had to." Andrew looked at Joseph as though he knew the words he had to say would destroy Joseph's world.

"He tried, but they fought dirty."

The young minister stared back, not understanding.

"Someone come to the school the same day as your daddy. A teacher, been off somewhere. Do you remember what happened back then?"

"The fall of 1918? It was the end of World War I. I guess the troops were coming home."

"Yeah, but that's not all."

He searched his mind. What else happened at the end of the war?

One of the guards sneezed. Joseph's memory was jogged. "Oh! The flu? The Spanish influenza." Joseph knew of the flu epidemic. Its horror blended with the other traumas assailing him after his capture. He remembered the headmaster of his school raving in front of the assembled students, screaming something he didn't fully understand. He knew he was talking about evil. He was saying that they had done something wrong and God had sent a terrible curse. After that, armed guards surrounded the school keeping everyone out—and in. No one in his school got sick. He knew of the epidemic, but it hadn't touched him directly.

Andrew continued, "Your daddy rode in the day that teacher come back. That night, the teacher's sittin' at dinner with all the teachers, coughin' and sneezin' all over.

"The next day, one of the kids spoke in our language in class. Jus' got up an' talked away." A bitter snort of a laugh. "They beat him so bad, he couldn't stand up. They put him in the infirmary. I went to see him. That sick teacher was in a bed, shakin' and screamin', out of his head. He was in with everybody. The sick kids and teachers were all goin' in and out. The nurse. Nobody ever seen nothin' like it." Andrew put his hands over his eyes as though trying to erase a memory.

"Blood come out everywhere, his nose, his ears. His eyes. It's like his insides turned to blood." Andrew grimaced. "His face, right here, around the eyes, turned blue, and that spread. First his face, then his hands, and then everywhere. He turned blue, then black. When he died, he was black. He didn't last 'til night, it happened so fast.

"The teachers got it first. When they died, most of 'em was black. Nobody knew what the sickness was, and nobody could do nothin'. The kids got sick next, the older ones first. Everyone's screaming and crying from the pain. Hell come to the school.

"They put the kids out in a tent and took the infirmary for themselves. Your daddy went in the tent took care of the sick kids as long as they was alive, and then he laid out in back and tried to bury 'em when he could. He brought the sick ones water and wiped off the blood and sweat. A day or two, that's all they lasted, if they got it bad. Your daddy kept goin' into that tent like it was nothin'. Smilin', even, so the kids wouldn' be afraid. I never seen no one that brave." Andrew cursed.

"Them sons a' bitches that rode in with him ran away. They knew what was gonna happen. Everyone was gonna get it." Andrew looked directly at Joseph. "They did, too, 'most everybody. Your daddy got sick. Took a coupla days. I don't know why he didn't get it sooner." Joseph Bishop was in free fall, mind spinning and spiraling downward.

"I saw him die." Andrew propped his elbows on the table and clenched one hand into a fist. He wrapped the other hand over it, knuckles turning white. He dropped his forehead to the point formed by his clasped hands, looking like a man in prayer or making a forced confession. Joseph stared in horror. "I watched, at the tent door." He scowled. "I watched all of it. I didn't do nothin'." He rammed his forehead into his clenched fists, striking himself. Joseph leaned forward to stop him.

"Don't touch the prisoner," a guard barked.

"But Andrew, you were so young. There was nothing you could do ..."

"Don't tell me what I could do. I was too scared to help. And I lived." His ribs rose and fell as he labored to release the words. "He died like all of them, blood all over and turned black. At the end, he's talkin' to things that ain't there, people that ain't there. I can't remember what he said, because they took my language away. But he was talkin' to our People, to people that gone on. They was there, I could feel 'em. He called your name, and your mama's. And the holy man's.

"He got quiet, and he died." Andrew looked up, a lopsided smile on his face. "Didn't matter that he was good, or brave. Or if he stayed and the others ran. He died like a' animal, covered in blood." Something in Andrew's expression made Joseph realize how dangerous his friend could be. "It don't make sense. Why should I live and he die?

"I went crazy right then. Ain't been right since. I been runnin' and rippin'. Doin' all kind of things." He leered at Joseph, who recoiled from the evil he saw in his face. "Oh, you don't know how bad I am, friend Joseph. You don't know what I done. Shit, I don't know what I done. How many I killed. And you thinkin' I'm just a poor unfortunate ..." He laughed, but went on with his tale. "Missionaries come after and told us the flu was God's will. What kind of *God* would will that?" He cursed.

"They put us in one grave. That's where your daddy is. In a' unmarked grave in a fallen-down Indian school somewhere. They closed the school and moved the ones who lived away. I didn't know what happened to our band for a long time." He stopped speaking, jaws clamped.

"What happened?" Joseph asked.

"Our agent wrote a letter to the school where they moved me. Not us! Me! I was the only one left. They stole fifteen of us." Andrew swore viciously. "Counting you and Sally and Raymond and me, only four of us was alive. The white man's protection sure helped us. And now, just you 'n' me 'n' my sister're left."

"And Raymond!"

"When did you hear from him last?"

Neither needed to say more.

"You wanna know what the letter said?" Joseph indicated that he did. "The agent said your daddy hid the band real good. They would never a' found them where they was—except for the buzzards. Buzzards led him right to the camp." His laugh was a snort. "The cowards that ran took the sickness home. Hid up there, they couldn't get help. Any of 'em made it through the flu, starved. Your daddy hid 'em so good, they all died." A snort that might have been a laugh escaped him.

"Our band was safe where he put them— but he went out to save *you*. If he forgot about you, they'd all be alive, most likely." He paused so that Joseph could comprehend the hideous truth.

"Then you come here tryin' to get me to believe in God." Andrew half-rose, and the guards stepped closer. He sat down. "You come in here so sure you knew what was right—you never asked me what I want. I don't want your God. I want what your daddy saw when he was dyin'. Our People come for him, our ancestors. Our God. That's what I want.

"An' I want all this to be over. Get out of here. Leave me die in peace." He stood up, shouting. Joseph was horrified. He thought they were friends, but the expression on Andrew's face was one of hatred. Andrew kept shouting as the guards dragged him away. He screamed until the steel door clanged and cut off his voice. "Don't come back here … I don't want your God. Traitor …"

Joseph Bishop left the prison and went to his dorm room. He sat on his bed all night, head in his hands. His family and all his clan died because his father came for him. He had a religion that he knew nothing about—and he was a traitor to his People. He had grabbed his captors' ways and never thought of what he'd lost.

The next morning, he packed a bag and left the white man's world forever. It was 1937.

11

Jon—we already have lobster. It's in coolers in the motor homes!"

"That's dead lobster ... it's been cooked. It's been traveling. This is live lobster." Jon looked at Mark as though he were subhuman. They stood by the cargo bay of Will's jet, surrounded by ice chests that Jon had snuck on board. While Mark and Jon argued, Delroy West waited, leaning on the handle of a flat luggage dolly. He turned his face away, but his shaking shoulders betrayed his laughter.

"Jon, we don't need any more lobster. We have five times as much food as we need," Mark Kenna sputtered. "We don't need this."

"Yes, we do. I have a lobster barbecue planned for tonight. We cannot have a welcoming barbecue with dead lobster! It's wrong! Just wrong!" Tears sprang to Jon's eyes. He was like jelly. Mark didn't know why they'd brought him. He sure as hell was making Mark's life difficult.

He and Brooke worked it all out. She wasn't on his case—Brooke would never be on his case—but she'd made their financial situation very clear. Ocean was starting school, and the other two were just behind him. They couldn't keep wearing last year's thrift shop T-shirts and tennies. They needed better clothes to fit in with the other kids, even in the Santa Cruz Mountains. Raven and Sky would need braces—anyone could see that. And he didn't want his kids to be "those hippie kids from the dome." Mark knew what that was like from his childhood. For the first time, his perfect life was under attack. He had to make more money.

When Mr. Duane gave him the job of handling logistics this week, he knew this was his chance. He had to make sure his boss realized that he could do more than drive. He wanted to talk to him about some ideas for Numenon he'd had for a long time, and tell him about his education. Maybe he could get a professional position. The week had to go perfectly. That would be hard, because everyone knew what a fanatic Will Duane was about details. And food ... And neatness ... Mr. Duane was almost as much of a nut case as his cook, when you got to know him.

"Look, Jon, we don't need all this stuff ..." Mark looked at the containers. In addition to cases of live lobsters, Jon had snuck huge ice chests of—Mark opened one—"Dry ice! What do we need dry ice for? We have refrigerators with generators. And extra gas if they don't have hookups. We don't need this!" Mark had driven himself crazy thinking of every little thing, and now this maniac threatened to ruin it.

"If you don't bring it, I won't go. You can cook for yourselves." Jon crossed his arms over his chest. "Just because we have to spend a week in the wilderness does not mean we have to give up style. Or good taste." Jon waved at the lobster containers, the tops of which were opened an inch or so. Mark could see antennae moving inside. "That's good taste: live lobster. Do you understand how I feel about this? This *camping*? I hate it! I hate the country. Having to stay at Will's place in Woodside is hideous. All those trees dripping caterpillars. We'll have to camp on the *dirt* where we're going." He waved his hands frantically. "We'll have live lobster, or I won't go. So— load that gurney!" He turned to Delroy, who took a step toward the lobsters, his eyes on Mark.

"No, Delroy!"

"Load everything if you want me to go. I'll go back on that plane and you can cook for yourselves. Do you know how to make flawless, low-cholesterol, béchamel sauce? Do you think Mr. Duane will like your cooking?"

Mark threw up his hands. Jon was crazy. You wouldn't believe what he had packed in those motor homes. "We might as well bring it," Jon said of every nutty addition. "We'll use it."

Mark was the majordomo. He and the other drivers were to take Mr. Duane and the professional staff to the campsite, keep the camp clean, and help Jon once they got there. Serve and cook, do whatever needed doing. At the week's end, they had to deliver their charges back to the Tucson airport and drive the motor homes back to the San Francisco Peninsula. This was his big chance. Mark was terrified of Mr. Duane's reaction when he saw the stuff Jon brought. But Jon overpowered him—everything went.

"We have room, Mark. We have five motor homes. And the trailer, don't forget that! What difference does it make what we take?" Jon said, well aware of Will Duane standing at the top of the jet's ramp watching them.

Mark looked up, "I'm sorry, Mr. Duane." His boss seemed more amused than angry. Mark turned back to Jon and caved in. "OK, OK," he said. "Bring your live lobster."

Jon smiled graciously. "You'll be glad. You'll see. We need the lobster. And we need the dry ice." He frowned. "I don't really know why … but we do. Delroy …" He gestured to the older man to proceed.

Delroy West loaded three Igloo chests of live lobster and four of dry ice onto one of the flat dollies and headed to the terminal and the motor homes. Jon turned majestically and followed the lobster. Mark put the rest of the luggage on his dolly, shaking his head. Jon hadn't been right since 'Rique died. Mark didn't know anyone who'd died of AIDS. He knew a couple of guys who got it, but AIDS creeped Mark out so bad that he kind of, well … he stopped seeing them. One had died. The other was hanging in there. Mark kept tabs on him, long distance. He'd seen the news reports about AIDS. Living cadavers, covered with sores. What a way to go. He knew Jon didn't have it—yet—because Will wouldn't let him cook for him if he did. Knowing that was a relief.

Jon missed a lot of work when 'Rique was dying and didn't come back for a long time after he died. The cook was sort of together now, except that he'd started dyeing his hair weird colors. He cried easily. It must be hard, not knowing when it would happen to you. It would happen to Jon. Mark knew how Jon and 'Rique had lived.

He turned his attention to the job in front of him. Mr. Duane, the professional staff, and the two secretaries would travel in the *Ashley III*, Will's supermotor home. He drove the *Ashley*. The professionals were supposed to

work while they traveled. Mark had been told that it was a five-hour drive
on bad roads to this Mogollon Bowl. They'd go east to New Mexico and
then follow the maps that had been sent to them. The other four motor
homes would serve as housing and a kitchen for the rest of them, and
would be driven by the other drivers. Of the bunch of them, only Jeff Block
was Mark's buddy. They played in a band together.

Mark handpicked the drivers to have the most rockin' week possible.
He and Jeff Block played in the Counter Continuum with a few other guys
back home in Santa Cruz. Actually, it was Mark's band. He was the leader of
the "world music ensemble." Because of the combination of instruments they
played—everything from sitar and tablas to African drums and violins—the
band sounded like crazed Irish monks would if they crashed off the coast of
India. Mark and Jeff Block were the kings of the hippest place in the world,
Santa Cruz, California. Only thing they could do better than surf was drum.

Mark was excited about this Native American thing. He figured those
Native drummers were up there with the best. He couldn't keep from grinning. Just because he was on a mission that would change his life didn't
mean it couldn't be fun. He even brought a little weed, despite Mr. Duane's
warning about the Indians' rules. It would be fun.

When Mark put out the word to get drivers for this trip, he empha-
sized "rockin' time." He couldn't bring the band, but he wanted to get guys
who played something so they could jam. They all said they could play
something; maybe he should have auditioned them. Well, it should work.
Between his band, surfing, and his job as a driver, Mark had everything a
man could want. He had his lady, Brooke, and their three kids. They hadn't
bothered to get married. Why wreck a good thing?

He walked to the terminal, looking at Jon's back. Mark had put Jon
with Rich Salles for the trip because he thought Rich might be gay. He was
quiet and supposed to be an artist. He never hung out with the other guys,
bullshitting and having beers. He never talked about women or the wild
things they saw as drivers. Maybe Rich would heal Jon's broken heart. Mark
pushed his loaded cart back into the terminal, watching Jon Walker saun-
tering next to his lobsters.

Jon was white, but the way he walked reminded Mark of some of those
African tribal guys you saw on TV. They were really tall and thin, and they

walked kind of loose, like their bones were made of rubber. He couldn't take his eyes off Jon. A lot of gay guys up in the City were good-looking, but Walker was beyond that. He was beautiful.

Thinking that, Mark yanked his eyes off the chef and hustled into the terminal like something was chasing him.

12

Grandfather gasped as he recalled what had occurred so many years before. Sixty years had passed since Andrew Waters was executed. He found out that Andrew's sister, Sally, was dead—the victim of a drunken boyfriend's rage. He had no idea where Raymond was. The school records said he'd left long before graduation. Joseph Bishop was utterly alone. Lying on his bed that morning, Grandfather felt the loss as strongly as he had in that long ago time. The Great One was merciful. The boat of his mind took off at full speed, not stopping. He went with it, whizzing back in time, back before his birth.

Grandfather floated in that bliss of nothing, the bliss of existence before time and flesh. Then the boat of his mind moved away from that heaven, moving forward through his life slowly. He soon felt the joy of those early days when he was inside his mother, protected and fed by her body, sustained by her love. Grandfather touched the buffalo robe beneath him. He stroked the rough brown fur between his thumb and forefinger as he had so many years before. As he moved his fingers, the old man entered that other time. He had been delivered from his mother and lay naked next to her on a buffalo robe. He was a tiny baby, perhaps two months old.

He could feel her love as she picked him up and burped him. She talked to him in the old words until the peace he felt numbed his mind and he slept, going back to the blissful place he had known before he knew her. When she finished cleaning and wrapping him, his mother would lie down, holding his tiny body against her. She folded the coarse brown wool of the buffalo robe around them both. He would sleep, half in the world of people, half in the other world, the world he knew before. He slept that way, rocked by the soft movement of his mother's breath, held in the human world by the beat of her heart. What his mother gave him sustained him through all that happened. It let him live until he could meet the one who led him back to the light.

Grandfather smiled as he thought of those days. The fullness of remembering was tinged by the sadness of knowing what would come. He knew that what his mother, his father, and his band gave him was more valuable than gold. That what happened with his mother on that robe kept him alive. Grandfather stroked the buffalo robe with his left hand as he thought. The buffalo had always been sacred to his People. To Grandfather, it was far more than sacred. To Grandfather, the buffalo was life itself. The tunnel of his mind was closing. The sights and sounds of the past disappeared. It was time to attend to the present. Time to leave the world of memory and enter the world around him.

Grandfather and the robe lay in the lean-to, as they had this week for the previous ten years. As they did when he was in his hogan at home. In the winter, he put another robe over himself. That was all he needed. Grandfather didn't have a watch, but he knew it was around four thirty in the morning. In a while, he would begin the morning rituals with the others. They would chant, then sit quietly to greet the dawn. He did this every morning, Meeting or no Meeting. Others or no others. The old man lay waiting for the instructions from Spirit World that would come to him, waiting and watching the patterns of his mind.

What he expected didn't happen. Orders for the week to come did not materialize. Again his mind slipped back to the old days, to 1937. Not too many months passed before the fugitive seminarian, Joseph Bishop, wandered into the desert alone. Was he looking for his family's home? Was he trying to die? Grandfather knew he'd been called to that place. He could no more resist the call than go back to his studies in Oakland. He was almost dead when Great-grandfather found him lying facedown in the sand. He had been walking in a direct line from the highway to the old shaman's hogan—a hogan that no outsider knew existed. Joseph's new teacher brought the young man to his home. Great-grandfather recognized his student instantly. This was the student who had been born to come to him, the student he had been born to teach.

When Joseph Bishop recovered, he began to talk to Great-grandfather. He laughed, lying on his bed in the Mogollon Bowl so many years later. It seemed a joke. Great-grandfather spoke almost no English. Yet Great-grandfather understood what he said in those early days, that young Joseph knew. The black coals of the shaman's eyes glittered and glistened, reflecting the sparks of the nuclear reactor that lived inside his bony frame. Joseph Bishop told his teacher everything he knew. He spoke to him of philosophy and theology. He spoke of history and science. He told the old holy man about things that affected him greatly. About his family and what happened to them. Joseph spoke of the English philosopher David Hume and his writings refuting the possibility of miracles. He spoke of Immanuel Kant and Descartes, of Hinduism, Buddhism, the Tao, and everything that he had studied in places forbidden by the seminary. He told about Jesus finding him, the Christian saints and what they showed him, and how different it was from what the missionaries said. The old shaman's eyes twinkled and glittered and sparked. Joseph Bishop knew that he understood. That reactor inside was stoking up.

Later, when the young man could see the spirits and ancestors who clustered around his teacher, he saw them sparking and flashing too. They understood what he was saying. Something happened in the desert long ago. They knew. The ancient shaman, the ancestors, the spirits, and young Joseph Bishop knew that everything was intertwined. They didn't have to be physicists, like those who combed their lands looking for stones that popped and fizzed, stones they called "uranium." Creatures of Spirit already knew that everything in the universe is interrelated. That you can't change one tiny part of it without changing all of it.

The young man called Joseph Bishop disappeared. In his place grew a warrior who would be known as "Grandfather" as an old man. In those early days, his teacher called him a secret name, known only to the ancestors and themselves. His friends called him Joseph. Just that. No other name. Grandfather smiled as he lay on the buffalo robe. He liked the name, Joseph. The husband of Mary. Caretaker of the Holy Mother of God. He liked the changes that were coming to him.

Once his People's spirits found him, they loaded him up good with things to look at and think about. Vision after vision came to him. For years, they rolled over him. He danced, laughed, and wandered in a state of bliss. He missed all of World War II. Didn't even know it happened. The world he was in didn't permit war.

He had the most important vision in his early days with Great-grandfather. The vision of the world where love was king. He lay on the buffalo robe in the early morning darkness and it burst upon him as strongly as it had that first time. He could see a world so beautiful and won-derful—so good. It was on the other side, just over there. All he had to do was haul it back over here and everyone could have it.

He saw a world that respected the value of every soul; where bosses respected their workers and treated them right; where the workers respected their bosses and did their best; where everyone worked together to do the job. He saw a world where the rich didn't hoard, where people shared what they had and helped each other. Where race didn't matter at all. Where how people looked didn't matter.

The old man's chest heaved and tears ran down his cheeks as he saw that world. He could see it, clear as day, there, just over there. It was so beau-tiful. He saw it for the first time long ago. Now it was always there, beyond his sight, beckoning to him, driving him mad with longing to bring it here. Sometimes he would try to tell the people about that world, and the intensity of seeing it and wanting it to be real would trip him up. His tongue would curl and the words wouldn't form. He'd try to describe his vision and people would look at him like he was insane or a dreamer. Grandfather wasn't a dreamer. That world was real and it wanted to be here so desperately. It was calling to people to make it real.

This week was the culmination of his life. It was for this that he had been born. If he could move one heart this week—just one—the little pebble at the top of the mountain that controlled it all would shift, and if it shifted, the others would shift. The reaction would go on, inevitably, because everything was part of the same thing. From one end of the universe to the other, from the beginning of time, it was all one thing. That one little pebble could sweep the world that was into the sea. Grandfather knew this. If one heart could be moved by what happened this week, or by what it heard or felt, then that world he saw could come to be. Which brought him back to why he was here, and what mattered. He existed to be the tool of the Great One who lived and breathed and moved in him. Who held him up and would see him through. The One that said,

"The play of the universe is mine, old man, not yours. The play unfolds according to my will."

13

Melissa Weir veered off as the three young executives entered the Tucson terminal. "Where's the ladies' room?" she asked a worker standing by the entrance. She followed his directions and found herself alone in the bathroom. Melissa looked in the big mirror covering the wall over the sinks. She was wearing her taupe gabardine suit. Its shoulder pads gave her a look of greater authority and size. Melissa was tiny, her physical size belying her personal impact. She wore an off-white silk blouse under the suit's double-breasted jacket.

She looked at herself in the mirror and watched her almost-belligerent stance crumble. Her shoulders dropped, then rolled forward. She grabbed the edge of the sink and dropped her head over it as the sobs came.

She couldn't believe it. She kept shaking her head in disbelief. She just couldn't believe it.

Melissa had intended to splash some water on her face and go back to the others, but once she started crying, she couldn't stop. She hung over the sink, letting her tears fall into it, guarding her clothes. She couldn't mess them up; she had to work. She couldn't look as if she'd been crying.

"Oh, please help me," Melissa moaned to no one. "Please help me!"

Betty Fogarty and Sandy Sydney walked into the terminal. Some workmen nodded at them. Sandy smiled back, sweetly. Betty had seen Melissa go into the ladies' room. The rigid set of her back tipped Betty that something was wrong.

"Sandy, you get settled into the *Ashley*. I'll be right there."

Betty was shocked when she saw Melissa. The girl was hysterical. Betty didn't know what to do. She had no idea Melissa could be like this. Melissa was huddled over the sink, cheeks covered with tears, nose running, face blotchy and red. The little thing was sobbing and shaking. She saw Betty and looked like she wanted to run, but she had nowhere to go.

"Oh, Betty," Melissa sobbed. "I started to cry … and now I can't stop."

Betty's mother's heart went out. She put her hands on Melissa's shoulders. Melissa immediately cried harder. She and Betty hugged each other in that peculiar manner known only to professional women who wear extremely expensive clothes. They stood facing each other about a foot apart. They leaned forward so their cheeks almost touched and patted each other's shoulders. It was a parody of a hug, but both knew they had to keep their clothes presentable. Being a professional woman with feelings was not easy.

Melissa cried for quite a while. Betty kept saying, "There, there. There, there. It will be all right."

As she comforted Melissa, Betty thought, This is The Bitch of Numenon? Harvard's Answer to Nuclear War? They all had nicknames at Numenon. She was The Holy Mother. Betty Fogarty had cried many a tear in many a ladies' room during her time with Will, but she never expected to see Melissa Weir like this. Melissa was legendary in her toughness, one of the most hated and feared people in the corporation. In six years, Melissa had made herself into one of the highest-paid women in the world. She had a talent no one had suspected when she was hired right out of the Harvard Business School. What the Woz was to computer engineering, what Jobs was to marketing, Melissa Weir was to making money. She could make money in a garbage pile. Melissa searched through Numenon and found divisions that weren't making Will as much money as they could. She fixed them. Knees shook when Melissa appeared, all over the world—and heads rolled.

Betty knew Melissa. She was as ambitious, tough, and driven as everyone said, and smarter than anyone but Will Duane himself or Doug Saunders.

She had risen through the corporation faster than anyone but Doug. Betty wasn't one of the ones who saw her as a shrill bitch. She knew the inside story. Melissa had caught some of Numenon's big names running little kingdoms inside the corporation. She sacked them fair and square. They deserved it, but she had made enemies.

Melissa also had staunch supporters. She played tough, but was totally honest. Everything she did was legal and ethical. She was color-blind when it came to people, and she cared about principles. She cared, period. That brought her friends.

Betty was Melissa's friend. She'd gotten to know the younger woman very well since the ... incident. The headquarters was still buzzing about it, even after six months. Betty never thought that Melissa was responsible for what happened to Doug. She came to her while Doug was still in the hospital, white faced and upset. Her garbled description of that night revealed that she didn't know what happened. Betty believed her. Besides, how could Melissa do that to Doug? He was way over six feet tall and worked out all the time.

Rumors circulated. You could hear any explanation you wanted. Doug was the worst in terms of spreading tales, but who could believe him? Betty thought that a third person had been in the conference room. That person attacked Doug and then escaped in the crowd at the reception. She thought Melissa couldn't remember because someone gave her that date-rape drug she'd read about.

Will would say nothing, even to her. He ratcheted up security throughout the headquarters and sent someone to Doug and Melissa's houses to upgrade their systems. Industrial espionage was a fact of life at Numenon. Computers were hacked into, files disappeared. People had accidents, and Will increased security ... If legal proof that something happened didn't exist, that didn't mean it hadn't. You adapted or left.

Betty was surprised that Will had picked Doug and Melissa for this trip. They'd scarcely spoken during the months Doug had been back at work. Putting them in such close quarters created an explosive situation. But that was Will. They were his favorites, his kids. Wanting a happy family, Papa Will overlooked details like the fact that the kids hated each other.

Betty and Melissa looked into each other's eyes. It was one of those rare moments when each saw the other's soul. Betty looked into the eyes of

Numenon's dreaded female dragon and saw a scared, overwhelmed little girl. Her hands still touched Melissa's shoulders. The little thing was skin and bone! She'd lost so much weight since it happened. As Melissa looked into Betty's eyes she saw a fifty-five-year-old woman who'd given her life to a cause and just discovered that it was worthless. They both could have wept forever. Instead, Melissa got some toilet paper for her eyes.

"I couldn't believe it, is all," she said, dabbing away. "Could you? I mean—why we're here?" Betty shook her head. Melissa started to cry again. "I thought it was *real*, Betty. I thought we were going on a *real* retreat. I'm so stupid." She visibly struggled to rein herself in.

"I thought Will had changed. I thought that he invited Doug and me so we could, maybe ..." Melissa broke down again, leaning over the sink, "... maybe Doug and I could talk about what happened ... Maybe we'd work something out ... I thought Will cared. I thought he was trying to make peace." She struggled to control herself. "But he doesn't care about us. It was about money all the time. Just money." She wailed, heartbroken.

Betty thought, Oh, the hell with them. They can wait. She needs to cry about this.

The dam had burst. Melissa showed no signs of slowing. Finally, she was able to say, "I was so scared, Betty. He scared me so badly. I didn't mean to hurt him. I yelled at him, that's all I remember. Then, everything that happened after ..." Her face was drawn. "Everything Doug said—it's not true, Betty. I'm *not* what he said I am." She searched Betty's face to see if the secretary believed her.

"Then this. I thought it would be a healing trip. But we're going to this thing to rape the Indians, Betty. That's what we're doing, we're raping the Indians, like we always have."

Betty went rigid. Before landing, Will had told them the real reason he'd dragged them on this wild goose chase. Numenon had the mineral rights on a big hunk of the desert somewhere near where they would be camping this week. It wasn't on the Indian reservation, but butted up against it. The old medicine man leading the retreat lived on that reservation and was the high muckety-muck there.

It was such a stereotyped story of corporate greed that Betty found it hard to believe, but Will's face and posture as he told the tale backed up his words 100 percent. This was why they were there. Numenon's optioned land held some rare mineral. Betty hadn't heard of it, but it was going to be used to make the new computer chips. The latest technology. So, naturally, Will had to have that mine so that he could make a few billion more badly needed dollars. The mining process would destroy the area and render it useless forever.

Will didn't see this as a problem. The problem was that the land happened to be an ancient burial ground and protected by law. Betty was outraged. Everyone knew how the Indians revered their burial grounds. Every Hollywood movie about Indians ever made went on and on about that. Betty had researched a brief she'd present to Will and the MBAs on the trip. She knew more about the area than anyone on the team.

This wasn't just a burial ground, it was *sacred* ground, ancient and highly revered. The Indians hadn't managed to get it included in their reservation, although they'd been trying for years, because the government had seen the mineral wealth there. With the rise in "Red Power," the government was requiring Numenon to get Native American consent before mining. Betty knew this, and was aware of just how shaky the validity of their task was.

"So," Will told them in the plane, "we're here to get the mining consent. The old guy leading the retreat is the only one with the power to get it for us. That's the mission: Get the consent. I'll do most of the talking, but I need you for support. We'll try to do a full week's work while we're here. But this shouldn't take long. Maybe we'll be able to go home early."

They all had looked at him. Melissa paraphrased, "We're going to this retreat to schmooze some old Indian into giving us the rights to destroy their holy lands?"

"Yes," Will replied.

Betty thought Melissa would blow up, but she held it together. Will was in one of those moods where you bite your lip and take it. In the bathroom, Betty nodded in agreement. "Yes, we're here to rape the Indians." Her lips tightened. Betty Fogarty made a decision.

"One more week, Melissa. Let's finish the week, then call it quits." She owed Will a week, but that's all. Horror bathed her. She had to call John and tell him it was a mistake. She'd be right back. Just give her the week and she'd quit Will forever. Please.

"Let's take it day by day, Melissa. We can always get someone to drive us out if it's too bad. But let's try to finish the week. The retreat might be good, regardless of Will." Betty looked at Melissa. The moment had passed. They were afraid to make that intimate contact again. She continued, "I researched the old guy who's leading the workshop. I called the All Faiths Theological Seminary in Oakland. They know all about him. He went there, if you can believe it. He's supposed to be the real thing, a real holy man. They said his teacher was great, but 'Grandfather' is supposed to be greater. It might be all right."

Inside, hope flared. *I want to meet him. I need to meet him. Something is calling me to this place we're going.* Betty couldn't form the thoughts, but they were in her mind.

Melissa pulled her sunglasses out of her purse. It was still the middle of the night, but no professional woman could show signs of tears. Certainly not at Numenon.

They walked out of the restroom and Betty pulled out her cell phone.

"It's an hour earlier in California," Melissa said.

She looked at her watch. She'd call John when they got under way.

14

A voice boomed in his mind, *"The play of the universe is mine, old man. The play unfolds according to my will ... All the universe is my play."* Grandfather sometimes forgot that he didn't run things. When this occurred, Creator reminded him of the truth. He was part of the play of the universe, the Great One's tool and creation.

He sat in his bed in the Mogollon Bowl, feeling the people around him. Many warriors slept in the darkness. He felt each soul, each essence. Many more were coming to the Meeting. Thousands of spirits moved toward him from every direction. They bore different emotional tones: anger, sadness, hope, despair, resolve, and enthusiasm. He could feel his visitors from the corporation, struggling forward like the rest. Such great work, finding one's way home.

And that is why he did the work in front of him. It was his part in the play called the universe. He picked up the evaluation forms from the ground beside his bed. They had fueled his furious answering of questions the night before. The feedback came from people who had actually been to the Meeting, not those who wanted information about it. He was so upset when he read it—he almost worked all night.

Paul had attached a note to the report: *I've been hearing from people about how you come across at the Meeting. The people from Numenon don't know anything about you or our teachings. Or anything about Spirit. I thought if you knew about how our people see you, it might help you to get through to them.*

He began reading—Paul had pulled phrases from the responses—*Sometimes Grandfather spaces out when he's talking. He just sits there with his eyes closed and doesn't say anything ... He looks like he's drunk or stoned ... I don't understand why he cries when he talks about Great-grandfather—he died years ago. He seems really unstable ... Once he gets going, he talks too much. He talks and talks. He told a bunch of the same stories last year ... The cere-monies are too long. They're boring and nothing happens.* It went on and on.

He was appalled. He couldn't imagine any of Great-grandfather's stu-dents saying such things about him. They understood his greatness, even if they didn't understand everything he did. No one would ever criticize him. But his modern students ... Didn't they know that he went into ecstasy when the Great One spoke to him? That's when he received messages, and sent messages to others. That's when the people at the Meeting were being blessed. He felt the bliss of the One and all the universe most of the time. And some thought he was drunk.

Didn't anyone realize that *bliss* is the hallmark of Spirit? That anyone touched by Creator was marked, forever different from ordinary people? Were his People so ignorant? The newcomers he could under-stand, but those who had been to the Meeting for years? Paul had read these responses. Did *he* think his teacher was drunk rather than intoxicated by Creator's presence? Didn't Paul realize he was receiving or transmitting messages from Spirit World when he was in that state? Grandfather con-sidered. He'd transmitted many messages to Paul over the years, and he knew that Paul hadn't received a single one. Had he gotten nothing of his teachings either?

And then he went on to Paul's schedule for the Meeting, which also bore one of Paul's notes. *I thought if the Meeting was on a schedule, like a management seminar, the Numenon people—and the people I talked to, our People—would be able to relate more. This is just an example. You can set up the program any way you want.*

He examined Paul's agenda. The document provided daily schedules, with a suggested theme for each day. It also specified what he should say, how he should stand, and what he and the spirit warriors, his most serious followers, should do. This travesty aped the instructions he got from the Great One each year.

The report ended with more of Paul's wisdom. *If people know what to expect, they can get more out of the talks. That's why I suggested topics. Oh— don't worry about the sanitation problem. I really handled that one. You can see what I did in the morning.*

Before going to bed the night before, he crumpled the manuscript and threw it on the ground. Paul had not the faintest idea of what the Meeting was about, or who *he* was. The realization stunned him, yet he already knew. Some of them smiled indulgently when they saw him, like he was a living doll, a shaman doll. They told stories about him like he was a character in a novel or a movie. They tried to reduce him to something their minds could comprehend—and dismiss.

Anger surged through him, as it had the night before. The Meeting had brought him a congregation of fools who fed on fireworks and action, who didn't hear his most basic teachings.

What did he have to do to reach those who saw him as an enter- tainer? Would they listen if he stood on the stage, screaming? Dressed like their rock stars? Half naked? What did he have to do so that people understood what Powers really were? Would they hear if he shouted, "Who I *am* is the *content* of the Meeting! What I *am* is what you're here to find. See this, or leave!"

Taking control of his feelings, he decided to say and do things *his* way this year. He wouldn't tailor anything to reach those who couldn't under- stand. They'd get it, or not. And he'd take the time necessary to tell the truth, not hurrying to suit their warped minds, minds addicted to electronic images that thought in terms of fast and faster.

He looked at the crumpled report. Paul had been trying to be helpful, and proved that he knew nothing. A management seminar was completely wrong. These people who would have him speak for twenty minutes instead of delivering all the Great One told him to say—these people would see him for what he was, the living flame of his lineage. Great-grandfather's message in flesh. They would find out that meeting a true shaman was a rare thing. Spending a week with him should have them on their knees, tears of gratitude falling like rain. Who were these people who ...

The directions for the Meeting jolted him out of his rant. Creator filled him. The shaman shut his eyes and went into the inner world. Great-grandfather was there, so were the ancestors. They told him everything he was to do that week, very quickly. He gasped.

"Really?" he said in that inner world.

"Do it," they replied.

"The People won't like it," he said. "Nothing like this has ever been done before."

"So what?" they answered. "Do as we have told you."

He got out of bed and lit a kerosene lamp, rummaging for a pen. Picking up Paul's rumpled sheets, he sat on the bed and went through them one by one, making changes, adding and subtracting items. He acted as though he was taking dictation, because he was. When he'd finished, he straightened the pages and set them carefully on his altar, bowing his head to the sacred objects there. I will do as you wish, he thought.

Grandfather turned out the lamp and crawled back into bed. He had never been to a management seminar, but he knew the directions he had received were for one. They followed the form of Paul's outline. The Great One made changes in Paul's schedule, for an even more shocking effect. These were the most revolutionary instructions he'd ever received. The new people would understand, but the traditional people? What would they say?

If anything would ignite the Meeting, this was it. Did the ancestors know what was at stake? Did the Great One? Did they know how inflamed the world was?

Of course they did.

He thought of Paul Running Bird. He hadn't been far off in anticipating what the Great One wanted. He had spent a long time making that report, which demonstrated how much he cared for him and his work. Maybe Paul had more to him than he thought. He was one of the Meeting's Founders and worked hard handling all the details every year. Grandfather knew that

Paul was a deeply flawed man. He was eaten up by envy and had every mental weakness, yet he'd been loyal all these years. He would watch him carefully this year, and have the other warriors watch him too. Perhaps Paul could be a spirit warrior. Heaven knows he wanted to be one enough.

Grandfather burrowed into his bed and pulled the buffalo robe over his head. He was to give a management seminar? He couldn't comprehend it. He couldn't believe the Great One would order this thing. But it was true.

He already could hear the gossip coming back from this Meeting.

With a groan, he willed himself to sleep.

15

Gil stopped racing with Doug Saunders the minute they got out of Will's sight. They stopped as if by agreement just inside the terminal. Gil veered off into the men's room. He ran into a stall and closed the door, shaking. Hearing that they were on the trip to get some Indian's permission to destroy sacred lands stirred ancestral memories.

After that, he couldn't get his stomach to settle down. This wasn't what his grandfather was about. This wasn't work for a warrior. He'd left Gabriela and the baby with that woman to do something terrible. He couldn't stomach what Will Duane had done to all of them.

He stood there, trying to get control of himself. He couldn't calm down, his emotions were gyrating. Suddenly furious, he decided to tell Will what he thought of his plan. They'd either change it or he'd go home. He'd get back to Gabriela on a bus if he had to.

As he thought of his wife, a sense of dread crept over him. Something was wrong at home. That fancy nurse wasn't working. He'd known Gabriela was terrified of her from the moment she saw her. Maybe the baby had been screaming since he'd left. Maybe she was throwing up. Choking. He could see her turning blue. Panicked, he pulled out his cell phone. It wouldn't work in the concrete building. He burst out of the bathroom into the deserted corridor. Everything was closed; it was still dark. Which way to the motor homes? He looked up and down, disorientated. He finally turned right and walked briskly, looking for a pay phone and the exit.

After walking a while, he realized he was going in the wrong direction. Spinning around, Gil noticed two men in the back of a darkened fast-food restaurant. A bottle sat on the table between them. One of the men waved at him.

"Hey, Gil! Ol' buddy! Come over and have a drink!" Doug Saunders lolled on a bench, shit-face drunk.

"Doug!" Gil was horrified. He hopped the cable separating the fast-food place from the hallway and ran to his friend. Despite their rivalry, Doug Saunders was one of the few people he cared about at Numenon. Their mutual affection was the product of one of Will's management training excursions. Will sent a bunch of them river rafting with a management trainer. It was supposed to make them bond as a team. Unfortunately, no one anticipated what that year's major snowmelt would do to the river. Their adventure became a near-suicide. During a harrowing twenty-minute period when the raft flipped twice, he and Doug saved each other's lives. Now they were bonded. They watched each other's backs in the more dangerous waters of Numenon.

"Hey, man! I tried to find a bar, but they were all closed." Doug was in great spirits. "My friend Evan here let me join him." Doug poured vodka into a soft-drink cup and downed it. "Evan, this is my ..." He fumbled the cup, spilling the last bit of vodka on himself. "Shit ... This is Gil, my buddy from work. My *only* buddy." His words were slurred and his face was red. Had he been there long enough to get that drunk? Gil remembered Doug's hostility getting onto the plane. Maybe he had been drinking before they left.

"Doug, you can't be around Will like that. He'll fire you." Gil stage-whispered.

"You aren't afraid of that pussy, are you? He won't fire me, or you, or Melissa. We're his *kids*. And who pays any attention to his 'no drugs, no drinking' bullshit anyway? He never tests *us* or the programmers or anybody who has to work three days straight. And, fuck, if they do test us, someone tells me when before. I'm sure they tell you too." Gil couldn't deny it, but he didn't do drugs or drink so it didn't matter. Doug tossed back another cup of vodka and kept talking.

"Everybody's on *something*. You know that. We just don't do it around Will." He turned to the other man sitting at the table. "You ever been to Silicon Valley? To the real upscale parts?" The guy shook his head. "Man, it is a trip. You go to any of those parties in the hills—it's coke city. I've seen parties where they had a *sugar bowl* full of the stuff. Everybody uses it. Don't get me wrong— I *love* coke. You can work on it—you can keep up with Will Duane on it. Christ, I'd like to know what *he's* on. I've never seen him slow down. He's the only guy who can party more than me." A belch rolled out of Doug's mouth.

He giggled and kept talking. "I mean ... I use coke once in a while, to keep up. It's nothing to me though, I'll never get hooked. I've seen what it does. Shit, I saw Will's daughter. Jesus, what a mess! Twitching like a bug. Nose bleeding all over ..." He poured another paper cup for himself. "Sure you don't want a drink, Gil?" Gil indicated no. "Well, when I first got to Numenon, I thought I'd marry Cass Duane. I'd be the one to grab the boss's daughter. Shit, I would have married Will's *mother* back then, if it got me closer to the old man. But when the shit hit the fan with Cass, forget it ... I got enough problems ..."

"Doug, we've got to get going." Gil had to get him out of there, and end this conversation. This was heresy in Numenon. No one talked about Will's family.

"Will has his no-booze, no-dope policy because of his ex and his daughter. Dope fiends and drunks, both of them. The wife was worse than his daughter." Doug leaned over to confide in Evan, who was all ears.

Gil stood up, "Doug, come on ..."

"No. I want to finish this ..." He raised his cup and downed its contents. "Did you ever notice that Will calls Cass *Ashley*? She hates that name. She likes Cass, from her middle name. That's so weird.

"Well, Cass Duane taught me to stay away from that shit. Coke's nothing to me, just like a cup of coffee. I won't have any trouble following the Indians' rules. I even quit early. I haven't done any coke in days."

Gil grabbed Doug's arm and hauled him to his feet. "You *will* get fired if Will sees you this way," he half-whispered viciously. "No golden parachute, no severance bonus, no nothing, Doug. You'll lose your stock options. He is serious about drugs—for us, anyway. Let's get out of here." He half-dragged Doug to the front of the place, trying to figure out how to get him over the cable. Doug wove on his feet, spewing obscenities.

"Fuck Will Duane! What an asshole. What do you think of what we're really doing on this trip, Gil? Getting permission to mine our Indian friends' holy lands! That's a good one, isn't it? I gotta say, Will had me going for a while. A spiritual retreat? Fuck. It was *money* all the time ... That's the great thing about Will—you always know where his head's at."

Gil looked back at the table and saw Doug's "buddy" writing furiously in a notebook with a smile on his face. He looked like he'd stumbled into the story of the year.

"What are you doing?" Gil turned on him.

"Uh, I'm just writing out a list of calls I gotta make. I'm a rep ... for Qualify ... The software company?"

"You never saw us, you hear me? You never heard any of this. You understand?" Gil looked at a camera in the ceiling by the cash register. "We got you. Any word of this anywhere, even on a note to your grandmother, we're after you. You'll never work again."

Evan looked at the camera, terrified despite his drunkenness. Everyone knew about Numenon's surveillance capabilities. "Hey, I was jus' doin' this guy a favor. He asked me for a drink, I gave him one. You don't need to get heavy." Despite his small stature, Gil could get much heavier than that, a fact that the stranger seemed to appreciate.

"Listen, Evan. You know how we do it at Numenon. You play nice, and we play sort of nice. We can also play *nasty*. Remember that. Now give me that notebook." Evan turned it over to him meekly. Gil turned back to his task of getting Doug out of the hamburger joint. Doug had become pale.

"Gil, I don't feel so good."

He grabbed him, finding and undoing the snap on the end of the cable so they could leave. He draped Doug over his shoulder and pulled him out of the restaurant. Doug kept talking, without inhibition.

"I feel so fucked up, Gil. Since it happened. And before ..." They got to a bench on one side of the corridor and Gil sat Doug on it. He was too big to carry. To his surprise, Doug began choking with the pathetic sobs of a man at the bottom.

"Doug, Doug, it's OK. Quiet down." Gil looked up and down the corridor, hoping that Will Duane was anywhere but there. "Talk to me, Doug. Just talk slow and quiet."

Doug's wailing slowed and finally stopped. "Look at me, man. I'm a mess. Seven years at Numenon and I'm a fucking mess…"

What could Gil say? It was true. That thing with Melissa undid both of them.

"It's been six months from hell… Six months ago, I saw an article in the paper saying that Jennie got married. It killed me, Gil. You knew how we were. I loved her. We split up, but I always thought we'd get together again…" He looked up with hopeless eyes. "You remember her, don't you?"

Gil nodded. Jennie was beautiful, smart, and classy. And in love with Doug. They lived together, and he cheated on her. Gil knew that was practically by Will's decree. All the top execs followed Will's example with women. He was the only one he knew who didn't cheat on his wife. Jennie walked out on Doug with reason. He thought they'd get back together?

"That was the last time I was happy, Gil—when I was with her. I blew it. And then I go out and do that to Melissa. Shit." He ran his hands through his hair, frantic. "All that stuff I said about her wasn't true."

"What really happened?" Gil couldn't help himself. He wanted to know; everyone did.

Doug touched his nose and presented both sides of his face to Gil. "It looks OK, doesn't it, after the surgery? I mean, it looks almost the same. Better, maybe." Gil agreed. "I just want to apologize to her and get the fuck out of Numenon. That's why I came on this trip. I'm done…" He never said what happened in that room. Gil was about to ask again when Doug went on, "I don't know what happened. It wasn't her; I could see her on the other side of the room, screaming at me. She was mad, but she didn't do it. She never got near me."

People were approaching. Doug looked like shit, with snot all over his suit and his face swollen and red. He acted like he might puke. How could he get him on the *Ashley* and keep Will from firing him on the spot? Doug's appraisal of Will's tolerance for drinking was skewed by the amount of alcohol inside him. Gil knew their surrogate father would fire any of them for a tenth of what Doug had done. He fired his own daughter for being high at work. He fired her and threw her out of the building himself. That was a Numenon legend. Gil looked at his watch. They were supposed to be on the road by now.

How could he get Doug sober and to the *Ashley*? How could he get him past Will's booze radar? Doug was right; Will's experiences with the former Mrs. Duane and his daughter had made him crazy about drugs and drinking. Numenon was a bastion of abstinence compared with the rest of the Valley. Doug seemed to sink into himself, scratching at his arms, and jerking spasmodically. "Stay here, Doug."

Gil took off on reconnaissance. He spotted a wheelchair and grabbed it. One problem down. What about cleaning him up? He looked back at Doug. He was lying on his side on the bench, knees drawn up, shuddering convulsively. He *couldn't* clean him up. What else, then?

A janitor was mopping the floor with muddy brown water. Gil stopped, thinking. Bingo! He got it. He approached the janitor and said, "Would you like to have this?" He held up a fifty.

"Get away from me! I don't do shit like that ..." The guy backed off, putting his mop between him and Gil.

"No, no! I want you to take that bucket to that guy over there ... See him? I want you throw the water all over him, and then throw the *bucket* at him. Don't hit his face—he just had plastic surgery. Then run. I'll cover for you."

It cost a hundred and fifty.

"FUCK! YOU FUCKING ASSHOLE!" Doug screamed when the bucket hit him and screamed again when he slipped in the water chasing the janitor. The fall added a nice bruise on his jaw and a tear in his pants to his camouflage.

Perfect, Gil thought, jamming Doug into the wheelchair. "It was a vandal, Doug. Just kids pulling a prank. Let's get to work."

Miraculously, Will bought the story. He turned away from the dirty water smell, saying, "Jesus, you're a mess, Doug. Go take a shower. We're waiting for Melissa and Betty. You've got time."

Mark Kenna opened the motor home that Gil and Doug were to share so Doug could shower and put on a clean suit. "Just work your way back in

there. The shower's got water, but it's not hot. Can you find your stuff?"
Mark's nose crinkled. He thought he smelled booze on Doug, but no one
was stupid enough to drink around Mr. Duane.

In the shower, Doug sobered up enough to know that Gil had saved
his ass. He let the cool water run over him. It stung on the bruise on his
shin, and felt worse on the gouges on his arms. He itched everywhere,
couldn't stop scratching, couldn't stop moving. His tongue felt like it was
twice its normal size. Everything bothered him, every noise, every light. Get
it together. Get it together. Apologize to Melissa, and get the fuck out of
Numenon.

He felt better in clean clothes. Doug looked around at the motor home.
It was jammed with all sorts of stuff. Palm trees. Carpeting. What was all
this? Who brought all this junk? Was everyone crazy?

16

The herd spanned the horizon, brown woolly backs rising and falling with the terrain. The noise as they galloped was as loud as the voices of the Thunderbeings. Their hooves pounded so hard that he bounced off the ground. He had to bend his knees and spread his feet to stay erect. The animals swallowed everything before them. Trees disappeared like twigs. The buffalo covered the sky. They covered the land.

He was directly in their path.

A huge bull cut in front of them, so close to him that its profile blotted out the herd. It was white and hairy, as tall as a mountain. He reeled as the energy coming from the creature struck him. And then it was gone. The herd bore down on him …

Just before it ran over him, the stampeding buffalo turned into a horde of his followers, leaping from their benches at the Meeting. They screamed, intending murder, their knives and fists raised. When they struck him, he flew backward off his seat.

Then he was flying high above the sacred Mogollon Bowl, flying in the air, looking down. Thousands of bodies lay sprawled across the land, his People and the outsiders. The bodies were still. Vultures circled with him.

He fought his way out of sleep. The buffalo robe on his bed seemed to hold him down, smothering him. He leaped up, grabbing the knife he kept under his mattress. He spun, searching for an attacker. He found one. His attacker had been his mind. He'd had a nightmare.

What did such a thing portend, coming on the first day of the last Meeting? For years, his visions and dreams had come true. What did this dream mean? He lit his pipe and raised it to the four directions, praying for the wisdom to make a correct interpretation.

It required no interpretation. The Power was very near, moving with the force of the universe. The White Buffalo would help him and give him power, as would all its ancestors and descendents. The Great One stood behind him this week, and supported him in all he did. That was good.

The rest was not so good. The end of the dream was not new. Each year as the Meeting began, he sat in front of the crowd and smoked his pipe. The same vision came to him every year. Screaming with rage, waves of his students attacked him. And now the vision had come as a dream.

Since this was the last Meeting, it followed that this thing would happen in the coming week. Would they tear his body apart? Would they destroy all that he had worked for? So it seemed. He didn't mind dying, everyone did that, but it bothered him that he might die before accomplishing his mission.

But it was inevitable; he knew what would happen before he agreed to give the Meeting. The play of opposites was inescapable. One thing was always linked with its opposite. Truth called out lies; good brought forth bad. Spirit blazed in some and showed its shadow face in others. The Meeting was a gathering of spiritually powerful people, doing what the Great One willed to create great change and great good. The Power coming so close, appearing to so many, would call forth darkness. He knew that evil always lurked at the Meeting, searching for receptive hearts, for people who wouldn't take the goodness offered them. He'd known of the stalker for ages, since he was stolen as a child. The evil one was always there, looking for a way to claim souls.

The Meeting was no different. Many could only apprehend superficial things, the surface. Gross power. Their own self-importance. They created the world the way *they* saw it. They surfaced so fast at the Meeting. By the end of the first year, there were leaders, followers, in-groups, bad guys, good guys. Traditions. Special names for everything. The Founders were the people at the original meeting where he laid out the new retreat. That became known as The Founding Meeting. All in capitals, very important. By the end of the first week, the Meeting could have been a political party—like in Washington. But Washington probably was more peaceful. Maybe it was like a *religion* ...

Every year he was given what really mattered that first morning—what he should do and say, day by day, word by word. The little stuff, how to organize people, set up the camp, arrange food and lodging—that's the part he let his students handle. Did they love it! They acted like their special ways and words bore the stamp of the Great One.

Darkness appeared almost immediately, showing itself in the way people split into groups and fought for his attention. It breathed in the festering outrage at what he did and said. The criticism. People said the Meeting wasn't authentic. They said *he* wasn't authentic, maybe not even an Indian. He rolled his eyes, thinking of his wrinkled brown form.

The gossip was beyond what he could have imagined. Every year, he'd return to his hogan knowing the Meeting had been a success. Everyone left high as a kite, having received some vision, some insight—some gift that would help each one live a better life. He'd go back to work, praying, chanting, and healing.

The rumors would begin rolling in. The elders would call on him. Most of the elders had been at the Meeting, so they should already have known what happened, but they'd still ask, "Did this happen?" "Did that happen?" "Did you do this?" The rumors were like a jigsaw puzzle that someone almost finished. It was coming along great, but the person doing the puzzle lost patience and jammed the last few pieces in any way he could. The final picture didn't add up, but the pieces were all there. That's how the gossip came back, sort of the truth, but not the truth.

The rumors would be funny if they didn't have consequences. He stopped touching women when he healed them at the Meeting, because people said he touched them in a bad way. It wasn't true, but for the sake of peace, he stopped touching the women and only touched the men. Now they said he was a ... wentke ... gay. Now, some men were afraid to come to him for healing. That was just the start.

The gossips made the spirit warriors into a secret society with the mission of taking over the United States government! He didn't know how they got that idea. He talked about the plight of his People. He talked about the injustices they had suffered. He also said that he wanted it all back, everything. They called him a radical. This was ridiculous. He wanted to get everything back legally and peacefully. He didn't consider that radical at all.

He needed to set everything straight this year. He didn't want to take over the United States government. The FBI wasn't after him, watching him constantly. Their file on him in Washington wasn't as long as your arm. The CIA wasn't after him either.

There wasn't any mission; the warrior training was it. The spirit warrior trained to be a good vessel for Spirit, not to win any outer battle. The state of the warrior called to the Great One. It called to the ancestors. Spirits crawled all over them at their special, warriors-only trainings and into the year. What else did they want? No, he would dispel all this nonsense this week.

Would they kill him? They seemed to be trying, some of them, trying to kill him with words and gossip and innuendo. Trying to kill his message, if not his body. This week, they might succeed.

He knew what happened was inevitable. Not only did light attract dark—people were all the same. Most people of all colors wasted their lives on trivia and missed what was most important. He knew that everyone was the same in their inner hearts. Each person carried the full range of feelings and states, from the most holy to the most depraved. Only those committing themselves to the Path would master their smallness and rise to the heights.

Some of his students were dedicated to the good of their People and the world. Those were the spirit warriors. A larger group was basically decent and honest. They understood the path to the Great One, and walked it—when they remembered. When they forgot, they got lost in the world and its enticements. Some of his People seemed lost—lost in gossip and fault-finding, lost in envy, anger and lust, lust for power and recognition, for control. Grandfather knew that only a few would truly understand what he had to say this year despite the thousands coming. Only a few would take his message in correctly and make it theirs.

So much for the part of the dream where he was attacked. He would be. The sad part was that he hadn't completed his mission, getting back everything his People once owned. He had a feeling his special visitors would know how to help with that. It was one reason they were invited.

Now, the other part, the thousands of bodies he'd seen. He took a long pull on his pipe and considered. Were they dead? Had he seen the Meeting's outcome? Or was it something else, something they could fix? He didn't know. He did know that everything he saw in his visions came to pass.

The sound of grating stones deep in the earth came to him. He'd heard that sound before. The underworld was opening. Death would walk with them this week.

17

Sandy Sydney walked through the airport terminal toward the motor homes waiting on the curb. The silk of her dress swished against her thighs, titillating her with each step. She loved how she felt wearing this dress. People were such fools not to enjoy their own bodies. She had never understood that until she went to Europe and met Carlo. The people in Silicon Valley were insane. They worked 90 percent of their waking hours and then rushed off to "boink" each other frantically—thinking that was real sex. The men at Numenon who were mad for her were simply starvation cases who got a good meal for the first time.

She straightened her shoulders, her spine supple and erect. A gentle smile lit her lips. "You walk like a goddess," a lover had told her. Two airport workers leered at her as she wafted through the terminal. She knew what she looked like and the effect it had on men. Her outfit was plain and modest, her skirt almost floor length. Nothing could hide her body. That's how she planned it. She was perfectly proportioned, curvaceous and classy. Her hair fluffed and fluttered around her face, as her skirt did around her ankles.

She smiled at the men when she drifted past. Her smile was a benediction and a promise. As she expected, one of them paid homage with a shrill wolf whistle aimed at her back. She smiled wider. Men were such fools. So stupid and easy to manipulate. All it took was a look or a smile and they'd do whatever she wanted. They'd tell her whatever she wanted to know. And Sandy used far more than just a glance. She could get *anything*. Her hips swayed as she walked. Another whistle followed the first and she almost laughed out loud. Those idiots wanted her, but they'd never have her. She was for those who were "Beyond the Best"—the corporate slogan. She was custom-made for Numenon and for the work she was doing.

One more week of this nightmare, then she could go home. She had been isolated in this wasteland for almost a year. Her darling Carlo had asked her to do a favor. How could she refuse? He'd changed her life and made her what she was. He'd let everyone know what she meant to him. At the last party before she left, she stood next to him on the terrace of his villa wearing a brilliant gown he'd given her. He put his arm around her and kissed her, right in front of the crowd. Everyone knew she was his woman. Soon, she'd be his wife—he had proposed that night.

Of course, she'd do what he asked. When she'd finished this little task, she'd return to Europe and they'd be married. He explained that it wasn't really spying; he just needed her to find out some confidential information about Numenon and Will Duane. She was the only one in the world who could get what he needed. He explained that she must work in absolute secrecy. Will Duane must not know that she was connected to him, or even that she knew him. "He's a very suspicious man, my darling. A jealous and vengeful man. For your own good, don't mention my name. If it comes up, pretend not to know me." The tone of his voice warned her more than anything. If she were discovered, she would be in danger.

She'd worked diligently all year, sending her benefactor almost everything he wanted. That's how she thought of him—her benefactor. He was tall and handsome, and not that much older than she was, really. He was almost as good-looking as Will Duane, and getting ready to overtake him in wealth and power all over the world. Carlo just needed a little boost, a boost that she could provide. Sandy couldn't wait to return to him in Spain. Her lips longed to feel his kisses again. Loving Carlo on the phone was barely surviving. No one could do for her what he did. Her mouth compressed in a pout. She'd been foolish in how she'd run this "mission"—that's how she thought of it, a fun, secret mission.

"Oh, Mr. Duane!" She'd been so lost in thought, Mr. Duane almost walked past her. She began jogging next to him, trying to keep up with him. He always went fast. "I'm so happy that you let me come on this trip. I've always been interested in Indians." She smiled and spoke sweetly, as nice as she could be. He didn't acknowledge her presence, striding along with that impossible gait. "If you need anything, any help on *anything*, just ask me. I'm here to help ..." He was gone. She couldn't keep up with him, wearing high heels.

She stopped, furious. Why did he hate her so? She had tried for a whole year to get him to like her. To get him to ... But he wouldn't, he made that clear. She'd taken a year to do something that should have taken days. All because of something that happened during her first week at Numenon.

Her benefactor had friends everywhere, people who could recognize true genius and see who deserved to be the most powerful man in the world. Carlo's friends in Numenon made sure that Betty was in the cafeteria when she went for her initial job interview, setting it up so they could meet. That was arranged. But the way Betty felt about her was real. She had taken a liking to Sandy from the start, putting her on her personal staff. She introduced Sandy to Will Duane her first day at work. He greeted her warmly, sitting at his desk in his vast office. That was real, too. She was taken aback, because he was much better looking than he seemed in the photos she'd seen. He was much more charming, too. His charisma filled the room. Her pulse raced. The problem began with that.

Later that week, Will had a party at his house. Betty invited her. Will's house dazzled her. It was a modern palace. Pale marble and glass walls. She could see across the Bay from every room. She knew how good the art hanging everywhere was—she had worked in a gallery in Paris. This was the real thing. Like Will Duane himself, this splendid place was real.

Unknown and unnoticed, she explored Will's home, eventually finding what she wanted, her world. Walking across Will's fantastic bedroom, she was a little girl in a dream. She sat on Will's bed, seeing herself sleeping there forever. He *could* fall in love with her. Why not? She was beautiful. She could make him happier than anyone in the world. He would love her truly—for herself. They would be married, on the patio by the pool. She could see it ...

As she sat in his room, the fantasy seemed to be happening. She could feel her filmy veils blow in her eyes as she walked across the patio to the flower-decked altar. She laughed and adjusted them before continuing to meet Will, her groom. He beamed at her, totally in love with her. She was beautiful in her snow-white gown. No one had seen a more beautiful bride.

She decided to work hard for Betty and make it on her own. Betty believed in her so much it was easy. She had dreams of staying in California, giving up the life she'd found abroad, even giving up her benefactor—if Will would love her for herself.

What an idiot! Will not only didn't love her, he didn't *like* her. No matter what she did for him, he didn't like her. The happy scene was a lie, like so many other things in her life had been lies. There was only one way for her to get what she wanted, and this week she would use it.

The word "fucking" didn't describe what she did. Her services bore no more resemblance to fucking than one of Jon Walker's fantastic meals did to a Big Mac. She had made a substantial amount of money showing Numenon's top executives the real "Beyond the Best," and got more information for her benefactor than he dreamed possible.

She'd jump Will Duane at this retreat and have what her lover wanted in a day. Will was an attractive man. It would be fun. Murder flitted across her face. When she'd gotten what she wanted, she would hurt him as much as he hurt her by ignoring her. He would wish that he had loved her. He would wish that he'd taken her to live with him in his big house. She would hurt him for every man who had ever called her a slut or a whore. She would hurt him until he screamed for mercy.

Realizing her hatred showed, she forced herself to relax. When her face returned to its normal sweet expression, she looked around. As she stood on the curb by the motor homes, the dry desert air exhilarated her. She inhaled deeply, feeling the energy moving through her body. What her benefactor taught allowed her to live so much more fully. The pleasure she felt simply breathing was greater than many people could feel doing anything. She brought her lovers into her sensuous world, letting them sample the highest possibilities of physical delight. They were always grateful.

This morning, her senses were supercharged. She looked to the east, the direction they would be traveling. As far away as it was, she could feel the power of their destination. The Mogollon Bowl beckoned to her. It was a Power Spot, the strongest she'd ever known. She could feel the power of the holy man there. Her mind honed in on Grandfather's essence. He was a master, as mighty as her benefactor.

She stood still, her face composed like an angel's. She could feel the others at that camp. There were others like her there, others as sensual and powerful. She was almost orgasmic by the time she broke her reverie. She decided to take a little vacation before reporting back to her lover in Spain. A week with the Indians—she deserved it.

Sandy Sydney stepped into the *Ashley*, poised and self-possessed.

18

He had his orders. The Great One, Great-grandfather, the ancestors, and all the supernaturals had commanded him to deliver a management seminar. That was more shocking than his vision of dying at the hands of his followers. A management seminar? Was he so behind the times that the One had to *tell* him to modernize? To *get with it,* as the young people said?

Paul Running Bird had been a thorn in his side from the beginning, presenting the Meeting as something he *had* to do or let the young people down. Bothering him all year long with ideas and innovations to try at the next year's Meeting, harping about details. That wasn't his job. His job was to pay attention to Spirit and do what he was told. The rest was unimportant.

Yet Paul was on to something, even as he displayed his ego. The Great One had validated everything he suggested. Was his suspicion of Paul wrong? Was he really acting for the Great One? Look at their special guests this year. Paul played a great part in their coming. True, the whole universe had to move to get him to invite them, but Paul was the one who started everything when he visited him last September.

Remembering what had happened, he wanted to scream. "Rising Wolf!" he muttered. "That vicious son of a dog!" They always took names like that, all his kind. "Rising Wolf!" "Soaring Eagle!" "Giant Buffalo!" He would see "Rising Wolf" in hell before he'd let him come to the Meeting again.

Paul came to him last fall and told him what "Rising Wolf" was doing. He had proven his worth in telling him of the worst betrayal, the deepest insult, coming from the Meeting. Paul came to his hogan, not an easy task. He lived in the farthest corner of a remote reservation, while Paul lived and worked in Seattle.

"I want to show you this," he said, pulling an expensive color brochure from his briefcase.

He took it and read. *Stephen Rising Wolf—Apprentice to the World's Most Powerful Native American Shaman—Presents the Secrets of the Ancestors.*

The words set his blood on fire. He never told the ancestors' secrets, not to anyone. And the guy's name was Steve Bakalian, not Rising Wolf. The name Rising Wolf didn't come from any vision. It wasn't something he had given him. If Bakalian was one-sixteenth Indian, he would be surprised. His father was an Armenian roofing contractor from Lodi, California.

Stephen Bakalian had put together a seminar *selling* his teachings. He had no authorization to do that—no qualifications. He wasn't even an entry-level spirit warrior. Steve Bakalian gave himself the name Rising Wolf.

It should be Farting Weasel, he thought, scowling as he remembered the brochure. Bakalian put together a seven-day workshop. The workshop supposedly told all the secrets he'd learned from his teacher—who was shown in a sketchy drawing on the brochure, an ancient Indian with long braids. It was his likeness! No one had permission to use that. He would not allow anyone to draw or photograph him—it was against Great-grandfather's teaching. Yet there was his image on a brochure selling sacred truths. For his week of enlightenment, Bakalian was charging three thousand dollars a head, exclusive of food and accommodations.

"How can he do this? Why would he do this!" he shouted at Paul. "Why?"

On the back of the brochure was a photo of Billy Bob Burton smiling like his cheeks might break. He didn't know who this Billy Bob was, just that he wasn't a Native American. Paul explained that Billy Bob was the founder and CEO of Cherokee Corporation and the second-richest man in the world.

"But he's not Cherokee! Why would he use that name for his company?" He became angrier the more Paul divulged.

"Steve has been recording your talks for years, and taking notes on everything." This in itself was heresy. His teachings and rituals were not recorded; that was one of the Rules. Paul continued, "He and his friends put everything together as a book. He made a seminar out of it. Mostly whites go to it. They don't know the difference. He's doing great. His book's selling like crazy and his seminars are full. Look at this." Paul pulled another brochure from his briefcase.

Reading the headline, a scream of fury rose in his throat. His war cry ululated over the desert. It was a brochure for a new seminar. *Sexual Secrets of Native America. Rising Wolf presents the lovemaking lore of an ancient shaman. Fulfill the longing of your heart!* This seminar was two thousand dollars per person for a weekend at a discreet site, couples over eighteen only. His outrage was boundless.

"My People don't need lessons about sex! Everyone knows about sex. Fish know about sex. Dogs and cats know about sex. I don't teach about sex!" In fact, he seldom mentioned the subject at the Meeting. He read the brochure carefully. The wording was ambiguous, but it could have been interpreted to be the direct teachings of Steve's ancient shaman.

Charging money for something he knew nothing about! He *never* accepted money for his work. Gifts of gratitude, yes. Money, no. This was an insult to his lineage, to the ancestors, to the spirit of the land.

"There's more," Paul had told him. His hogan had neither a telephone nor electricity. He lived in a valley where cell phones wouldn't work. Paul drove them to a friend's house where they had a computer and the Internet. They had to go all the way into town. Paul showed Rising Wolf's elaborate Web site, featuring a fantastic photo of the great man himself, with that sketchy painting that looked like him in the background. The site advertised Steve's books, CDs, and videos, shaman sticks, bells and rattles, buffalo horns and skulls, as well as "Shaman Love Oils."

Also advertised were his seminars, now based in Austin, Texas. The Sexual Secrets courses were up and running, as were the Executive Seminars, with Billy Bob Burton's endorsement prominently featured. Paul told him the Web site was brilliant computer work. "And I know—I'm a computer jock, and an executive at Microsoft." Grandfather already knew this; Paul had told him many times.

"You can buy all this stuff or register for a seminar right from your computer," Paul showed him the order forms and how to put in a credit card number. Then he showed him the site's latest page. *Expect a new and exciting seminar next spring when Rising Wolf returns from his latest* spirit *voyage with his shaman. The shaman so secret that Native Americans hold his name in awe.* It showed a soft focus drawing of Wolf Man and what had to be him gazing off into the distance.

"He's promising a new seminar from the Meeting we haven't had yet?" He was apoplectic. Jesus turning the moneychangers out of the temple could not have been more outraged. Paul showed him how to e-mail Rising Wolf. He sent an e-mail that Steve Bakalian would never forget, telling him that he and his cronies were not allowed at the Meeting or anywhere else he was speaking or healing. Or even just standing around. The shaman e-mail denounced Steve and all his helpers, saying they weren't developed enough to teach what they were using and had no idea of its power. They could harm their students. He put the curse of the ancestors on Rising Wolf's work and lineage and all that he touched.

He lay in bed, smiling as he remembered. The Fallen Wolf drove them crazy on the reservation the next day, calling everyone he knew, trying to get them to go out to his hogan to talk to him. No one would. The great Wolfish Teacher himself showed up a few weeks later. Reservations at his seminars were falling off something terrible. He begged him to relent. He shrugged and said, "No." Rising Wolf begged to be taken back into the fold. "No." He finally left, not so repentant as looking for any way back in that worked.

Paul Running Bird had his own impurities. Because of what Steve Bakalian had done, Paul wanted him to set up a Web site of his own. He would have nothing to do with it. What he'd seen of the Internet appalled him. "So much information. How much of it is worth anything? It will distract people from the path." Paul asked him if he could set up something to handle information about the Meeting. "No."

Paul finally got Grandfather to allow him to discuss spiritual issues on his personal Web site and host a chat room. He would not mention the

Meeting or Grandfather or reference his teachings in any way. This subterfuge lasted about a week. After that, the whole Movement believed that
Paul's home page was the official Web site for the teachings.

Paul's Web site was linked to every Native page known. Soon everyone
knew about him and the Meeting. Worse, people started showing up at the
reservation. He would never turn his own People down, but others were
swarming around—kooks and weirdos in long white robes, chanting and
waving incense. All of a sudden, he was a well-known figure. It was against
everything he stood for.

That was it. He told Paul, "This is the last Meeting. No more." That
news hit the Internet, and now twice as many people were coming as the
year before. Paul had no idea how to handle four thousand people—how to
feed them, where to put them, and what about bathrooms?

Because of this catastrophe, he relented on another matter. A friend of
Elizabeth's needed a favor. Her name was Marina and she was a healer in the
San Francisco Bay Area—Silicon Valley. He had taken spirit voyages there.
If any place needed a good healer, it was that one. This was a very good
friend of Elizabeth's, and, as a very good friend of his most prominent warrior, he listened to her. The woman had a patient she couldn't handle. She
said that he was the only one who could help him—would he please take
the case for her? She had begged him repeatedly, writing letters and calling
the reservation office.

It took Billy Bob Burton's endorsement of Rising Wolf Turd and the
Internet disaster to get him to agree. If that fake shaman could have his
white man, the *second* richest man in the world, then Great-grandfather and
his ancestors could have *theirs*. He agreed to take her patient, if he did what
he was told.

His white man would arrive at the Meeting later that morning. In
return for the help he would receive, Grandfather was sure this man would
help him achieve *his* goals. Namely, getting back everything taken from his
People. He had read that Japan's economic growth after World War II had
made the war unnecessary. They could have bought the United States without
conquering it. That seemed like a good idea. He didn't want the United States
government. Who would? He wanted to take over the United States economy.
His guest would help them; he just didn't know it yet.

Those were some of the reasons his white man was struggling toward the Mogollon Bowl. But not the most important one. What clinched the invitation was what Elizabeth's friend told him about her troublesome client.

"He started Numenon," she said. Grandfather had never heard of it. "It's the largest corporation in the world." He'd still never heard of it. But the name interested him.

"Numenon?" he said, remembering his student days in Berkeley. "The great business chieftain named his company *Numenon*?"

"Yes." He could feel her smile over the telephone. She'd hooked him.

"*Numenon...*" The thing-in-itself, the absolute reality lying beneath the universe we perceive. How would a corporate executive know about the philosophy of Immanuel Kant? What executive would name his company after an abstraction that could never be known by a human being, pure being that all souls craved? Was this man a philosopher? He asked the healer to describe Numenon, and she did.

"The Numenon Ranger is the best personal computer made. I'm a Numo Nut—that's what they call the Numenon freaks. It's a cult, almost. I go to the Numo Fair every year. It's unbelievable—they take over San Francisco. Will Duane speaks. It's almost like a revival meeting. I use Numo's phone service, and their Internet connection... The movies they make are incredible. They win tons of awards. Their publishing wing..."

"What about the company's soul?"

"You'll have to meet my client."

So he did, as he and the healer talked on the phone. He turned his attention toward California, toward the valley hosting the new gold rush, the rush built on silicon. He sampled the currents of souls in that place, finding Will Duane's essence easily. Brilliant and clouded, tortured and ecstatic. Dark. Ruined. Vicious and loving. This man was at a turning point. Very soon, he would be claimed by evil—or good. If he were taken by evil, the world would perish along with his soul. If good claimed him, a new flowering could occur around the globe.

And then he understood. This student was coming to him as he had to Great-grandfather, almost dead from crossing the desert. Almost dead from the wounds he bore. Will Duane was in the same condition he had been in when Great-grandfather found him.

When Great-grandfather and he met, they knew they had been born to teach and learn from each other. Will Duane was seeking his teacher, in his own stupid, pig-headed way. He was the teacher Duane was born to find.

So, he returned Will Duane's phone call when it came. The call didn't come to him directly—he didn't have a phone. It came to the tribal chairman, who drove his truck to Grandfather's hogan to tell him of the famous man who wanted to talk to him. Grandfather didn't feel like riding in a truck right then, so he sent the Chairman back and walked into town. That took three days, because he had to visit everyone along the way. He was simply being polite. When he got to town, he couldn't call Will Duane immediately, because Maria Cross Eyes' sciatica was acting up and she needed healing. Then there was a feast. He had to conduct the ceremonies associated with it. It took a week for him to return Will Duane's phone call. Unfortunately, that was last Thursday, a few days before the Meeting.

He smiled broadly, remembering the controlled fury in the richest man in the world's voice. He agreed to all of his conditions and suggestions, as the old man knew he would.

He invited Will Duane to the Meeting because of the name he chose for his company, and because of circumstances too convoluted and strange to explain. His soul required it, as did the universe.

He allowed his special guest to bring his staff. "Bring anyone you want," he told him. "Just make sure they're your best." Your best warriors, the shaman meant. He trained *warriors*. His guests didn't know what they were in for. He couldn't stop laughing, even though people were sleeping around him. His laughter rippled like the sea, spreading out in waves. The desert itself laughed. Tears came to his eyes.

Oh, I'm going to give them the works! The *executive* package! I'm going to fry their brains! He knew the words the young people used. He remembered something else. Forgive me, Great One. *I* will do nothing. The Meeting is Yours, Oh Great One! What *You* will do to the white man and his friends!

He began to sing in a high minor key, "*Oh, Great One! They are coming! They are coming! All the warriors are coming! It will be as it was of old! They are coming! The warriors will ride in glory! Ride across the sky!*"

His song faded, leaving him sitting quietly, pulled inside by a force he knew well. As he sank deep inside himself, the shaman remembered the real reason this would be the last Meeting. The secret reason best kept to himself. He continued moving deeply inside, drifting down to the heart of his being.

The ancestors waited for him there. They touched him and laughed, blessing him and urging him on. One smiled, light beaming from his mouth. He moved quickly through the cave of the ancestors. As he approached the rear, a crack appeared in the cave wall. The light on the other side burst out at him, covering him with gold. The old man went through the opening and into the flames. He passed through them quickly, entering the blackness of nothing. Into the silence filled with a million crystal bells. He could feel it calling to him, the point outside everything. The point beyond the void spoke to him. Time stopped. He disappeared into the Power.

Down in the flats, Bud Creeman awoke. Grandfather's laughter rang in his heart, not in any outer ears. He sat up. The glow from the lean-to struck the younger man. Bud began to sink into himself, into his own being. The Power was upon Grandfather. The Power was with them all. It would be a good Meeting.

19

Will walked around the five motor homes before getting in. They made quite a display, lined up along the curb. Upscale corporate presence—exactly what Will wanted to impress upon the Indians. They were custom motor homes, identical except for the aerodynamic *Ashley*. Even the smooth-sided trailer pulled by the last vehicle matched. All were crème with a few touches of the corporate burgundy and gold. Each had the Numenon name in its trademarked font painted in gold on all sides, accompanied by the logo, an enigmatic face circled by flame that was recognized by most of humanity.

Will remembered when he designed it. For years, they couldn't come up with a logo he liked. Back in the 1960s, as he walked by a hippie store on University Avenue a statue of a man dancing in a hoop of flames grabbed his attention. His expression said, "I *know* the numenon. I *am* the numenon."

He bought the statue—some god from India, they said. That face became the Numenon logo. His designers kept telling him to update it, but that face still enthralled him. It was the numenon.

Mark Kenna approached him. "Is everything all right, Mr. Duane?"

"Fine, Mark. You've done a great job. She's in perfect shape, all of them are." He climbed into the *Ashley*.

Mark wanted to jump in the air and yell, "Yes!" After driving almost nine hundred miles from Palo Alto, he'd found an all-night car wash—the do-it-yourself type—and insisted that his drivers wash their vehicles before donning their official, crisply pressed uniforms. "He'll notice, believe me," he'd said to their grumbles. He was right. Mr. Duane ran a finger along each motor home.

All he had to do was keep it up and he'd have a better job by week's end. He stepped into the *Ashley* and took the driver's seat.

Will sat in his big command chair, his back to the wall separating his bedroom from the main cabin. To his left, Gil Canao sat on the banquette running along the wall. He looked like he wanted to jump out of the vehicle and hitchhike back to Cupertino. Next to him, Doug Saunders lolled and twitched. He was drunk and, by the way he kept moving and scratching, detoxing from cocaine. Will didn't buy that story about vandals for a minute, and he knew how serious Doug's drug problem was. Sandy Sydney sat opposite him, on the banquette she and Betty would occupy, assuming Betty appeared. Sandy kept flashing looks at him, crossing and uncrossing her legs, and making her intentions toward him clear: rape and murder.

The tension in the cabin acted like a catalyst. He could barely sit still, could barely stay in his own skin. He cleared his throat and put a hand to his tie. The eyes of every person in the vehicle focused on him. His tension ratcheted up. He wanted to tear off this monkey suit and run. He could run alongside the *Ashley* as far as she had to go. He could run five hours. He'd done it before. His knee bounced up and down, out of control. How could he sit in here with them until they got there? Will started to stand. Everyone stiffened, ready to follow him wherever he went.

He forced himself to sit back and relax. He was too tense to pretend to make conversation. Mark was at the wheel; the other drivers manned their respective vehicles. They were waiting for Betty and Melissa. Where were they? Someone had seen them go into the ladies' room.

He knew what they were doing—roasting him alive for what he'd said in the plane. He knew that Melissa had taken it too calmly. They were holed up in that bathroom, calling him every name in the book. Developing a strategy for dealing with him. Melissa would never come out screaming, but she'd corner him somewhere and deliver a sermon that would make him feel like shit. And Betty would take her revenge somehow. He'd never see it coming, but she'd nail him.

Will attempted to calm himself by letting his eyes travel over the *Ashley's* interior. Beautiful from its custom tires to its satellite-equipped roof. The *Ashley* was bulletproof. More than that, it could take a direct hit from a missile, in theory anyway. Will had spent more millions than he'd admit on her. Most of the rumors about her cost were low. Les Whitney, the famous New York designer of boardrooms and yachts for the rich and famous, created it for him.

His eyes traced the patterns made by the fine hardwoods of the cabinets and danced over the syncopation of color and line of the rest of the interior. Three paintings from his collection were hung in the stateroom, two more in his bedroom. The *Ashley's* beauty failed to calm him. His knee continued its frantic dance.

Betty and Melissa finally climbed in. Melissa walked deliberately to a seat next to Gil and sat down. She was wearing sunglasses in the dead of night. With trembling hands, she took them off and put them in her purse. She made eye contact with everyone in the cabin. Her face was swollen and blotchy and her makeup had been rubbed off. Her anguish and vulnerability were painful to see. Everyone knew why she had fallen apart.

The cabin was shocked into silence as Mark pulled out. Numenon had already changed. Someone had told the truth.

20

Grandfather moved through the rolling flames on the other side. He did not go very deep into the trance, only deep enough to discover what he should know. Animals flared out of the conflagration, neon-edged and dazzling. They were totems come to bless him. A bear, a Gila monster, supernaturals, kachinas—all as real as he was. They were going to show him something.

People thought he could see into the future. The truth was that he could only see what he was given to see. It was like looking into a hunk of swiss cheese. If you looked in some holes in the cheese, you could see all the way to the other side—and very clearly. If you looked in other holes, maybe you'd see something, but just parts of the whole would be shown, you'd have to put the pieces together. If you looked in other holes, you saw light, but nothing more. Grandfather didn't see anything he wasn't shown, and then only as clearly as the Great One wanted. Still, everything he saw in that state turned out to be true. It had been that way for years.

The sensations came so fast they shocked him. He was with Wesley Silverhorse. He could feel what Wesley felt, smell what he smelled, and hear sounds like he had Wesley's ears. The shaman could do everything but see through Wes's eyes.

Wesley Silverhorse was inside a woman. He was rutting inside her, having sex. He could feel it like it was his own body. Wesley and the woman were ecstatic, enraptured. He pulled back. This was too much. He didn't want this intimacy with his favorite or anyone else.

The old man couldn't stop the experience. He was inside Wesley's body. Oh, it had been so many years since Grandfather had felt that softness around him. Forty-four years since his wife left, since he'd been where Wesley was. He wanted to stop what was going on, but the Great One wouldn't let him.

He thought of his wife, his Rebecca. So beautiful, so smart. They were doomed before they started. It couldn't work. But they loved each other so much that they married anyway. They were soul mates, like all the others who would marry at the Meeting. They would never split up. He and his wife had never divorced.

Yet they hadn't seen each other or communicated for over forty years. He knew she was living and well, better off than he was, maybe. A success. Rich. Respected. He could feel her in his heart. Where Rebecca was, he didn't know. He didn't even know what name she used. She was as powerful as he was. She hid herself from him. They had to separate; they would have killed each other. They tried to stop fighting for almost seven years, but it was no use. They had their beautiful daughter, Emily, Leroy's mother, who died of the cancer when Leroy was four.

He would never forget his wife. Here at the Meeting, he remembered her as he saw the joy of the couples he married. He would never divorce Rebecca, nor take another woman. He would never be able to live with her either. She drove him out of his mind.

He had studied with Great-grandfather for many years and had been tested in ways that most would call cruel. He thought he could handle anything, but nothing prepared him for marriage. If she opened her mouth a certain way, parts of himself he didn't know existed came out. Terrible parts that he thought he'd left behind. He blushed, ashamed. He could not forget what happened between them, and what he did that caused her to leave.

When he recalled that truth, the reverie let him go. He was supposed to remember his wife. Did he want to reconcile with her? Is that what the Great One was asking? It seemed impossible. They fought so much. What use would it be, anyway? They were so old. Grandfather didn't know how old he was. Many years over eighty. Rebecca would be in her late seventies. A voice arose from his depths,

Do you want to reunite with Rebecca? Do you want another chance?

His heart leaped, not bothering to outline the futility. Oh, yes! More than anything.

The old man was at once in the golden flames of the other side and fully aware of what was around him. Grandfather could be in a trance and give a talk. He could be in a trance and be twice as alert as anyone in the room. He was in a trance most of the time these days and no one could tell. Knowing how people at the Meeting could interpret what they saw had taught him to be careful this week. Only on occasion did he go so deep as to lose sight of where he was.

His eyes narrowed as he thought about what had happened. He'd had a vision of Wesley. It wasn't happening now, because Grandfather could feel him approaching the camp in his old truck. His vision was of Wesley in the near future, having sex. Good. Wesley had been with the shaman since he was six years old. He was Grandfather's favorite, a spirit warrior of spirit warriors. The vision said Wesley was getting married this week. The young man kept the rules so well, the only way he'd have sex was if he was married. Grandfather smiled. Wesley Silverhorse was thirty years old and a virgin.

Things would be better for Wesley if he was married. A wife would relax him. The other warriors wouldn't think him such a prick. Grandfather smiled again. He knew what the other warriors thought of his favorite. They said Wesley was a pain. What they said was true. Wesley was demanding of everyone around him. He had to do things his way or not at all. The other warriors tolerated Wesley, because they knew that none of them could beat him or even match him. Yes, Wes was an uptight fanatic and a maniac. That's what it took to do what he did.

Wesley would probably succeed Grandfather, over his real grandson, Leroy Watches. Leroy would have to change plenty to take his place, and he didn't see that happening. Wesley would succeed him, if Wesley survived. He kept Grandfather's rules to a T, all but one. He had trouble in one area. It was hard to resist—addictive. Rodeo was Wes's problem. He liked bucking

horses and bulls. Wesley couldn't stay away from rodeo. Grandfather for-
gave him, because he knew why he did it. If it were the thrills that drew
Wes, Grandfather would have forbidden him from participating.

It was the money Wesley wanted. Winning a purse was the only way
he could make fast money when he needed it, which he always did, usually
to save the ranch. Wesley's family lived outside the town of Smallbone,
Wyoming, an all-white burg in the middle of nowhere. They were the only
Native American ranch owners in that part of the state as far as Grandfather
knew. Ever since Wesley's daddy, Cal Silverhorse, got a hold of that ranch
almost thirty years ago, the family's lives had been about keeping it. The
locals and the bank would just as soon the Silverhorses skedaddled back
to the rez. That ranch and the rodeo killed Cal Silverhorse. Grandfather
would be lucky if it didn't claim Wesley too. Wes would tell Grandfather he
wouldn't rodeo any more, then go out and do it when money got tight—
which was always.

Wesley was coming. Grandfather could feel him, and the strength of
his will to be there. He was nearing the Bowl, coming to his teacher. Wesley
loved Grandfather more than the rest. He loved him as much as Grandfather had loved his own teacher. Tears came to Grandfather's eyes thinking
of Great-grandfather. Oh, terrible day that he died. Terrible day!

The Great One brought him back to his purpose. Grandfather needed
to see the other brides and grooms the Meeting would create before Wesley
arrived. That was one reason so many came to the Meeting. Here, at this
blessed Mogollon Bowl, the earth revealed things. That's all his "selecting"
partners was about. The people who were supposed to be together were
obvious here—he simply recognized and blessed the fact, as they did. He
could hardly keep the soul mates apart once they recognized each other.
They had lots of weddings at the Meeting. People came, hoping to meet
their soul mates and marry.

Grandfather had a hard time with this concept. Soul mates. The words
were like so many associated with him—not his. They were words the
people at the Meeting came up with to suit their own needs. The truth was,
most human beings were more interested in finding their perfect mate than
in finding the Great One. And was that so bad? Had not Creator made
people so that they could love each other? Had not Creator instilled the

desire for happiness, a mate, and love in every soul? For children? For some, the mate was the Great One, and these men and women of God remained unmarried and happy. Or alone, and happy, like he was.

He tried to tell his followers that the soul needs no mate. It is perfect and complete all by itself. Grandfather was fine alone. He missed his wife sometimes, but he was fine alone. The people who belonged to the Great One were fine alone. They might be married, but they didn't need their mates. Anyone who had the Great One in his heart would be satisfied and need no one. Yet people persisted in thinking they needed a perfect soul mate. Somehow, the presence of the One brought out this longing for perfect human love more strongly. Well, they got as close as they could come here. Who was he to say that finding a true mate and marrying wasn't the best outcome a person might have at the Meeting? The most spiritual? He married all the couples that Creator told him were meant to be together.

After the Great One showed Grandfather what to do at the Meeting, he was always shown who was going to be married, but never to whom. The One liked to play with the shaman, driving him crazy guessing who went together. He was pulled deeper into the trance. Faces swam before him. Ten, twenty, thirty, fifty, a hundred people. Sometimes, a couple would know each other for ages and—nothing. Then one day, Wham-o! A door opened and they knew they were soul mates. They would be married later that day. Grandfather thought that was how it would be with Wes—she would be someone he'd known. Kit Jay, he thought. Maybe her.

Ahah! Grandfather understood—that's why Rose Silverhorse didn't come with Wes to this last Meeting. Rose was a powerful healer. She knew that her oldest child, her favorite, the one who helped her raise the other six, would be married. She couldn't stand to see it. He understood. Poor beautiful, lonely Rose. Now she would be alone on the ranch that killed her husband and tormented the rest of them. All of her other kids ran off the minute they finished high school.

Grandfather slipped back into the reverie, marking the faces before him. All would be married. That's why they required blood tests of everyone coming to the Meeting, for the marriage licenses. They needed them fast, once that energy hit. Grandfather was an ordained minister, a justice of the peace, and a holy man of his People. The weddings he did were legal, handled on the reservation, recorded right and proper. People came to the Meeting to see God and marry their true mates. They came to make lasting marriages. None of the hundreds of couples he had married here had divorced. Some had wild times, but they lasted.

The Great One revealed more faces to Grandfather. More surprises, and then an outright shock. They'd had the Numenon crew take blood tests, too. What would the richest man in the world think if he knew what would happen within his own camp?

21

Melissa's appearance stunned everyone in the *Ashley* into silence. Everyone knew why she'd been crying. Will Duane looked at the young woman, stricken. She could have lectured him on corporate responsibility and social values for hours with nowhere near the impact of her tearful face. He looked at his protégée and ached inside. He wanted to jump up and take her in his arms, comfort her and tell her why they were really on this trip. He longed to tell her the truth, but he couldn't, and he couldn't tell any of his staff. He sat, rigid.

Why did she have to look so much like his daughter? Will moaned inwardly. The first time he saw Melissa Weir in the Numenon hallway, it was like seeing his Ashley when she first worked there. When he first saw Melissa—was it eight years ago?—it seemed as if she'd been in his life forever. He could see her form in his mind's eye back then, walking down the hall with Betty. Melissa Weir had the same squared shoulders, the same mannish way of walking as Ashley. She even had on the same type of suit that his daughter wore. Will's heart jumped when he saw her—then and now.

Ashley Duane was tall—five foot ten. She was slim, but very strong and athletic. She had dark, wavy hair and her large, dark blue eyes matched his. Melissa Weir was a diminutive version of Ashley except for her very curly hair and enormous gray-green eyes. Both women had refined features, high cheek-bones, and heavy, arched eyebrows. They could be sisters. It was Melissa's no-nonsense attitude that hooked Will harder. She was like Ashley at her finest, totally professional, and achievement orientated beyond even his expectations.

Melissa Weir hadn't been with Numenon six months when Will moved her to his private staff. Everyone thought he was sleeping with her. The few who didn't were sure he favored her because she looked so much like Ashley. Neither and both were true. Melissa rose in the corporation because she came up with a plan that made him more money than any of his major executives. For eight years, she'd surpassed her own projections. Melissa earned everything she got.

Will Duane wanted to take her to bed, but not the way anyone thought. When he saw Melissa Weir, he saw his Ashley as a young child. He could see the vulnerability, the fragility, in the MBA that no one else per-ceived. Will longed to cuddle her the way he never had his infant daughter. He wanted to do everything with Melissa that he hadn't done with his own girl. He wanted to make Melissa/Ashley's haunted look go away; he wanted to make her well and happy.

Melissa was so much like his daughter, except for two things. Melissa Weir was emotionally stable and she wasn't a drug addict.

He fired his own little girl! She was too volatile to keep on board. He could see it as though it were happening. Ashley's hands shook as she packed the things on her desk. Her long, fine hands moved rapidly, putting pictures in a box. She glared at him, but held her tongue. She had on one of those expensive navy blue suits and a silk blouse. She still looked fine in those days, as long as you didn't look too closely.

Will blinked and another scene danced before him: log walls, garlands of evergreens, and white lights. He could see the tall Christmas tree at his Montana ranch. Ashley's partially shaved head with its dragon-tattooed scalp leaped out of the holiday decor. Ashley's eyes blazed as her dark purple lips funneled obscenities into his heart. The language she used! Will cringed in his motor home chair as the memory struck him.

Ashley swore at him on Christmas Eve. She cursed him until he climbed into the ranch Suburban and left. That was three months ago. He had been shaken from the moment he saw her. The big sweater she wrapped around herself couldn't hide the skeleton under her clothes. His daughter was dying. Will Duane put his face in his hands, turning a moan into a loud yawn. He looked through his fingers at the other people in the motor home. Did his staff notice his weakness?

Will hadn't slept the night before, barely more than that for the three previous nights, not much more for the past two months. Not since Marina … He never thought she meant it; he never thought she'd throw him out. Will twitched in his chair, thrashing about for something to relieve his pain, something to make himself feel better. He looked up, and the others responded by focusing their attention on him. He'd better take control. He'd better get everyone to work. But he couldn't think of anything to do, he couldn't organize his mind.

22

Grandfather sat quietly, losing consciousness of the world around him as the parade of faces to be wed marched before him. The dawn was nowhere in evidence. The shaman came back to his senses at the sound of Wesley's beat-up truck faltering across the campground. How the kid avoided running over people sleeping on the ground, he didn't know. The truck drew closer and wheezed to a stop nearby. He heard Wesley stumbling around outside his lean-to, trying to set up a tent. By the sound of his movement, he knew Wes was hurt worse than last year.

"Come in here, Wes. You can sleep here," he whispered.

Wes entered, trying to hide his face, even in the dark. He struggled to put down a sleeping bag. Grandfather could see he was having difficulty moving one side of his body. He lifted the blankets of his bed. "Come in here, Wes." Wes did, curling up on his good side as far away from his teacher as he could get. Grandfather touched him, and Wes began to shake.

"What happened this time, Wes?"

Wesley was crying. Grandfather had never seen him cry, except when his father was killed. Something devastating had happened. He took a while to speak. "They sent me a bad horse …"

"And it hurt you?"

"She. A mare. I got her saddled, no problem. I got on her, no problem." He started to draw a long breath, then gasped. Broken ribs, thought Grandfather. "The owner and his ranch manager were there at our place, watching by the round pen. You know them—the Rocking W Bar? Mr. Williamson?"

Grandfather did. Williamson was the richest rancher in half the state of Wyoming. He had a string of fine horses and his own training staff. The old man was immediately suspicious that he'd send a horse to Wesley.

"I was up on her," Wes continued, "and she exploded. I couldn't feel it coming—usually I can, but this mare, no." Wes turned to look at Grandfather, wincing. "She *wanted* to hurt me. I've never seen one that bad. She tried everything she knew, then turned around and bit my leg. She bucked worse than any rodeo horse. When she couldn't throw me, she threw herself down."

Wes spoke and Grandfather touched his head, seeing what had happened through Wes's eyes. Wes's mind communicated directly with his teacher's. Grandfather could see the stockyard of the Silverhorse ranch with the unfamiliar truck and trailer in it, the round pen, the three men, and the horse. A pretty mare—dark bay. Nice hip, pretty head. Grandfather liked a pretty horse.

Wesley kept talking, even though Grandfather could watch the scene in his mind,

"She threw herself down—into the round pen walls—on purpose. She tried to crush me against the wall, and then she rolled on me. My mother got her off me, or I'd be dead. The mare stepped on my face when she got up, Grandfather. Look." The old man could see the bruises in the moonlight. "She hit my face with her hoof. An inch, and I'd be dead."

Wes clutched him. His tears were from emotional injury as much as physical. "I thought they were finally sending me good horses. They let me get on her without telling me ..." Grandfather sat and listened. "They knew I wouldn't take her if I knew. So I almost got killed." He shook his head. "They hauled me into the house afterward. They said they were sorry, but they didn't get a doctor.

"My mother heard them talking as they loaded the mare in the trailer. They were trying to figure out what to do with her next. She'd almost killed a couple of guys at their place!" Wesley stopped, struggling to go on. "They brought her to me. *I* can be killed to see if a bad horse can be fixed."

Grandfather patted him softly. What Wes said was true. He never understood why the Silverhorses didn't get it. The ranchers had sent all their bad horses to them for thirty years. That's how Cal Silverhorse kept going. Why didn't Wes suspect? Why did he still hope to be accepted? An Indian *never* would be accepted in Smallbone, Wyoming.

"What else, my son?" The old man asked, tenderly. Placing his hand on the boy's head, Grandfather could see the images in Wes's mind as though he were there. They were images the healer had seen many times before. This was a seminal trauma in Wes's life, one that wouldn't erase easily.

A much younger Wes was at a rodeo watching his dad bull clown. It was an ordinary fairgrounds somewhere: bleachers, bucking chutes, dirt, and noise. Cowboys and cattle. A young red-haired cowboy came out of the chutes hard, riding a ghost-pale Brahma bull. He got bucked off, landing on his feet. The kid's hand was stuck in the rigging, which didn't release. The bull bucked in a circle with the cowboy tied to him. He was getting yanked around. He could fall at any time. The rigging finally let go, and the young man ran off, but lost his footing before he got ten feet. The bull was on him, mauling him. Out of nowhere, a clown ran in and distracted the animal.

Touching Wes's head, Grandfather could see the bull turn after the clown while other cowboys picked up the fallen rider. The clown dashed for a big metal barrel a few feet away. He was small, so he could jump inside it easily. The race looked easy. The clown would escape. Except that he didn't. Almost at the barrel, the clown stumbled. The bull threw him high in the air. The clown floated over the animal's back like a paper airplane. It looked like a joke—a grown man gliding like that. He landed headfirst in a heap on the ground. The bull turned and went after him. His sawed off horns made him look like a hammerhead shark. He drove one side of his ghastly skull and then the other into the clown. The cowboys tried to get him off, and couldn't. The rodeo manager finally shot the animal, which collapsed on Cal Silverhorse's body.

Wes Silverhorse, aged sixteen, watched his father die. He brought his father's body home, told his mother what happened, buried his dad, and picked up where Cal Silverhorse left off. The young man raised six brothers and sisters and helped his mother keep the ranch going. Those activities accounted for years sixteen to thirty of Wes's life. He worked like a maniac.

All that kept him from becoming one was his time with Grandfather and the Spirit he found inside himself and in the land around him.

Wes had just watched his father mauled to death for the thousandth time. He continued to cry as Grandfather spoke, "Talk to me, Wes."

"We've had the ranch for thirty years, Grandfather. We have the prettiest place around. We do everything right—and no one likes us. They won't even come into our house. I've spent my whole life trying to prove that I'm good enough. That they should..." Wes struggled to express his thoughts ... "send me good horses, and buy the horses we raise. That I deserve to ..." He stopped cold.

Grandfather interjected, "Be treated like a human being?"

"I almost died, Grandfather. If I died, my whole life would have been working that ranch. I get up and work and go to bed. The only thing in my life that I love is what I do with you." He corrected himself. "No. I love my family, too. I worked and I raised them. I did it for them. But I'm so tired." He fought to get the words out. "They got to finish school; I wanted to go so bad." Grandfather knew how much it had hurt Wesley to have to drop out of high school when his father died. "I thought they'd help me when they graduated, but they didn't. They left. It's all on me now. Me and Mama ..." Wes forced out the real point.

"I don't want to die to save our ranch."

Grandfather's heart leaped. Was it going to happen? Was Wesley going to let go? He couldn't be free until he did. "Save our ranch" was the problem. The old man had heard those words a thousand times from Wesley and the rest of his family.

He looked at Grandfather. "We got behind with the bank again. We're going to lose the ranch."

"You took in outside horses to try to save it." Wesley nodded. "Including the one that almost killed you." Another nod. "What else have you been doing, Wesley?" Wesley looked away. "Rodeoing?"

"Last fall."

"What?"

"Bronc riding."

"—And?" The old man was insistent.

"Riding bulls."

Grandfather shook his head. "What else? Bull clowning?"

Wes nodded, ashamed. He had promised his teacher that he wouldn't do what had killed his father. The old man grimaced.

"Wes, do you *want* to live?"

"Yes! That's why I came here. I don't even know how I got here. I'm afraid I'll die before I've done anything—or had anything that was my own." Fear shook him.

Grandfather knew what Wesley wanted: a wife, a family, a little money; simple things that everyone wanted. The family's poverty had sapped his energy and hope.

"What are you willing to do to get what you want?"

"I'll do whatever you say."

"You may lose the ranch."

"I know. I talked to my mother. She doesn't care about the ranch. She'll move back to the rez. She doesn't want to lose me, too."

"You'll do what I say?"

"Yes. Whatever you want." He meant it.

Grandfather smiled. "Good. You'll stay with me after this Meeting, unless I tell you otherwise. You'll do what I say." His voice became a command, "I forbid you to rodeo again, ever. No bull clowning, ever." Grandfather had never been so strong in his prohibition. "I forbid you to take horses for training unless I approve them."

Wes nodded, looking relieved.

"Good, Wes. Now let me get to work on you. Take off your shirt." He lit a kerosene lamp while Wes stripped off his shirt, moving slowly and wincing. Grandfather was horrified when he saw Wes's face and side. He was right; the mare would have taken off his face if she'd hit him a fraction of an inch closer. As it was, a gruesome, purple bruise covered his cheek and temple. Wes's side matched his face; it was purple from below the shoulder. "Take off your pants, Wesley." The bruises extended to the knee. Seeping abrasions were covered with homemade bandages. Grandfather didn't ask if he'd gone to a doctor. They didn't have insurance and couldn't afford a doctor.

Grandfather shook his head, then got to work. Rose Silverhorse had done an admirable job. She was a great herbalist and healer, but Wesley needed something stronger. Grandfather would patch him up for a couple of hours, then finish the job later. The old man went to his supply of herbs and medicines at the back of the lean-to; it was the most important thing he brought to the Meeting. The shaman made an herb poultice and laid it down Wes's entire side, with a smaller one for his face. Mixing herbs and other ground substances with water from a bottle, Grandfather made an elixir. "Drink half of this now, Wes, the other half when you wake up." The old man sat while Wes drank his medicine. When he was done, Grandfather gave him a large ceramic jar of ointment with a cork stopper.

"This is for your hands. You can start using it now."

He sat back, waiting for Wesley to realize what he had said. Wes started to turn toward his teacher, but stopped when his side hurt. He lay back on the bed, breathing hard. The old man smiled as he noticed him begin to tremble. It was very different in character from his earlier grief-stricken shaking. His breathing deepened. The jar of ointment for his hands had meaning for the spirit warriors. By giving him the jar, Grandfather had told him he'd had a vision indicating that Wes would be married at this Meeting. It was a code. Most working cowboys and ranchers had hands that were collections of calluses, scars, and cuts in various stages of healing. Like those of his compatriots, parts of Wesley's hands were hard as horn; the rest resembled sandpaper. He couldn't touch a bride with hands like that. Grandfather's ointment healed and softened nicely. The warriors knew that when they received this particular gift, the end to their waiting was at hand.

"Really, Grandfather?"

"Yes, Wes. My vision says you should meet her this week. You should be married by the end of the Meeting. Does that help you? Do you feel better?"

Wes nodded and continued to quiver. Grandfather smiled, "Don't worry about your shaking. It's energy wanting to be released. It will be, soon enough."

"Do you know who she is, Grandfather?"

The old man shook his head. Wesley already knew the answer to his question. "No. That isn't revealed. You will know; when you touch her, you will know. Listen to your heart, my son, it will guide you. You'll feel it when you touch her."

Both of them knew that once the partners had touched, the urge to consummate their bond could become so intense that it would drive them crazy. Not literally, but they'd get pretty uncomfortable until they got married. Grandfather had been known to do four or five group weddings a day at the Meeting to keep things calm.

The Meeting was the only time that Grandfather insisted that everyone follow the warrior's rules; he figured that everyone could live like a warrior for a week. The only exceptions were the newlyweds. They were permitted to have discreet sex during the Meeting. This was an accommodation to reality, as Grandfather could no more have stopped them than pulled the moon from the sky. He didn't want moaning newlyweds in tents or swaying campers distracting the other people attending the Meeting, so he banished the lovers from the Bowl and parking lot.

Fortunately, geography accommodated the People's needs. Immediately after being married, couples ran off to the numerous caves found in the cliffs behind the Bowl and were seen again only when they got hungry. Grandfather smiled. People who were dignified to the point of being stuffy got pretty lively once they touched their mates.

He patted Wes. "You've been very good, Wesley. Things will change quickly now. The important part is that you're not trying to make the world run in a way it doesn't want to go or hold on to what should be released. What you want will come to you on its own." The old man fell silent.

Wesley lay back, wondering. Grandfather could practically hear his thoughts, "Will it be the girl I met last year? What tribe will she be? Will she like horses as much as I do? Is it Kit Jay?" His student had a great incentive to get well now, an hour after arriving.

He smiled at Wesley, lost in thinking about his bride. Grandfather indicated the jar. "Put some on now, Wesley." The young man opened the jar and put some ointment on his palms, rubbing it in. The ointment was also medicinal, providing a release of tension. Wes's breathing turned to gasps as he let go. He was a wreck. That was good. Grandfather knew they usually needed to hit bottom before they changed. Wesley continued to talk, knowing Grandfather could read his mind anyway.

"I've worked for so long, Grandfather; I can't do it anymore. I've been so lonely; I've waited so long. I see her in front of me, dancing. I want her to touch me, Grandfather. I lie by myself at night. When I lie on my bed, my skin feels so alive. My lips, all of me—I can feel the life in me, wanting her." Grandfather stroked his head.

"She longs for you, too, Wesley. You've done very well. You're a young man, and you've controlled yourself well. More than that, my son, you haven't settled for less than what is due you. You haven't used some girl who isn't for you to satisfy yourself for a moment."

Grandfather looked at Wesley with pride. He had a great destiny. The old man knew it the moment he first saw Wes, when the boy was six years old. Picking up the poultice on his cheek, the shaman could see the bruise was fading. Good; the medicine and poultices were starting to work. "Wesley. Sleep now. I'll have someone set up your camp and move your truck. Meet me at the Wedding Cave around ten, I'll do a real healing then." He stroked Wesley's body lightly to put him into a deep sleep, then covered him with his blankets and turned out the lamp, leaving for the morning ceremony.

Grandfather whistled as he walked. He always forgot how beautiful Wes was. The only man he had ever seen who was better looking was Benny, Wesley's younger brother. What a joy Wesley would be to his wife! Wes was not too tall, but was perfectly formed. He's just bone and muscle, Grandfather thought, like a fine horse. Wesley's face was chiseled planes and angles, precise curves, and brilliance. His black eyes sparkled with humor, his white teeth flashed. The intelligence and sweetness of his expression outshone his looks.

He's the purest student I've ever had, thought Grandfather. Despite his life, there's no meanness in him, no whining, no complaint. People ask me how I pick my favorites. They're the ones who've suffered most and come through without bitterness. They're the ones who've worked the hardest.

With a light step, he walked to the amphitheater to begin the morning chant. Stars filled the skies. What a good beginning! Wesley could live the life that was meant for him, instead of struggling to complete his father's.

The shaman nodded to the participants to begin the morning ritual.

23

Will frantically tried to regain the edge of his mind; he had to cover his confusion and weakness.

"Why don't we have some coffee?" Sandy Sydney saved him. Her little-girl voice reminded him of Marilyn Monroe's. Sandy got up and straightened her skirt. Betty started to get up to help.

"Oh, let me do it, Betty. It's no trouble." Betty smiled at her beautiful protégée. Sandy went to the *Ashley*'s granite-countered kitchen area. Jon Walker had supplied everything they might need for their journey: coffee, juices, snacks, and sandwiches. All were ready with minimal need for preparation. She pulled out four vacuum-bottle carafes. They were labeled "black," "cream and sugar," "low-fat and sugar," and "nonfat." No "decaf" at Numenon—faster was the only option.

"Who wants what?" Sandy's coffee service was as efficient as her work. Despite her looks, Sandy Sydney was as effective a secretary as her resume would lead you to expect.

Betty smiled as Sandy handed her a mug of "low-fat and sugar." Sandy was her most brilliant hiring choice. She had walked in off the street almost a year ago. Betty liked to visit the employees' café from time to time. She made herself accessible to everyone at Numenon. The café was the place to do it. Betty knew her power was based in part on the finger she kept on the company's pulse. A year ago, she was drinking coffee in the employees' lounge—the best coffee in the West, thanks to Will's penchant for fine food. His "Beyond the Best" credo extended throughout Numenon. A lovely young woman, demurely dressed, sat down near her. They ended up talking, and the girl told Betty she had an interview for a secretarial position in a few minutes. It was Sandy Sydney.

Betty could see herself in Sandy's bright freshness—and she had looked like Sandy twenty-five years ago. I ended up taking her into the interview myself, Betty recalled. I told personnel to call me if she passed muster. The young woman's skills were beyond excellent. Numenon hired her on the spot.

Sandy's résumé was extraordinary, but her life story was even more astonishing. An orphan, Sandy wasn't able to go to college immediately. She started out at a secretarial school in the Midwest, then worked as an executive secretary for a couple of years in Chicago. Through the generosity of a family friend, she was able to go to Wellesley, graduating with a double major in art history and literature. After that, she spent a year studying art at the Sorbonne. She made practically straight As throughout. Betty had carefully verified Sandy Sydney's application. It was all true. The young secretary received a phenomenal recommendation from her previous employer, the American owner of a Parisian art gallery. Sandy was all she presented herself as being.

"Do you remember her?" Betty had asked someone in the registrar's office at Wellesley.

"Who could forget her?" was the reply. Yes, who could forget Sandy Sydney?

Betty had Sandy assigned to her office, guiding and supporting her the whole year. What a year it had been! Sandy learned incredibly fast and remembered everything she was told. She was so quick to please that she almost seemed to be a mind reader. Within weeks, Sandy made suggestions to improve the efficiency of the secretarial staff in Betty's domain. In three months, she had reorganized the secretarial system in the headquarters. In six months, Sandy had learned all the Numenon software and developed improved tracking methods for projects and documents throughout the corporation. In another year, Betty thought that Sandy would be able to easily do her job. That's what Betty wanted. She wanted to retire.

If it weren't for the financial handicap her parents' deaths had put upon her starting out, Sandy Sydney could have been another Melissa Weir—Betty was convinced of that. She arranged a private interview for Sandy with Will to see if Sandy could somehow qualify for a management-track job.

Will obliged her by talking to Sandy and then told Betty, "She's a nice girl, but without an advanced degree and more quantitative background, she'll never get ahead in the Valley. Tell her to go back to school. Otherwise, she'll be a secretary for the rest of her life."

Like me? thought Betty.

Will insisted on having Sandy stationed as close to him as possible. Betty knew this was so he could ogle her. All the male executives did, and made comments. Sandy was more than beautiful—she was breathtaking. Her figure was lovely. Even though she dressed modestly, she couldn't hide the way she was built. The moment she appeared in the office, the rumors started to fly. A girl who looked like that was in for it, Betty thought. She didn't pay any attention to the gossip about poor Sandy.

Sandy's nickname among the men was "Tits." She was exposed to the full brunt of Numenon's sexual double standard. Will forbade sexual harassment, as legally mandated. He instituted a policy of "look, don't touch, but be sure and talk about it with the guys."

Despite Will's prohibition against physical contact, Sandy had complained to Betty of repeated fondling by a number of executives. Betty told her if she wanted to press charges, she'd help her every way she could. Sandy was so grateful that she teared up. "Not unless it gets worse, Betty. Thank you so much for caring." Betty spread the word that her protégée was thinking of taking legal action. Sandy stopped complaining of the fondling, but still was the target of "jiggle jokes" and stares. They said terrible things about her. Betty smiled at her young helper and Sandy beamed back.

Melissa Weir got up while Sandy was serving coffee and went to the *Ashley*'s bathroom, taking her purse. She looked at herself in the wall of beveled mirrors. Most designer show houses couldn't claim bathrooms as opulent as the *Ashley*'s. She found the small linen closet and took out a washcloth, beginning the process of cleaning up the damage done by her crying fit. She washed her face and looked in the mirror again. A scared little girl looked back at her. That would never do. Her makeup case came out.

Melissa didn't have time to shop. She had employed a wardrobe consultant since she started making real money. The consultant edited her clothes and turned a serious graduate student into a model of female corporate competence. Three or four times a year, she would bring a number of new wardrobe pieces to Melissa's home, all calculated to keep her image up to date. Melissa did not have a vast wardrobe, but what she had was stunning, utterly appropriate, and ultraexpensive. She could go anywhere in the world at a moment's notice—and did. The consultant also supplied Melissa with makeup artists, hair stylists, manicurists, and, most important, the name of the best massage therapist on the Peninsula.

Together, they turned Melissa from a mop-headed intellectual to Numenon's most stylish female executive. Like clockwork, the manicurist and hair stylist visited Melissa's townhouse in the quaint town of Saratoga, checking in for touch-ups and major events. Melissa learned their skills as well as she did everything else.

In minutes, Melissa had reconstructed her face. Her makeup was subtle, classy and gave her an air of utter command. She blotted her lipstick and smiled at the face in the mirror. Melissa Weir, MBA, the Bitch of Numenon, Harvard's Answer to Nuclear War, was back. No trace remained of the little girl who'd cried.

Melissa walked back to her seat like she owned not only the *Ashley*, but also the sector of the globe on which it rested. The minute she sat down, Sandy Sydney rushed to her with a mug of coffee.

"Here you are, Melissa. It's how you like it—nonfat milk, one sugar." She smiled sweetly as she offered the mug.

"Thank you, Sandy." Melissa's tone could have frozen the Pacific Ocean. Not only did she have her Bitch of Numenon voice on, she had her Bitch of the Universe act operating too. Sandy blanched, then flared. For a moment, razor blades floated in the air between the two women. Sandy turned away.

Melissa had no use for Sandy Sydney. First, she was a liberal arts major. That reminded Melissa of her fuzzy-brained, intellectual parents, the Doctors Weir. Melissa hated her parents and everything they stood for. Worse, Sandy was the epitome of the kind of woman Melissa hated in every other way. She'd put her considerable brains and talents in abeyance to travel through life on that sex kitten act. The baby girl voice. The sweetsie clothes. The subtle come-ons. Those breasts. Melissa sipped her coffee and fumed; Betty was so naive that she thought Sandy's figure was natural. Melissa wanted to tell her, "No one looks like that, Betty! She had it *done!*" She couldn't be that gorgeous by herself.

From what Melissa had heard, Sandy had the morals of an alley cat. She'd slept with most of the upper executives at Numenon. She had them at each other's throats, leaving their wives and giving her money. Melissa loathed her. Besides, anyone who wore pink as much as Sandy Sydney had to be mentally ill.

After Melissa's rebuff, Sandy turned away from the group, her face contorted. You bitch! she thought. You think you're so great with your MBA and your big staff. I'm as smart as you are. She'd seen Melissa's scornful glance at her breasts. They're all mine, Melissa. They've gotten me more than your stupid MBA. They got me through Wellesley. I had to *work* my way through school, bitch. I use what I've got, but you're the same as me. Will thinks you're his daughter, that's why you are where you are. Sandy composed her face and sat down, demure as always.

Doug Saunders smiled for the first time in weeks. If they were lucky, those two would square off this week. He'd never seen two women who hated each other more. A nice catfight would liven things up. He didn't know whom he'd bet on. Doug knew what Melissa could do if pushed; he felt his nose. He suspected that Sandy was far less of a wuss than she looked. He looked at Sandy and thought, Melissa has you pegged, Tits. You're bad news. He had suspicions about her that he needed to tell Will as soon as he could.

Will spoke and everyone jumped. "We might as well get to work. Betty, did you bring the briefs?"

Betty went to one of the cabin's floor-to-ceiling cabinets and opened the door. Five bound journals were stacked on an eye-level shelf. A massive computer, Numenon's latest, took up the rest of the cabinet; the *Ashley* carried five such machines. The motor home's secret was revealed. Every nook and cranny, every corner and drawer was jammed with electronic gear. The *Ashley* cost so much because of its armaments, not its doodads and design. Equipped with solar panels, the motor home was a war machine, a tool of corporate domination. Will Duane could run his empire indefinitely from the *Ashley*. She had more computer capability than most corporate headquarters. The satellite receiver in the roof let him do it anywhere on the planet.

"Well, let's get to work," Will said when everyone had his or her report. "This brief carries all the information on the site we're going to mine. It details the process of mining, and the uses of ..." He waited as they opened their briefs. "I've also outlined some possible negotiation strategies, our walk-away point. A few tidbits we can throw out that might interest them that cost us nothing. We'll do a mock negotiation after I discuss ..."

24

Bud Creeman was a worried man. He was always worried, but this morning's apprehension was beyond the ordinary. He felt like a small animal had crawled inside him and was gnawing away at his guts. The varmint was so frenzied that he had to keep his mouth clamped shut for fear it would start screaming if it saw daylight. To handle his distress, he did what Grandfather told them to do during the warriors-only summer trainings. Focus on what was happening around you so hard that the fear or pain or whatever it was disappeared.

He focused on Grandfather. It took all his concentration to keep him in the front of his mind. He began to breathe long and slow, the way Grandfather showed them. When he did that, the creature inside him seemed to settle down. In a minute, he was calm. He and Paul Running Bird stood about a hundred feet from the shaman, on the Pit's sloped area.

It was light now; he could see Grandfather sitting on a buffalo robe in the middle of the low stage. The stage looked pretty much the way it had the ten years Bud had been coming to the Meeting. A ramshackle thing made from leftover plywood and boards, it ran along the back of the Pit's flat area. They'd fixed it up some this year, on account of the guests and it being the last Meeting. Grandfather had finished chanting and sitting in silence; now he was talking to the early birds.

This year, he had everyone line up down the central aisle. He was sitting close to the edge of the stage, leaning forward to talk to each person as he or she got to the front. The Power was on him so strong that people in line looked stoned just from being around him. They laughed and chatted normally in the rear of the line, but became silent the closer they got. Up front, some cried or looked blissed out. Others fell at his feet when they got up to them. Paul said that more than seven hundred people were there, waiting for their moment with the holy man; the line went clear to the edge of the Pit, past the wooden benches where everyone would sit.

Bud didn't join the line. He and Bert had picked Grandfather up at his hogan yesterday and drove him to the Bowl. They had spent five hours with him, just the three of them in the truck. Bud was in charge of the horse part of the Meeting, as usual. When their People lost their land, most lost all contact with horses. Grandfather knew how important horses were to the People and how they bolstered the experience of Spirit. He made sure that anyone who wanted to ride could, and he came down to the stable area several times a day. Bud would have many chances to talk with Grandfather.

That Sunday morning, he watched the others meet the shaman. Grandfather never let anyone, even the most humble, get lost in the shuffle. He welcomed each person in turn, petting their heads when they needed it, holding their hands, listening to problems and news. Calling people by name as though they were old friends, even though he might have seen them only once or twice. He acted as though the person before him was the most important person in the world—which he or she was, right then.

People brought Grandfather all sorts of gifts: food, moccasins, belts, and knives. "Wonderful! Look at this beadwork! Wonderful!" he exclaimed. Everyone knew that he liked the old crafts best, beading, quillwork, and leatherwork. Some gifts he kept, and some he gave back to the giver, a great blessing. Some years, he would give everything away at the end of the Meeting. Those who gave him something knew they received much more than they gave.

Bud watched the old man's face. Love poured from his eyes, his lips, even his cheeks. Every inch of Grandfather's body was a blessing. Bud savored the tenderness he could feel his teacher lavish on each person he saw. Bud thought he was beautiful, though he'd never say that out loud.

Grandfather was a tiny man, not much more than five feet tall and thin. His size surprised Bud the first time he saw him, but now he was used to it. Looking down at the top of his teacher's head didn't feel so strange. Sitting as he was on the stage, new people couldn't tell how small Grandfather was. When someone did a double take over his height, which they definitely would when he stood, Grandfather would laugh and say, "I'm taller than Geronimo, and he held off the United States Army!" Geronimo was only five feet tall; Bud hadn't known that.

Like always, Grandfather wore a tunic belted at the waist, and beaded pouches for medicines and charms. His knife. Fur and bright ribbons bound his long white braids. Bud smiled when he saw his new shirt. Grandfather had found the package in Wes's truck. Every year, Wesley's mother, Rose Silverhorse, made Grandfather seven new shirts for the Meeting, one for every day. Wesley made silver buttons for them. They looked like the designer shirts worn by the rich people who owned the ranch where he worked, but Bud recognized the flowered pattern on Grandfather's shirt. It was one of Rose's old tablecloths. He'd eaten off it in the Silverhorse kitchen.

Grandfather also wore new moccasins. Fred Perce made them for him every year. They were the traditional design, up to the knee, beaded and tied. He looked like a rich Indian decked out by Hollywood, He had the concho belt that Wesley made, flowered shirt, braids, beaded moccasins, and a tall hat with feathers in the brim. He looked like a photo, exactly the way you'd expect an ancient shaman to look.

Bud never expected the joy that radiated from him, or the compassion—the energy. He could never believe how he felt when Grandfather was around. When he walked in, it was as though the lights went on in the heavens. He stood up straight and strode out—like a warrior. Grandfather was ancient, but he would outlast any of them.

That was as much paying attention to the world around him that Bud could muster. He squeezed his eyes shut, trying to forget. All he could do was remember. His Bert had winced all the way from Texas. Damn it! His old truck didn't have a single spring that wasn't broke; Bert felt every bump along the way. He wanted to buy a good truck for her; he wanted to buy her a Rolls-Royce. That's what she deserved. Grandfather had noticed her grimacing yesterday.

"How are you, my Bert? How long do you have left?" Two weeks, she'd told him. Bert would attend the last Meeting, ready to pop or not. Bud had no idea how big a woman could get at the end of pregnancy, or how big his Bert would get. He wanted to cry seeing her shuffling around, holding her belly. How would that baby get out?

She wasn't worried, nor was Grandfather. But that's how true sprit warriors were. As for Bud, he was a wreck from all of it, proof of his lowly status in the world of Spirit. He pulled his hat off and ran his hands through his hair. These days, it always seemed sweaty, not matter how cold it was. Not that it would be cold this week. They had the Meeting before Easter because the Bowl was one of the hottest places in the country. A couple weeks from now, all the newcomers would be fainting from the heat instead of complaining about it.

He wanted to be able to buy a better truck and get a nice house. He wanted enough money to buy his wife a present once in a while. After eleven years at the Rock'n Bar B Ranch, he had graduated from the crummiest little trailer house in the back of the staff quarters to a rusty double-wide in the middle. Bert deserved more than that. He could see her face as she looked in that store window in town. There was a maternity blouse she wanted so bad. He couldn't buy it—he needed the money for gas. Tears welled in his eyes.

Before he cried and really embarrassed himself, Bud forced himself to pay attention to what was going on around him again. The Pit was where everything happened at the Meeting. People said that the Mogollon Bowl got its power because a meteor hit it ages ago. That accounted for its shape. It was a shallow bowl several miles across. The Pit must have been where the meteor actually hit; it was a bowl within a bowl and perfect for what they did in it. The Pit's real name was the Amphitheater, but who could say that twenty times a day?

About as big across as a couple of football fields, the Pit sloped down gently to a flat area at the far side. Thousands of people could sit in it and see Grandfather, who sat on a low stage in the back of the flat area. They did powwow dancing and whatever demonstrations Grandfather cooked up in the flat area. The power of the Bowl was most intense in the Pit; it was where most people had big experiences and visions, though these could come anywhere.

Over the years, they'd built semicircular rows of benches from scrap lumber going up the slope like a stadium. Rickety frameworks for tarps and other shades covered some of the benches. It got hot, even before Easter, so people brought their own sunshades. These days, most brought those nylon ones with aluminum legs. Some more traditional people brought palm fronds and put them over a wooden framework. Grandfather had a pole shade covered with palm fronds up in front. The Pit would be a sea of moving humanity tomorrow, partially visible under a hodgepodge of beach umbrellas, nylon shades, tarps, and fronds. Right now, it was as calm as it would get, with just the people standing in line.

Bud was edgy and tired of waiting. His feet hurt. Paul Running Bird wanted Grandfather to check out his riding. Paul had told Bud how he'd taken lessons all year and wanted a better horse *this* time. Bud replied that Grandfather would have to decide that. No way Bud would put his nose into this one.

Looking around, Bud saw more than one person wiping away tears. Grandfather had the same effect on them. Grandfather looked straight at him; their eyes met. Something like a spark flew from Grandfather's eye into his. He felt like he'd been struck, like Grandfather's glance tore open his soul.

And that's when he saw the humanity in the pageant before him. It was a river of love. People cared for each other; people loved each other. People felt so much that tears welled up naturally, part of the depth they were touching in themselves. Tears were flowing down his face and he didn't notice. Tears, with questions attached.

How could people do what they did when *this* love was possible? How could some people be so good, and others be so cruel? How could what happened to Abbie occur? He couldn't hold it back anymore. What had happened before he left exploded in his mind.

Bud could see himself walking into the barn; Abbie stood in the crossties, her head down, sides heaving. Sweat ran off her like she'd been squirted with a hose. It puddled on the floor. She looked like she had had shaving cream sprayed around the edges of where the saddle pad and girth had been. More shaving cream dripped off her chest, landing in globs on the rubber mats in front of her. Her nostrils flared; he could see their red interior easily. She trembled with exhaustion as she panted.

Ace Parnham and one of the younger trainers were standing next to her. Ace looked up, looking guilty and surprised for an instant before his smirk bounced back like his face was rubber. Bud would have never known. He had had to take Bert into town for a doctor's appointment that day. He wasn't supposed to be at work that afternoon.

She was the best horse Bud ever trained, more cow in her than any horse he'd ridden. Abbie was a temperamental mare; horse shows were hard for her to handle. She needed to mature. He'd made a project of her; he loved the mare. Abbie didn't like to be pushed or shoved around; she needed to be respected. He found the key to her, and she worked for him like no other horse had.

She was a top prospect for the coming show season. Bud felt sure he finally had the horse that would get him known as a trainer of great show horses. That was the only way he was going to move up—get out of the trailer house and into a real house. Abbie wouldn't work for anyone like she would for him. Ace had seen him ride her; he knew. He asked his boss if he could show her. "We'll see. Maybe," Ace said. That was as positive as he'd ever been on the subject of Bud going into the show arena on the back of a horse. Bud had been excited.

They took Abbie out when he wasn't around and rode the crap out of her. Now, as he stood waiting in the Pit, all that he'd felt and couldn't express flooded back. He wanted to beat that lying, thieving, son of a bitch Ace Parnham's face into the ground. He could see him grabbing his boss and beating that white head in; he could see his blood flowing over the cement. The most famous trainer in the country! What kind of trainer did that to a horse? He heard Grandfather's voice inside him, *"Just watch, Bud. It's your mind. You don't have to act."* Bud watched. That wasn't all that happened that day.

Ace had turned to him and said, "She'll never make a show horse. We're selling her."

"Why?" Bud stammered. "You've seen me ride her."

"John took her out. She acted like a rodeo horse, practically killed him. He had to teach her some manners." John looked at Bud, his sneer barely hidden. Bud almost took the bait; his fists clenched.

Ace stood there, daring Bud to say something. Take a swing, anything. He was waiting for any excuse to fire him. Mr. Baynes, the financier who owned the ranch, was off in Dallas. He'd accept anything Ace said. *He* was the famous trainer; Bud was just his wife's pet Indian.

Bud turned away and took Abbie out of the crossties, attaching the lead line to her halter. "I'll walk her out." He cared for the mare, running his hands over her; laying them on the spur marks that covered her sides. *Rodeo horse*, he thought. Do that to any horse and they'll buck. He opened her mouth and saw the bruises on her tongue, the fruit of John's great hands. Bud was sick. Ace's hatred of him had ruined a beautiful animal.

And she was ruined. Some part of Abbie had closed up and died. Bud put his hands on the mare, did every healing trick Grandfather ever taught him. He talked to her, stroked her. Something came over him that he'd never felt before. As he ran his hands over Abbie, something enveloped him. He felt energy flow from him; it was as real as her distress had been. He healed the suspensory ligament that was torn in her right rear where it wrapped around the fetlock. She'd be sound again, but she would have been ruined without what he did. He knew that Wesley and Grandfather could heal like that, but never thought he could. Yet, with all his stroking her, the mare would not open her heart to him. She had shut down.

Tears rolled down Bud's face. He couldn't stop them; he made no effort to stop them. Abbie would be sold—either while he was gone at the Meeting or when he got back.

Bud couldn't go back to that place. He needed a new job, a better job, a real house, and more money. He needed so many things. What was he to do? All he knew was horses; he was lucky to have the job he had. He barely had made it out of high school. How could he take care of his wife the way he wanted to? What about the baby?

25

Mark Kenna was so shocked he could hardly drive. For the previous hour, he had listened to Will Duane give a presentation on the real reason they were going to the retreat. Oh, man! Mark thought. I can't believe it. I *can't* believe it. They were there to talk the Indians into giving them permission to mine their sacred lands. Mark had thought they were going to a spiritual retreat—all the drivers did.

If you knew Will Duane, it made sense. If Will had a religion, it was management training, and not only the classroom, communications skills type. Mark had driven the three MBAs in the *Ashley* and a whole bunch of their colleagues to every ridiculous scam you could imagine—all in the name of management training. Bonding as a team, group problem solving, management circles, whatever. They'd rappelled down mountains in Yosemite; camped out in Alaska; stood on telephone poles in the desert of Arizona; swung across a hotel atrium in Colorado. It seemed like Will Duane would try anything if it would make his favorites better managers. No matter what he did, none of them could reach his standard, so Will sent them off to more training.

Mark thought the Indian spirituality deal was real. Probably all the top Fortune 500 firms would be out at the rez next year. He had laughed about it to the other drivers. No one on the staff batted an eye at Will's latest escapade.

But this! After his presentation, Will led the staff in a session discussing negotiation strategies to achieve their goal as soon as possible. They hoped to be out by Wednesday. Mark noticed that "the staff" participating in the discussion consisted of Will, Doug Saunders, and Sandy Sydney, surprisingly. The others were silent. Not Will and company. They thought up great team strategies to convince the Indians to give their consent, offers of meaningless perks and bennies that cost Numenon nothing. Beads and mirrors—that's all they were.

Doug Saunders, that soulless bastard, led the pack. Mark thought he looked drunk when they started out, but he perked up at the scent of blood. He kept talking about his experiences on some reservation and what stupid, drunken slobs Indians were. And Sandy Sydney was much smarter than Mark suspected, almost vicious in her approach. Mark couldn't see their faces, but he could tell Doug and Will were impressed with her by the tones of their voices. Mark felt sick. These were the most skilled negotiators in the world. He had never heard anything as polished as the speech Will Duane practiced on the group. How could the Indians stand up to them?

He barely could keep his hands on the wheel. Oh, man. He couldn't believe it. All he wanted was a rockin' week—some fun with the Native brothers. Oh, man. As he drove, everything Mark Kenna had stuffed inside himself about his boss rose to the surface. He had his wild side and had done plenty of everything before he settled down with Brooke. He hadn't been critical of the Numenon executives he drove, even when it was to a company condo with women he knew were other people's wives or fancy whores. It was part of the Numenon image—high rolling, high performance in every respect. Numenon epitomized the work hard, party harder lifestyle of Silicon Valley. Will Duane had slowed in the last couple of years, but he would always be the Valley's reigning cocksman, based on the previous forty years.

Mark had blocked out so much about his boss. The shady stuff hinted at or picked up in fragments as he drove. The women. Will Duane had been with so many, Mark couldn't count them. He'd driven the billionaire to rendezvous from one end of the Peninsula to the other. Mark was disgusted.

Yeah, his boss was the best manager in the world; a genius in business and everywhere else; the richest man and self-made, if you didn't count the hundred million dollars his dad left him. What was that compared with the fifty billion he was worth now? Will Duane was the guy who built the most effective organization in the history of capitalism. Everything they said in the books and magazines about Will Duane was true, Mark knew that.

His mind abruptly admitted the rest. Will Duane was also what everyone who was too smart to write about it said—the Prince of Fucking Darkness. Will Duane would slash anyone who crossed him; he'd screw your grandmother so he could tell you about it. And Will Duane always won.

Oh, God! Oh, God! Mark ranted internally. Why am I here? The idea of what they were doing was bad enough, but the expressions of the voices in the strategy session made Mark sick. They're like sharks circling for the kill, he thought. He felt like pulling over and throwing up. Doug Saunders was talking about what drunken bums Indians were, again. What an asshole. Saunders was worse than Will.

He got sicker and sicker as he drove. After an hour and a half of driving on paved roads, they turned off onto a dirt road indicated on a hand-drawn map some Indian guy faxed to Betty. It meandered into the desert, getting vaguer as it went. Mark finally followed a path through the wilderness. It was still dark. Every once in a while a car or truck would pass, driving so fast it looked like a pogo stick bouncing over the rocky desert. He tried to wave some of these drivers down to ask for directions, but no one would stop. They glared at the custom motor homes, sometimes flipping them off. All looked like Native Americans. Mark's mood plummeted as he realized what they were heading into—these must be their fellow retreat attendees. These people hated them already. What if they knew why they were there? What if they needed help?

The caravan finally ran into a sheer cliff face, which the map indicated they would. Some guy named Paul Running Bird drew the map. His card was imprinted on the fax, along with his large signature on the directions. The directions clearly stated, "*Take the path through the cliffs that I've indicated. The other ways are dead ends or lead to hours of delay.*" Four paths that would get them to the campground on the other side were drawn. One went completely around the bluff to the southwest; another skirted the bluff the same way to the northeast. Another "road" went straight through the middle, and the path marked "*Take this one*" with a big arrow was between the southwest passage and the middle path.

The actual cliff was foreboding. A rock wall rose almost straight up, at least thirty feet high. Its surfaces were striated by erosion. In the early light of the dawn, the dark wall looked menacing.

They stopped at the central opening in the cliff, the one they came to first. Will got out, followed by the rest of them. He seemed to sniff the air like a hunting dog. The canyon opening was narrow and looked like it could swallow them—they might be unable to get out if they went in. It curved almost immediately. They couldn't see two hundred yards up the ravine. They turned and walked back to the *Ashley*.

A couple of miles southwest, they found the opening Paul Running Bird had indicated they should take. It was broad and wide; they could easily turn around in it if need be.

Inexplicably, Will Duane ordered Mark to stop. He got out and sniffed the air again. Getting back into the *Ashley*, Will shook his head. "This is wrong. It's the wrong way. We should go back to the first one."

Betty piped up, "Paul Running Bird said to be careful because we could get very lost. He said the cliffs are tricky. He seemed like such a nice, sincere man, Will. He's been organizing the retreat for eleven years. I think we should follow his map."

Everyone got out and looked around. They agreed that they should take the pass before them. The written map was very reassuring. Will allowed himself to be outvoted. They drove up the canyon.

Will turned to Betty. "Now's a good time for you to present that brief you put together."

Betty smiled stiffly. She took out a set of one-inch-thick binders, one for each person.

"Yes. 'Know thy enemy.' That's the negotiation buzz word, isn't it?"

26

Paul Running Bird fidgeted irritably next to Bud Creeman; he wanted to get out to the horses. Most of these people were nothing. Why did Grandfather spend so much time on them? Many crucial details pertaining to the week had to be settled: where to locate their important guests' camp, for one thing. Paul fretted; he'd done his best to make the Bowl presentable. If he couldn't get any cooperation from Grandfather, it wasn't from lack of trying. He settled his new Stetson on his head, knowing that *he* looked his best. When could they get out of here and over to the horses?

For the past year, Paul had taken riding lessons from a top Western trainer in Seattle near where he lived. The trainer was a reined stock horseman. He said he thought Paul could become a good reiner; he had the seat and hands for it. Paul was sick of doing all the work he did every year for the Meeting and getting stuck with the lousiest horse. Last year, Bud said he needed to improve his riding if he wanted a better mount. And Paul had. This year, he would get what he deserved.

He watched the shaman greet the hordes and felt himself tear up. Anyone could see how great Grandfather was. Why did he have to be so stubborn? Paul kept trying to get him to modernize just the tiniest bit. It was "No!" to everything. He tried to tell him how many more people he could reach using the Internet and by putting on seminars and more retreats. He could fill the Bowl three times a year. Do some satellite broadcasts all over the country. Shoot, all over the world. Maybe charge just the tiniest bit for what he did. The old man seemed to think that putting on spiritual events cost nothing. That wasn't true. The reason they were able to have the Meeting, as grubby as it was, was *his* ingenuity at getting things free—or getting someone to pay for them. He did a mental inventory of the Bowl.

Thank God he'd ordered all those portable toilets. They were a lot of trouble to get out here, but what were they to do—let Will Duane see them using barely screened privies like they always had? The only reason they had the privies was that he hit up Elizabeth Bright Eagle to pay for them. Otherwise, it would be au naturel, the Native way. He'd scrounged up twenty additional golf carts. They would come in handy with the crowds. They were the same as the other carts he'd gotten—derelicts. But the junk-yard he got them from didn't know about Willy Fish, the Meeting's secret weapon. Willy was dumb, but he was the best mechanic in all the Nations. And the Mogollon Bowl and its electromagnetic energy had a few effects on machines that the scientists of the world didn't know about. Golf carts didn't even need charging out here. Paul was delighted with his abilities to get things for the Meeting cheaply or at no cost. He felt no one appreciated what he did.

He carefully took off his new, pale gray Stetson. It was the latest style, the "buckaroo" type. The hat's wide brim was generously curved on the sides and the crown stood up about seven inches, with the back taller than the front. He'd put some tasteful feathers in the band, gray and beige owl feathers. He couldn't get eagle feathers. He thought they were overdone, anyway. As he ran a comb through his short gray hair, he wished he had a mirror. What if he had something on his teeth? He knew he was a good-looking man, but the slightest flaw could spoil a first impression. How many new people would come this year? He'd written to hundreds through his Web site. He brushed a bit of dust off his jeans. He'd had his wife care-fully starch and press his indigo jeans and tailored Western shirt.

Paul remembered Selma's round form and beseeching eyes, always trying so hard to please. Groveling. Thank God she wouldn't be coming this year. Mark had the chicken pox and she couldn't leave home. Last year was the only year he'd let Selma come to the Meeting. What happened? First, Grandfather fawned all over her, ignoring him; and then the whole camp *loved* his wife. Topping everything, she had a wild vision right off the bat. Paul was still waiting for a vision. Any vision. Fourteen years with Grandfather and nothing.

If the old man hadn't gotten so mad about Stephen Rising Wolf, Paul would have been tempted to go to Austin for Rising Wolf's seminar. His friend at Cherokee, Inc. said he could get him in at half price. He wanted a vision so badly; he'd do anything.

Paul brought Stephen Rising Wolf's brochure to Grandfather to suggest that he do seminars too. He didn't see what was so bad about that. The old man could make a fortune; he was the real thing. Paul could manage Grandfather's workshops and product sales. They would go high end, all the way. The best. When he got the idea, he felt as though Grandfather's Great One was speaking to him. This was the break Paul was looking for. A high-visibility job bringing in big bucks. A chance to leave soggy Seattle.

In a frenzy of inspiration, Paul drove out to see Grandfather with some sample brochures he made up and a seminar all planned out. *Learn Native Spirituality from a Great Shaman.* He showed him Stephen's material first to demonstrate what could be done. The old man got so mad when he saw the brochure that Paul kept the pamphlets he had made in his briefcase, shutting up in the nick of time. Grandfather gave him more credit for telling him about Stephen Rising Wolf than he ever had for anything. For the first time, he felt that Grandfather appreciated his worth and how much he cared about him.

The way Grandfather responded to finding out what Stephen was doing showed Paul true greatness. The old fox went out and snagged not just Billy Bob Burton, the second-richest man in the world, but *Will Duane*. He was twice as rich as Billy Bob. Screw Rising Wolf! Paul would stay with Grandfather.

The shit the old man was getting about inviting Will Duane—he couldn't believe what he was hearing around the camp. People thought he was sucking up to the white power structure; selling out to corporate America; betraying his principles for money—this from people who didn't own a pot to pee in. Like that paunchy idiot standing next to him. He stole a glance at

Bud Creeman. God, what a slob! How could his People ever advance when they looked like that?

Bud had his eyes glued on Grandfather. Don't drool, big fella, thought Paul. He was feeling catty this morning, and loved it. At least he could *think* what he really felt; he always had to keep up such a good front at the Meeting. Bud had gotten married last year; one of those instant weddings that happen around Grandfather. His wife was pregnant in months, of course. Now it was hard to see who was more preggers, Bud or Bert. Their names were a scream—and they looked like potatoes! Paul looked at Bud, eyeing him without being seen.

Bud was wearing a faded, worn Western shirt and a cheap felt hat the same style as Paul's, but old. Dried sweat discolored the area where the brim met the crown; it looked like a horse had stepped on it a few times. Paul was practically apoplectic when he saw Bud's boots. Not only were his boots worn and dirty, but duct tape? Oh, my God! Paul could barely keep from shouting out loud. Bud Creeman had duct tape wrapped around the toe of one boot. He couldn't even get his boot fixed properly. The richest man in the world was going to see this fat slob with duct tape on his boot? This was as bad as open privies. What would Will Duane think of them?

Thank God this lunkhead wasn't going to decide which horse he got to ride, Paul thought. Grandfather would give him a mount that reflected his new capabilities. All he had to do was wait while the old man did his thing with the nobodies.

27

Betty Fogarty watched Will's presentation about mining and the subsequent negotiating session with disgust. The kind eye she'd always turned on Will's escapades had evaporated. Part of her antipathy stemmed from the telephone calls she'd made from Will's bedroom. Her phone worked fine, but she got no answer at home or at John's office. Her anxiety surged. Where was John? What if he really had left her? What if he had someone else?

When Will started foaming at the mouth over taking something precious from the poorest people in the United States, Betty was jolted. Hearing him rave seemed to open a door inside her. She knew his weaknesses, but now they flooded her awareness without the buffers of friendship and loyalty. Will was a maniac. He'd get totally crazy, absolutely over the top, then he'd get it back together. He'd done it a dozen times in the years she'd worked for him. She thought of the recent past. Will had been falling apart for the last two months—which meant that others in Numenon had noticed his declining performance.

She knew exactly why; she knew everything about Will Duane. She knew more than his poor wife, Kathryn, ever did. Will and Kathryn had divorced twenty-two years before. Betty had been there since, taking over the public aspects of Kathryn's role. Her job description made her Will's secretary, household manager, and nanny. Betty hired the staff for Will's estate, scheduled his personal appointments, and even balanced his checkbook. Will trusted her more than anyone on earth. I'm his wife with everything but sex and community property, she thought.

Because of her access to his checkbook, Betty knew when her boss's "sport fucking" turned to traffic with the pros. Sport fucking, she thought. It sounds so athletic and almost wholesome. Like duck hunting. She could see a man saying, "Darling, you don't mind if I go sport fucking with the boys this weekend, do you? It's the season." Before "sport fucking" became the accepted nomenclature, Betty thought Will and his friends were simply "screwing around." Betty didn't know how prevalent the practice was in Silicon Valley. She thought the "work hard, play harder" credo applied almost everywhere in the valley. The male-dominated Numenon had to be the champion in acting it out.

The men of Numenon simply followed Will's lead. In years past, the few nights they weren't working until all hours, Will and his cronies would pick up cute young or not-so-young things in all the best places, take them home, bed them, and dump them. Politely, of course. Will and his fellow predators were too classy to be vulgar. Beautiful women would line up for the privilege of being discarded, again and again. Who said money and power weren't the best aphrodisiacs?

Now that he used the pros, she knew what he spent on their services each month. She had cash delivered to a blue-blooded madam up the Peninsula in Hillsborough. By the amounts, Betty was sure the girls were the best in the business. She thanked God that Will had finally formally made sex the business transaction it always had been to him. She had been fielding calls from poor little widows and divorcees—and more married women than she liked to admit—for twenty-six years. Every silly one thought she had a chance at marrying the wealthiest man in the United States.

That's why she got the name of that madam and gave it to Will. She couldn't stand all those pathetic women calling. Stupid fools. If they had known his wife, they would know that being married to Will Duane was the booby prize. Poor Kathryn. Betty met her in 1971 when she became Will's private secretary. Kathryn Duane was a broken-down alcoholic then, and when the Duanes divorced three years later, she looked like a zombie, one foot in the grave, obviously on booze and God knows what else. She was supposed to be in an institution in Europe to this day. Betty knew why— she'd fielded all those calls from women since day one. And that poor daughter of his—exactly like her mother.

Betty sat holding her brief, surveying her employer with contempt. She knew what happened. She knew when he'd hooked up with Marina Selene; that's when the big checks started flowing out. Over two and a half million dollars to Marina in the two years they were together, and another million for her San Francisco restaurant. She knew exactly when Marina dumped him. Two months ago, the outflow stopped.

Betty Fogarty was way smarter than most, and she did her homework. She found out that Marina Selene was not the world's most expensive prostitute as was commonly believed. She was some sort of healer; everyone who knew the woman said she was wonderful. She was a San Francisco institution; naughty, but with a heart of gold. Betty was glad she got a chunk out of Will. I wish she'd taken him for more, she thought.

Betty worried about one thing. I hope she didn't dump him because he hurt her, she thought. Betty glared at her boss across the cabin, glad he couldn't hear her thoughts. You don't know that I know about Dawn, do you, Will? The little working gal you beat up three years ago. Like your lovin' rough, Willy? Not much happened in Will Duane's universe that Betty didn't know about, but she never knew how Will fixed that felony. It went away without a trace. Being the richest man in the world had some perks.

She felt great satisfaction as she watched Will's misery. Now you know how it feels to have someone hurt you. You son of a bitch! Betty was shocked at the strength of her feelings. The closer they got to the retreat site, the more emotional she became. She decided to give the information in her brief a slightly different spin. Same facts, different emphasis. When he asked her to speak, Betty spoke clearly and with no hesitation.

"Yes, 'know thy enemy' is the first rule of negotiation. By the time we've gone through these briefs," she held up an inch-thick document, "we will know our enemy as well as anyone can. Let's do our homework, people."

28

Bud Creeman felt Paul Running Bird's agitation as they waited for Grandfather. Something about the guy gave him the creeps. At this point in the Meeting, Bud's psychic abilities were not fully manifest. He could tune into Grandfather and feel if the old man needed him or wanted him; he could feel his wife's state of mind; he could sense the presence of the other warriors very clearly. By the end of the week, he would be able to read Grandfather and Bert's minds almost perfectly. He would have almost as close a connection with the other warriors, especially Wesley, prick though he was. Later in the week, Bud would be able to read the thoughts of almost everyone at the Meeting. He'd get glimpses of future events. That's if he took up where he left off the year before; he could have much stronger powers this year. Bud had been a spirit warrior from his first Meeting with Grandfather. He didn't realize that he was among the most developed of the warriors, a contender to be Grandfather's successor.

As it was, Bud didn't like standing next to Paul. Running Bird was one of those guys who worked and worked and tried to do everything right. By some interior flaw, Paul managed to undo the good he'd done with the nastiness that leaked out the cracks. Paul killed himself organizing the Meeting. It wouldn't happen without him, everyone agreed. But he'd always screw up, so all the people who mattered—Grandfather and the warriors—were ticked off at him. Despite his years of hard work, Paul hadn't been asked to be a spirit warrior.

The man was repulsive. The only people at the Meeting who liked him were the guys who hated everything. They kept coming to the Meeting for some reason—probably to complain to Paul. The back-of-the-Bowl crowd liked Paul—those were the no-goods who hung out in the rear of the Pit. 'Fonzo Ramos and his gang. That bunch barely kept from getting kicked out every year. Paul went around the camp, a lightning rod for gossip, complaint, and dissent. Bud wished Grandfather would throw Paul out before he did something really damaging. He'd asked him about it.

Grandfather said, "The fact that Paul does so much work shows that Spirit moves in him. It is working on his faults. Until he breaks the Rules, Paul can come to the Meeting."

Bud stole another glance at his companion. Paul was a handsome man, fifty-something, tall, and distinguished. Bud was never sure that Paul was quite as high an executive as he made himself out to be. He sure looked the part, though. His gray hair was cut short and looked real sharp. Everything he wore was new and the latest thing. He could be one of the guests of the ranch where Bud worked. All were perfectly dressed and none of them knew a thing about horses or ranching. Bud knew that Paul wanted a flashy horse so he could impress Will Duane. He also knew that if Paul didn't ride better than last year, such a horse would hurt him. Best leave the matter to Grandfather.

Bud was as edgy as a young colt at its first show; he'd been that way for weeks. That was part of the Meeting—everything you were worried about seemed to shake loose in the months and weeks before you got there. It would get worse until it exploded, usually about four days after you got to the Bowl. This was his tenth Meeting, but Bud still wasn't ready for the storm that attacked him this time.

"Purification," Grandfather always said. "The Great One is cleaning house. Cleaning you up so that It can come to you."

Bud knew he was a totally different man than he had been before meeting Grandfather. He had a steady job; he had a wife he loved. They had a roof over their heads, food to eat, at least some medical insurance. He was grateful, especially considering where he started.

Eleven years ago, he thought his dreams had come true. Ace Parnham watched him work horses in the round pen out at the rez. Nobody knew why a famous horse trainer, one who got his nickname by acing every major competition in the country, would come to the rez looking for talent, but Bud found out. After watching dozens of people work horses, the lanky, white-haired Ace saw Bud work a horse using the natural techniques that anyone who had any feel for horses would use. Nobody had any patent on it, but kindness to animals seemed to be a big new thing. Ace hired him immediately.

Once he got to the Rock'n Bar B Ranch, he discovered that he didn't work for Ace. They both worked for David William Baynes, a Dallas-based financier who was Big Money even in Texas terms. Ace managed David's five-thousand-acre boutique ranch. He trained Mr. Baynes' horses, making sure they won every time they set foot in a show arena. He also made sure that the Baynes family and their guests had a good time when they visited the ranch.

Bud Creeman was dropped into a life he didn't know existed: Dallas socialites, beautiful women, billionaires, international businessmen, bankers, computer entrepreneurs, oilmen, and horses purchased for hundreds of thousands of dollars. The Bayneses had parties that cost more than his tribe's annual income. He felt like an ant at the queen's picnic—he'd be squashed if anyone noticed him.

When he met Mrs. Baynes, Bud found out why he had been hired. "I feel so bad about what happened to your People," she gushed, batting her false eyelashes. "We'll take care of you! You'll have all the horses you can ride." The woman twittered on, blond hair poofed out, designer conchos sparkling. She was a river three miles across and one inch deep. Saving the Indians was Mrs. Baynes' latest project; he was the Ranch's pet Indian. No. Mrs. Baynes' pet Indian. The rest had no use for him.

Lonely and in over his head, Bud found a remedy that had been used by others in situations like his: booze. He timed his drinking so that he was sober when the Bayneses arrived on the weekends, then he'd hit it the moment they left. As time passed, the boundaries of drinking and non-drinking days slipped. The virtuoso round pen work that got him his job went by the wayside. Ace and the others looked at him with disgust as he stumbled around. Mrs. Baynes' love for *Dances with Wolves* was all that kept him employed at the end of that first year. Bud owed Kevin Costner a lot.

He was down to cleaning stalls when Ace gave him the news.

"Mr. Baynes is sick of your being drunk. He'll pay for one of those rehab programs—or give you two weeks' pay." He smiled, obviously hoping Bud would take the money.

That was why he went to the Meeting. One of his friends had told him about Grandfather and what he could do. "He can heal anything, Bud. The most low-down drunk, addicts—he can heal anyone. Even fix broken bones. I've seen him." Bud wouldn't have gone, except he had no choice. He knew alcohol was killing him, job or no job.

He told Ace he was going to a Native American rehab program. The week before the Meeting, Bud drank so much he couldn't work. His friend arrived from the reservation to pick him up and had to pour Bud into his car. He puked all the way to the Mogollon Bowl, but he was sober by the time he got to the Meeting.

That was the last drinking Bud ever did. He had no idea what Grandfather was or what the Meeting could do. Ten years later, Bud Creeman was the one who trained the horses at the Rock'n Bar B, not Ace or the others. He never missed a day of work. He never drank. In acknowledgment of his success, he got what he had—but not what he deserved.

Once Bud stopped drinking, Ace gave him a job the old trainer didn't like—"baby-sitting" the Bayneses. That meant giving riding lessons to the Baynes family and their multitude of guests and providing Western entertainment and barbecues. Bud did as he was told, and found that he liked it. More than that, he liked the Bayneses and their friends.

When Bud started working with them, they had seemed absurdly rich. Their clothes and cars and talk of country clubs and European vacations scared him stiff. After a while, he found his employers and their friends were just people trying to cope with what life threw them as best they could, like everybody else.

Being around horses punctured the illusion that some people are better than others. Horses don't care how much money you've got—they'll buck or shy or run off for a rich man same as a poor one. Bud's skill with horses and people won his employers' hearts and trust. He taught the socialites to ride and let them discover what horses truly were. Bud found that the lessons of the round pen applied to his students as well as the horses he trained. He went slowly when he gave a lesson and concentrated on everyone having fun. The Bayneses did—and they learned to ride. Bud laced the riding lessons with things Grandfather taught him; he started telling stories of his People and the West. The Bayneses loved that.

Ace didn't know about any of this since he was on the show circuit most weekends.

The bad trouble started when Bud arranged a campfire for the Bayneses and some guests by the ranch's fishing lake. He led the group in singing songs and talked about the old days. They had a wonderful time. Divisions between them fell as they became a group of human beings, Westerners, appreciating the history and land they shared. Bud taught them how to do war yells. Pretty soon, they were yelling to beat the band. Mrs. Baynes laughed so hard Bud thought she'd fall over. He'd never seen her let loose like that.

Ace came home right then. Anyone could see the campfire blazing out by the lake. Ace ordered the others to put the horses away while he checked out the "unauthorized fire." He was burning before he saw Bud Creeman. Ace's ancestors had been Texas Rangers. When he talked around the campfire with the Bayneses, it was about bloody Indian treachery when the West was won. Ace saw a no-good Indian moving in on his boss. He burst into the campfire circle.

David Baynes clapped him on the back and said, "I had no idea what a gem you had here!"

Mrs. Baynes piped up with, "You must have wonderful times when we're in Dallas. Sitting around the fire telling stories. You have so much in common!"

Ace's war with Bud began that night. He was fighting to hold his position at the ranch over an upstart, two-bit Indian. That his fear was crazy never dawned on him. Ace got Bud off the ranch when the Bayneses were coming—telling them Bud had started drinking again and he had to watch him like a baby. The Bayneses stopped asking Bud for lessons, believing the lies.

Bud suffered under Ace, but didn't do anything about it. Why didn't he go to Mrs. Baynes and tell her the truth? As he stood watching Grandfather that Sunday morning, he knew why he didn't go to the Bayneses and protest. He figured he didn't deserve any better.

Over the years, Ace got worse. He tried to goad Bud into taking a swing at him or doing something so he could be fired. But Bud held his temper. What Grandfather taught him and his own good sense kept him in control. Until he saw what they did to his mare. For the rest of his life, he'd see her shaking in the barn, covered with sweat and lather.

Bud stood by the stage, sick with grief and fear. He worried about everything. He was worried about Grandfather—he never looked *old* before. He worried about those white people coming. He felt like they were the Bayneses somehow. Would they be able to take it if they felt what he had a moment ago—the full strength of his murderous hatred for his boss?

What would they do when the thunder started booming all around camp? When the blue lights twinkled everywhere? When they looked down on the Bowl from far above and saw their own bodies? When they had visions and dreams and heard voices? What would they do if they came face to face with Creator? Bud was as worried for them as he was for himself. He looked blankly at the ground in front of him.

Moments later, Grandfather had finished with the crowd and approached Bud and Paul. Teasing, he bent over and looked up into Bud's face, smiling. He became serious as he realized how troubled Bud was. Putting a hand on Bud's shoulder, he said, "The Meeting is the Meeting, my son. No one has died yet. This Meeting is the play of the Great One. Trust the One to know what we need. See what the week brings, my son."

Grandfather turned to Paul Running Bird. "Let us see what a great horseman you have become, Paul!"

29

The most important thing to know in any negotiation is your opponent. That's what I've concentrated on in my brief. What is this Meeting we're going to? What is the Mogollon Bowl? Who is 'Grandfather'? Who are the people close to him—his movers and shakers? What are their strengths and weaknesses? Will asked me to put together some information on these topics. It's in this report. In the back you'll find an executive summary. It's a cheat sheet in case you forget names or whatever."

Betty spoke with easy authority and obvious intelligence. Had her father had a different view of a woman's place in business, Betty Fogarty could have ended up with an MBA and been the old guard's Melissa Weir. Even though she was "just a secretary," Betty Fogarty was the most powerful woman in Numenon. She controlled access to the richest man in the world. Betty used her position with the canniness of a five-star general. She held up her brief, its title, *Grandfather & Company*, showing through a clear plastic cover.

"It's less organized than what I normally prepare." She shot a look at Will. "But we only had three days to get ready. Some of this information came in late last night. I had to have publications pull the front end and rebind it to include the first part." Everyone could feel the barb she threw at Will. What he expected of them was impossible. More than that—it was abusive. They got it done anyway.

Because of the short lead time, they hadn't prepared the way they normally would. They hadn't read the brief the night before; it didn't exist when they left work. Betty knew the MBAs felt like football players about to go on the field without helmets or gear.

"Some information came in so late that I wasn't able to include it in your briefs. I *will* cover it. When you get to the Meeting, you'll have all the data you need to succeed."

Betty was performing an obligatory ritual. No one in Numenon went into a negotiation without *all* the pertinent facts, bios of the important actors, and knowledge of the issues at hand. Frequently, preparation included watching videos of their opponents, acting out negotiations, or even making a clandestine site visit. They always tried to set up the meeting site so the "sun was in the eyes" of their opponents—making sure they had every advantage. As Will said, "Life is a negotiation. Those who win, win. Those who don't, don't matter."

"This came in last night." Betty opened the cover and turned to a section right behind the table of contents. Titled "The Mogollon Bowl," the section consisted of a smudged report that looked like a photocopy of an antique scientific paper. A paper *typed* with a fuzzy ribbon. "The MOGO Anomaly" was barely legible on the title page, with a list of names under it, all followed by PhD.

"This is all I could find about our destination." She waved the short paper. "I got this after exhausting all other resources. This Bowl is a mystery. Deep in the heart of the reservation, it appears as a blur on satellite maps. No government reports are available on it. It might as well be in the darkest jungle."

"Nobody uses *typewriters* anymore," Gil commented, leafing through his binder.

"This paper was written in the late 1950s, the final report of a series— the rest of which are lost. We're going to the..." She pointed to the report's first page. "Mogollon Bowl" was one of the few legible phrases. "God knows how you pronounce it."

"It's pronounced Mow-go-yone in Spanish," Gil volunteered.

"You can find it on a map of the reservation, but that's all. No history, no detailed information anywhere. The Mogollon—*Mow-go-yone*—were an ancient Indian tribe, now extinct. There's a resurrected ghost town of the same name hundreds of miles away from where we'll be. A Mogollon Rim, in Arizona. There's even a rock band called Mogollon. But nothing about a Bowl.

"We do know that, like much land around Indian reservations, it's had a spotty ownership history. First it was included in the reservation, then not, and now, it's part of the reservation again. This report convinced the government to cede it to the Indians permanently. The scientists got around the pronunciation problem by calling the place 'MOGO.'" The group looked through the paper.

"I can't read it," Gil said for all of them. It was smudged. Only the equations and statistical tables were legible, plus a word or two of the text. The conclusion was clearly legible. "The authors submit that although 'the MOGO Anomaly' was experienced within hours of our arrival, exhaustive study has demonstrated it to be of no practical or scientific use and of no economic value. We recommend receding the area to the local Native..." The copy became illegible again.

"Give it back to the Indians, since it's useless," Gil snorted.

"Exactly, Gil. I got this from the USGS—the United States Geological Survey—down the street from us in Menlo Park." She smiled. Silicon Valley could supply everything anyone could need. "I thought, if I need a special map, they're the people to call. This was the only thing I could find. The young fellow I talked to said its original was written in the Bowl and had been sitting in their files all this time. It didn't fax very well. He tried to photocopy it, but it came out the same way." She looked at the smudged pages. It looked as though it had been edited so the bare minimum of facts were legible. The way the sheet had been smudged effectively edited it—but how could that happen?

"Is this 'MOGO Anomaly' dangerous, Betty?" Will asked. He had also conducted an investigation, but Betty had done better than he had in finding out about their destination.

"No, Will. The young man at USGS said it's like the Mystery Spot in Santa Cruz—you know, where trees grow in spirals and funny things happen with gravity? Weird, but not dangerous." Betty kept her eyes on

Will, knowing he could be as apprehensive as he could be hyper. "I also checked it with our liaison, Paul Running Bird."

"And he said 'MOGO' is safe?"

"He said that some people get emotionally upset in the Bowl, but it's never affected him in any way. Sometimes watches and things work funny, that's all. There's a legend that a meteor landed there, but that scientists have studied the area to death and haven't found it. Yes, Paul said it's perfectly safe."

Will nodded. "We'll see."

"Yes, we will…" Betty paused, holding up her report, opened to a smudged sheet. "Doesn't this strike anyone as weird? The cover letter that came with this fax was perfect, yet this document wouldn't fax or copy. The fellow who sent it to me said the original was perfectly legible. I'm making a point of this, because how weird it is didn't dawn on me until I got out of Will's car this morning at the airport.

"The thing that got to me was this—look at the date on the report. You can read it easily. The fellow at USGS told me the project's start date was exactly three weeks before the date of this report. Eight PhDs signed it. Have you ever seen eight academics agree on anything in three weeks?" She looked around at the group—they looked a little edgy. "Have you ever seen eight academics write a report this short about anything?" The group leafed through the document, alarmed. "And why would an almost fifty-year-old report typed in 'MOGO' come across like this in a fax?" Blank looks. "It doesn't make sense." The group studied the report in silence.

"Electromagnetic energy could explain it. The pages could have been permeated with a magnetic field in the Bowl that's stayed with them all this time." Mark Kenna's voice from the driver's seat surprised everyone. Heads swiveled to the front of the *Ashley*. No one had considered Mark as anything more than a pleasant smile that could drive.

"Really?" Betty said.

"Yeah. In Eastern thought, the earth's energy is called prana, or life force. This is tied up with the sun's energy, providing power for the whole planet. We're bathed in it. That's one kind of energy. Another theory is that there are lines, called ley—l-e-y—lines all over the earth. They're roughly straight and form the structure of the earth's *soul*—I guess you could call it. The spirit of the planet. I did some research on the earth's energy currents when I was in graduate school. And I took eco-psychology," he yelled, twisting his head to be heard. The *Ashley* veered as Mark turned his head to talk.

"Can I turn the speaker on, Mr. Duane?"

"Certainly, Mark."

With the intercom turned on, he could drive straight. Mark's entrance into the conversation enlivened the group. "I have a master's degree in transpersonal psychology," he explained. "I got it at UC Santa Cruz. I know about this stuff."

The three young MBAs stared at the back of his head without moving. Mark's MA obviously surprised them. It changed him from a nonentity to a real person in their eyes.

Betty watched it happen. She didn't want to absorb that mentality, but it was inevitable at Numenon. A smile played on Betty's lips as she noted Gil, Melissa, and Doug's stunned expressions. The labor market in the Bay Area in the late 1990s was so tight that anyone with a degree in a nonquantitative field was likely to find himself driving a motor home or waiting tables. Their MBAs saved them from that fate.

Their expressions hardened, and Betty knew why. Mark's degree was from UC Santa Cruz, known as a hippie magnet. The school's mascot was the *banana slug.* How could anyone take a degree from a place like that seriously? Could Mark know anything that would help them?

"You should know a little more about Mark," Will said. "He was first in his class." Betty and the others paid close attention to his words. "The faculty considered him a brilliant scholar and researcher. He gave the valedictory speech. And Santa Cruz is a very good school. If he'd gotten an MBA, he'd be sitting with you, instead of where he is." Will gave a little shrug, confirming that he knew everything about everyone, and that Mark was one of them, sort of.

Betty noticed Mark's ears flushing. Did he keep his education a secret because he didn't want to be like the MBAs, who flashed their credentials at every possible opportunity? Or had Will surprised him with how much he knew about his life? She didn't care; she wanted him to explain the mystery.

"Well, yeah, I did pretty well in school. Anyway, some people believe that the earth has ley lines, and power spots too. The ley lines are supposed to look like hourglasses in cross-section—high-frequency energy flies from them, both up and down, into the earth. If a sensitive person gets near them, he or she will think very clearly, and maybe become psychic. People can have all sorts of manifestations: spiritual experiences, revelations, and ecstasies. They'll remember old stuff like it was happening then. Almost anything can happen on a ley line, and has, according to some."

"Where did you hear about this, Mark?" Will asked.

"Uh … Shirley MacLaine." Everyone burst into laughter. Mark blushed as he grinned. "Yeah, the scientific community thinks it's absolute hokum, like the time machine under the pyramids." Everyone laughed again. "Some people believe stuff like this, you know, the guys with white robes that will believe anything. The 'woo-woo' people. Some places are supposed to be 'power spots' or 'energy vortexes.' They include Machu Picchu in Peru and Santa Fe, New Mexico. Though some people believe anything about New Mexico …" Mark spoke as though he was imparting secret wisdom. "Aliens and little green men land there all the time. I mean, all the fruits and nuts aren't in California …"

They doubled over laughing. Mark was like a bolt of light thrown into the cabin, brightening everyone's mood.

"So it's nonsense." Will looked relieved.

"No, not at all. The scientific community just doesn't accept the theories. When I was in school, I saw special photos of the earth showing energy radiating along those lines. You probably have, too. They've had programs on TV about it and I've even seen articles in newspapers. The scientific community doesn't know what to make of them. 'Just electromagnetic fields.' Well, they're more than that.

"I feel their effects, and I'm not a 'woo-woo' person. I've taken statistics. I've taken lots of math and science. That's why I'm not trying to convert people into believing in ley lines. My logical mind can't accept them. But I feel them, along with many people. That's 'eco-psychology'—how the earth and the human psyche interact. I took a course in it at UC Santa Cruz. It's taught all over the world."

"In credentialed universities?" Will barked.

"Extremely credentialed. But I wouldn't get up in a scientific meeting and say what I've told you. I'd get hooted off the stage. I'm talking about it here because we need to know. We'll need to know what's going on if the Mogollon Bowl is what I suspect."

"What do you suspect?"

"I think it's the strongest power spot on the planet. I can feel it."

Betty tossed in the rest of her questions. "Mark, how do you explain the fact that the Bowl isn't shown on satellite maps? Why did the scientists cut off their research so quickly? Why are the reports about it lost?"

Mark was silent for a moment. "What if the Bowl is the biggest energy vortex on the planet? What if it's the most powerful? Some people say that the earth is conscious. They say that not just people are conscious—awake and responsive to stimuli—but that other living things are, too. Animals and plants, of course. But inanimate objects too. Rocks, dust. The whole planet. Lots of people believe this, even if our scientists don't: Hindus, Buddhists, Native Americans, and aborigines all over the planet. Many spiritual traditions have at least sects that feel the whole planet is sentient.

"You read about the Indians' relationship with the earth, the *Dances with Wolves* thing. It's not just PR hype. Supposedly, indigenous people all over the world have responses to the earth that are much more powerful than ours. Pollution that we find offensive is painful to them. You read about Australian aborigines in dreamtime, their spiritual trance state, being able to ride on waves of the earth's currents and know what's going on hundreds or thousands of miles away.

"Anyway, if the Mogollon Bowl is a power spot, say the most powerful spot on the planet, maybe the reason no one knows about it is that it doesn't *want* to be known."

"How could a piece of land want something?"

"It's not the traditional Western view of the cosmos: It's our planet and we'll do what we want to it. So we can bulldoze it and blow it up and do whatever. This is a different worldview. Don't think of the Mogollon Bowl as dirt. Think of it as a huge organism with a mind and will of its own. Mind you, I'm not saying that's what the Bowl is, but if what I've been discussing is true, it could be.

"The fact that that report came out like that and that no photographs or satellite pictures of it exist demonstrates something. If it doesn't prove that it's the most powerful energy vortex on the planet, it certainly supports the idea. In Hinduism, the ability to conceal is one of the five divine powers. If the Bowl can conceal itself from electronic spying, maybe it can do things we can't imagine. If its energy is strong enough to render a paper typed there fifty years ago illegible—except where it wanted it read—that's something.

"Why was the study over so fast? Maybe the Bowl didn't like those scientists poking around. Maybe something happened to force them out. Do you know what happened to them? Were you able to contact any of them?"

"No. I didn't have time," Betty said. "Plus, it's been a long time. The report was written in 1959. It's 1997 now, so it's been almost forty years. Who knows if the authors are still alive."

"Do you know anything more about the Mogollon Bowl? You said a meteor fell there. What kind of meteor? What was it made of? When did it fall?"

"That's what's so frustrating! Everywhere I went, it was like information was blocked. And not by people. That kid looked all over for those other reports. That's why he was so late getting back to me. He called Washington. They were looking back there, but all the reports had vanished. No one knew why."

"That's what I'm talking about. Scientists would call this a meaningless coincidence. But—scientists don't know how I felt at Machu Picchu."

"You've been there?"

"Yeah, Brooke and I went when we first got together. Unbelievable place. Man, the way I felt." The ecstasy that grabbed him halfway up the mountain and stayed as long as he was in the ancient Inca city returned as he spoke. Everyone in the cabin could recognize it. "Scientists never felt what I did in Machu Picchu. I'd be stupid if I didn't believe after that. Not believe—*know.*"

Will's anxiety mounted as he listened. With his top-secret security clearance, his investigation was conducted at higher levels than Betty's. But she had done better than he had in finding out about their destination. Deep inside, something stirred. Be careful, Will, something warned him. He knew that the voices and intuitions he felt were real. As real as the stalker. Something evil was watching them; he could feel its presence. What was this Bowl?

"What else do you know about electromagnetic energy, Mark?" Will's voice was hard.

"Well, that's all we are. We're nothing but energy. This body," he patted his shoulder, "has so much space in it—the space between molecules and parts of atoms—that we're really just electric charges and space. I did research on this; scientists do agree on this one. That's why we react to power spots. People who are sensitive to their own energy flows can feel the differences when the earth's fields change."

"Can that energy be used for anything?" Will was probing, not wanting to reveal what he knew.

"Yeah. Picking up pencils, driving a car ... everything we do, we do because electronic impulses from our brains have given our bodies orders to do them. Our thoughts are electronic impulses. All the great art, scientific discoveries, and masterpieces of literature are the result of electrons rattling around in a sensitive brain, then being turned into brushstrokes or welding, or words."

"Could a person move something or touch someone at a distance? Read minds and heal in ways that doctors can't? Is that possible?"

"Sure. What I majored in, transpersonal psychology, is about the aspects of the mind that are above and beyond the personal psyche. Transpersonal psychology covers all the traumas and complexes that traditional psychology does, but also reaches the highest flowerings of the mind and soul.

"Anyway, we studied all the 'weird' stuff. Paranormal psychology, psychic abilities. People who can bend spoons with their minds, and move stuff. I never thought any of that was very useful, but I've seen it done. And it's been documented in universities all over. But there's way more that can be done with personal energy than bend spoons. Healing, for one thing.

"But to really explain that, you need a martial artist and a specialist in religious experiences *and* psychic energy. I know some stuff about this, but for understanding the esoteric stuff like kundalini and chi gong, I'd talk to Jeff Block."

"Who's that?" Will looked at Betty, signaling her to get contact information on him. They'd get him on the phone or fly him out.

"He's driving the motor home behind us. Jeff's in my band. He's got a MA in religious studies. He almost got a PhD," Mark said loudly for the benefit of the MBAs, "but he was too involved with his spiritual practices to finish his dissertation. They gave him the MA instead. If you want to talk about energy, Jeff's your man."

"Get him up here. Right now." The cabin fell silent.

"Who will drive his motor home, Will?" Betty asked.

He thought a moment. "We'll stop. Give the drivers time to stretch while we talk. Let's do it."

30

"Grandfather, try one of the new golf carts." Paul Running Bird hustled the shaman into the cart without indicating that he knew Bud was there. "I'll drive you down to pick out a horse for me." Paul took off. Bud had to jump onto the moving vehicle and scramble to stay on.

"I got these carts for nothing," Paul explained. "The junkyard guy said they weren't worth hauling away for scrap. He didn't know what the Bowl would do for them!" Paul laughed heartily. They headed southwest from the Pit to the trail leading to the horse area.

Bud turned around and looked at the familiar geography. This was where his real life began, where he'd learned what a man could be. Where he'd seen and felt things that he didn't know were possible. Where he and Bert met and loved. Things he couldn't understand anywhere else were simple in the Bowl. His eyes stung as the tears grew behind them. This was the last Meeting. No more of Grandfather's teachings, or the other part of it, the craziness that erupted here—the fistfights that came out of nowhere that Grandfather made manageable somehow. No more Grandfather raising them to the heights with a gesture or a word. Bud ached as he realized what he was losing with the Meeting—the Mogollon Bowl.

They still would have the warriors' trainings here, wouldn't they? When they drove in the day before, Grandfather told Bert and him that he was retiring. "I'm going to sit in the shade and do nothing. I'm going to talk with the other old men. I'm retiring."

That didn't mean really *retiring*, did it? He would still teach the warriors—certainly. Bud hadn't been able to bring the subject up on the drive in, but he wouldn't just cut them loose, would he?

Bud's eyes rested on the familiar landmarks, but touched them in a new way. Would he ever be back here? He looked to the north, where cars were starting to leap over the Rim like a stampede. Everyone entered from due north. That's because that side was closest to the main road—and because it didn't have a thirty-foot cliff rimming it like the other side. You drove right in from the desert, as fifteen cars were demonstrating. The People drove their stuff in, set up camp, and then drove back out, parking outside.

He knew the place so well. The Bowl sloped down very slightly from its Rim to the depression of the Pit. The slope was so subtle you could hardly see it, but you could feel it in your legs walking out. The Bowl wasn't symmetrical; the Pit where the meteor hit was the Bowl's deepest part, in the southeast of the Bowl's circle.

Bud thought the meteor must have come in like a slider, skidding sideways before finally landing in the Pit. It chucked up dirt behind it, like a baseball thrown sideways into sand. But the meteor threw up *lots* of dirt. The back of the Bowl was unlike the easy front. Anybody sleepwalking out there would go over a thirty-foot drop-off. The cliff was even trickier from the northeast to southern edge of the Bowl. Sometimes it was a simple cliff like in the southwest. In other places—the eastern and southeast edge—fingers of soil spilled over the desert behind it, making a maze of canyons, freestanding rocks, and caves. The People called it "the Badlands" and it spread out for miles outside the Bowl's Rim.

The Badlands were the Mogollon's dark side. Where people had visions and saw lights in the Bowl, the Badlands were the place that nightmares formed. Getting lost in the Badlands was usually fatal. Grandfather taught the spirit warriors how to track there, but except for a few well-known caves, the Badlands were strictly off limits. Bud never went in the Badlands; their secrets were for a special few, even among Grandfather's warriors.

The Bowl was pretty safe while the Meeting was in progress. The scorpions and rattlesnakes cleared out for the event, and even the poison cactus seemed to lose most of its bite. Grandfather explained it by saying that the Great One asked all of creation to cooperate with the work they would do. Bud knew for sure that all those critters came back afterward; the place teemed with snakes and such when the warriors met.

They were heading toward the Rim, which marked the Bowl's circumference. A gentle rise about four feet high and ten feet wide, the Rim made a path around the whole place and a good divider. You had to be pretty dumb not to know it when you hit the Rim, since you had to climb up onto it. Once on it, remembering not to fall off the outer edge should have been easy. People did, though, two or three a year.

They drove southwest from the Pit, toward the trail on the edge of the Rim. The Bowl was so flat that anything that stuck up became a landmark. The depression of the Pit was to their left; to their right and a little behind them sat the camp headquarters, two decaying cement-block buildings almost in the center of the Bowl. Bud felt sad just looking at them. Was it his last time here?

Paul stopped the cart so Grandfather could see the fruit of his labor. Hundreds of turquoise portable toilets were arranged in neat rows south of the camp headquarters. A sea of plastic privies stood ready to serve. The effect was ludicrous.

Grandfather gazed at the tableau and said, "Very good, Paul. We will be much..." His words faltered, "...*better* this year." He managed to say it without guffawing. Bud had to put his hands over his mouth to keep from laughing. What the hell was Paul thinking of? Everyone at the Meeting could have their own toilet, he had ordered so many of them.

Paul studied the scene. "I didn't know how many to order. Maybe I got too many."

"It will be fine," Grandfather assured him.

They looked over the scene for a moment. The camp headquarters were the only permanent buildings in the Bowl. The two square concrete buildings and the decrepit generator behind them were all that was left from the final scientific study of the Bowl's unusual geomagnetic characteristics.

Bud smiled again. Those buildings were part of the Meeting's lore. Every year, the old-timers who lived on the rez regaled one and all with eye-witness accounts of the scientists' hasty departures.

"The last bunch ran out like rabbits." The tales *still* produced riotous laughs around the campfire. "Some study; they left in *three weeks*. That's the record." Some of the very old people had seen several teams of scientists fold 'em and run. They debated as to exactly what triggered the stampedes. The massive lightning strikes or the moaning often heard in the Bowl were deemed the most likely causes.

The Bowl had been ceded back to the reservation permanently, sporting a couple of ugly buildings. The headquarters housed the community bathrooms and an office; the generator supplied the only electric power for a hundred miles.

"Where shall we put the people from Numenon, Grandfather? You saw their fax. They wanted water and electricity," Paul said. "I put them there." A large empty space next to the headquarters was barricaded off. "But you're the boss." Paul sounded worried about his choice.

"That is fine, my son," Grandfather replied. Bud wondered about that, because it was the worst spot in the Bowl. Everyone gathered around the buildings—that's where the showers and water were. If the plumbing backed up, the smell was pretty bad—and the plumbing always backed up. Elizabeth would set up her hospital tent there too, so everyone who had a bellyache, or thought he did, would stand in line in front of her tent, talking. Bud had set up his tent down there because he wanted Bert to be close to a doctor. A person would have to have a compelling reason like his and Bert's to camp next to the headquarters.

Paul drove away, leaving the headquarters behind them. Bud could see Grandfather's lean-to behind the Pit, up a pretty steep rise on the Bowl's far southeastern Rim. Farther to the southwest was a tall and lovely traditional tepee. Grandfather sometimes held the weddings in front of the tepee. It wasn't traditional to this area; one of Grandfather's friends from the Plains had given it to him. It immediately became a beloved part of the Bowl. Bud's throat tightened; that's where he and Bert were married. Sadness rose within him. He'd never see the tepee again. Paul drove along, chattering, and took the trail to the horse area.

They climbed the slight incline to a path that went to the Rim. So many people had used it over the years that the incline was eroded. The golf cart climbed it easily. Bud held on as Paul navigated the tortuous switchbacks down the thirty-foot cliff on the other side of the Rim. The path—perhaps ten feet at its widest—lurched across the cliff face. Miraculously, they made it down. Bud looked back, thinking he'd hate to try to drive a car down.

The horse facilities were about a quarter of a mile from the switchbacks, across the plain. Spirit warriors swarmed all over. Last September, at their last warriors' meeting, Grandfather made a big deal over the horse facilities for the Meeting. "I want a round pen," he'd said. When asked what it should be like, he replied, "Ask Bud." So the guys built a round pen to Bud's specifications, working weekends and days off from their regular jobs. "We should have corrals," Grandfather decreed. Again, Bud designed the corrals; he didn't see much sense in it since this was the last Meeting.

But if Grandfather gave a direct order, everyone knew that a good reason was behind it. So they had primped and fixed since September. It was worth it, everyone agreed. The horse facilities looked slick. A fenced arena had been built behind the tack shed. Next to it, twenty corrals held horses brought in for training. The round pen was fifty feet across, constructed of solid lumber eight feet high. The walls angled out a little to allow for a rider's foot if he was riding a horse inside. The pen had a raised platform outside its perimeter so people could stand and watch horses be worked. Across from the round pen, the tack shed and corrals were arranged. Even the decrepit tack shed had a face-lift. Bud could see new gingham curtains through the windows. The windows even had glass.

"Well, Paul. Show me how you ride." Grandfather turned to Paul Running Bird abruptly. "Where's your horse?" Grandfather's words were kind, but his eyes were sharper than an eagle's.

"I guess I'd better go catch one," Paul stammered.

Bud started to go help him, but Grandfather caught his arm. "No, my son. Let him do it." When he looked into Bud's eyes, all the feelings Bud had inside welled up. He thought, Are you really quitting? Is this the last we'll ever see of this place? Bud realized he loved the Bowl as much as he did Bert or Grandfather. It was a place that got inside you, that changed you. That loved you, in a way he couldn't explain, just like he loved it. All that quivered in him, and he didn't say a word.

"My son, everything will be all right. It *is* all right, you'll see."

He knew that Grandfather felt his fears like they were his. The rich folks he worked for talked about being in therapy and how good their therapists made them feel after talking to them for hours, but this was better. Grandfather *understood*; you didn't have to throw words at him. Bud bent over the cart's front seat, hiding his face. His shoulders shook as his feelings released.

"You stay here, my son. I'm going to watch Paul. Come when you want."

Paul walked to the tack shed and got a halter and lead rope. He headed out into the field behind the tack shed. Guys were fixing the old fence that kept the wild horses contained. Behind the fancy new arena was the old dirt area where they rode in previous years. It had pretty good footing—dirt covered with ten years of manure and sand. That's where Paul would ride; he wanted to try some fancy maneuvers. The new arena was too hard for that.

The wild horses were already in. No one brought them in. A few days before the Meeting, horses would start showing up out at the stable area. They were usually the same horses, though new ones appeared and old ones disappeared. Paul surveyed the animals; he glanced back quickly to see if Grandfather was watching as he made his catch. The old man was. Good. Paul picked a pretty gelding, dark bay. He still had most of his winter coat, but he looked sleek and shiny. The gelding bore the unmistakable stamp of Wesley's stallion. Wesley brought his stallion to a few of the Meetings to "refresh the herd." They'd turn him loose with the mares and they'd all be pregnant by the end of the week. Paul loved to watch that stud horse work. He could still see him, up there, pumping away. Boy! To be a stallion.

Better keep my mind on my business, Paul thought. The gelding was eyeing him and moving away. Paul would love to use this horse for the week if Grandfather let him. He picked him not only for his looks, but also because Bud Creeman had ridden him the last three years. Paul had seen Bud ride him. This horse would show him off proud.

He could see the gelding knew he had him marked. The horse looked at him and moved off. Paul followed him, keeping even with his girth. The horse pulled away from the others, not trying to get away very hard.

Paul saw him relax and give in. Paul walked up to him and offered him the back of his hand. The gelding sniffed it delicately. Paul marveled at how easy it was as he buckled the halter. Picking up the lead line and arranging it as his trainer had taught him, Paul looked up to see if Grandfather had seen his spectacular catch.

The old man was laughing with a bunch of the guys, standing by that idiot Willy Fish and a mule. Paul's joy evaporated.

31

Kundalini is a Sanskrit word meaning coiled. According to Hindu and Buddhist texts, kundalini lies dormant at the base of the spine in most people. When it awakens, it begins to move upward, purifying the person and causing spiritual experiences." Jeff Block's face was calm and serious as he made eye contact with each person in the *Ashley's* stateroom.

He'd done lots of public speaking for his guru and felt comfortable with his topics, but not his listeners. They'd been parked in the middle of a canyon, God knows where, for who knew how long, while Will Duane grilled him. He was glad that Mr. Duane introduced him at the start; without that, the others never would have listened to him.

"Jeff is even more high-powered than Mark. He's an ABD—a PhD who has completed his program, all but the dissertation." His boss gave a huge sigh. "I hate to see PhD candidates stop before finishing their degrees. But Jeff did very well down at UC Santa Barbara. He might have been sitting where *I* am if he'd kept on and gotten his degree in business. But he dropped out for a good cause, doing volunteer work in India, I understand."

Jeff had smiled wanly at the sideways compliment. He quit the program to do seva, selfless service to his guru. Guruji needed help organizing his world tour and Jeff was the only devotee who knew how to do it. He earned enormous spiritual merit during those years.

But the MBAs wouldn't understand that. They stared blankly when Will introduced him. He didn't like giving morons an impromptu class on the secrets of spiritual life. He knew the MBAs were very smart, but it was in a canny way that ignored everything that really mattered. Their scrutiny made him feel nervous, which made him wonder how he looked.

He wasn't vain; he just knew that looks mattered. Jeff did a quick inventory. He was taller and thinner than Mark, but just as tan and fit from all the surfing they did. His erect posture and graceful movement testified to his hatha yoga practice. His uniform was perfectly pressed. He looked fine. He stopped himself from touching his chauffeur's cap.

"I need to clarify some terms before we go further. The chakras are centers of energy aligned along the spine—seven of them, up to the top of the head. If they dissected you, they would not find chakras, but anyone who works with energy—acupuncturists, oriental medicine practitioners ..."

"From all over the world, not just China or Asia," Mark interjected. "This energy isn't owned by one tradition."

"That's right," Jeff said. It bothered him the way Mark kept interrupting, like he couldn't teach by himself. Mark was that way all the time, in the band, even when they were surfing. Jeff was surprised that Mark didn't have an MBA—he was so pushy. Jeff fingered his cap's brim unconsciously. He knew what Mark was up to—he'd get a better job this week even if it meant screwing a friend. Jeff had realized the potential this jaunt held in terms of their careers. Well, he'll have to beat *me* first, he thought. We'll see who comes out on top. He quickly picked up the thread of what he had been saying.

"Everyone has kundalini, whether it's active or not. Its manifestations appear all over the world. Australian aborigines have a trance state they call dreamtime. They can foretell the future, see things in the future—know all sorts of things when they're in dreamtime. Christian saints in ecstasy have experiences that a yogi would call kundalini manifestations.

"As the kundalini rises, many people see a brilliant column of light moving up their spines. The column often has a brighter golden tip ..."

"*What did you say?*" Will Duane practically jumped up and grabbed him by his shirt. "People see a *column* of light?"

"Yes, sir. It's a classic kundalini manifestation. The golden tip is pretty standard, too." Will stared at him so hard he felt like stepping back.

"A standard manifestation? Standard? Standard!"

Jeff had no idea his boss would get so worked up about kundalini. "Yeah. Lots of people see the column of light."

Will began tossing questions. "What does it feel like when this energy starts moving up? It must be intense, right?"

"Yes, Mr. Duane, the awakening and unfolding of kundalini energy are very intense experiences. Many people would find them frightening. That's probably why it doesn't occur more often."

"So it's rare?" Will raised his eyebrows, sitting back with a smug smile.

"Yes and no. Among the general population, yes. Among those who consider themselves on a spiritual path, it's not so rare. My meditation school has millions of practitioners all over the world. I'd say most of them have manifestations of kundalini. These differ from person to person. Some see the column of light. Others might have a sense of a transcendent Being protecting them. Or visions. I'm sure that other meditation schools and spiritual groups have many people with awakened kundalini. Plus, kundalini yoga is taught all over; you can take it practically anywhere."

Jeff did a mental calculation. "I'll bet that at least ten million people worldwide have personal experiences of kundalini. And that's just now. Countless people have had such experiences throughout history—and many have written about them."

Mr. Duane gasped. "Ten million people? Why doesn't anyone know about it?"

"They do, in yogic and other spiritual traditions."

"But why don't they teach about it?"

"The theory of kundalini has been taught all over the globe for thousands of years." Jeff found Will's intensity scary. He wanted to calm him down. "It's nothing new."

"But why didn't I know about it?"

"Did you ever ask anyone or go where spiritual ideas were taught?"

"No."

"'Ask and ye shall receive,'" Jeff said.

"I never *asked*," Will whispered. He was thoughtful before launching another barrage of questions. "Can people start seeing the column of light and all the rest by themselves?" Mr. Duane seemed disconcerted. Jeff hadn't expected his reaction. "How does it get started?"

"A shaktipat guru can awaken dormant kundalini easily if a seeker is ready. That's the safest and easiest way—the guru's energy will control the unfolding kundalini. That's important. It's a big experience that goes on for years." Jeff fumbled as he tried to explain. "Other ways exist. They do all sorts of exercises in kundalini yoga classes, with breathing mostly, to awaken kundalini. And it awakens spontaneously for some people."

"How does it awaken spontaneously?"

"Well, it's a matter of spiritual connection. How much you love God, or spirit—however you conceptualize the divine. I know people who had their kundalini awakened when trauma occurred. It's sort of like—they needed a divine intervention, so it came. If your soul is orientated toward the inner realm, Spirit will come to you."

Will sat back, chewing on a knuckle. Jeff could practically see his thoughts. He realized his boss must have had kundalini experiences; he wouldn't have reacted the way he had otherwise. Jeff had a hard time believing it; Will Duane was the least spiritual man he knew.

"Tell us everything we need to know about kundalini." Will's eyes bored into his.

He told him everything he knew, starting with more about the chakras. "As it moves upward, the energy strikes the chakras, causing them to spin and emit lights and sounds, and produce bliss."

"How can you be sure of that, Jeff?" Will asked.

"If it happens, you'll know it!" He laughed. "It's like sitting on a volcano. You can see and feel the chakras exactly where the charts show them. They vibrate and send off colors. It's amazing."

"You've experienced this?" Will asked. He nodded, as did Mark.

Gil, Doug, and Betty stared at him like he was from a different planet. He was. Jeff felt as though he set back his spiritual development every time he went to work. The people he drove made him sick—he could feel their vibe even through the glass separating him from his passengers. Sex, money, power, and greed were what they were about. They were perfect examples of people living from their lower chakras.

He worked at Numenon for three things: the pay, benefits, and all the time off. He surfed and played in the band with Mark when he wasn't driving, but mostly he worked for his guru. Seva, or selfless service, was a major part of his spiritual practice. That and mantra repetition. His mantra got heavy mileage when he was driving for Numenon. He had repeated the sacred words to protect his spiritual state from the people he worked for. And now he was telling them his secrets.

"Yeah, I feel the energy all the time. But I've been meditating for more than twenty years. I started when I was a little kid." He did not want to talk about his spiritual life, but he needed to. He had to show them that he was more spiritual than Mark. Jeff touched his cap self-consciously. Talking about this made him nervous, which showed up as concern for his hair. OK, it was vain, but he loved his hair.

"When did you start seeing lights and so on?" Mr. Duane looked interested, not judgmental.

"When I met my guru nine years ago. I'd been raised with meditation, my family lives in Santa Cruz, everyone there meditates or *something* ... But it wasn't until I met Guru Maharajiva that I began to have real spiritual experiences. He awakened my kundalini, and the things I've talked about started happening."

He clutched the brim of his cap, holding on for his life. Jeff got around the Numenon dress code by cutting the sides and back of his hair very short. He stuffed his ponytail under his driver's cap, managing to hide a two-foot long, sun-bleached mane in a corporation known for its conservative and well-enforced dress code.

"Take off your cap, Jeff," Mr. Duane said. "It's just us here."

"Uh, I'll leave it on ... I got a bad haircut last time." They laughed. Everyone seemed to be in a jolly mood. That was because of Mark. He couldn't put people at ease like Mark. Jeff never felt like "just us" at work. He wasn't one of the popular drivers.

"Mark tells us that you know all about personal energy, tai chi, and so on," Mr. Duane looked at him like he was an expert himself. His boss always seemed like the most assured person in the world. It was more than the fact that he was an arrogant jerk. Mr. Duane didn't know a thing about yoga or spirituality, yet he did. His energy filled the cabin. Anyone could feel it. How could a man whose personal life was repulsive broadcast energy like that? "Tell us everything you know, Jeff."

He talked about the types of spiritual seekers, how an intellectual might be drawn to study God with his mind, while a bhakti yogi—a lover of God— would be drawn to devotional practices. "It's like the difference between St. Thomas Aquinas and St. Francis. Different people, same end result."

"What's the practical result of this stuff?" Mr. Duane seemed irritated when Jeff finished. "What does it *do*?"

"Well, a person with his or her kundalini awakened becomes sort of like ... uh ..." Jeff searched for an analogy.

"A superman—or woman!" Mark interjected. "Kundalini is power. People with risen kundalini can do more, for longer, with better results, than any people on the planet. They can have superhuman strength, all sorts of psychic abilities. Do stuff you wouldn't believe. Very, very few people who have had it rise all the way ..." Mark touched the top of his head ... "to the top—and stay there."

"That means they're enlightened," Jeff barked, fighting for his position. "They are jivanmukta, merged with God while still living on this earth." Mark's interference made Jeff more vehement than he would have been. "We should spend our lives seeking the company of enlightened beings! We should spend as much time with them as possible. Most of what we do is worthless! We chase ..."

"Enlightened people have enormous powers, which have been documented all over the place." Mark cut in again. "It's not just in religious writing, either. People like the psychologist Abraham Maslow wrote about those who have achieved the highest state a human being can attain. An individual can have these powers without professing religious beliefs."

Jeff glared at his erstwhile friend, who had redirected the discussion to present what their boss wanted—the worldly and nonreligious aspects of spirituality. He was sucking up to the godless Will Duane.

Mark kept going. "You read about what these people can do—heal, mostly—and it's amazing. But they can also do other things, like projecting energy long distances and striking opponents who are far away. That's bona fide research, documented by scientists. These people can predict the future and know what their followers are doing a continent away. Some masters can influence the weather, and blow things up ..."

The MBAs gasped. Will was very attentive.

"How, Mark?"

"Well, that's rare."

"Enlightened beings do not go around blowing things up." Jeff's exasperation sharpened his tone. "They're *saints*. They exist to bring people to God. That's it. And they're not for hire!"

Will put his hand to his mouth. Jeff thought he'd rebuke him for his outburst, but he simply asked. "Do you have a guru like that, Jeff? One that can jump-start people's kundalini?"

"Yes." But that didn't fit Jeff's feelings. He had devoted most of his adult life to his guru. Soon after meeting Guru Maharajiva, he'd had what he thought was shaktipat, the awakening of his kundalini. But was it the real thing?

What he was feeling now was much more intense than his earlier experiences. He could see almost invisible beings, American Indians, floating around his motor home as he drove. In his mind's eye, Grandfather smiled at him, welcoming him. That had never happened with his guru. Was he being torn from his roots, or shown something he needed to know?

His girlfriend had told him that what he was doing—going to a retreat given by another guru—was blasphemy. He told her it was just work; he wasn't going to see another teacher, or to the retreat. But he was, in every way. The retreat and Grandfather were coming to *him* as he drove. Mr. Duane was talking; Jeff made himself focus.

"If one of these saints got his people's kundalini going, he'd have a movement of superpeople doing his bidding after a while. You could say he had an army, a private army of superwarriors sworn to follow him. They could take over the world ... or at least the country."

"That isn't how ..."

"It's not militaristic." Mark butted in again. "It's not like that. They're devoted to peace ..."

"But they could make war?"

"Yeah, if they wanted to, but they don't. They want people to love each other. They want a perfect world." Jeff spoke rapidly.

"You've got one of these gurus?"

"Yeah, I do." He was lying. Jeff was no longer certain his guru was so great. He could feel Grandfather's presence in the cabin where they sat. Where was Swamiji?

"Betty, get this guru's contact info from Jeff. I want him here."

"No! He's in India on retreat. You don't just call up a guru and order him around ..." Jeff was appalled.

By the grace of God, someone knocked on the door.

"Come in," Will barked.

"S'cuse me, y'all." Delroy West's tall form filled the doorway. "I know you're workin' hard, but we got to get to this campsite. We got a full day's work once we get there, settin' up. We been drivin' a long time." He smiled ruefully, holding his cap in his hand and looking tired.

"I'm sorry, Delroy," Mr. Duane said. "You guys must be exhausted. Get ready to pull out while we do a quick wrap-up." Del retreated and Will turned to Jeff and Mark. "It seems to me that this Grandfather may be one of those gurus who gives people a power boost ..."

"A shaktipat guru," Jeff said. "They're the rarest teachers in the world. Grandfather *is* real." Jeff wanted the group to see *him* as the expert, because he *was* more spiritually developed than Mark. So he revealed his secret, something he hadn't told anyone, especially his girlfriend.

"I called one of my religious studies professors at UCSB about this trip. He knew about Grandfather. He said he's the most powerful holy man on the planet, maybe the most powerful in hundreds of years. He said that it's a miracle we're invited—he never sees outsiders—and I should count my lucky stars that I got to go on this trip."

Was the thrill of anticipation he felt wrong? "And also, my professor said that he thought that Tyler Brand, one of the other professors at UCSB, was one of Grandfather's followers. But he didn't know. They're very close-mouthed." Jeff played his trump card.

"That may be so," Betty Fogarty said. She took over the cabin with a few words. "We'll find out." Her deadpan reaction ruined the effect of his great piece of intelligence.

"The people we're going to see wouldn't call their teacher a guru. That's a term from India." Mark added, determined to spoil Jeff's moment. "They have an entirely different vocabulary and system of thought. Systems, really, since spirituality is individual and interpretations of it vary by tribe."

"Yeah, fine. So this guy may have powers that we can't conceive..." Mr. Duane interrupted brusquely.

"Actually, that's not true. We all have all those powers, and become aware of them sometimes." Mark spoke forcefully, without his usual nice-guy act. "Holy men and women may be in touch with the source of power—that many call 'God'—but this power isn't foreign to us. As Jesus said..." Mark paused, as though he were thinking, What *did* Jesus say?

"He said stuff like we'll do more miracles than he did. He said spiritual abilities are innate. You read of spontaneous cures to cancer and horrible diseases. This kind of paranormal stuff is very ordinary. We all have premonitions and visions. It's just that we don't pay attention to them."

Will sat silently before he spoke. "OK. If this is true, we're heading into the eye of the hurricane. Anything could happen. What else should you know?"

"That whatever is going to happen in the Meeting is already happening. The seeds of whatever changes we make are in our lives now. They show up as our weaknesses and problems. Whatever they are, they'll get hotter and *louder* as we get closer to the Meeting. We will feel lousy, emotionally. Tempers may flare..."

"Whenever I go to India or to do some job for my guru, everything inside me starts screaming. Whatever I'm afraid of *leaps* out in my life and hits me in the face. That's part of the process," Jeff threw in.

"So, if you're an arrogant jerk, you'll be twice as arrogant a jerk on the way to meet a holy man." Mark said, making eye contact with everyone, including Will. "But the holy man won't care. He will see you as the perfect child of the universe."

After meeting Mark's eyes, Will slumped in his chair. He finally said, "Well, thank you, Mark and Jeff. We'd better get going." He could barely speak. He knew he was an arrogant jerk. He was worse than that. Mark, his employee, had called him a jerk to his face, and he let him get away with it.

Why? Because the two men who had just spoken were so different from him and his Dream Team that they might have been another species. They had something he lacked, that he needed.

They knew about the column of light. He couldn't believe it. He'd thought he was a freak, the only one who had experienced its beauty—and joy. But he wasn't ... Millions of people knew about the light, Jeff said. Millions. Could he meet them? Were they potential friends?

He couldn't imagine having friends. Will was badly shaken, glimpsing a reality he couldn't conceive. You're always talking about thinking outside the box, he thought. You're really outside the box now. His eyes narrowed as he thought, This is data, just like a financial statement. Use it. He reviewed the information.

Jeff had said that people who'd had traumatic experiences could have their kundalini awakened. Will could remember himself as a child cowering in his bed, shaking, and stifling his sobs. The Light had come to him after such an episode. He needed a divine intervention, and got one. He remembered what Jeff said word for word, but didn't understand the last part. "If your soul is orientated toward the inner realm, Spirit will come to you." He didn't believe in God—why should he? He thought Karl Marx was dead right about religion. It was the opiate of the masses. And the upper classes, too. Believers were delusional. Why had the Light come to *him*?

His gaze lingered on the door after Jeff left; he watched Mark take the driver's seat. These men knew things he didn't; he wanted them to teach him. He felt better about approaching Mark; he was funny and easy to be around. Jeff wasn't as easygoing, but he had an ascetic quality that Will found riveting. Will knew all about the ponytail he was trying to hide. Who cared? Will picked up on the rivalry between the two drivers instantly. It didn't bother him. Rivalry was normal.

Could he tell these men of the visions he'd had all his life? Could he tell them of the dreams and premonitions? Could he divulge that every major decision he'd made in business had had its root in a vision? What about the stalker? He hadn't been able to ask them about evil.

Could the power they described be used for evil? What he'd learned from the FBI and Pentagon made a lot of sense when you thought in terms of men and women with supernatural powers.

What was he doing thinking about all this crazy stuff? He shook his head, trying to dismiss what he'd heard.

It wasn't crazy. Mark and Jeff were well-versed scholars with advanced degrees from University of California campuses. The *New York Times* reported that people performed surgery in China using acupuncture for anesthesia. Even *The Wall Street Journal* would have an article about the earth's energy flows once in a while. It had to be true.

Could he talk to them about Kathryn? About the things that hooker, Dawn, revealed? Could he talk to anyone about what troubled him?

He had no one to talk to. No wife. No family. Everyone in Numenon was either a toady or looking to rip his belly. His peers outside Numenon were his competitors. The only person he had was Betty, and his need to keep her near him had almost ruined her marriage. Isolation was the hardest thing in his life. It went with the territory. He was the boss.

Will looked at the back of Mark's head as he drove the motor home. Could he confide in him? No. He could never confide in an employee of such low rank. What could Mark do at Numenon that would justify hiring him as a professional? A high-ranking professional? Someone he could really talk to?

He shook his head. Fascinating though it was, he didn't see a practical use for what they'd discussed, except for the stuff about blowing things up. That could be useful in a corporate setting.

32

Grandfather watched Paul approach the gelding. The horse he picked was a very good choice. Beautiful, well trained, the horse was perfect for his skill level. Paul moved quietly. Excellent. He kept watching until he saw the horse give in. The job was done. Paul made the catch so well that Grandfather decided he'd let him have that horse this week. Paul's horsemanship had improved greatly; his teacher was very good, whoever he was.

Several of the young warriors approached him, bouncing along like frolicking pups. The men and women who worked with the horses were his all-time favorites. Grandfather *loved* horses. Lisa Cheewa, Steve Lame Dog, and Stanley Begay came up to him, laughing.

"Grandfather! We have a name for ourselves!" they said all at once. Figuring out something to call the warriors who specialized in horsemanship had been troublesome. They had proposed several names that Grandfather had vetoed. He smiled and said, "What is it this time?" Usually they came up with real doozies.

"Horse masters!"

"That's fine. Use that name. Why are you laughing?"

"Lisa's been reading all these new books about horses and riding. We had to be careful not to step on anyone's toes."

"Yeah," said Lisa, "everyone has a name for their method of working with horses. They're all selling seminars"—that was a bad word to Grandfather—"and workshops, tapes, videos, books, you name it, all telling you how to ride your horse. We didn't want to get into trouble by picking a name someone already has." The three youngsters were silly, like colts that had been locked up all winter.

Lisa went on. "Yeah. We wanted to call ourselves 'horse mumblers'."

"—Or 'horse babblers'," added Stanley.

"Horse murmurers'," said Steve.

Bud Creeman got in on it. "How about 'horse chatterers'!"

They kept going. "'Horse twaddlers'!"

"No, 'horse drivellers'."

"Nah. 'Horse patterers'."

"Forget it! 'Horse jabberettes'!" Lisa grinned ear to ear. The four of them were cracking up.

Grandfather was silent. He thought that living alone in the desert, he might be missing something. This must be an in joke. Was there something about talking with horses that he didn't know?

Bud's mood had visibly improved. While they were watching Paul, Grandfather told him that he was assigning Bert's sister, Roxie Crow Moon, to be with Bert all week. Roxie was a third-year nursing student who already worked for Dr. Elizabeth Bright Eagle part time. Bert and their soon-to-be-born baby would be safe, and Bud was acting frisky as a result.

"Now, you know, you better get a copyright on that horse master name. All them others are copyrighted already," Bud said solemnly. "You could get in trouble just saying them without permission."

"Really?" Lisa didn't believe him, but she knew he worked for rich people. Maybe he knew something she didn't. "'Horse babbler'?"

"Oh, yeah. Everyone's trying to cash in on not beating horses. It's a big fad," Bud could have been a judge—he was so serious. "Yes, but don't you worry, Lisa. You know how fads are. They'll be back to beating them soon enough."

"Bud! That's not funny!"

"I know. But gee, you put two words together these days and you got someone with a patent mad at you. What happened to the time when people rode horses because they liked them, and helped other people because they liked people too? Everybody wasn't tryin' to get rich teachin' you how to clean a horse's hoof the natural way."

Grandfather noticed something very interesting by the new corrals. A crowd had gathered around Willy Fish and the best-looking mule he had ever seen. Willy Fish was normally a joke around the spirit warriors. When they talked about Willy Fish, they said things like, "He's dumb as a post!" Sometimes, in the evenings, the warriors sat around the fire and discussed how many posts it would take to make "dumb as Willy."

Grandfather knew that Willy wasn't stupid. He had a good job as a mechanic in a big garage in Tulsa, Oklahoma. He could fix anything that had an engine; he had a house with a yard—he didn't own it, but didn't owe any back rent either. He had two nice kids, smart kids. He had a wife that half the single warriors would love to call their own, Rocky Fish. Pretty woman. She wasn't flashy, but she had the power and integrity that the warriors prized. Rocky and Willy Fish—those were their real names, strange though it seemed.

Why did everyone think Willy was so dumb? This was his eleventh Meeting—he'd been to all of them. For all the previous Meetings, Willy Fish went straight to the back of the Bowl. There, he oohed and aahed over everything the men there said, taking it like it was the Native gospel, not paying any attention to what Grandfather said at all. Not even seeing or apprehending anything of Grandfather's state or the fact that ancestors and supernaturals swarmed all over him and the Bowl. The spirit warriors just scooped up visions in the Bowl.

Not Willy Fish. He didn't know who was worth listening to and who wasn't. He practically kissed Paul Running Bird's feet. Willy Fish was so dense that he didn't know that his own wife was a topnotch spirit warrior and had been since her first Meeting. He was so thick that he didn't know that five hundred guys would take her the minute she turned her back on him. That defined dumb in the ways of the world.

Grandfather tried to keep the way the others thought from influencing him, but a question that came to him. What was someone like Willy Fish doing with a mule like that?

Willy explained to the crowd, "I adopted him! Got him right off the Internet. He was a victim of nature! You remember all those tornados the first of the month? They tore up the farm he came from. The folks that owned him said, 'Take him, we don't got nothin' left.' The rescue people brought him clear from Arkansas." Willy's expression indicated that he didn't know that Arkansas was adjacent to his home state of Oklahoma. "I saw his picture and, I swear, he just hauled me in. I went out to the rescue camp and adopted him." Willy heaved a huge sigh.

"I went to see him every day—well, for three days—until they said I had to take him out of the camp 'cuz they didn't have room. I brought him home. I didn't think the neighbors would mind him in the backyard. But they do. That's why I brought him here—I thought one of you guys might want him. He's a real nice mule. I call him Butch." Willy went on talking, not noticing that the mule had edged closer. "Rocky *loves* him! I thought she wouldn't like him, but she does." The instant Willy stopped talking, Butch stepped on his left foot.

"Ow! Get off," Willy howled. The mule leaned on Willy's foot.

Grandfather approached the animal, stepping close to him quickly and saying something in a Native language. The mule jumped off Willy's foot and stood with its head down.

"Oh! I think he broke my foot." Willy jumped up and down on his good foot.

"No, he wouldn't do that, Willy. He was teaching you. He has his own ways of teaching."

"He was teaching me?" Willy's eyes glowed when he looked at the mule. It was a glossy chestnut, an unusual color in a mule. He still had his winter coat. Its long guard hairs waved in the wind, making him look like a long-eared teddy bear. Willy gazed at him adoringly.

Grandfather walked up to the mule and blew in his nostrils. He appeared to be whispering in his ear. He scratched his neck, working out some kinks. The mule dropped his head, his lips relaxed. Everyone, including Willy, could hear him say, "Oh, man. What a touch he has." Willy Fish jumped a foot and stared. The mule talked! It was silent speech that came out of its body, but it talked.

"All horses and mules talk, Willy. We need to learn to listen so we can hear what they say." Grandfather saw Willy's reaction to the mule's speech and was pleased. He was waking up. "This mule will teach you something great this week, Willy. He has been sent to teach you."

Everyone stepped back and looked at Willy with respect. He blushed.

Over by the tack room, Paul Running Bird burned. Grandfather wasn't even watching. He tied the bay gelding he'd caught to the hitching rack, using the proper knot. Paul saddled him. He did it like a pro, every step perfectly executed. His trainer would have praised him up and down—he would have brought the whole class out to see. First, Grandfather praised every nobody in Native America, and then he ignored him for a mule. He led the horse out and walked him in a couple of circles to see if he wanted to buck. He adjusted the girth and then carefully got on. Paul sat down on the saddle so lightly the horse couldn't even feel it. He sat for a full minute, stroking his neck and talking to him, letting the horse adjust to a rider being on its back. This was a fine horse, even if Grandfather didn't notice him.

He cued him to walk out, glancing at Grandfather. The old man was rubbing the other side of the mule now. Paul rode the horse over to the unfenced area they used to use as an arena. He was really into this horse, remembering that it hadn't been ridden for a year. Remembering how Bud had ridden it. Paul could tell when the horse was warmed up enough, and he cued it easily into a slow jog, which the gelding picked up perfectly. Paul looked at Grandfather. Damn him! he thought. A bunch of heads went up around the old man and turned his way, but Grandfather didn't move.

Paul jogged the horse, reversing him and doing circles. The horse was the best-trained animal he'd ever ridden. When it came time to lope, the horse picked up the three-beat gait perfectly. Paul was in love. He liked the horse so much that he didn't notice Grandfather watching him and smiling.

Grandfather looked away. Knowing that Paul would feel nervous with someone watching him, he observed him riding surreptitiously, with glances rather than stares. Paul made circles with the horse in both directions, then he made a figure eight, breaking the horse down to a jog to change leads between two intersecting circles. He did a few more figure eights, then headed the gelding down the arena doing serpentines. He looked up. A crowd of people was gathering by the side of the flat area where he was riding. Paul kicked the horse and made a flashy sliding stop; he was enchanted, enthralled. Grandfather looked over and saw how much fun Paul was having. Good. He might make a horse master and a spirit warrior yet.

Willy Fish sidled up, wanting to talk to him. His dark eyes were so earnest, he reminded Grandfather of a little gnome. He was short and square, but not heavy. Stubby. Very strong. He looked like some sort of cute forest creature you'd be tempted to bring home, but wouldn't because you knew it could never be housebroken.

"Grandfather, I don't know what to do. The neighbors hate my mule; one is going to get the health department after me." Willy was in a state. "I've never had nothing like Butch. I was going to give him away, or turn him loose out here, but I can't."

Paul looked over at Grandfather. He had one arm around Willy's shoulder and was listening intently. Rage flashed through Paul—with all the work he did for the Meeting, you'd think he would get some respect. Willy was a freak! Paul sneered at Willy's cheap, gaudy Western shirt and jeans. Undoubtedly, if Willy squatted, his crack would show in back. Paul grabbed his reins. "Whoa!" he shouted. The horse came to the flashiest stop anyone had seen. The crowd grew. He sat back and cued the horse to spin to the left, using his right leg for motivation. That horse spun like a merry-go-round on hyperdrive. Another murmur went up. Paul looked at Grandfather. He was still paying attention to Willy.

He booted the horse to the other end of the arena, hauling on him to stop this time, not cuing him. Shocked, the horse opened its mouth wide and slid. It bounced a few times before stopping and standing, trembling. He didn't let go of its mouth, so it shot backward. He yanked the horse around. It didn't spin so well this time, but the crowd didn't notice. He ran the horse to the other end of the "arena" and slid it the same way. Paul looked for Grandfather. He was still talking to Willy, goddamnit! The crowd applauded his performance. Paul made another run.

Everything Paul did, Grandfather saw. He heard every thought, even while counseling Willy. "Willy, this mule is a supernatural. He's come to help you. I think many things will happen for you this week. You must spend as much time as possible with this mule." Grandfather smiled. "This will be a good week for you."

The old man nodded at Bud, who had been watching Paul aghast. Bud whistled and someone in the arena yelled, "Whoa!" The horse whoa'd, almost dumping Paul.

Paul grabbed the reins and kicked the horse at the same time. "You stop when I tell you to stop!"

"No, Paul." Lisa Cheewa walked up and took the horse's reins. "Grandfather wanted you to stop. He signaled to us to stop you. Get off." Her face was stony. Paul didn't know why she was angry.

Grandfather was standing next to the horse, looking at him with cold eyes.

"Well, how did I do?" Paul beamed, remembering those stops and turns.

"Look at your horse, Paul. Your horse will tell you."

The horse was sweaty. It stood with its head down, panting. It held the left rear foot up.

"Look at its heel, Paul."

Paul picked up the horse's foot and looked. Oops! He'd slid it too much without sliding boots. The heel was blistered and the ergot—the vestigial hoof at the back of the fetlock joint—was torn off and bleeding. Paul flushed. Well, it was a natural enough thing. He was excited; Grandfather wasn't watching him. He had to do something to get his attention.

"Look at his mouth, Paul. Touch it." Paul did. The horse pulled away; its mouth was sore. One corner was flecked with blood. Paul froze.

"Well, I messed up a little. I was nervous."

Grandfather nodded. He had seen every bit of Paul's ride, beginning to end. This man was an egomaniac. When he spoke, everyone standing around ducked, feeling the power of the shaman's emotion. "Paul, you have it in you to be a great rider. What you did catching the horse and bringing him in was wonderful, the way you saddled and got on him was perfect. What you did early in your ride was excellent. And then, when you thought I wasn't watching you, you got angry. You hurt that horse. You would destroy him in a week. I'll give you a horse to ride, Paul, but it won't be that one."

Paul's cheeks flamed. Grandfather smiled at him and patted his shoulder.

"It is not bad to make mistakes, my son. It is bad not to learn from them. I'll give you a good horse. You've learned much this year. If I see you doing well with this horse, we'll see what else you'll get."

The shaman walked into the desert a few dozen yards. A couple hundred horses stood out there in groups. He closed his eyes and stood silently for a few minutes.

Everyone watched as a horse walked toward him from far out in the desert. It was a horse no one had seen before, a strange horse. It walked over to Grandfather and put its head on his chest. They stood like that for some time, apparently talking. Grandfather turned around and the horse followed him. They made their way back to Paul.

"This is your horse, Paul," Grandfather said.

Paul had never seen such an ugly horse in his life. It was a washed-out beige; its mane and tail were dark, but not quite black. The mane stood up like a long scrub brush. It had a stripe down its back. Uglier than its color was—everything else about it. This horse had big feet, short, stubby legs. And the ugliest monster of a head Paul had ever seen. It looked prehistoric. Tiny round ears and this humungous snout—Roman-nosed didn't even start to describe that proboscis! Grandfather was insulting him on this week of weeks.

"Grandfather, I can't ..."

"Yes, you can. It's this horse or no horse." Grandfather was stern. He gave people what they needed, not what they wanted. Paul's ego was out of control. He'd hurt an animal in his greed for recognition. "You can't hurt him, Paul. Look at his legs." Paul finally understood and was shamed. Grandfather didn't trust him with a good horse.

"I was nervous, Grandfather."

"This horse, Paul, or none. If you decide to take him, I have a special job for you."

A special job? Paul was interested.

"I want you to lead Bud and Willy on a scouting trip. The Numenon people are late. I want you to find them and bring them in."

Paul's eyes went wide—Grandfather appreciated him after all! "Yes, certainly. I'll do that, right away."

"Oh, Paul, one other thing."

"Yes?"

"You'll have to break your horse. He's never been ridden. You might want to ask Bud for help." Paul's mouth dropped. "You'd better hurry." Grandfather indicated the thunderclouds gathering in the West. "Looks like a storm's coming."

33

Will mulled over what Mark and Jeff had said. He felt like he was tottering at the edge of his universe. Behind him was the world of business that he understood, and before him was a world as alien as Mars. Or was it? Many would say his world *was* Mars—the home of the god of war. But he wasn't so different from Mark and Jeff. The visions and dreams had shown him the other side.

People moved around the cabin as they got ready to pull out. Sandy served more coffee. The delay gave him time to think. Supermen? Super-human powers? That was the stuff of cartoons. Yet he knew of it from what the Light had shown him. Will ran his hand through his hair. An army of people like him? How tight a spot were they in?

He knew a few things even Betty didn't, having researched Grandfather on his own. He wouldn't report his research results to the group—the infor-mation was classified and he *never* told everything he knew, even to Betty.

When he talked to the old Indian on the phone, Will was bothered by the man's secretiveness about himself and where they would be staying. Will wouldn't go anywhere that he hadn't checked out. He made a few phone calls and ended up talking to someone at the Pentagon; from there, he was directed to the FBI. The bureau chief referred him to Albert Wexler, the senior FBI officer in charge of Native American investigations. He ended up talking with the FBI man about Grandfather and the Meeting, but said nothing about the Meeting's location.

"Mr. Duane, this so-called medicine man is a dangerous revolutionary." Wexler was dead serious. "We've been tracking him for years. He is an enemy of the United States government and maintains a squad of trained killers. Their intention is to take over the United States. We have a file on him as long as your arm. We'd bring him in, but he's slippery as slime. We recommend that you terminate any contact with him. Don't go to his so-called retreat."

Will couldn't do that. He had to go to the Meeting. When the FBI man couldn't dissuade Will from going to the Meeting, he asked, "Will you wear a wire?"

"For a week?"

The agent then pumped him for information on the Meeting's location. Something told Will to lie, to get them offtrack. He followed that intuition—he had a very bad feeling about Wexler. "I think it's in Arizona. At some fancy hotel outside Scottsdale. My secretary knows where it is; I can ask her. I'm sure there aren't too many hotels outside Scottsdale that have had big Native American spiritual workshops."

Will didn't know it, but Grandfather's ancestors could have orchestrated his answer. The bureau found that only one hotel in the Scottsdale area had hosted a large Native American retreat. Stephen Rising Wolf held one of his early seminars there. The bureau started a file on him, and began watching him night and day.

To get the FBI agent off his back, Will agreed to take along a red phone. A safety measure, he was told. The Army, Air Force, National Guard, CIA *and* FBI, state militia, and highway patrol would come running at the push of a button. The phone also contained tracking devices that would finally allow the bureau to pinpoint the location of the Meeting.

"We've known about this tea party for ten years; we can't seem to get a fix on it. You'd think someone would blab, but no one does," the agent complained. "We try to track it on surveillance satellites, and let me tell you, some weird things have happened." Wexler chuckled. "Of course, I *can't* tell you what happened. It's classified. Even for you."

Will sat in the *Ashley*, brow furrowed. He looked at the red phone sitting on the counter. Why couldn't they pinpoint the location of the Meeting? Today's satellites could practically look behind your refrigerator. Why couldn't they see the Mogollon Bowl?

The memory of Mark's voice rang in his ears. "What if the Bowl doesn't want to be photographed? What if it's the greatest power spot on the planet?"

That *was* crazy. On the other hand, what if the Bowl *knew* he was carrying a surveillance device? Could it tell? Could a hunk of real estate know anything? Why did the scientists leave so fast? This was too weird—Indians with super powers? Able to read minds and project energy across space? Come on, what was this?

And what about jolly old Grandfather? Was he a revolutionary with a private army of trained killers or a sweet old healer? And how did he know Marina? One reason Will brought them on this goose chase was because his only hope of getting Marina back was to prove himself a good guy to the old shaman. How did *she* know him? Was she one of his army? Red flags went up everywhere.

Will rubbed his chest, suppressing a groan. What had he gotten them into?

"No, thank you, Sandy. I don't want anything." He waved her off. Betty had collected her brief and began speaking again. Will listened attentively. Maybe she knew something more. But Betty looked as perplexed and upset as he felt. He knew how conservative she was; all the talk of kundalini and shakti-pakti must have her half-crazy.

"Well, that certainly was interesting," she said. "I don't know how useful it will be ... Oh! I'm sorry Mark! I forgot you were here." Betty flushed. Will knew why she blushed; he shared the same prejudice. The professionals usually treated the drivers like robots. "I forgot, you *believe* all that ... I just ..."

"It's hard to believe until you experience it," Mark said. "Of course, I was born and raised in Santa Cruz, so it comes naturally."

Will smiled, despite his misgivings.

"OK, this is the rest of what I've got about Grandfather and his troops," Betty opened her report. She was glad to take control again. All that crazy nonsense. "Paul Running Bird supplied me with data about notables in 'The Movement'—which is what Grandfather's followers call themselves. I did a little more looking myself." She smiled—her sleuthing abilities had paid off.

"First, this holy man called Grandfather. Paul supplied me with absolutely no information about him, other than that he is old, a master who lives in the desert and never sees anyone but Native Americans. He doesn't talk about his past. His own People know nothing of it, other than the fact that he studied with his teacher, known as Great-grandfather, for decades. He became the head when the older man died. I got on the phone and I found out that what Paul didn't tell me is typical. Great Native holy men and women exist, but they are kept under wraps by their tribes— because of what happened to them in the last four hundred years.

"Then, I got lucky. I was referred to the All Faiths Theological Seminary in Oakland. They knew of Grandfather. He has a couple of degrees from them. I tracked down an ancient professor emeritus who knew him. He said that he disappeared from the seminary in the thirties, but came back after the Second World War and got a master's degree, and his real name is Joseph Bishop. The professor said, 'He'd returned to that aboriginal mumbo jumbo. A great academic turned into a witch doctor.'" Betty felt like a private eye hot on the chase. "The seminary gave me the name of a retired professor of anthropology, Beatrice Salkind. She had some amazing things to say. I thought they were crazy—I still do—but they make more sense in terms of what Mark and Jeff said.

"Dr. Salkind spent some time with Grandfather in the sixties. She said he's absolutely the real thing—able to move heaven and earth. She met him when she was interviewing people on his reservation for her doctoral dissertation. She broke her leg out in the middle of nowhere. The family she was with called for Grandfather. When he touched her, she saw an orange light radiate from his hand all through her. She felt as if he knew everything about her from the moment she was born. She seemed to pass out from bliss. When she woke up—her broken leg was healed and she felt great."

The group looked at Betty, disbelieving. "OK. You don't have to believe it. I didn't either, but maybe what Jeff and Mark said is true. Maybe some people can do things like that. Dr. Salkind repeated again and again that it's a miracle that we're allowed to go to the Meeting. She said, 'Expect your whole life to go crazy before you meet him; that's normal. Grandfather acts like a magnet and pulls out your shit.'" Betty rolled her eyes. The language these Berkeley types used, even *old* Berkeley types.

"But that's just what Jeff and Mark said, too. I know *my* life seems to have … taken a turn." Betty stopped in consternation.

Will frowned. Betty's research corroborated what Jeff and Mark said about supernatural abilities. It seemed to say these powers were used for healing. But *all* of them were benign? He looked at the red phone again. He didn't want to bring it, but he couldn't say no without appearing unpatriotic or, worse, getting the FBI on *his* tail. He knew that if he picked up that phone, the full might of the United States military would sweep down. They'd be saved, but his chance of getting what he wanted would be ruined. He couldn't get rid of the damn thing. If he attempted to dismantle it, it would be activated.

Betty was speaking again. Will sat up and listened.

"The last section in the brief gives some information on other big-wigs—and there are some big ones. First, there's a married couple, Tyler and Leona Brand." The brief contained a newspaper picture of a couple. He was a tall, gray-haired, craggy guy—serious and distinguished looking. She looked like a Joan Baez to Betty, but darker and taller. Betty wondered if any of the MBAs could remember Joan Baez. Betty never cared for her politics, but she sure could sing.

"Dr. Tyler Brand is a professor of religious studies at UC Santa Barbara. This must be the professor Jeff was referring to. Even his fellow professors don't know about his involvement with Grandfather. That's how secretive they are." She raised her eyebrows significantly. "He's the author of eleven books and is considered a leading authority on Native American religious beliefs—and Eastern religions, of all things. We have all of his books." Betty pointed to a bookshelf behind glass doors. "He's listed in *Who's Who in America*. His wife, Leona Brand, is just as high-powered. She's a mover on the Board of Supervisors in Santa Barbara County. She's expected to run for Congress in two years—and win.

"Then there's Paul Running Bird—"

"Our liaison?" asked Will.

"Yes. He's an executive at Microsoft," she flipped to Paul's pages in the brief, complete with an eight-by-ten full color, professional portrait and his resume. Paul's write-up on himself was three single-spaced pages, compared with the paragraph he'd provided for the others. "He sounds like an up-and-comer. If he vets out in person, I think we should hire him, Will. He's got all the credentials. I brought tons of employment applications."

"Fine. We'll hire him if he's as good as he seems. Is that everyone?"

"No. Two more very prominent people are invited—plus the four thousand others they expect to attend. Jesse Creed, PhD, is also one of Grandfather's followers ..."

"Jesse Creed!" Melissa exclaimed. "Oh, my God! He is fantastic. I have all of his books." The group looked at her. "He's the most amazing poet. They call him 'the most soulful man in America.' His next book is supposed to be a shoo-in for the Pulitzer."

"Well, he's on the guest list. Here's a picture of him," Betty flashed a studio shot of an intriguing-looking man with a narrow face. "It's a few years old, Paul Running Bird said. Dr. Creed is invited, but may not show. He's been awfully busy, Paul said. Teaching and writing his book.

"That's the cast of thousands—except for the thousands. Paul said they expect more than four thousand people to be there this year. I've covered the most prominent individuals, except for one. We'll have to be surprised by the rest." Betty looked at them, eyes twinkling. "There's one more person I want to 'introduce.' The most visible of Grandfather's people. Does anyone watch *Oprah*?" They looked at her blankly. None of them had ever watched the show, including Mark Kenna.

34

Putting the ugly horse under saddle took about an hour. Bud led him into the round pen with Paul Running Bird as guys clambered up the scaffolding around the pen so they could watch. Bud didn't notice the crowd; he was too intent upon teaching Paul.

"OK, Paul, you got him moving," Bud said, lobbing tips at Paul when he needed them. The horse was walking around the pen with Paul standing about eight feet away, moving in a smaller circle even with the animal's flank. Bud watched the horse like a predator, nodding his head in approval. That was a fine horse! Funny looking, but legs like nobody's business. Bud dropped his head and looked under the horse. Good. No one had cut him. Some idiot might look at his head and think he didn't deserve to keep his balls, but, boy, watching that horse move, and watching how he kept his eye on the two humans in the pen, Bud would never cut him. The horse never lost focus.

"Now, step back and see what happens," Bud said. As Paul did so, the horse swung into the center facing Paul, the way the broke horse he'd caught earlier had. The dun horse stood, ears pricked, body rigid. "Step back again," Bud whispered. Paul did and the horse dropped his head a bit and stepped forward.

Soon, Paul was touching him all over with a coiled lariat, then his hand. The next thing, the horse was saddled, and Paul was stepping up on the stirrup on either side. His getting onto the saddle followed that. The horse never once misbehaved. Paul was in awe of his own attainment, looking like he wanted to kiss himself, when Bud said, "Take him out of the pen, Paul. Ride him at a walk around the stable here. Make some big, wide turns. Go slow."

One of the horse masters approached Bud as Paul rode off. "You sure made that look easy, Bud," he said. Bud smiled his self-effacing smile.

"Grandfather did all the work. Didn't you see them talking out there in the field? Grandfather told that horse the whole story. All Paul had to do was fill in the blanks."

The guy's eyes widened as he realized what happened. Then he became apologetic, indicating something behind him. "Grandfather told me to say you only had to ride her this once. Just to decide what to do with her."

Bud looked up and saw another one of the horse masters approaching, leading—if you could call it that, the horse was jumping around so much— a flashy black-and-white mare. Oh, no! Squirrel Brains! Bud groaned. She broke Joey's leg last year! With Bert expecting, Bud couldn't afford to get busted up.

"Grandfather said that he'll heal you himself if you need it. He just wants you to try her." The other guy had almost reached them with the mare when Paul Running Bird, who was two hundred feet behind her, waved to someone. The mare sprang forward like a lion was on her tail and knocked over her handler. Bud reached out and caught her lead line as she ran past, marching the mare into the round pen before she had time to think. A dust cloud rose over the pen, and the pen's scaffolding gallery was soon jammed to capacity with people who wanted to see a real rodeo. Bud never swore once, but the words seemed to hang in the air.

Paul watched the scene as he circled the barnyard on his horse. Look at that, he thought. It was so typical. That mare was magnificent. She had a flashy coat, beautiful long neck, and the prettiest head he'd ever seen. And the way she pranced—so refined and spirited. Bud showed up at the Bowl once a year and got to ride that beautiful animal. He worked for the Meeting year after year, slaving away, and Grandfather gave *him* an ugly piece of crap. He kicked his horse out of spite. It leaped forward. He almost went off the animal's back end. Paul looked around. No one saw. The piece of garbage had more to it than he thought—he'd have to be careful.

In due time, Bud burst out of the round pen on the mare. If he wanted to be a good trainer, he would have made her go in and out of the gate until she walked out in control. But he didn't want to be on her. The mare was junk, pure and simple. Oh, she was pretty. She had pretty everything, except anything that mattered. She had no bone to speak of; her legs were matchsticks; she had long, long pasterns and itty-bitty feet. Worst—the mare had no mind.

Bud sighed—slowly, you didn't dare move on this horse or she'd spook—and looked over at Paul Running Bird. Boy, Grandfather sure gave him a good one—look at the bone on that old boy. Look at his feet, those tendons, that short back. That dun stud was a horse that would work until he was thirty—unless some jerk wrecked him. Bud would have traded places with Paul in a minute, except that Squirrelly Girly would kill Paul.

Just when he thought he was home free, Carl Redstone came roaring up in a golf cart. Squirrelly erupted, as Bud knew she would another hundred or so times that day.

"Grandfather wanted you to have this," Carl said holding up a large, heavily fringed buckskin pouch stuffed with something. Carl was so big that his approaching the mare would be a challenge by itself. The problem was exacerbated by the way the pouch's fringe flapped with every movement. It also smelled funny, like some of Grandfather's famous herb blends. The mare didn't like the smell. She jumped around so bad that Bud thought he'd have to get off and blindfold her before he could take Grandfather's pouch. Carl took care of that by reaching out and putting his hand flat on her neck. She sighed, dropped her head, and passed into bliss. Being a healer and warrior and healer came in handy. Carl was one of the best; he could tranquilize anything with a touch. Bud took the package and tied it to his saddle.

"Did Grandfather say what this was?" Bud asked.

"No."

"Did he say what I was to do with it?"

"He said to tell you that you'd know when it was time. He said when you saw what was in it, you'd know how to use it. Don't open it before then, and don't lose it." Carl took his hand off the mare and backed away. He was heading back to the camp before Squirrel Brains realized he was gone. Bud was mystified, but figured he'd find out about the pouch soon enough.

Bud, Paul, and Willy Fish headed out to find the lost billionaire. Willy's smile practically lit the desert, he was so proud of his mule. The animal moved forward with animation, its big ears pricked forward. People waved good-bye to the strange cavalcade, and the movement of a dozen arms made the pinto mare spin and snort. Bud swore silently. He'd already made his evaluation of her. She'd make a nice rug in someone's house. The guys yelled after him, "I hope you've got insurance, Bud!" Bud laughed and raised a hand to wave them off, and the mare tried to run away. This is going to be a long ride, he thought.

They proceeded across the desert, looking like the Three Stooges on horseback. Paul, leading on his dun stud, followed by Bud on Squirrel Brains, with Willy bringing up the rear.

Where could they be? Paul thought. He had estimated the Numenon crew's arrival around nine a.m. It had to be close to twelve by now. Paul looked around. They had circled the Bowl from the south and were on the flat desert to its west. Swarms of vehicles of every description approached the Bowl from the north. That was where the central pass deposited them. It was a straight shot through the pass, across the desert to the Bowl. Everyone unloaded their stuff in the Bowl, and then turned around and parked outside. How could the Numenon people possibly get lost? He'd faxed them a map.

Paul's heart grabbed. Had he made a mistake? He was busy when he drew the map—his office was hopping. He had become aware of a tendency he had to occasionally do things that might be interpreted by others who didn't know him well as possibly being counterproductive. He was proud of this insight. Grandfather always told them to watch their minds, saying that their greatest friend and greatest enemy lay in their own heads. Well, sometimes Paul did things that might lead to negative consequences for others—or

even for himself. He sometimes shot himself in the foot, if you wanted to
be judgmental. But he certainly didn't want the Numenon group to get
lost—they mattered more than anyone who had ever come to the Meeting.
Paul looked around. Where were they?

Bud scanned the horizon, sitting easily in the saddle. He relaxed and
went inside himself. The minute he did, his attention was drawn due west.
The corporate people were in the west. But why would they be there? That
southwestern canyon was a deathtrap; it was open and wide at first, but it
narrowed down after a while. If you were in it during a flash flood, that was
it. Kids used to go out there and party until two carloads of them drowned
one spring, right about now. If a storm came, a thirty-foot wall of water
could careen down those canyons in the blink of an eye. Why would the
Numenon people be out there? Bud knitted his brows. Paul sent them
directions. Surely he warned them?

Bud became aware of something as he rode. Grandfather's image was
plastered a foot from his face, like the old man was sitting on his horse's
head talking to him.

Bud, my son, I have work for you, Grandfather's voice rang in his ears,
audible only to him. Listen silently in your mind. Listen to Willy and Paul;
hear their minds. Tell me what you think of them. Tell me if they should be
spirit warriors. Bud's eyes widened. He'd never done anything like this
before. It is easy, my son. Think of me, like you are now. Pretend you are
connected to me—think a message to me about them. It doesn't matter if I
don't get it—we're just playing.

Grandfather gave more mentally transmitted orders: I want you to find
the Numenon people and bring them in. See what you can learn of them.
Send what you find to me with your mind. Tell me who is weak and who is
strong; what they brought with them, who will succeed this week. Send me
reports of them with your thoughts. We will talk when you return and see
how much I understood.

Bud wheeled Squirrel Brains and headed her straight west. "Let's try
over here." He felt as if he and Grandfather were connected with a phone
line and the old man could hear everything he thought. Bud knew Wesley
could do things like this; and he himself could read people's minds at the

end of the Meeting when he was within sight of them, but not like this, at a distance.

It's time, my son, Grandfather's voice spoke softly in his mind. Time for you to become who you are.

35

Did anyone read *People* magazine in February?" Betty got blank looks. "We're culturally deprived. We're probably the only people in the United States who don't watch *Oprah* or read *People*. Well, the most illustrious member of Grandfather's entourage has starred on both. Dr. Elizabeth Bright Eagle was on *Oprah* twice, the second time a few weeks ago. She just won *People's* Woman of the Year award, edging out Mother Teresa." They chuckled.

"She's a one-woman social welfare machine. A graduate of Stanford Medical School and on the medical school teaching staff, she has a private practice on Welch Road in Palo Alto. When she's not tending to those, she travels to the reservations, trying to address her people's health needs. She picked up a master's in public health along the way. The woman is amazing. I have a tape of her appearing a few places. Do you want to see it?" They nodded. The group was getting tired from the barrage of information and needed a change of pace.

"This will perk you up. Mark, could you lower the window shades so we can see the screen?" Betty picked up a hand control and pushed some buttons. A screen dropped from the ceiling in front of the wall of cabinets holding the computers and opposite the seating U. "I'm going to start the tape without any introduction. You'll know where she is."

Images were projected on the screen. In seconds, they knew where the film was taped. The United States Senate Chamber. The elegant, imposing room, rife with history, was well known to Numenon's top people. Most of them had been there, either testifying—Will, mostly—or serving as backup staff. It was never a fun place to speak. An imposing Indian woman was in the hot seat. She was heavyset, but beautiful all the same. She had perfect, ramrod-straight posture; her steel gray hair was bound in a neat bun at the nape of her neck. She wore a black velvet shirt, silver earrings, and a small squash-blossom necklace. She could have come from a Gorman painting. No one recognized her, but they knew that she dominated the Senate like nobody they'd seen. The room belonged to her.

"The United States government created my People's poverty." She spoke with calm authority. "As if being massacred and forced onto reservations wasn't enough, the United States government *managed* us to death. The General Allotment Act of 1887, the Indian Reorganization Act of 1934, and the Termination Policy of 1953, systematically reduced us ..." She summarized the legislation and what it did.

"My People lost 63 percent of their land. We became the poorest ethnic group in the United States by a long shot, engineered by legislation and the way it was managed." The word "managed" hit the professionals hard, Will harder than the rest. Management was his god.

"Because of the corruption and stupidity of the Bureau of Indian Affairs, we were able to keep the *worst* land. Even though everyone could see what was happening, the plunder of our land and resources continued for years ..."

The people in the *Ashley* watched, rapt. Her impact was amazing. She sat still and poised, with her face grave, and her voice level. In the corporate world, none of them had seen such a powerful woman.

"Unprecedented numbers of Native Americans served in World War II. We were rewarded with the Termination Policy of 1953. That act dissolved the state of being an Indian. What did this mean?

"Consider the Menominees, a Wisconsin tribe with a good logging and lumber business. They were bullied into terminating in 1961. They turned from a tribe into a corporation. The members became shareholders; the reservation became a county. They owned a county that they could not mortgage;

their corporation was supervised by local non-Indian businessmen; and
most of their trust fund's shares were controlled by white bankers."

Will blanched. "Is that possible?" he asked Betty. "It sounds illegal."
She stopped the tape.

"What she says is true, Will. Read your brief when you get time. Wait
until you find out about the Indian school system. It ripped families apart
for more than fifty years. Can you imagine anyone taking *our* children
away? Listen to the rest..." Betty hit play.

"If some of the tribes have trouble governing themselves, it's because
of the 'modeling' they've received for four hundred years. A few examples?
The Bureau of Indian Affairs negotiated mineral and oil leases at flat rates
instead of percentage royalties. Navajos got ten or fifteen *cents* per ton for
their coal, while the market price rose from two *dollars* a ton in the fifties
to *twenty dollars* in the eighties—"

"What! They got fifteen *cents* when the market price was twenty
dollars!" Will barked. This was sacrilege. On the screen, the doctor kept
speaking.

"The BIA *lost* two *billion* dollars in tribal trust funds... Just couldn't
find it... So sorry."

"What is she talking about?" Will leaned forward in consternation.
Betty stopped the tape while he spoke. "That isn't how the government works.
They diddle money away all the time, but not like that. Powerful congressmen
ram billions into pork-barrel legislation. They stick into upcoming legislation a billion or *four* for some stupid thing their constituents want. Congress
has to pass the whole bill to get the part they want into law. The pork barrel
money isn't subject to control or rational analysis. But the government
doesn't just *lose* money. It wastes it, hides it, or subcontracts it to some asshole
who couldn't keep track of his socks."

"They don't *lose* money. Do they?" Will looked around the cabin, panic
on his face.

"I don't know, Will. Let's listen to the rest." She restarted the tape and
Dr. Bright Eagle's image began speaking.

"One tribe formed a delegation to protest legislation that would have
destroyed their livelihood. Their superintendent ordered them back to the
reservation. Another tribe was prevented from hiring lawyers to defend..."

"They couldn't hire lawyers! Couldn't protect their livelihood!" Will erupted again. "What is this? I know what happened to the Indians, the massacres and all that. But this is really bad. Everyone should be able to hire lawyers! The Indians were exercising their rights as property owners!" Will looked horrified. "This is anti-American. Everyone has the right to engage in commerce and the right to own property. What she's saying is against capitalism." He kept emoting.

"The government *lost* two billion dollars? Christ! I'd lose Numenon if I did that. How could that happen? Where were the checks and balances? The control?"

Betty paused the tape, hoping it wasn't too much. She knew what Will could do if he became too upset. What Dr. Bright Eagle was saying struck his core values. Regardless of Will's reaction, everyone needed to know this before they got to the Meeting. She started the tape again.

An ancient senator whose social philosophy had been formed almost a century before and who was famous for his sexist and racist views spoke. "Didn't we give you those casinos to make up for that nastiness so long ago? Aren't y'all living in fat city these days?" He never did say, "little lady," but the words were there, hiding behind his drawl.

Dr. Bright Eagle sat a bit straighter. She looked at him and softly spoke a few words in a foreign language before answering.

"What did you say?" the senator blustered. "We can't have any blasphemy here."

The doctor cracked a tiny smile. "I said, '*What goes around, comes around*,' in my language." A look of not entirely friendly amusement appeared on her face before she spoke again. Her words were like bullets. "You didn't *give* us the casinos. My people worked hard and long to get them, using the governmental system skillfully and lawfully. The citizens of gaming states have passed—and continue to pass—legislation to enable us to create and expand our casinos and associated businesses. In most cases, the population at large has overwhelmingly supported Indian independence, which our casinos can provide."

"Well, why are you talking about your medical problems, an' social problems? Poverty. I thought y'all were eatin' high off the hog." "Little lady" always hovered behind his words.

"Some of our People wanted to keep their traditional cultures and values, and didn't want the challenges that the casinos posed. These tribes chose not to participate in the activities permitted under the Indian Gaming Regulatory Act of 1988. So, while they may be culturally rich, some of our Nations remain economically poor.

"The casinos do not benefit equally all the tribes that have them. Those located in wealthy, urban areas can do very well. My Nation's land is in eastern Oregon. We don't have a casino; there's no one out there to go to one.

"Casinos haven't made all of us rich, Senator, only *some*. They've done nothing to address social problems resulting from four hundred years of mismanagement, genocide, and discrimination ..." Her gaze was like a laser, moving from one senator to another, spending plenty of time aimed directly at the camera. The people in the *Ashley* pulled away from the screen, she was so powerful.

Betty stopped the tape. "She's living proof they're not all drunken losers living off casino earnings."

Gil looked intrigued. "What was the date of that Senate hearing?"

Betty consulted her notebook. "September ninth, last fall."

"That old senator died two days after that tape was made."

"How do you know?"

"It was headline news, and I remember things like that." Seeing the perplexed looks, he clarified, "People of color remember it when guys like that die."

Betty was surprised; she always thought of Gil as one of the gang. That he was Asian didn't occur to her.

"I wonder what she really said to him," Gil mused.

36

Grandfather had gotten away with it all morning; all he had to do was finish the week and his secret would be safe. He smiled as he drove the golf cart up the switchbacks to the Bowl from the horse area, waving to everyone. No one noticed when he called all the People to him earlier. They'd never formed a line to talk to him. Before, he'd always gone around to greet everyone. No one spotted the fact that his left leg didn't work so well, that he'd lost weight, or even that he was taking a cart. The old man jammed the pedal down and it roared off. He liked this cart.

Thousands were there already, setting up camp. His eyes scanned the Bowl. He saw a huge, brand-new tent going up by the headquarters. Next to it, a truck pulling a horse trailer was being unloaded by a swarm of people. Grandfather's eyes narrowed. Elizabeth Bright Eagle had arrived. That was her hospital tent. Roxy Crow Moon, Elizabeth's student nurse and Bert Creeman's sister, had brought a load of supplies in her horse trailer.

Grandfather couldn't figure out why Elizabeth brought all that stuff. She could heal anything with her hands; she could do anything one of those X-ray machines could with them too. Elizabeth usually did her teaching and gave people shots and exams at the Meeting, but not this year. Grandfather had arranged for other doctors to do her work. He assigned her to take care of the spirit warriors and the Numenon crew; that was all. She didn't like it. But Grandfather was still the boss, he still knew a *little* more than she did.

She turned around and looked at him. She could feel his presence without being told he was there. Fooling her would be hard. Well, might as well face the tiger. Grandfather drove the cart toward her. She could hardly work for the people clustered around her.

"Oh, Elizabeth, we saw you on *Oprah!*" Faces glowed at the doctor like she was God herself. A half dozen proffered back issues of *People* magazine with Elizabeth's picture on the cover. "Would you sign this?" She smiled and signed.

When he stopped, the crowd that inevitably followed him merged with the crowd surrounding Elizabeth. He hid behind the people, admiring her. He loved every student, but this Bright Eagle—he knew how she would soar from the moment he first saw her, more than thirty years ago. She was a sad young girl, crying in the back of a Berkeley church. He knew what she would be even then. Grandfather was as proud of the doctor as he would be if she were his daughter.

Trying to avoid people, he inched forward. Elizabeth looked up when he was twenty feet away. She smiled at him, her smile blinding as always. Then she froze. She stared at him, the warmth fading from her face. Damn it!—he couldn't fool her. She launched at him through the human sea.

As he stepped off the cart to greet her, his left leg buckled. It was nothing, nothing at all. Someone grabbed him and set him on his feet before he hit the ground. Elizabeth was there, face ashen. She reached out to put her hand on his throat—the hand that could heal broken bones in an instant—and knew everything.

Grandfather reared back like the lion he was and turned on his heel, walking a short distance from the crowd. She followed him, people surging after them, but he stopped them with a raised hand. Smiling reassuringly, Grandfather maneuvered Elizabeth so that her back was to the group.

Bright Eagle! His voice ripped into her mind; outwardly, he was silent. *You are a warrior! You will reveal nothing! Nothing!* Elizabeth placed one hand on Grandfather's throat, the other on his heart. The lion's voice roared to her soul, *Smile! Act as though you are happy!*

"He's healthier than last year. How you do it, Joseph, I'll never know!" Elizabeth heard her voice speaking cheerfully.

The onlookers drew an easy breath. They knew that Elizabeth could find any illness with those hands, and heal almost all of them. Grandfather was fine, even though he seemed thinner this year, because she proclaimed it.

She fought down panic as the lion spoke to her again. *I will not have what happened before. I will not have it. Do you remember?*

She did. When Grandfather had his heart attack five years earlier, Elizabeth had him airlifted to a hospital in Las Cruces. When the People heard what happened, they followed him to the hospital, camping in the parking lot. When he was stabilized, she transferred him to Stanford Hospital, where she could care for him. They followed all the way, filling the big court in front of the hospital, camping everywhere. Crying in the lobbies and corridors. Her house had so many people staying in it, she had to go to a motel. They refused to keep the hospital's visiting hours, jamming the place with humanity. People thought he was dying and went crazy. It was a horrible mess.

I will not have the fuss, Bright Eagle. It is nothing that an old Indian should die. That's all I'm doing, Bright Eagle, just dying.

Elizabeth smiled brightly, nodding as though Grandfather was talking to her with spoken words. His voice bored into her mind.

There is time, Bright Eagle. I have three or four months. You will stay with me a week—after this Meeting is over. We will say what we need to say then. Now, no one must know.

Grandfather smiled at her and addressed the crowd, "This year, Bright Eagle will be lazy. She will not work so hard. You will help me. You will go to the other doctors. You let her go hike now—go, Bright Eagle. The others will set up your tent. Go now, say hello to the desert." He shooed her off. Elizabeth left, too shocked to protest.

She knew the real reason this was the last Meeting. Elizabeth half-ran to the Bowl's rim and followed it past his lean-to. Out of sight of the lean-to and the people, Elizabeth stumbled along the Rim, not seeing, not hearing her own sobs. "Oh ... God, oh, God—it's not true!" She walked out to the end of one of the fingers projecting into the Badlands, and faced the desert.

Yet, she knew it *was* true. Her hands were never wrong. The arteriosclerosis was massive. His heart was shot. The arteries in his head were blocked, not just the major ones—she could unplug those, but also the tiny little capillaries that she couldn't reach. The blood flow to his brain was blocked; he was having a small stroke as she touched him. Her teacher and dearest friend, the person who was her whole family—the person she had loved so much—*Joseph* was dying.

Four months. He didn't have *four* months! If he had two, that would be a miracle. She slid onto the ground, holding her knees to her chest, her feelings rising out of control. She thrashed from side to side. How would she live if Grandfather died?

Dr. Elizabeth Bright Eagle, *People*'s Woman of the Year, star guest of *Oprah*, Congressional hearings and political battles, began to dissolve. Cracks appeared, hunks broke off. She could have kept herself together that week, before she knew that Joseph was leaving her.

37

D o you want to see more of Dr. Bright Eagle?" Everyone did. Betty
started the tape again.

This time, a TV chat show set appeared on the screen, with
the lacquer-faced presenter smiling in the middle of it. "I'm excited to welcome
today's guest, Dr. Elizabeth Bright Eagle." He clapped while a heavy-set
woman walked to her seat next to him. Seeing her walking showed that
Elizabeth was *big*, but moved easily and gracefully with a warrior's carriage.
Her gray hair was in a bun, as before. This time she wore a tiered, burgundy
velvet skirt and matching silk blouse and silver earrings, and a massive
silver concho belt. She looked even more like a painting.

The presenter was astute and lively; the doctor, serious and dignified.
She took over the show in two minutes. The camera seemed to have no
choice but to rest on her. She gave a straightforward explanation of the
health problems on the reservations as well as the problems associated with
poverty, isolation, and lack of hope.

"She covered this in the Senate Chamber," Betty said, hitting the fast-
forward button.

Will watched the screen as Betty fast-forwarded. A few clips of the
doctor and her staff on various reservations came and went. Dr. Bright Eagle

mesmerized him. Even on fast-forward, she was very still. Her hands moved, but she was like a mountain. Elizabeth Bright Eagle could have been the center of the universe. She transfixed him; she was beautiful and Will Duane loved beautiful women.

Betty slowed the tape. "Watch this." Dr. Bright Eagle was focused on the presenter, who said, "We had so much fun putting together information on you that we decided to go back in time." The orchestra trilled as he proclaimed:

"This is your life—Dr. Elizabeth Bright Eagle!"

A thin, dark man in a western suit limped onto the stage. The doctor reacted instantly. She couldn't have been more different from the somber creature she'd been. "*Vic!*" she exclaimed. "*Vic Norton!*" She got up, grasping his shoulders and looking into his eyes, then hugged him as though he were her dearest old friend.

Subtitles along the bottom of the screen read: Vic Norton, Dr. Bright Eagle's team roping partner.

The host spoke with him, "I understand you and Elizabeth participated in rodeos together in the sixties?"

Vic nodded, "Yeah, we sure did. Elizabeth was the best team roper in the state. The only thing she could do better than rope was ride. Well, she could shoot better'n both of 'em. She had a sharp shooting and trick riding act that you can't see anymore."

The presenter went on, "Here comes..." More and more people came out, each greeting Elizabeth with tears. One thing was obvious—people *loved* Elizabeth Bright Eagle. Family followed.

"Join me in greeting the Lewis family of Remedy, Oregon. They've lived on their ranch in the Bonheur Basin since time began!" The crowd cheered as an adorable, tiny, old Indian woman and her equally old but tall and gaunt husband hobbled on, followed by an entire tribe of relatives. Elizabeth's family. Will teared up seeing them. They were so real. This was *America* on stage.

"Here's Dr. Charlie Lewis, straight from Johns Hopkins Medical School where he teaches. Dr. Lewis is Dr. Bright Eagle's older son..." After the applause, the host explained, "We tried to get your younger son, Dr. Sam Lewis, but he was unreachable in the wilds of Nepal. Doing post-doctoral work, folks! Dr. Bright Eagle has two smart kids!"

When all the people settled in their places and the rumpus died down, a tiny little girl toddled forward with a bouquet. "Gammie!" she cooed, handing her grandmother the flowers. Elizabeth took them and put the child on her lap. The Numenon crew sat in awe. She had a high-achieving family and *grandchildren.* Will's jaw dropped. He wanted grandchildren more than anything.

"Here comes the good part," Betty announced. The presenter was quieting the tumultuous applause.

"Would you like to see what Dr. Bright Eagle does best?" The crowd went crazy again. A big screen lit up. He turned to Elizabeth and said, "We've seen how you work; some of your friends thought the world should see how you play."

A beautifully edited tape played on a screen on one side of the stage. It was made up of old 8 mm film, home video clips; you name it. The tape filled the screen, starting with black-and-white footage, which must have been from the early sixties. A much younger, thinner Elizabeth stood by a horse. In one motion, she was on the horse and it was barreling down the middle of an arena. The camera caught her pulling herself up to standing, and piloting the horse around the arena while standing behind the saddle with her arms outstretched. She pulled a pistol from her holster, then stood upright on the loping horse. She fired at a series of targets on the unoccupied side of the stands.

After that, the film moved forward through time rapidly. Toward the end, her shooting style appeared to be controlled mayhem. The Numenon crowd watched with pounding hearts as gunshots rang in their ears. In what proved to be the last segment, Elizabeth Bright Eagle wore a caped coat almost to her ankles. She was in a dusky field surrounded by huge evergreen trees. Fog wafted through the upright trunks and over the scene—*spooky* didn't come close to describing the setting. Two person-shaped targets were set up next to each other at the end of the field. The camera panned on Elizabeth's face. The look in her eyes was terrifying. They expected the screen to burst into flames with her intensity.

Elizabeth pulled her coat back over her hips, exposing twin pistols. They were big, like antique guns from the movies. Before anyone could blink, the guns were in Elizabeth's hands and blazing. She walked forward, shooting at the targets, advancing steadily. When the guns ran out of ammunition, men on the sidelines threw her new ones. She caught them without looking up and kept blazing. The most frightening angles showed Elizabeth from dead ahead, shooting, shooting, shooting. Her face was terrible. The woman was a killer. The reports echoed around the *Ashley's* cabin. The last scene showed the targets. Their centers were gone. There were no misses.

After the film, the TV show's camera focused on Elizabeth. She obviously did not like her martial abilities being shown in public. Elizabeth composed herself, her face transforming from avenging goddess to superdoc in a second. Looking directly into the camera, Dr. Bright Eagle said, "Now my patients will know—when I say 'stop smoking,' I mean it. When I say, 'lay off the booze,' I mean it. When I *say* what I *say*, I *mean* it." The woman was terrifying. The tape stopped.

The Numenon cabin was silent. They stared at the screen.

"What is she, Will? A one-woman army?" Gil said.

Will shook his head, thinking of the research he'd done that he wouldn't be reporting to the group. Seeing Elizabeth Bright Eagle shoot, he had no doubt that Grandfather maintained a secret militia. The question was not were there more like that where they were heading. The question was: how many more?

He looked back at the screen, hoping to see more of that terrifyingly attractive doctor. She was a success in everything. She was beautiful. Her kids turned out great. She had grandchildren. He thought of Dr. Bright Eagle with longing. Not one word had been said about a husband or partner. No, that was foolish. He would be alone the rest of his life; he couldn't have a partner. And the woman was a killer.

"I don't know what she is, Gil. Do you have any more about this holy man and his people?" Will's voice was as sharp as his eyes.

38

He'd awakened barely in time to get to the wedding cave at ten as Grandfather asked. Looking at his ruined side when he got out of bed, Wes could see that what Grandfather had done earlier had helped. His bruises were fading and he could move more easily. But not painlessly. Carefully putting on his jeans for the ten-minute walk, he saw his tent was set up next to Grandfather's lean-to and that his truck was gone. Someone had helped him out.

Wes was still shaky from the emotion of the early morning. His eyes teared a bit as he saw his tent so close to Grandfather's; he would be next to the old man for the rest of his life. He touched his cheek with his hand, noticing both that his face hurt less and that his hands were soft. There was an instant's response time as he remembered, and his body stiffened. A surge of sexual energy passed through him. Celibacy hadn't been hard for Wes, not until the last six months. Now, the craving for sex was almost unbearable.

He walked down the switchbacks behind the Bowl to the cave, nodding as he passed his fellow spirit warriors. They carefully guarded Grandfather's most private healing space. The cave was also used as a marital cave. He smiled. Hopefully he'd be there soon for his wedding night. The cave was accessible from the plain behind Grandfather's lean-to, carved by nature into the rock cliff marking the back end of the Bowl. Its entrance was well hidden in the maze of blind canyons. While the Bowl was open and welcoming, much of the world behind it was closed and frightening. Unless you knew its secrets. One of its secrets was a series of hot mineral springs used by the People, and the reason no one worried about water—they had plenty of fresh water that the water truck took around every day. Sitting in the baths was one of the most satisfying parts of the retreat. Wes frowned. He hoped the outsiders wouldn't be told about the springs.

Wesley loved this area. He was a master tracker and liked hunting in obscurity as well as in light. In the lowlands, the colors were darker and murky. Burgundy, brown, and black. Muted sounds echoed. Clear vistas existed only away from the Bowl to the west and from the pastures where the horses were kept. Close to the Bowl, enormous tormented rocks loomed overhead. Miles-long passages could lead the unwary to their doom.

He took a deep breath and sighed as he entered the cave. The cave's primal quality soothed his soul. It had a hide fastened over the opening for privacy. The cave burrowed deep under the Mogollon Bowl, merely one exit from a subterranean maze. Natural air holes pierced its vast interior, keeping the air fresh. An underground mineral hot spring existed beyond the healing area; air holes provided some light there. This was a wonderful honeymoon chamber.

The healing room where Wes stood had low shelves holding Grandfather's supplies: herbs, jars, and bottles of unknown substances. A mortar and pestle. Stone bowls and implements. A primitive stone table and benches and a mattress covered with a quilt were the only other furnishings. Kerosene lamps—an innovation Grandfather had permitted in lieu of the traditional torches—ringed the cave, providing dim light. Lamps illuminated petroglyphs—ancient cave paintings—covering most of the wall surface. Their topics showed that the cave had been used for healing—and lovemaking—for thousands of years.

Looking at the drawings and shivering, Wesley took off his clothes. How many days until he would be here with his bride? Soul mates were often married the same day they met. A chant was scheduled for tonight. He would make the rounds, and if his future wife was at the Meeting, he would find her … perhaps tomorrow night they would sleep here? He lay on the bed and covered himself with a sheet and quilt—another change. Grandfather always used to use buffalo hides. Wes put himself into a trance state, awaiting Grandfather's arrival.

Some time later, the shaman entered. He looked at Wesley lying relaxed on the bed. Grandfather was about to do what he liked best—heal. Others had created the Movement and built up a big hype about him. Called him the greatest healer ever, created this overblown Meeting with thousands of people coming to see him. He thought it absurd. He was a healer and teacher. That's all he ever wanted to do. He'd rather be in his hogan a few miles away, singing to Creator by himself than at this Meeting. Even though some of his true friends came here, the old man knew everything he did would be watched and criticized. Yet, if he helped one person, it would be worthwhile.

If those circulating the rumors saw what he was about to do, the Movement would be over in the time it took to whisper, *"Did you see ...?"* Good, he thought, I never wanted it.

Grandfather puttered happily among his pots and supplies, selecting a number of herbs and gourds full of liquid. He sat next to Wes, removed the quilt and said quietly, "I'm here, my son." The massive bruises Wes had sustained were visible in the dim light. Grandfather burned several herbs, passing them over Wes's body while chanting. He set them next to the young man and carefully rubbed a strong smelling liniment into the bruises. "All right, my son, we will begin."

The old man ran his hands over Wes's body about five inches above the skin. He appeared to be listening as he did so. Ah! he thought. The energy is blocked here ... and here. He could feel the functioning of Wes's organs, the strength of his life force, the progress or status of any disease. And he could tell the extent of the injuries inflicted upon him. The shaman plunged in without hesitation, sinking his hands directly into Wes's body. He mended two broken ribs, healing traumatized internal tissues and bones. He simply wiped away the blue-black bruises and all the pain. When he was done, Wesley looked like he'd never been hurt. Grandfather smiled and looked around; he knew the source of his power. He couldn't always heal this completely. The Great One wanted this boy healed fast. He must have important work to do this week.

Now the hard part, thought Grandfather. "Let me in, Wes," he said softly. Wes had been stoical throughout, now he winced. "I know it hurts, my son, but I must do it." He touched Wes's breastbone with one hand, putting the other hand below his navel. He lightly wiggled the hand on his chest. Immediately, it sank within Wes's flesh. Grandfather could see his heart clearly. Ah! There it is, he thought, taking a deep breath. It's grown so much since last time. He could see a soft black mass around Wes's heart, intertwining with it, choking it. Killing him. As he'd done every time they'd met for the last four years, he reduced the mass, pulling and cutting pieces away. He worked for some time, loosening tendrils and stubborn shoots of the main growth, putting the refuse in a stone bowl. When he was done he said, "Wes, it's growing faster; you'll have to be treated more often. But you can survive, my son, and live a good life." With that, he withdrew his hands from Wes's heart and placed them softly on his chest and abdomen.

When he had discovered the black mass in his beloved Wesley, Grandfather had grieved. The boy was afflicted with a dreadful disease, a crippling, deadly illness, an invisible killer. Wesley Silverhorse was a victim of depression. Whether he inherited it or it was caused by the trauma of his father's death or as a result of his struggle to survive, Wes was hard hit by it. Far different from healthy sadness, Wes's depression mixed self-doubt, inability to feel pleasure in life, and a sense of worthlessness. He was a potential suicide, which only he and Grandfather knew. He did crazy, wild stuff to cover the pain eating at him. Riding bulls, for one. Yet with all this, Wes Silverhorse remained the most dedicated spirit warrior.

Grandfather was glad Wes had finally been willing to let him direct his life. Now he had a chance. The shaman glanced toward the hide covering the cave's entrance. He was going to do what had started and fueled the rumors. He was going to give Wesley pleasure. With his hands on the young man's torso, Grandfather began to let his energy run into Wes. Wes reacted immediately; his body convulsed. "Relax. It's all right." Grandfather did this with very few of them anymore. Only with the very discreet and with those who needed it. Until his life and depression stabilized, Wesley needed it badly.

Only energy passed between them. Wes allowed Grandfather into the deepest reaches of his mind, soul, and body. After several minutes, he raised his head and looked at the shaman, eyes deep and dark. He was breathing heavily. "Let it happen," said Grandfather. A cloud of sexual energy flew from Wesley's belly, filling the space and drizzling on them like a fog. Wesley lay back. "It's all right, Wes. Let it go." This happened twice more. After that, pure, sweet energy flowed up Wesley's spine and between him and his healer. At the end, Wesley was limp, and all his energy passages were opened. His energy was flowing; he could feel and enjoy life.

Grandfather carefully withdrew his hands. He stroked Wesley's head and smiled at him. "Are you OK? Do your practices every day? Chant? Have you been doing this?" Grandfather knew he hadn't. "You must, Wes; you'll get sick if you don't. You know that." The old man lit herbs over the material he had removed from Wesley's heart. Dropping the herbs on the mass, it burned quickly. "When you're married, Wes, I'll teach your wife to do what we just did with you. It's more important than sex for you."

Wes dressed while Grandfather put his herbs away. He had an open, deep-eyed look, like people have after powerful spiritual experiences or very good sex. Grandfather opened his arms and hugged him. Their hearts merged. They looked at each other as, as close as two human beings can be. "Go to my lean-to now, Wesley, and sleep. You need rest."

He thought for a second, and then said, "Do you think you'll be up to doing a horsemanship and martial arts demonstration at four?"

"I should be."

"Good. I want you to do one for Will Duane and the people from Numenon." Wesley recoiled, then nodded—he'd never turn Grandfather down. "I want you to give a show like you've never given. Show them everything, except those things that are only for you and me." Wes's eyes widened. "Yes. Wes. Work as though your life depended upon it." Grandfather knew it did depend upon it.

Before he could object, Grandfather gave him a special touch that induced sleep. "You have time to get back to my lean-to, my son, before falling asleep. Leave now." Wesley did. Grandfather watched him go. He knew Wes would have never been able to sleep if he knew he was to perform before whites. The young man wasn't exactly prejudiced. He simply had very good reasons not to trust white people.

As Wes walked back to the lean-to, his face bore a soft-focused smile. He had that deeply relaxed, loose-jointed way of walking usually seen on honeymooners. Wes felt very good. Last night, he was so hurt he could hardly move. Today, he'd be doing a strenuous demonstration in a few hours. His depression was gone. Grandfather had worked a miracle. He threw off his clothes and climbed under the buffalo robe. That's all he remembered, sleep took him so fast.

39

I've been sitting on this next bit of information primarily because I didn't know what to do with it." Betty's mouth was tight and her posture rigid. "Paul Running Bird faxed this to me just before I left last night. You won't find it in your briefs." She held up a sheet of paper. "He said he'd forgotten to mention it. I can certainly see why!

"I couldn't sleep because of this." Betty drew a deep breath. "Apparently, a large number of people get married at the Meeting. Grandfather is fully qualified to marry people—he's an ordained minister, a justice of the peace, and a Native holy man. The marriages are perfectly legal and recorded on the reservation." The group's faces were blank when they heard the news. This changed as what she'd said began to register.

"We'll get *married* this week?" Gil asked, incredulous. "I'm already married.

"Well, I assume that people who are already married are exempt. But listen to this," she looked at Paul's fax, before speaking. "The people who marry are not just those who've known each other for a long time. Often, they're people who meet at the Meeting. *That* year." She looked up. Their faces mirrored her consternation. "That's why we had to take those blood tests—in case some of us get married."

"Betty, that's ridiculous," Will said.

"I think so, too. But Paul spells it out in great detail. Grandfather checks out each couple for suitability before tying the knot. Not only that, but none of the marriages blessed by Grandfather have ended in divorce. All of them, hundreds, maybe thousands, of these marriages have lasted. Marriages between *strangers*!" Betty's mouth compressed tighter.

"It occurred to me that some of us, might be affected by this ... *mania* or whatever it is." Betty looked at her boss. "Will, we need a policy on this. This affects corporate functioning. You're the one to set the policy. Do you have a position on this marriage thing?"

"Pretty near any position will work, Betty." He smiled broadly, a smirk, really.

The group laughed, looking at each other nervously. Will's tone was unsettling. Despite their boss's reputation as a Lothario, he didn't operate on the job. Sex on Numenon property or between employees was verboten, just like drugs and alcohol. His policy on sex didn't hold up in practice any better than it did with the other things. It did restrain Will. Whatever he might indulge in elsewhere, he didn't do it with anyone from Numenon headquarters. (Except for Doug. Will's womanizing romps with his younger sidekick were the stuff of legend.) Those who had been at Numenon long enough—Betty—knew that that woman's successful lawsuit years ago had knocked the on-the-job sexuality out of Will. Why was he smiling like that? The rest of them began grinning. His ribald attitude was contagious.

"Will, this is serious. And I don't get it. This is a spiritual retreat. Why should people be getting married frantically? And going off to," her expression indicated that Will's attitude had not rubbed off on Betty, "do things in *caves*. Grandfather won't allow the newlyweds to remain in the campgrounds for fear of disturbing others. The ensuing activity is apparently ... um ... *memorable*." Paul's fax had been characteristically comprehensive. "Will, we need a policy on this. This is not something I expected when I was getting ready for this trip." She laid her hand next to her untouched sandwich. Sandy had dashed around giving them lunch after the video.

"I don't understand. Why all this sex, when sex is forbidden? And marriages between virtual strangers. At a holy site and a spiritual retreat?" A tense silence settled on the group, until Mark broke it.

"Have you ever heard of tantric yoga, Betty?" He didn't ask permission to speak or use the microphone this time.

"No."

"Jeff talked about yogic energy and its awakening. In people who are dedicated to a spiritual life, people with committed spiritual practices and awakened kundalini, the energy moves *up* the spinal column, creating visions and spiritual experiences as it goes. It purifies them at higher and higher levels. In regular people, or people not so disciplined and pure, the energy goes down."

"Down? What do you mean?"

"To the sexual organs."

Betty gasped. "What do you mean?"

"The energy becomes sexualized. It can also become sexualized in spiritual people—not all of those dedicated to God are celibate. Many are married and have families. Our spiritual ancestors knew all about this. Masters taught their disciples how to control the energy and direct it upward if they weren't married or how to incorporate it in their sexual lives if they were." Mark spoke quickly, effectively keeping Betty from cutting in. "In addition to all the types of yoga Jeff talked about, the old yogis also taught about the yoga of sexuality, tantric yoga. People practice it all the time. You can find tantric yoga workshops in every good-sized town in this country. All over the world, for that matter."

"Are we going to some kind of orgy?"

"No. You read the Rules. Everyone got copies of them. This is a very chaste event."

"Except for the newlyweds."

"Yes. Who are married people."

"Who might have just met each other!"

"How many of those marriages fail?"

"None."

"That's because they're soul mates."

Betty scoffed. "That is a fairy tale. Everyone has that fantasy. A love written in the stars exists somewhere—all you have to do is find him or her. Industries exist because of that ridiculous myth: romance novels, movies."

"It's not a myth. Neither is tantric yoga. If you've experienced it, you *know*." The certainty in Mark's voice silenced them. He also became still, remembering.

The first time, they were in his dome with just a few candles warming the darkness. Outside, the wind brushed the redwoods. It sounded like a fairy godmother whispering, "Hush, hush." They sat on his bed, Brooke astride him. He could feel himself deep inside her. She wrapped him with her legs, and pulled him close. "Just let it happen," she said. She was the one who practiced yoga. She had a guru and had meditated for years. Her chest rose and fell with his, their warmth intermingling. "Don't move," she said. "Or just enough to stay hard."

Time slowed. All he could feel was her. He knew she was wonderful, but not like this. Not the silkiness and softness. Something came from her, something good. He couldn't name it; it just came from her, like a wave. A gentle pulse from her heart to his, and then back again, from him to her. He kept breathing with her. Something rose inside him, from the small of his back, from his butt. It rose up. All Jeff's talk about his guru and kundalini couldn't have prepared him for the sensation. It was like a fire hose was attached to the base of his spine. Something too powerful to stop erupted inside. His back arched and a guttural sound burst from him. Brooke groaned, too, and moved around him.

"Like Shiva and Shakti," she whispered. Shiva was one of the Hindu trinity, the god in charge of destruction. Shiva swept what didn't need to be into nonexistence—so something new could take its place. Shiva was associated with procreation, because of the creative surge that follows removal of the unnecessary. Shakti was his consort. Brooke had taught him that much about yoga. This was their favorite position, the god and goddess.

Then it got wild. The room changed, it was like a different place, barely related to normal reality. Something arose from them. A blue tube. *Tube* was the only way to describe it, but that didn't really fit. It was powder blue light. He could see through it like billowing smoke, but it was a cylinder. It came out of them, from down there where they touched, and rose. It rose to the dome's ceiling, and began to move around, all over the room. Undulating. Spiraling. Wrapping around and touching both of them.

He rocked back and groaned. Nothing was like this. It was like meditating. They were in an altered state, but it was more real than reality. And wonderful. It was physical and spiritual pleasure at once, and he was with *Brooke*. He flew, the blue thing banged around them, and Brooke surrounded him. And both of them flew. Puffs of this blue stuff came out his heart and went into hers. All night long, all night. They finally fell in a heap wrapped around each other.

God! He wanted to cry, thinking of it. It wasn't sex; it was magnificent. And it was for *them*. God was playing with them, playing all night. He maybe came twice all night, and that was great, but the really great part was that God came to *them*, to him and Brooke. Their loving was so simple. He didn't need all that … stuff he'd done with others.

They'd been together ever since. They had a happy life; they had the kids. And sometimes the blue light came back. Not always. If you gave up the dope, it would happen more, a silent voice said to Mark. If you … No! He didn't want to hear it, not here. He knew about his faults. The bliss was God's. He could see the blue light. And Brooke …

"So tell us about tantric yoga." Will's voice jolted him.

Mark chuckled, a deep, rich sound laden with his experience. *"Oh, man*. Whatever you've heard about tantric yoga, it's *better*." Mark laughed, a full out laugh that seemed to last forever. What happened that night filled Mark's laugh. The laugh told them all about tantric yoga.

When he spoke again, it was a warning. "The thing is, it only works if you truly love the person you're with. There can't be any lying or betrayal between you. The minute that appears, poof! The energy and bliss go. You have to be in a very pure state." That's why he'd been faithful to Brooke all this time. He knew what would *really* kill it. And it wasn't really hard being true to her—she was the best. The only one for him. Mark thought of something else.

"You know, if people are following the Rules and go to the Meeting with the intention of meeting God, it doesn't surprise me that a bunch of them get married. In a big crowd of like-minded people, spiritual seekers, living the way Grandfather demands, I'm surprised if *most* of them don't find their soul mates. If not the first year, maybe the next. Or the next. Soul mates aren't a myth; they're real. Stopping that energy once it's aroused is impossible. Grandfather does the only thing he can to keep the Rules. He marries the soul mates and lets them express their love."

Mark fell silent, remembering. Brooke. Brooke. She was the love of his life. His soul mate, he was sure of that. As beautiful ten years later as she had been that night. He watched her in his mind's eye, walking through the redwoods. Taking care of their kids. Painting at her easel. His woman … his wife.

Except he hadn't married her. Why didn't he do that? He should get her a ring, and take her to a judge. Or whoever she wanted to marry them. Throw a big party. Give her what she deserved. What *they* deserved.

Her father had said to him, "When are you going to make my girl an honest woman?"

And he laughed it off. "No one gets married now. Why spoil a good thing?" He was too hip to get married. He had his band. His stash. Shit! He even brought it here. He knew the Rules. Mark vowed to flush it the minute he could. He kept the motor home pointed straight, despite the stinging of his eyes.

"I gotta pay attention to the road for a moment, Mr. Duane. There's a lot of rocks."

Mark's throaty laugh traveled around the cabin like a slap, striking each of them differently. Doug had been riding along, scratching his arms and wondering why his tongue felt so big. Mark's laugh told him that the driver knew more about sex than he did. Doug had never laughed about anything sensual without a smutty tone. Mark's laugh wasn't like that; he *knew* something that Doug didn't. Some joy, some depth. Something clean and purifying about *sex*.

Doug ran for the bathroom. There he choked and remembered Jennie five years ago. That was the last time he was happy—five years ago with Jennie. He cheated on her all the time. The Numenon way. He was Will's protégé, his true son. Doug swayed over the sink looking at himself in the mirror. Hating himself. His arms started itching so bad that he couldn't concentrate on hating himself. He pulled up his sleeves and gouged in a frenzy. His forearms were dripping blood by the time he could stop himself. He put some cold water on them and carefully daubed them dry. Then he searched through the cabinets for bandages.

Gil felt terror. Gabriela was home with that monster. He'd abandoned his wife and baby. What had he done? The demons in his mind began whispering stories of disaster. Every unguarded moment, his mind presented him with more horrors. The baby drowning in the bath; Gabriela crying; that nurse beating them. He couldn't stop the thoughts. He should be with them. He loved her. What had he done?

Betty stiffened. It wasn't her fault if John couldn't ... For most of their married life, he couldn't. *She* wasn't the one who drank ... John said it was her fault because his disease made him blame others. Her therapist told her John's dysfunction wasn't because of her. No, she wouldn't believe it was her fault, even though she felt so ugly that no one would want her.

Melissa heard the sound in Mark's voice. She knew all about kundalini and tantric yoga. Tantric sex, for that matter. Books were written on it. She had many of them. Personal growth was her hobby. No, it was more than that. She was very serious about her inner state. She'd been to all the major personal growth workshops: Lifeline, the RoundTable, and New Beginnings. Plus The Beloved Relationship Seminar. She'd visited all the meditation masters who passed through the Bay Area. At least one was visiting all the time. She had wanted to ask Jeff who his guru was, but didn't want to break in with a personal question. People were touchy about their gurus, she knew that, but she'd probably met him, whoever he was.

She studied mightily and impressed her workshop leaders with her honesty and willingness to share. Why not? She'd gotten an H—*honors*—in interpersonal relations at Harvard. That should guarantee her an A in life.

But she wasn't getting an A, Melissa knew. She was awful. Shrill. Horrible. Mark's chuckle shot her illusion of herself as the New Age queen. What she knew was from books. She didn't know it from being with real, living people. Mark did. He was a better lover than a joke like Doug, she realized. Maybe better than Will.

She had never had a lover because she wasn't lovable. She drove everyone away. She was awful, controlling. Stiff.

Scared. She was afraid of everyone. Melissa grabbed her purse and slipped into Will's bedroom. Doug was in the bathroom trying not to let anyone hear him weep. She looked around the room. Fortunately, Will had some bottled water on the bureau. She pulled out her flask of pills. One or two? Her breath rattled out of her dry mouth. Her doctor said she could take two. She'd only done that at night, but this was an emergency. She poured two into her hand and swigged them down. In forty minutes, she'd feel fine. Klonopin had a slow absorption rate, but it did the job.

Sandy Sydney was furious. That little shit, Mark, was divulging her professional secrets. He was giving away the source of her livelihood, at least until she and Carlo were married. That was low. And he was not telling the truth about one thing. You didn't have to be in love with the person you were with. You didn't have to even *like* them. And you certainly didn't have to be *faithful* to them. Sandy could make the blue lights fly wherever, whenever, with whomever. *That* was Carlo's greatest innovation. He remodeled tantric sex, or just *sex*, as his followers knew it.

Carlo figured out a way to separate the love from pleasure, the spiritual from the bliss, and let his people have a ball. For money, if they wanted. She made herself settle down. She could feel Mark's state; she knew where he had been. It excited her. She had to get control. No one could see her aroused here. Self-control. That's what Carlo taught. When she composed herself and looked demure again, Sandy had another thought. This Meeting should *really* be fun.

Will heard Mark's chuckle and knew that whatever tantric yoga was, it was real. Whatever a soul mate was, it was real. He knew that Mark knew something essential about life and sex that he didn't. Will put his face in his hands, trying to look sleepy rather than anguished.

Kathryn. His wife, the woman he'd failed completely. He didn't know where she was. He couldn't apologize. Her lawyers said that she never wanted to see or hear from him again. They gave him an international 800 number that he could use if their daughter had an emergency. He tried calling it. Some asshole with an Italian accent always answered. "No. The lady will not speak to you." He made up lies, said Cass was sick or there'd been an accident. "I will get back to you if your story is verified." The guy never got back to him.

Two years ago, when he found out what really had happened to Kathryn, he called that number a dozen times a day. He wanted to apologize. "I will tell her you are feeling remorse," the Italian said every time. Jerk. He never heard from her, even so he could say he was sorry. He knew she'd had a lover, someone named Carlo. He didn't know all that had happened until that bitch Dawn wrecked his life. He had the 800 number traced. It originated in the Vatican, and there was nothing he could do to find out more.

He called his wife's lover. By that time, Will knew him well. Carlo Piretti was one of his competitors, one of those European noblemen crawling all over. Usually they were penniless and looking for someone with money to give them back the glory of their family's past. Carlo wasn't like that. He had kept up and modernized. Now, he was one of Will's biggest competitors. They were waging a tough battle over the European markets. Twenty years ago, he was Kathryn's lover.

When he found out what her summer jaunts to Spain were really about, his first reaction was relief. Someone finally had taken his drunken wife off his hands. Carlo was already rich; he didn't think he was after Kathryn for her money. He didn't know why he wanted her; she was such a… He couldn't stand thinking of her; all he saw were drunken scenes.

And then she left for Spain one summer and disappeared. She sent Cass back to him, a thirteen-year-old mess. He tried to find Kathryn, but not too hard. If she wanted to go, fine. He'd had enough.

But when he found out what really happened from Dawn, he searched for his ex-wife with a vengeance. He put everything he had into it, and found nothing. He called up Carlo and asked if he knew where she was.

"No, Will—I may call you that, sí?" The guy was totally poised, talking to the man whose wife he'd stolen with one of those accents women love. "She left *me* too. The lady was so—sick. I tried to help her, you must understand. I put her in a hospital, but she did not stay. She left, taking the little girl, and disappeared. I think she had another man. She must have found someone more powerful than me. He would have to be, to hide from me in Europe. I am very sorry, Will. I wanted her to be happy." The guy's sadness and indignation over being dumped sounded so sincere. No, he *was* sincere. No one could lie to Will; he knew every time. Carlo was telling the truth.

"I searched for her, but I could not find her. I wanted to know that she is all right, sí? She was a lovely woman, in the beginning." Carlo was so earnest and charming that Will believed the man who'd cuckolded him. Not only believed him, but felt good about him. "If you find her, please tell me. It will set my mind at ease."

Will continued to search. Kathryn was alive, he knew it. And if he found her then, he would have let Carlo know where she was.

Even Marina didn't make him forget his wife. He thought about Mark's laugh and a wave of hilarity swept him. If he was Kathryn's soul mate, she sure must have a twisted soul. Will wanted to dash into the bathroom or his bedroom and hide, but his employees occupied them.

"Mark, does everyone have a soul mate?" he asked.

Mark took a moment before speaking. "I suppose. You'll know it if you meet her—or him. The thing about soul mates is, they're not the woo-woo, romance-pulp thing. Off into the sunset, happy forever after. Your soul mate fits *you*. He or she complements the state of your soul. Your soul mate will give you the lessons you need to grow. Life with a soul mate may be harmonious, or it may be awful."

"You get what you deserve," Will said. Kathryn was *definitely* his soul mate.

"Yeah. That's it. The law of karma. What goes around, comes around."

They rode in silence. During that time, Will's attention was drawn inside. He closed his eyes and dropped his forehead to his hand. The truth came to him. Carlo Piretti was the best liar in the universe. He *had* succeeded in lying to him. Piretti didn't know where Kathryn was, but he knew what had happened to her, and at whose hands—his own.

Kathryn had run away from him—she'd escaped and gone into hiding. Carlo had tried to charm Will into telling him where she was. He'd succeeded—he would have told him, if he'd known. Piretti would have captured her again. Will shuddered.

Something opened in Will, hatred deeper than any he'd felt before. Rage flamed inside him, white hot and raw. He would destroy that son of a bitch. He would take him down.

40

He found he could read the minds of the men riding with him like billboards. He could hear their thoughts and see the images in their minds. Bud Creeman's eyes widened. He allowed himself to drift to the rear as they rode west; that way, he could listen to his companions' contemplations without them noticing his reactions. Willy Fish was in front of him, carrying on a mental conversation with his mule. Bud fought back laughter.

I don't understand it, Butch, Willy thought to the mule.

Bud realized that the mule's name was Walden. He didn't know how he knew that, only that the mule was trying to get his name through to Willy and failing. The animal was becoming annoyed.

Willy went on, thinking. People laugh at me. They think I'm dumb. Rocky's mad at me all the time and I don't know why. When we got here yesterday, there were guys hanging around our tent, smiling at her; I never noticed that before. I bet they'd like to take her from me. I felt like 'Fonzo and the guys were laughing at me, too.

These were all things that everyone except Willy knew. Bud realized he was having an avalanche of self-discovery. The mule seemed to understand this also, crow-hopping in delight. His small bucks jostled Willy.

"What are you doing?" Willy cried. He wasn't much of a rider.

Bud turned his attention to the mule. Grandfather once gave a lesson to a crowd of people who'd been riding for a while. "Can you hear your horse talk?" he asked. They shook their heads. "Have any of you been bucked off a horse?" They all nodded vigorously and smiled; anybody who's been riding any length of time has been bucked off. "I guarantee you, your horse told you what he was going to do before he did it." The rest of the lesson was about listening to your horse. *Most* of Grandfather's lessons about horses were on that topic.

Bud knew about the kind of talking every horse did with pretty near every inch of its body. He knew how to listen for that kind of speech. But what he got on this particular ride was almost like the mule was talking in human. He wasn't speaking words, but Bud could feel what was going on in its head like it was his own. Honing in on the animal, Bud realized it was up to no good. Grandfather had said the mule was going to teach Willy powerful lessons this week. Recalling the smirk on the creature's face, Bud hoped it wouldn't be a lesson involving broken bones. He sidled quietly over and whispered to Willy. (Anything louder would have Squirrelly Girl standing on two legs.)

"Willy, you take a deep seat in the saddle, OK? Pay attention to that ol' mule of yours. I know you like him, but you ain't had him long. He had a terrible shock with that tornado. And he's not used to the country around here. This desert may scare him to death. You wouldn't want him to hurt you by accident."

Willy's eyes widened. "That's right. He lost his home and everything. He could be real scared."

"You take care of him and keep him awake, now. If he does any more of that hopping around, call me. Quietly." Bud eased away from the mule. He expected that an atom bomb wouldn't scare that mule, but he wanted Willy to stay awake. If he was going to get bucked off, at least he should see it coming.

Willy went back to "thinking to Butch" before Bud was ten feet away. I'm sorry about what happened to you, he thought. Losing your home an' everyone you knew. I'm so sorry. Bud could feel Willy's compassion for the animal. I'm afraid I'm gonna lose my home, too. I'm afraid Rocky will leave me, Butch. She'll take the kids and go; I'd die if she did. I love them so much. He patted the mule's neck. You know what? I think she's a spirit warrior and didn't tell me. Willy heaved a sigh. I'd like to be a spirit warrior more than anything. That's all I've ever wanted. But they'll never take me. I'm too dumb.

Bud stifled a laugh and sent a thought message back to Grandfather saying that Willy was a sweet man, and a good family man. He'd make a good warrior. He was waking up, too. Figuring out that he was dumb was a great step forward. Most dumb people just inflicted it on others and never realized that the stupidity emanated from them. Then he turned his attention to Paul Running Bird. He got a sour feeling in his stomach.

Paul Running Bird looked to the west, thinking, Did I send them the wrong directions? He remembered the scene in his office when he drew the map. He was fending off a power play by one of his fellow execs. It wasn't his fault. He was distracted. He couldn't remember what he'd faxed, and he didn't have the original with him—damn! This week was so important! Paul had been thinking about it since Grandfather told him Will Duane was coming. He would impress him and get a better job with Numenon. He'd be free of Seattle once and for all. His mind flashed on the gray Seattle skies, the rain, and the damp. His fat wife; his whiny, sickly children. He'd hire a shark and make sure Selma sucked as little blood out of him as possible when they divorced.

He would get his dream job at Numenon and move to California. He'd buy a great condominium in the sunshine. He knew how Numenon was supposed to be—the executives' hip, wide-open lifestyle.

Bud Creeman followed Paul's mind, seeing his fantasy. He was living in a fancy condo development with lush planting and a pool in the middle. It was night; the pool was softly lit. Paul was in the hot tub with a flashy blonde, sitting close and whispering. Bud's mind zoomed in. He saw that Paul had his hand in her bikini bottom and was talking dirty.

Bud could feel Paul's eyes narrow as he contemplated the desert ahead. How could they get so lost? Paul thought. His heart froze. What if he sent them a bad map? He was sure his name was on whatever he sent. Did he do it again? This would be the worst one yet. He reeled. Did he screw up his chance to escape? A groan escaped his lips and he frantically searched the horizon.

Bud felt sick. He'd met Selma Running Bird last year; she was lovely. A little chubby and depressed—but a nice person. Paul wanted to dump her? He communicated all this to Grandfather, adding that Paul would never make a spirit warrior. Bud could feel Grandfather's receipt of the message and subsequent command. Find them!

He looked to the west. He couldn't see too far; rocks and projections from the bluff stuck out into the desert as they did from the back of the Mogollon Bowl. The cover allowed them to watch without being seen.

Eagles circled overhead in the distance. Bud saw them and smiled—the Numenon crew had *never* been lost to Grandfather. He had the winged people watching them. When he spotted a moth-eaten old coyote, Bud laughed out loud—spooking his crazy horse. He knew that coyote! Grandfather had the four-leggeds watching, too; he wouldn't be surprised if even the cactus were on the job.

Bud redirected the other two men. "Over here," he said, moving southwest where the caravan would have to exit the rocks. Willy and Paul changed direction as he did, accepting his leadership.

They rode silently for a while, so intent on the terrain that Bud nearly missed what happened. He glanced back to see Willy's mule levitate three feet off the ground. Willy catapulted out of the saddle, landing hard next to a big, bushy cholla.

"Oh," Willy cried, rubbing his behind.

"Hee-haw! Hee-haw!" The mule's loud bray had Bud's mare spinning in circles. He was *laughing* at Willy.

Bud kicked Squirrelly over to Willy and swung off, helping him to his feet. "Are you all right?"

"Yeah," Willy said shakily. "I was thinkin' about somethin' else. Butch must of gotten scared."

"That's what must have happened, Willy. You pay attention to him and keep a little hold on his mouth. Are you OK to keep goin'? We got a job to do."

"Yeah. I think so." He rubbed his hip like a little kid. "Sure hurts, though."

"Sometimes it does smart."

Bud was furious. Holding his mare's reins in one hand, he whirled on the mule and grabbed him by the side of the bridle, shaking it. Listen here, you, he thought furiously to the mule. He doesn't know about you, but *I* do. You do one more thing to him, and I'm gonna see you don't pick on any beginners for a while. Bud didn't *say* the words, but he knew the mule got them. The animal stepped back, wide eyed. He dropped his head, his lower jaw moving in the way that meant, "I hear and obey," in equine. Bud continued silently, Act like a normal animal for a few more hours, we got some people to find. That's more important than whatever game you're playin'.

He turned to Willy. "I think he'll be OK now. Can you get back up there?" He helped Willy back in the saddle and mounted Squirrelly. "You OK?"

"I don't think I broke anything, but it sure hurts." Willy rubbed his behind, on the edge of tears. "I thought Butch liked me."

"He does like you, Willy. He's just got a screwed-up way of showing it. His name is Walden. He doesn't like being called Butch."

"Walden? That's a weird name."

"Yeah, and he's kind of a weird mule. Just call him Walden. Do you think you got any cactus spines stuck in you?"

Willy felt around where he'd landed. "No. It just hurts."

Bud thought directly to Walden's mind. People are learning that you don't have to hurt animals to teach them. Maybe you should take a lesson. The mood of the ride had darkened, just like the sky in the west over the mountains. Bud was angry and ill at ease. He turned back to the mule, thinking, You try anything like that again, and *I'll* ride you.

Walden ducked his head and behaved.

After they'd ridden for a while, Bud asked, "You able to keep going, Willy? Do you want to go back?"

"No, I want to find them. That's our job." The sky seemed ominous; the air, thick and oppressive. "I didn't know it was gonna be this hard. Everything's scary."

The trio pulled together and ventured forward slowly, Bud leading and following his intuition. His intuition said something bad was going to happen.

41

The memory of Mark's laugh lingered in Betty's mind. She couldn't remember expressing such uninhibited joy, and certainly not about sex. It wasn't her fault. She struggled to compose herself so she could present the next segment of the brief, never thinking of excusing herself to take care of her feelings.

Her manicured hands rested on her report, which lay on the granite table before her. Betty stared at her fingers, unaware of their tremor, unaware of the quick breathing that dried her slightly parted lips. She had to finish the material she'd prepared. This was the most important presentation she had to make, for her and the Indians—and for Will.

Betty stared at her hands. The words "Indians and Alcohol" topped the page above her enameled nails. She had all the data, all the facts. She could talk about the disastrous effect alcohol had had on Indians since they had come in contact with it. She could describe the difficulty of defining alcoholism. When does a drinker become an alcoholic? She had all sorts of figures, showing estimates of the percentage of active alcoholics by tribe, and how many times the national average each tribe's identified alcoholic population was. Betty could cite statistics on Indians' alcohol-related child and spousal abuse, crime, accidents, disease, and death; she could lay out exactly what alcoholism had cost Native Americans.

She wasn't aware of any of it. She was frozen, feeling what her life had been. Seeing only the mental image of their living room years ago, with its seventies orange and avocado sofa and the burnt-orange high-low carpeting. The room was empty, like a crime scene after the police and bystanders left. Only a yellow plastic ribbon cordoned off the area, saying: A disaster happened here.

Her speech was supposed to start off with a clever opener. "Make a list of ten adjectives to describe the word 'Indian.'" Betty expected everyone's list to contain the word "drunken" or some variant. The stereotype was that prevalent. She didn't move, didn't speak. Couldn't. Even though at Numenon, you *did it,* whatever it was, even it if killed you. You *performed.* She was frozen.

A figure materialized on the sofa. John, facedown. His right forearm lay limply on the floor, its hand pointing to his empty glass. The empty bottle lay next to it.

Of course, John drank—he was Irish. Of course, his family drank. Drinking was part of their culture. She loved it in the beginning. His family was so different from hers, wild and riotous rather than cold and controlling. John's parents weren't drunks, but she couldn't remember either of them without a drink in hand.

At first, it was so much fun. They'd go up to Lefty O'Doul's on St. Pat's Day and get smashed with friends. John was the life of the party. She didn't go with them much after joining Numenon. You couldn't drink at Numenon; you couldn't keep the pace if you drank. Plus, Will hated it. Betty knew about Kathryn's drinking long before she began as Will's private secretary. Betty was the one who arranged Kathryn's hospitalizations, three during the last years of their marriage. Betty's position with Will depended upon her efficiency, and her willingness to arrange certain highly confidential matters. Covering and lying, that's what she did.

Betty had planned to discuss why Indians had such problems with alcoholism; for one thing, there were genetic reasons. Indians didn't like to talk about it—they hated to feel marked. But we're all marked, Betty thought, anxiety striking her. They told her at the hospital where John was treated that if a child had one alcoholic parent, the probability of that child becoming an alcoholic was 50 percent, rather than the national average of nine. And if both parents were alcoholics, the child had a 90 percent chance of succumbing to the disease. Ninety percent! How could anyone fight that? A few drinks would become a habit, and then a disease.

Her own children had a 50 percent chance of becoming alcoholics.

When she took her job at Numenon, Betty had defied everyone: John, her parents, her in-laws, and extended family. Just because she got pregnant didn't mean her life was over. She could go back to work with two small kids—lots of women did. Unlike Betty's father, her husband understood her need to make something of herself. It was 1968, and John's response was, "Hell, if she can make more than me, I'll quit and let her support me. I'll go golfing!" Her father laughed at that.

John was her rock. Betty smiled sadly as she remembered, hardly aware of the people around her. And they were hardly aware of her. They had all the alertness of individuals who'd awakened at one in the morning, traveled for hours listening to presentations, and then wolfed down lunch. Even Will nodded and jerked awake. The others looked at her through half-opened eyes, if they weren't asleep. Her reverie took Betty back.

Things happened. She changed. She became Will Duane's private secretary. That took precedence over everything in her world. Very soon, she was making more than John. For years, Betty didn't notice his drinking increase. She noticed nothing but Will Duane. Betty made herself indispensable to him.

And John became indispensable to her. All through grade school, he drove the kids around. He'd cook dinner or go to the deli. Then it crumbled. Her rock lay facedown on the sofa. She approached him cautiously when she got home: "John. It's time for bed, John." No matter how hard she shook, he wouldn't wake up. He became belligerent if she tried too hard, cursing at her and striking out. She covered him and left him on the couch. Betty walked up the stairs and to bed, as alone at night as she was during the day.

John lay on the couch for nine years, passed out.

She loved that burnt orange carpet; it hid the stains from when he threw up.

Who was to blame? Was anyone to blame? Those years were so many whirling leaves. Images flew. Taking the kids to school. John picking them

up. Keeping up with the kids was hard work—school plays, science projects. Helping John. He couldn't seem to get his paperwork done, so she'd do
it on weekends or when she got home. The kids grew older—more worries:
cars, drinking, and pot. Hurry, Betty! Run, Betty! She'd dash from Numenon
back to the house.

John never struck her. He simply became more and more angry as his
partners forced him out. He wasn't producing. She couldn't save him; she
couldn't do his job when she got home from doing hers. He accused her of
sleeping with Will. That was ridiculous. Betty was the only woman on the
Peninsula who *wasn't* sleeping with Will Duane. John got angry when she
came home late, if he wasn't passed out.

When she thought about those years, she remembered them as
peaceful and normal. The professionals called it *denial*, she learned.

They seemed to be on a speeding train. No one could get off, and no
one could stop it. In 1974, Kathryn Duane shipped Cass back from Spain
and left Will for good. Betty thought Will would be relieved, but he was
devastated. He was so wired he couldn't sit still. He tried to keep Cass with
him at home, but he was so nutty he couldn't be a father. So he sent her to
a boarding school. The school was around the corner. It should have been
all right.

Will was practically bouncing off the walls. Raving. Betty covered for
him at work. The man was falling apart. What he said scarcely made sense.
Betty hid it from the other employees, the executives, and the stockholders.
She covered for Will everywhere. When she got home, John was facedown
on the sofa.

Will climbed out of the hole Kathryn dumped him in crotch first.
When he realized his wife really was gone, he plunged into the scene that
started in the sixties, but hit its stride in the seventies. Love was never free
for Will Duane. He usually paid top dollar for it, whether in champagne or
flowers or hotel suites. Years passed.

Betty's brows knit as the *Ashley* bounced across the desert. The pictures
kept coming. Now her house was 1980s pale. The avocado and gold sofa
had turned to mauve leather with a canvas floor cloth in lieu of a rug. So
practical. Wipe it up. No stains. Even if he lost control and peed when he
was passed out, you could wipe it off. The kitchen and the floors were

whitewashed oak. John was home only for dinner and to crash. They sat tensely at the table. No one said anything, even if he cursed them, even if he fell face first into the roast.

Why? Why didn't they speak up? They tiptoed around and pretended it was normal. The kids stayed away from home. She worried about drugs and birth control. Should she take her daughter to the doctor? No time.

The economy got shaky; Will's womanizing escalated. For the first time, Will's nightlife intruded into his work. Betty had to call security to get rid of an assortment of bimbos who showed up at the office. *She* was the one who supplied Will with the madam's name and got him started with professionals. *She* was the one who structured her work contract to cover so much of his personal life. She had to take over—an empire was at stake.

Meanwhile, John started disappearing. He'd show up every few days, stinking and bruised. Between the kids, her work, and trying to cover for her husband with his partners, Betty was a one-armed paperhanger with a fire on the stairs. And Will Duane was on a kamikaze course.

That famous night, Will called about three a.m. "Betty. Can you come over? I'm ... I ... don't know." He wept on the phone. She ran over. Will was completely unglued. He'd sit, then pace around talking as fast as he could. He'd start to talk about something, then change his mind and talk about something else. He didn't make sense.

"—I never realized what I was doing. Ashley was just over there ... I could have ... We did all right, didn't we, Betty? In the Malaysia thing. We came out fine. What's up for tomorrow, Betty? We can do it, can't we? We always win." He hunched over, unable to hold back his tears. "Ashley wouldn't see me today. I went to the dorm, and she wouldn't come out. Do you think we should expand in Asia ...?" All rapid fire as he dashed around the room. She couldn't calm him down.

She called his doctor. They converted his bedroom into a private hospital that night. Nurses, medications, restraints. Everything. No one ever knew. Will had been the richest man in the world for years—no one *could* know. He was "hospitalized" in his bedroom for two weeks. The doctor called it "exhaustion." Betty covered it up at work. She visited Will every night once he was coherent and worked until midnight with him. Will couldn't get well unless he knew everything was all right at Numenon. Then she'd go home. And John would be gone. Run, Betty! Run!

The accident happened at the end of Will's hospitalization. John was storming over to Will's place, determined to have it out with him for taking Betty away. He cried all the way to jail. He didn't mean to run the light; he didn't mean to hurt that man. Betty knew her husband was a good man. It was a felony DUI nonetheless. He was ordered into treatment.

They all went into treatment. That was when the real work started, she thought. But not the pain. That had started years before; they just hadn't felt it. Now, they felt it, all of them. When John got out of the hospital, his partners threw him out. It cost so much. They had to pay legal fees and medical costs. The insurance jumped because of the felony... everything... They almost lost their house.

Betty gazed at her hands, oblivious of the others seated around her. The group had come out of its stupor and stared at her, horrified. No one had seen Betty Fogarty the way she was. Betty didn't see her trembling fingers. She was blind to the tears splattering her table. Betty felt only the shaking confusion inside, the images fighting each other. More memories than she could contain.

She had such hopes for this speech. She wanted to tell the group, anyone who would listen, anyone who could hear, what a dreadful, horrible disease alcoholism is. How it scars everyone it touches; it destroys families. Kills. She wanted everyone to know that it wasn't only the problem of Indians or dark people with bottles in bags. Alcoholism struck everywhere, in the best homes, the best neighborhoods. It took good people who weren't bums. She wanted to move the group, to make them feel what it was like so they wouldn't judge the Indians so harshly. She wanted everyone to know how hard alcoholism was to treat. How much it hurt.

Betty wanted to communicate all that, but she couldn't say a word. She stared at her brief, gasping. When Will put his hands on her shoulders and lifted her up, she jumped and cried out. He put his arm around her and led her to the *Ashley's* bedroom. "Let's go in here, Betty," he whispered. "It's been a long trip."

She clung to him, "Oh, Will. I'm so afraid. *Will it happen again?*" She didn't know she was crying until she tasted the salt of her tears.

Will held her. Betty suffered a breakdown a year after John's DUI. She was hospitalized for a month, and missed three months of work afterward. No one knew but her family and him. He covered for her at work, just as she had covered for him.

42

Bud Creeman focused his attention on the Numenon caravan. Grand-father wanted him to appraise his guests, so he would. He and Paul rode across the open desert. Willy was lagging; Bud suspected that his unplanned ejection from Walden hurt him more than he said. He yelled back, "You OK, Willy?"

"Yeah," came the dispirited answer.

"You tell me if you need to rest." Not hearing anything, Bud looked around. This was the most beautiful landscape in the world as far as he was concerned. The desert's dusty red floor was punctuated by tousled rock for-mations and cactus; in the distance, the rocks joined to form a ring of mountains, a painted backdrop as colorful as an Easter egg.

Thunderclouds threatened in the distance, looking like they'd take over the sky by late afternoon. Now, at one p.m., the unrelenting daylight bleached the landscape of all but the strongest colors. Come dawn or dusk, the desert's splendor would be more apparent—rocks and mountains would be tinted mauve, rose, rust, ocher, and sienna; Easter colors, perfect for this week before Easter, the prettiest time of year in the Mogollon country.

The corporate caravan labored clumsily through the canyons, out of sight, but not out of Bud's mental reach. He could see that image of Grandfather before him, a couple of feet from his nose. That seemed to give him access to things he couldn't see otherwise. Like the five ungainly shoe boxes, the lumbering motor homes, plus the equally ugly trailer, bouncing their way up the gorge.

Bud tried to tune himself in to the vehicles and see if he could get any insights about their occupants. He tilted his head in wonder. He felt separate things, entities, inside the boxes. They had distinct "flavors." Those were the people—he could feel them. He tried to halt Squirrel Brains to concentrate better, but she wouldn't stop if Paul's horse was moving. Paul wouldn't stop. Nothing would stop him but arriving at the caravan. Bud would have to ride his nutty horse and see what he could pick up.

OK, Bud, he thought, what do you sense? He focused on the "flavors." Most of the Numenon crew was in the first vehicle; that must be Will Duane and his staff. In each the following vehicles, one person rode, except for two in the last one. He tuned in deeper, trying to get the information Grandfather sought. Two women and eight men … Bud's forehead wrinkled in dismay. These people were miserable! Only one in the front of the first vehicle—must be the driver—seemed OK, but Bud could sense an impending breakdown in him too. Grandfather wanted to know who was weak and who was strong, so Bud concentrated harder. He could feel what had to be Will Duane, unmistakably the strongest of the group, in the first motor home. Still, the man was a fragile shell. Several of the rest were almost as powerful, but every one of them was in trouble; Bud couldn't say who was in worst shape. This was good. This was how Grandfather liked people to come to him, ready to meet Spirit, ready to meet themselves; but first they had to crack.

Who could succeed at the Meeting? Bud "listened" some more. Every single one of them could—and every one of them could fail. Something else occurred to him … There were ten *people* in the vehicles, and something else. That something else was so horrifying, so terrible that Bud could only wonder what it was. Nothing he'd ever encountered in his journeys with Grandfather was as malicious as this thing; it wasn't human. It rode in the first vehicle, and it seemed not quite formed to Bud, as if it were in a process of metamorphosis. What had these people brought with them? He didn't feel any fear from the people in the first vehicle, so either the creature was totally under their control or they didn't know to be afraid of it. He sent this message off to Grandfather right away.

What else? The old man wanted to know what they were bringing with them. Bud tuned in to inanimate objects. No booze, that was good. One driver had a little weed; and one of the women had some pills with her. She had a problem with pills, not serious yet, but getting there. About *fifty* knives were stored in what seemed to be the kitchen car. Who needed that many knives? It didn't make sense. What else were they carrying? Bud concentrated deeper still—and was sure he'd lost his mind—chests of live lobsters? All that food? They could feed the whole camp with what they bought. More and more crazy stuff. His mind shut down when it hit the motor home jammed full of palm trees. *Palm trees*? That couldn't be right, he had to be mistaken. And then there was the trailer—

Bud beat a hasty retreat from his psychic activities, after sending the message on to Grandfather. He had to be wrong; corporate America couldn't be so crazy.

43

O nce in the bedroom, Will sat on the bed and held his arms out to her. Betty let him hold her, but she couldn't cry on his suit; her control was that ingrained. Will took his jacket off and held his secretary and friend. He had never held her before. Betty was amazed at how tender he could be; she could almost feel his heart radiating warmth from his chest. She knew that he remembered everything that had happened during those years, exactly as she did.

Betty cried in earnest. Will held her tenderly and stroked her hair and back softly. She realized for the first time why all those women had chased after him. Being in Will Duane's arms was wonderful. She looked up at her boss. Was she falling for him? What was happening?

"Why don't you call him, Betty?" Will said, pointing to the phone next to the bed. "Call John and work it out."

"How did you know, Will?"

"I know you, Betty, and what would make you this upset."

Betty looked grief-stricken. "He said he was leaving me, Will; that he was sick of taking a backseat to you. John said he'd leave me if I went on this trip."

"Call him, Betty. Don't let that happen." Will kissed her forehead and got up to leave the bedroom. "Take as long as you like."

Will walked into the cabin and said soberly to the group, "Betty has some problems at home that she has to deal with. She'll be out in a minute. I think we're all feeling touchy. We'd better be extra nice to each other. This may be a hard week."

Gil was shocked. Will Duane actually acknowledged that Betty had a personal life that could pose problems, and that people had feelings that needed to be taken into account. This never happened at Numenon.

The MBAs all took a course called "interpersonal relations" while completing their graduate studies. The students' nickname for the course was "touchy-feely." It was developed when business theorists observed that businesses fail because managers don't know how to deal with people, not because they don't know enough linear programming or statistics.

Once they got to Numenon, they found touchy-feely was ignored. Instead, hiding feelings, backstabbing, manipulation, and, most of all, putting on a false face were the rule at the bastion of enlightened management.

Gil remembered his professor saying that all the techniques he taught could backfire if they were used in a hostile environment. That summed up Numenon. Gil would never expose his tender feelings there or share anything that was sensitive. Betty's tears and Will's acknowledgment of them were shocking admissions of humanity.

"Why don't we take a little break while Betty freshens up? Anyone want some water or juice?" Much to everyone's surprise, Will served them.

44

The people at the Meeting will know this material cold and have very strong feelings about it. Because of that, you need to know it, too." Betty's voice quavered. After ten minutes in Will's bedroom, she had made her way back to her chair carefully, trying to hide her pain and confusion. When she picked up at her brief and started to speak, she realized she couldn't do it. She hadn't reached John; nothing was resolved. Betty held herself rigidly so she wouldn't fall apart again.

"I'm not up to leading this." She shook her head sadly. "Maybe you can have a group discussion. I'll throw out the main points." They nodded solemnly, and she went on, her speech punctuated with silences and sighs.

"Everyone knows that Indians have been dying since they came into contact with us. *Dying*, not *vanishing*. Nothing romantic about it. No one knows how many died—there were no census takers back then. Estimates of the number of deaths exist, but they're just guesses. This isn't..." John's image came to her and her eyes filled. She couldn't go on. Betty looked for someone to take over. "Gil, could you read the top paragraph on page 27? It's in italics."

Gil found the page and began to read, "... *After a few days, the illness became so severe that death came only hours after its first signs. Once those signs appeared, the afflicted persons became terribly agitated. They had so few hopes of surviving that almost half took their own lives, using their knives or guns. Some leaped headfirst off a tall cliff, breaking their skulls on the rocks below. Their blood and brains covered...*" Gil stopped. "That's disgusting! What was it?"

"Smallpox. It's an eyewitness account by an artist passing through in the 1830s. The Indians had so little immunity that the disease almost didn't look like the smallpox we know. He wrote more—it's in there—about a cholera epidemic. Starving dogs *ate* their master's rotting bodies... I can't talk about this now. What I want to say is that the Indians didn't just die, they died horribly."

"I've read reports that more Indians died during the 'settlement' of the Americas than Jews were killed in the Holocaust." Melissa had an interest in the Holocaust because of her family. She had been shocked when she read how many Indians had been killed by her fellow Americans.

"That's true, Melissa, but it wasn't quite the same. What happened to the Indians was awful, but it happened over hundreds of years—and it wasn't high tech, like the concentration camps were for the time. The biggest cause of death was disease. The West was won by mindless germs, not heroic Indian fighters, as some would have us believe."

Betty jumped when Will leaped up and ran into the bathroom. Now what had she done? Was he that disturbed by her reports of the settlement of the West?

Will was having a hard time listening to Betty. Not because of what she was saying, but because of her obvious anguish. Knowing that Betty's marriage was over seemed impossible. He knew that they had had problems, but whatever their difficulties, the Fogartys were ideals to him, They were his windows to the normal world. Will didn't know another couple who had been married for thirty years, raised children, and weathered hardship. He could not imagine a world in which Betty and John weren't together. When he held the trembling Betty in his arms, he felt her despair. She and John were breaking up because of *him*.

He had returned to the stateroom in a daze, leaving Betty trying to reach John on the phone. He handed out snacks because he didn't know what else to do. He couldn't believe it. John had left Betty *because of this trip*. He had to stop it.

As Betty spoke, he realized that he *could* stop it.

Will dashed into the bathroom, pulling out his cell phone. He couldn't get a signal. Going to a panel on the wall, Will punched in some numbers. He felt the ceiling shudder and movement on the roof as the satellite dish deployed. Good, the satellite system worked. He tried to call John with the satellite. He couldn't get a signal that way either. No signal with a satellite receiver? Where were they, anyway?

Will turned to the bathroom window that filled the wall over the Jacuzzi. A high-style metal screen covered the bulletproof glass. The screen provided privacy as well as additional security. He punched some numbers into another set of controls. The screen rolled up into the ceiling, revealing a clear window.

"Oh, my God!" A red rock wall rose less than twenty feet from the vehicle. The canyon had been at least a hundred yards wide when they entered it. He leaned over and looked out the window. A cliff loomed high overhead. That's why nothing worked; they were in a hole. Why hadn't anyone noticed?

Then he got it. The window shades in the cabin were down for the video. The lights went on automatically. The way they were sitting, no one in the cabin could see how tight the canyon had become. No one but *Mark* ... Why didn't he alert them? Will wanted to chew him out.

But should he? Were they in danger? An Indian gave them the map— surely he knew about the canyon narrowing. Betty had said he was overjoyed that they were coming. He wouldn't send them into danger. If no immediate peril existed, Will decided to talk to Mark quietly and not alarm anyone. He opened the door to find Betty talking in an almost inaudible voice.

Guilt flooded Will. He had destroyed the only marriage in his world that had lasted more than ten years.

45

Mark kept tabs on what was going on in the cabin as well as he could through the rearview mirror. He could see what Betty was doing, using history to get through to all of them, especially Will. He was the one who mattered. Betty was *in* a negotiation, not practicing. Her delivery was perfect. You could almost feel the Indians' pain in the tone of her voice. More likely, her suffering was due to whatever upset her earlier, but her presentation sure got everyone's attention. Maybe things would turn out OK. Maybe Will wouldn't do that mine, after all.

He began to feel better. He'd scored some points earlier. He could tell that the others now regarded him a little more as a group member than just as a driver. All he had to do was keep it up, and he was sure he'd get a better job. He heard Will say they'd hire that Paul guy sight unseen. Maybe everything would be OK.

He looked at the vehicles behind him through the mirrors on each side of the vehicle. The digital clock on the dash was flickering oddly. He tapped it. They should have been there hours ago. Then he noticed the canyon walls pressing ominously close, with less than twenty feet clearance on each side. Why hadn't he seen the canyon narrowing? He had been so involved in what was happening in the cabin that he hadn't paid attention to his job.

The only reason everyone hadn't noticed was that the shades were down and the lights were on. He might have ruined his chances for a better job!

Then it struck him—he hadn't done his job. He hadn't checked with the other drivers since they left the airport. Who knows what problems they might have? He glanced in the rearview mirror. Betty was having people read from her report. No one would notice him whispering. He picked up the headset for the shortwave, punched a button and spoke. "Jeff? Jeff? Can you hear me?"

A sullen voice replied, "Yes, Mark. I can hear you."

Jeff Block had been trying to make contact with Mark on the shortwave for an hour, with no answer. Didn't he see that the canyon had slowly narrowed? The change was almost imperceptible, like a well-designed trap. They couldn't turn around anymore; they couldn't get out without backing up.

Jeff wanted to scream into the speaker, "Mark, you idiot! Look what you've done!" He stopped himself because he was afraid that Will Duane might hear. Plus, he could have honked the horn, stopped, or flashed his lights. He could have done something to signal Mark about the cliff walls. What was the matter with him?

Jeff remembered a newspaper story he'd seen. Some people had been hiking in a ribbon canyon in Arizona; a flash flood drowned them all. The hikers couldn't escape the twenty-foot wall of water that roared down the canyon out of nowhere.

"Mark, look out the windows. What if there's a flood? We'll be trapped."

Silence; then, "The sky is blue, Jeff. It's sunny. There won't be a flood." More silence.

"We gotta get out of here, Mark."

"I know, Jeff. The map's wrong, we should have been there by now... We have to keep going, there's nothing else to do." More silence. "Are you OK, man?" Mark asked.

"No. I'm not OK. I keep thinking about how you cut me off when I was talking in there. Everything I had to say, you one-upped me."

"What? I did not."

"Yes, you did. You do it all the time. Even when we're home." Jeff knew his irritation was more apparent than he wanted it to be. He was a yogi, not a stupid pothead like Mark. He kept himself under control.

Mark's voice was even tenser than his. "Look, I'm a little upset. I'm sorry if I cut you off or anything. I didn't mean to."

"Yes, you did."

"Well, maybe sitting up here with them rubbed off on me. They're so competitive I caught it too. I'm sorry."

"You do it all the time. I hate it."

"Are you OK, Jeff?"

Jeff remembered what had been said of the Mogollon Bowl. Maybe its influence extended outside of the Bowl too. Jeff's voice caught. "No. I'm not OK. I keep thinking about all sorts of weird shit. Can anybody hear me?"

"No. What kind of shit?"

"My life. How I ended up in a dead-end canyon driving a motor home for some rich guy. That sort of shit, Mark."

"Yeah. You're right. I've been up here listening to these people. There's a lot more that you don't know about why we're here. We'll talk when we get there. I'm going to check in with the others. Call me if you get freaked out."

"I have been calling you, every ten seconds. Stay in touch, OK? It's weird out here." He hoped Mark couldn't hear his voice trembling.

Jeff was more upset than he let on. His guru was the center of his life. His life *and* his girlfriend's. Michelle was even more of a devotee than he was, if that was possible. She said his going on the trip was heresy. Was it?

Grandfather was a real holy man; Jeff knew that by the images that kept appearing in his mind and the energy boiling up his spine as he drove. He wanted to meet this holy man desperately. He felt like his life was funneling him toward the Meeting. That terrified him.

Of all the Numenon people, he had the clearest idea of what it was like to be around a spiritual master. He knew how wrenching close contact could be. If the Meeting was as good as he felt it would be, his whole existence could be changed at the end of the week. What would that mean? Would Michelle dump him if he told her he had a new teacher? Or could they work something out? Would she still love him if he told her their teacher was good, but not great?

He thought of something worse. If his guru wasn't a sadguru, a true guru, he wasted the last eight years working for him for nothing.

Then it struck him what his service to Guruji really had cost him. His PhD. He tried to get his dissertation committee to give him more time to complete his work, but his committee chair said they couldn't. "It's department policy, Jeff."

As planning for Guruji's world tour took longer and longer, Jeff felt wrenching pain as his dissertation's final deadline came and went. He got an MA, but not the PhD he deserved. Why couldn't they give him a little more time? They said his topic was brilliant.

Diddling around for his guru took his life. He deserved a title that fit his abilities. *Dr. Jeff Block.* Credentials that would let him teach at any school he wanted. That's what he wanted—to be a professor.

What he got was a driver's cap and a motor home heading up a canyon in the desert. Jeff felt like he was falling off the edge of the universe. Who could he talk to about it? Who could understand his dilemma in this bunch?

After talking to Jeff, Mark called Hector Carillo, the next driver in the procession. "Hector?" he said into the mike.

"Sí?" Hector replied in Spanish, uncharacteristically.

"Are you all right back there?"

"Sí. Yes," the clipped reply came back.

"Things are cool?"

"Yes, Mark. Things are cool."

"Great. Hector, we're a little bit lost, but we're getting out as fast as possible. Call me if you have any problems."

"Of course, Mark."

Hector swore under his breath, thinking in Spanish as he did when alone. Didn't that stupid Norte Americano see that they couldn't turn around? If the canyon dead ended, they'd have to back five motor homes out, caravan style. It would take hours. They were a *little bit lost*? They were very lost; they should have been there hours ago. Hector's mood floundered. His mind had been repeating a singsong since they left California.

"Los Indios son dulces… Los Indios son buenos… Los Indios son suaves… Los Indios… Pobrecitos…" "The Indians are sweet… The Indians are good ... The Indians are soft and kind ... Poor little ones ..." Images of the highland Indians of his native Peru flooded his mind.

His mental chant to the Indians stopped. The vision of his ancestral home came to him and took Hector's breath away. The hacienda's colonial majesty demonstrated four hundred years of his family's dedication to the land. The Carillo clan had been los ricos—the rich, colonial imperialists. They lost everything in the Peruvian reforms in the late 1960s and early 1970s.

Hector's chest tensed. Why was he on this trip? He'd lost a way of life so his government could help the poor Indians. Why should he play his guitar for them?

Hector would have spat, had it not been impolite.

Mark called Delroy West, the driver following Hector.

"Del—you OK?" He hissed into the mouthpiece.

"Yeah, man."

"We're a little lost, but we're gonna be fine."

Delroy was silent. He was kind of a scary guy, Mark thought. The oldest of the drivers, Delroy looked close to fifty. A movie-star handsome, African American guy from back East, he was like an almost over-the-hill action hero—or villain. He could play the bad guy just as well. Or a shuffling bumpkin if he it suited him. Sometimes he had a Southern accent, and sometimes he sounded like the big city. Del was not someone Mark wanted mad at him. His silence was ominous.

"Delroy! Are you still there?"

"Yeah. You see we can't turn around, man? If we can't get through, we have to back out."

Mark tried to make amends, "Yeah, I know. I've been kinda busy up here. Look, I'm sorry. I'm trying to get us out of here as fast as possible. Hang in there; this can't last. We have a map."

Mark switched off the set. He could feel Delroy's rage. Yeah. He'd screwed up. The sun was shining now, but afternoon thunderstorms were common in the desert. If they had to back out, it would take hours. If there was a flash flood, what Jeff had feared could easily happen.

Delroy cursed as he drove. Stupid fuckin' college kid! He'd buzzed him a dozen times—with no answer. Stupid fuckin' kid! Turns off the intercom! He was probably too busy kissing Duane's ass. They were targets for anything. Delroy didn't have to imagine Indians above them on the cliffs—there were many more dangerous things in his world. Nothing made him more anxious than being unable to escape.

Then he pulled himself in. He liked Mark, especially since he gave him and Denneesha free tickets to their show at that club in Santa Cruz. Paid for their dinner, too. That was nice. Those guys could rock, especially that tall one with the long hair, Jeff. He'd never forget Denneesha up on the table, doin' her moves. "I didn't know white boys could play like *that*, Del!" she yelled. The place took off—everyone climbed on the tables. Mark was a nice kid; he just didn't have a brain.

Del had had a bad feeling since he left Palo Alto, like he'd never have good times like that again. Like everything he'd worked for—his job, his woman, their apartment—all of it would be torn away. Not a thing he could do to stop it. Every mile they drove, the feeling got worse.

"Just leave the lines open, Mark," Del whispered into the mike. "Stay hooked up, man."

Mark didn't have to ask Delroy what he felt—it came through the earphones like a pickax. He was pissed off and scared. Mark could read feelings like some people did music. Peeking over his shoulder at Will Duane, he set the shortwave for a wide band broadcasting outside the *Ashley*. He spoke into the mike while Betty told them exactly how bad the Indians had had it. Hopefully, the passengers wouldn't hear him whisper into the mike.

"This is Mark Kenna with the Numenon party. We are lost. Repeat: We are lost. We need help. Can anyone hear me?" The set weeped and tweeped, making a horrible shriek in his ears. The instrument panel jumped around, then acted fine. Mark talked into the microphone—and the instruments went crazy again. What was happening? One last try.

"This is Mark Kenna with the Numenon party ..." A piercing noise had him pull the headset off. The shortwave wasn't working. Could it be the canyon walls? Must be that. One more time. "This is the Numenon party. We're lost and need help ..." Piercing noise. The Numenon party. It felt like the Donner Party, the infamous group of pioneers that tried to cross the Sierras too late in the year and got stuck in the snow. Those who survived did so by eating those who didn't.

Mark looked in the rearview mirror. Betty was still speaking softly, leading the discussion. Sandy Sydney passed out snacks. "Boy, Jon really took care of us," she said of the food. Mark realized how much she loved to eat from her tone of voice. You'd never know it—Sandy was very slim. "Jon's the best cook," Sandy purred. "This week will be a treat. You're so lucky, Mr. Duane, to have him cook for you all the time."

Mark glanced into the mirror. Sandy was coming on to Mr. Duane very subtly. And Will Duane did not like her. Mark swerved the motor home. "Sorry," he said to the ruffled passengers. Shit! thought Mark, I'd better keep it together. During the years he'd been driving, he had dulled so much that he didn't notice things he would have noticed immediately when he was studying counseling. His ability to understand how people acted and felt was flaming brightly again. Had he lost touch with himself that much?

"Mmm," said Sandy Sydney, "Even a sandwich made by Jon Walker is yummy!"

Jon Walker! Mark jumped. He'd forgot to call Rich Salles to see how the lovebirds were doing. As Betty began a new part of her presentation, Mark put on the headphones one more time. Gritting his teeth in case the noise returned, Mark whispered,

"Salles! Salles! Are you there?"

"Yes, I'm here. Where else would I be?" came back loud and clear—and pissed off. Mark realized they could use the shortwave between the five vehicles, but not to contact the outside world. "I've buzzed you a dozen times, Kenna. You didn't answer. We can't turn around, did you notice that?"

"Yeah. I did. Hey, I didn't see the pager light. I've got the sound off up here because they're giving presentations."

Rich Salles was so upset he could hardly talk. "We're in trouble, Kenna," he finally got out.

"I know, Rich. I called the Indians for help," Mark stated both truthfully and untruthfully. "We'll get out of it. We went the way the map said—it's got to widen out somewhere soon. An Indian drew the map. He's been here a million times." That seemed to calm Rich down.

"Well, watch for my light, Kenna," he grumbled and disengaged.

Mark couldn't figure out why he didn't see the pager light that was supposed to go on when the sound was muted. It was plenty bright when they tested everything at home. What was going on with the equipment? Not wanting to lose his job immediately, he kept driving. His chest was tight like when his allergies bothered him. He peered out the windshield nervously.

46

Rich Salles had been thoroughly pissed from the minute he found out that Jon Walker had been assigned to ride with him.

Goddamn it, he kept saying to himself. Mark put *Jon* with me. What Mark Kenna thought of him was obvious. Put the faggot with the faggot. Maybe they'll make baby faggots. Jon's dyed hair was like a red flag, enflaming the driver's outrage. Rich was planning on leaving Numenon, and this made it definite. He couldn't take any more of the place and its mentality, its reptilian brain. Subhuman.

All Numenon's about is sex, Rich thought. Half of what these Numenon jerks talk about when I'm driving is their conquests. A guy who doesn't tell everyone each time he has sex, they think he's gay. If they're not talking about sex, it's power. Toys. Me and mine. What I made last year. My net worth. Rich drove for a while, disgusted. Kenna thinks I'm gay because I'm not like them.

Rich needed to go on this retreat. The worst crisis of his life stared him in the face. He looked out the window at the vehicle in front of him. He was exhausted; he needed a healer. Mark's request for drivers for a music-oriented, spiritual retreat in the desert sounded like the perfect thing back in Palo Alto. Rich could play the mandolin very well. The rumors were right; he was an artist. The Southwest light and desert colors called to him. He'd brought a ton of art supplies; and right before they left, he felt better than he had in weeks. Ready for art and spirit and playing in a band with the guys. Now he didn't want to go.

When I got my master of fine arts, I never thought I'd be driving a motor home with a bunch of jerks, he thought bitterly. I thought I'd be painting and showing and selling my work. Not making a lot of money, but surviving. What a joke! I can't feed my cat on what I make painting. All I can do in the Bay Area is drive a bunch of maniacs. The conversations Rich overheard among the Numenon executives made him sick. Sandy Sydney's anatomy was a topic of conversation with all of them—as well as her companion of the night before. They've never known a woman who's pure. They've never loved anyone like that. He thought of his Carrie.

After Mark called him on the shortwave, Rich glanced into the rear of the motor home in the mirror. Aside from all the *palm trees* Jon jammed in it, the cabin was empty. When they started out, he was so pissed that he had refused to speak to Jon. For hours, the cook sat silently on the cabin's one available seat. Rich looked into the rearview mirror and saw that Jon was bent over, holding his handkerchief. A minute later, the driver heard the door to the bedroom closing and muffled sobs. Then it was finally quiet. That was how things had been since.

Rich didn't know whom he was madder at, himself for being a jerk to Jon, or Mark for getting them lost and putting him in this shitty position. Rich felt like a criminal for the way he'd treated Jon. He wasn't close to anyone who died of AIDS, but he'd heard it was awful. Jon and 'Rique were together for eight years, someone said, and they said he died in Jon's arms. And they were both celebrities, for Pete's sake. He'd seen Jon on the news after 'Rique died. They ambushed him outside the hospital.

Hearing Jon weep made Rich feel better about riding with him. Jon was more real than the rest of those jocks at Numenon. Rich didn't usually feel such incendiary anger. The closer they got to that damn retreat, the more screwed up he felt.

47

Jon knew what was bothering Rich. He didn't want to drive with the only homosexual in the group. No big deal, he thought for the first hour of their morose ride. He'd had the same sort of thing happen to him since he was a teenager.

Rich's foul temper made Jon feel silly. He wished he had nail polish to pull out, or that he could samba around the cabin in a hat with bananas. Silliness gave way to anger. Does he think he's so gorgeous that I won't be able to restrain myself? he thought. Why should I want *him*? He couldn't get a date in San Francisco.

Loneliness began taking bites out of his shaky composure. He had wanted to ride with Rich; he was the most sensitive of the drivers. Jon knew he wasn't gay. He wanted company, not sex. He needed a friend, but Rich obviously thought that having to drive five hours with a gay man would brand him for life. Would people in the other motor homes think they were driving along fucking? Jon shook his head. Why would *anybody* think he'd be interested in sex now, after the last year and a half?

He pulled out his handkerchief and wiped his eyes, wishing he were driving with a friend, someone who would put her arms around him and comfort him. Jon thought of Melissa Weir when he needed a true friend. That's what she'd been when 'Rique was sick.

Melissa was Jon's only buddy at Numenon. They were an unlikely couple, the Bitch of Numenon and the goofy gay chef. They were very good friends, but most people didn't know that. He met her at Ao Punto four or five years ago when Will Duane hired the restaurant for a Numenon function. Jon came out of the kitchen after dinner for a "compliments to the chef" drink and was invited to stay at the party. Jon gravitated to Melissa. Her intelligence and style won him over. They talked for a long time, during which he told her about his partner, 'Rique Maldonado.

Much to his surprise, she practically shouted, "*The* 'Rique Maldonado? You're his—"

Jon filled the awkward pause with, "Partner."

Melissa practically jumped up and down. "I've seen his work in all the magazines. *Architectural Digest, Elle, Metropolitan Home*—you name it. He's great. His room at the San Francisco Show House is always my favorite, and last May ..." She revealed how much she loved design and knew 'Rique's work.

When he came to work for Will Duane three years ago, he and Melissa became close. Jon cooked for Will Duane every day, either at the company offices or at his home. Will entertained a lot in those days. Jon was busy, yet still had more time to be with 'Rique than he had when he was executive chef at Ao Punto.

Shortly after he started at Numenon, Melissa asked him if he'd like to take a dance class with her. "I'd go alone, but I don't like to be mauled," she said. Jon was surprised. Why didn't she go with a date? Or to meet someone?

He'd realized Melissa wasn't gay after talking to her for about two minutes; he guessed her virgin status long before she told him. People thought she was gay because of the way she dressed and moved, but she had to dress the way she did to survive at Numenon. Plus, she was so intense that she came across as masculine.

They became dance partners and won a few contests down the Peninsula. They had fun together. She'd had him and 'Rique over for dinner many times. Jon would cook while 'Rique admired her townhouse.

"Incredible!" 'Rique would say in his cute Guatemalan accent. "Where deed you find thees?" Melissa ate it up. Interior design was her passion and she was very good at it.

"I owe it all to the Smithsonian! My father is director of the National Gallery. My mom is an archeologist with the Museum of Natural History. I've been force-fed culture since birth." Many of Melissa's things were museum quality. Tapestries, fossils, rugs, architectural fragments. Some of the furniture.

"Where deed you get these theengs?" 'Rique asked. She told him about a few stunning buys she'd made when her father tipped her about little-known sales.

Their first dinner cemented them as more than dance partners. Dinner was great, courtesy of his virtuosity in the kitchen. They had lots of wine— *lots*. 'Rique admired Melissa's flair for design. "The pieces are wonderful, true. But you put them together like a master. Most professionals could not do thees."

Charmed by the compliment, Melissa said, "Would you like to see my best work?" They nodded and she ran upstairs with the two of them following.

"My bedroom," Melissa threw open the double doors. The room was breathtaking. From the high ceilings to the custom, hand-wrought iron bed and its fine linens, the room was the work of an expert. Melissa stood by her nightstand, beaming. Jon and 'Rique stood by the foot of the bed, shoulders touching, weaving on their feet. They were beyond well lit. They were also very worldly. Both had been around San Francisco—and LA, New York, Paris, and a few other urbane capitals—a great deal. They looked at each other. Had she invited them up for something?

Melissa seemed to catch the shift in their mood—they thought she showed them her bedroom as an invitation to a ménage a trois. She bolted downstairs. He and 'Rique followed her, finding her in the kitchen, shaking and terrified. The tough corporate star was a frightened child, backed into a corner, scared speechless and immobile. They couldn't go near her—she looked like she'd be hysterical.

Jon would never forget how 'Rique treated her. He talked to her softly, "I'm sorry, querida. Do not be frightened; we weel not harm you." Very slowly, 'Rique touched her hand. She eventually let him hold her. It was one of the tenderest scenes Jon had ever seen. Melissa's tears stained his silk shirt, and 'Rique didn't mind. When she finally calmed down, she was so embarrassed.

"I'm such an idiot. I don't know why I acted like that," she said.

"It's all right, querida. No problem with us."

And it was all right. 'Rique fixed the mood of the evening. He could do that—take the most screwed-up situation and fix it. He said that was as important as design skills in his business. They had dessert and chatted and when they left, both men hugged Melissa. Jon felt her against him, fragile as a little bird.

Driving back to the City, Jon said, "What would make her act like that?"

'Rique was silent. Then he said, "Rape. She have been raped many times."

Jon was shocked. "Wouldn't she know? Wouldn't she remember?"

'Rique shook his head. "Not if it was brutal. Or if she was young." He was silent again. "She will remember some day," he added later, nodding his head knowingly.

"How do you know?" Jon had asked.

"She reminds me of my little sister, Carmen."

'Rique never talked about why his family left Guatemala. Jon knew they had come to the United States as political refugees, and he knew they were upper class and lost everything. That's all he knew about them. Until the grieving family sued him after 'Rique died, then Jon found out about them. 'Rique left him everything he owned and his family wanted it.

Jon and 'Rique made love when they got home after that strange night with Melissa. 'Rique seemed sad, but he held Jon in his arms and loved him sweetly. "Dance with that woman, Jon. Make her happy. Think of me when you dance."

He knew it was thinking about what happened to his sister—and presumably Melissa—that made 'Rique say that. He could be so sweet, trying to assuage others' pain.

Sitting in the Numenon motor home heading across the desert, Jon remembered that and was overcome with grief. He headed into the bedroom and threw himself on the bed.

Jon cried when 'Rique died, and before, he'd cried in therapy. He'd been to grief groups and cried. He'd been to an AIDS partners survivors' group. He'd been to so many fucking groups and cried so fucking much. But nothing helped. The loneliness was still there. The hole in his heart kept screaming. The pain. The emptiness.

Whether they were open or closed, images hovered in front of Jon's eyes. The way 'Rique felt at the end as Jon held him. His body was so light and fragile, like a child's. A child of skin and bones, covered with sores. Tufts of hair stuck up here and there, with 'Rique's scalp showing through. 'Rique stopped talking days before he died; he stopped making sense weeks before that.

He wasn't dead, though. He moved. He grimaced. He taught Jon the difference between being dead and alive. 'Rique lay in his bed at the end, breathing. His rib cage—and it was just that, a cage of ribs, the only part of him sticking up off the bed. The rest of him was bones. His rib cage expanded and contracted, air going in and out with vigor. 'Rique was alive.

He'd raise his hand. The way he held it reminded Jon of a stalk of asparagus, with the fingers pulled together to make a point. Slowly and deliberately, 'Rique would reach out and grasp the slats of the bed for a moment or two, and then just as deliberately, he'd withdraw his hand. He wrapped his fingers around whatever was there. Jon would put his arm out, and 'Rique would twine his fingers around his wrist. It felt good, even if 'Rique didn't know he was doing it.

"'Rique, it's Jon." he'd say. He thought that 'Rique knew he was there. He had sort of a burst of something sometimes. Brightness. Jon thought that meant he knew he was there. He talked to him all the time, joking. "OK, 'Rique, it's time to go dancing. Stop all this lying around." They told him hearing was the last sense to go, so he kept up the patter.

At the end, it was like something opened up and 'Rique went through it. He left. His body was still. That was the major difference between being alive and dead. A dead person doesn't move; a living one does.

'Rique *left* him—that made him furious. After everything they'd been through, 'Rique left and he was stuck with *life*. Worst of all was the fact that 'Rique looked better after he died. His face was blissful—not just peaceful—blissful. He wondered, was he happy to leave me? Or was he just glad that the pain was over?

Melissa drove him to the hospital the last few days; he didn't trust himself to drive and he was staying at her place anyway. She saw 'Rique's body and said, "Look, Jon. Look at his face. He's not suffering anymore."

But that was the point—what was life but suffering? *Life* was the problem—not death. When you were dead, it was *over.* 'Rique left him with the mess. All of it. His sisters. Finances. The press. Oh, the press. He loved the press.

'Rique was famous. Jon was a well-known chef, but the whole world knew 'Rique Maldonado. 'Rique started as the boy wonder designer for San Francisco's elite; he segued into doing their offices and boardrooms. Then he designed and manufactured the furniture for the whole sixty-story corporate headquarters, not to mention their yachts and planes. 'Rique was a phenomenon. He was just getting started—the new clothing line was a sensation. So many communities loved him ... He was gay, Latino, West Coast, San Francisco-based. His death was a major event. Careers could be made with a good story on how 'Rique died.

Ronny Hertlin, the station's token gay reporter, stuck a mike in his face as he staggered out of the hospital. Jon had cried over 'Rique's body until he could barely stand. He just wanted to go home. Melissa scouted out the exits, trying to outsmart the press. They were clustered in front of the hospital.

"I found one exit that's clear, Jon. This way."

And there was Ronny with his fluorescent white teeth and film crew. He stage-whispered with such sincerity, "Please accept my condolences ... How do you feel, Mr. Walker? Was he peaceful at the end?" Would you give me an interview? I'll give you the whole hour. Just up my ratings and tell us everything. Cry for us, Mr. Walker. Spill your guts.

Jon refused to do interviews, but others didn't. He still gritted his teeth when he turned on the TV and saw some jerk sitting with Ronny or one of his plastic buddies, talking about his life with 'Rique. "Oh, I knew him *intimately ...*"

And that was the problem. They did know him intimately. Everyone knew 'Rique intimately. He was impossible. Jon ran his hands through his hair. "We loved each other," he whispered. They did. But 'Rique was impossible.

The blissful look on his face disappeared after a few hours, leaving a husk and the sound of 'Rique's breathing echoing in his ears. His last breath was no different from those before—but there wasn't any other after it.

"He died in my arms!" Jon whispered. "He was here, and then he was gone."

But he wasn't gone. He was with Jon all the time, day and night. During the day, 'Rique's last hours played and replayed again. The sounds and sights, the catheter, the tubes. His 'Rique. What happened to his beautiful 'Rique? The love of his life.

When Jon slept—if he slept—'Rique was there. In his dreams, Jon ran through corridors and looked behind doors. 'Rique was just out of sight. Just there, over there. No, there. No, behind him. "'Rique? 'Rique?" Jon would cry in his sleep, frantically searching. He was always hiding out of his sight. "Oh, 'Rique! Please, wait for me," Jon cried. The nights were more horrible than the days.

Why did I come on this trip? Jon thought, trying to pull himself together.

Jon knew perfectly well why he came. Will Duane paid him five times what he usually got. Jon needed the money; he'd missed so much work. They didn't have as much money as everyone thought, even as famous as 'Rique had been. And then there was the Maldonados' lawsuit. His "in-laws" were suing him. Jon couldn't stop shaking. The other visions came back, and he was wandering the streets of San Francisco, covered with sarcomas. Starving. Alone. Dying of AIDS, while 'Rique's poor rape victim sister lived in the chic warehouse he and 'Rique had remodeled and shared. Jon pulled a blanket around himself. Oh, help me! Please help me!

His therapist's words came to him, "Jon. You're catastrophising. It's a well-written living trust, Jon. 'Rique left you safe and well off; the lawsuit will come out fine. You have the royalties from your cookbooks; you have good medical insurance. You'll be OK. Even if they won everything, you'd be OK. And they won't win."

'Rique's sisters had approached him at the funeral, faces like monstrous fish, bubbling something at him from a world beyond hell. Jon couldn't understand what they were saying. Finally it came clear—they were suing him. He had no legal relationship with their brother. They were 'Rique's lawful heirs, and they wanted it all. Jon scarcely knew their names.

His therapist had held him together for the last six months. She talked to his and 'Rique's attorney with him, she went to the reading of 'Rique's trust with him. Jon couldn't think well enough to understand what was happening. "The trust is a good document, Jon," she said. But he couldn't remember that all the time. He had to remind himself. Every time he got another letter from

'Rique's family's attorney, Jon went into a panic. He had to run to read it with her, or he couldn't understand it. "You'll be OK," she said.

Jon had to trust that.

Oh, God. He was so alone. Everything was too much. He couldn't believe 'Rique died of AIDS. No one died of AIDS in *1997*—that was the eighties. Now, they had treatments, drugs. Protocols. 'Rique did them all, took them all. His pager went off round the clock. Taking, doing, going to this hospital and that. Nothing *helped*. Other guys' viral counts were down to zero; 'Rique died.

He knew it was a matter of time; his turn was coming. Why were they so stupid? Neither of them needed to play around. They loved each other. They made each other happier than anyone else could. But 'Rique couldn't be faithful. And Jon wouldn't stay home if 'Rique was with someone else. So they partied separately in New York or LA for the first four years they were together. Pretending it was what they wanted and needed to do, that it made them happy and free.

We were faithful the last four years, Jon thought, lying about it even to himself. He hadn't been faithful. Not totally.

Jon had himself tested every three months since 'Rique got sick. He was always negative. But one day, he wouldn't be; he knew that. What would he do? Who would have a HIV-positive chef? What if he cut himself near the food? What if he gave someone AIDS? Jon couldn't do that. He never, never wanted anyone to go through what 'Rique had suffered.

Then those fucking Indians had them blood-tested—of all the invasions of privacy! They said everyone who went to the Meeting had to be blood-tested by their doctor. He protested, but Will said they had to do it. So Jon went to that Indian doctor's office on Welsh Road. Dr. Elizabeth Bright Eagle. At first Jon was excited to go there; he'd seen her on *Oprah*. She was fantastic, talking about her projects on the reservations.

Was she ever different in real life! Fat as a pig; meanest face he ever saw. Fancy offices in the best building on the road—she had to make a fortune. He walked into her office, scared stiff. The nurse took him into a private room. Dr. Bright Eagle came in beaming. They talked for a few minutes and then she picked up his arm. Then she felt his pulse, and all the life went out of her. She knew something—Jon was sure. The doctor became all business. She drew the blood and said, "We'll let you know as soon as we get the results back. It will probably be at the Meeting, since you're late getting in." He left in a state of shock. He was HIV positive; she knew the minute she touched him. Jon didn't need the blood test results—he knew too.

Why did he come on this trip? He put his arms around himself and rocked back and forth on the motor home's bed, looking out the window at the dusty red canyon walls moving past. The canyon walls were so close to the window. Oppressive. Jon moaned as 'Rique's face appeared on the red rock. "No. Don't do this to me." Jon whispered, "I can't live without you, 'Rique. I don't want to live without you." He felt himself panicking, throwing himself at nothing.

Nothing—there was nothing out there. He whispered to the empty room, "Please help me. I'm so afraid." He lay back on the bed, crying softly and shaking. Soft, dry breath moved in and out of his mouth. "'Rique. Don't leave me. I don't want to be here without you." Breathing. "Please, help me."

Jon must have dozed. When he awoke, 'Rique was there with him. He couldn't see him, but he knew his lover was there. Jon whispered, "'Rique?"

"Yes, querido, I'm here." Jon could feel him stroke his head.

"Oh, 'Rique, I've missed you so much." Jon clung to a pillow, and 'Rique held him.

"I know, my darling."

"'Rique. I don't want to be here without you."

"Shh! Shh! Querido. Quiet." Jon heard 'Rique whisper to him, "It won't be long, my love. It won't be long. We'll be together again." Jon stared, terrified. 'Rique calmed him, gentled him, and said, "Don't fear, my darling."

"'Rique, I don't want to die. Not like you did. I can't do it," Jon moaned.

"You won't, querido, you won't suffer. I've taken care of that. I will be with you. I love you."

Jon lay on the bed and 'Rique talked to him, caressing him softly. "Querido, the world is not ours. Something moves the world; something moves us. We do what we do, and we get what comes from that. But who we are is beyond this. It's so different here than we are taught, querido. So different. We will be together, my darling. Here, where I am." 'Rique's voice mesmerized Jon. "Remember me. You will soon be free—two years or less,

Jon. You will not suffer. Listen to your heart, my darling. Spend this week like precious gold, like it was our love. Jon, querido … I will be with you."

Jon could feel 'Rique touching him, loving him as he did on earth. He could feel the love in his partner's soft strokes, touching his whole body, and he drifted off.

"Sleep, my love," 'Rique said. "We will be together soon."

48

The population had been savaged. Bodies of those killed, and those dying or wounded, were found in every shelter or lying in the open. The blood of children and women, bodies and skulls broken by axes and knives, soaked into the ground. The brains of an infant oozed onto its dead mother's gory breast." Gil stopped reading. A baby's brains oozing? He stared at Betty.

"A San Francisco newspaperman wrote that the day after the massacre. I know it's hard to read, Gil, but it's history." Betty's voice was soft. "Disease was the primary cause of the Indians' deaths, but murder was the second major cause. I used firsthand reports to illustrate this section." She stopped and wiped her eyes, sighing heavily.

"I'd never read things like this. And I just don't understand it. The hatred. The massacre Gil read about took place in 1860, on an island near the City of Eureka in Northern California. The Indians used the island once a year for a peaceful religious ceremony. People in Eureka could hear them screaming, but no one went to help. The next day, some went out to see what happened. That's when that reporter wrote that. It was 1860. Eureka was a town; the people who did this weren't early settlers."

A pall hung over Will. Part of it was Betty's subject matter, and part was her tone. The grief and pain in her words were there because of him.

Because of the mine he'd proposed, and because John left her. Her despair was an indictment. It was his fault.

His eyelids twitched from exhaustion. How many hours had he been awake? He looked up and saw the canyon walls through the windshield. He was the only passenger facing straight ahead; only he and Mark could see the walls creeping closer. He'd almost forgotten that he needed to talk to Mark. He could feel his dry breath moving up and down his windpipe, puckering his lips. He needed to move, do something, but he had no will to do it.

The stalker was in the cabin with them. Sniffing them. Who was ripe for a fall? Who would give in? Darkness surrounded him as though he were in one of his nightmares. Will grabbed at the book in his jacket pocket, grabbing for anything that might protect him. He felt the embossed Numenon logo on its leather cover. He'd discovered the book in his nightstand when he got into the *Ashley*. He'd slipped it into his pocket. They used to call it *The Numenon Bible*. He hadn't seen one in years.

He fingered the familiar volume, the only corporate handbook to receive a major literary award. It was Immanuel Kant's *Prolegomena to Any Future Metaphysic* packaged by Will Duane. Kant's work had had an enormous impact on him as a young man.

When he started Numenon, he commissioned a famous philosophy professor to write an introduction to the *Prolegomena* and get him the best English translation of Kant's seminal work. Then he hired a ghostwriter to work with the academic and render its message into language that a normal person could understand. Finally, he hired a *cartoonist* to put it in terms *anyone* could understand. He had the three versions bound together, put the Numenon logo on the front, and gave one to everyone he hired. He entered it in the competition for the National Literary Honor Award, and it won.

He smiled. How many realized numenon was spelled incorrectly? It was supposed to be noumenon. He had dashed the word off and handed the paper to his attorney when they were incorporating. He didn't bother to check the spelling until he saw it on the logo and signs. Too late to change the spelling in the corporation's lean early days. "It's a lesser known spelling," he said to the three people who'd noticed in thirty years. Which it was, that he checked. The philosophy was correct too.

In *The Prolegomena,* Kant spelled out his famous Kantian Dilemma. We can never know anything as it truly is, because we only contact existence through our five senses. We can never know the thing-in-itself, the numenon, the ultimate reality beneath the experienced world, except through inference. So we have to make the best inference to the world-as-it-is that we can.

The best was Numenon, the corporation that would change the world. His corporation. Everyone thought he was so hip and cool with a corporate bible, even if they couldn't understand the cartoon version of what numenon meant. He *was* hip, back then. He made a big deal of his almost-major in philosophy in those days. He hadn't thought of it in years. What had happened?

He pulled away from the group. As he did, the gloom that had followed him caught him. Images appeared in his mind: white sky, dark stone towers sharp against the brilliance. The stone towers with their hard edges. The cold wind off the lake. His legs reddening as he ran across miles of green grass. The nanny clutched her paddle back in the house; she was too slow to catch him once he got outside. His parents believed that children *liked* discipline, that he needed and liked beatings.

Will shuddered. The memories only came in dreams. Why were they coming now? He clutched the volume in his pocket, searching for protection, searching for how he had felt when he had it made.

Leaving Chicago and breaking his father's grip took everything he had—all his fortitude and planning, and his power. But he did it—Will went to Stanford University, instead of the University of Chicago as his father wanted.

When he found himself walking under brilliant California skies, past buff-colored stone buildings with Spanish arches and murals of glittering tile, Will felt as though he could do anything, as though his life until then was a mistake he could fix.

His studying philosophy started out with a mistake. He went to the wrong freshman orientation. A professor stood in the front of the auditorium and said, "Why are you here?" for five minutes. He said it in different tones of voice, directed it to different people, and the crowd at large. He yelled his question. The room squirmed with embarrassment. Will understood what he was asking and was electrified, "Why are you here, in this room? Why are you alive? What are you doing with your time on earth?" He needed to know these things. Why was his father the way he was? Why had he been born into his family? Why did people hurt others?

He signed up for a class and ended up two courses shy of a major in philosophy when he graduated. Officially, he'd majored in political science and minored in economics. He had to major in "something practical" or his father wouldn't pay his tuition. But philosophy was his love and his battle cry. He needed to learn what it taught, and studying it was a direct strike at his father.

Old Mr. William raved when he saw the courses Will took, but he kept taking them. His father couldn't dominate him anymore. It looked like Will might win, for a while. Will clasped the book in his pocket. Philosophy had been his key to freedom. He abandoned it.

Wham! Will jumped as Betty slammed her binder down on the granite table in front of her. The noise startled everyone. They stared at her. Betty looked back with watery eyes, trembling.

"No one's listening! I can't do this if we're not committed to it."

"We are committed, Betty." Will tried to placate her.

"Then pay attention! You're talking about doing something that will change the Indians' lives—don't you think you should find out about who they are?" She was on the edge between exploding and breaking down. "Can't you care about why we're here—can't it mean something?" The group was silent, stunned again. No one at Numenon let his or her helplessness show like that.

"*I* care about it, Betty. And I know some Native Americans." Mark Kenna's voice came from the driver's seat. Heads swiveled to the front of the *Ashley*.

"Really, Mark?" Betty said.

"Yeah. I was active in some environmental issues when I was in school. I got to know some Indians in Nevada. We were trying to stop a nuclear dump. I got to be buddies with a few of them."

Betty asked, "What were they like?"

"They were real nice if they didn't think you were there to screw them," he replied.

Will blanched. The purpose of their trip undoubtedly fell in the "screwing them" category.

Betty reiterated, "They're a little touchy, Mark?"

"Real touchy." Mark added, "I've taken a Native American history course and a Native American spiritual traditions course." Will raised his eyebrows. Mark would come in handy.

"Please, give us your insights, Mark." She turned to the others. "The massacre Gil read about is part of the 'removal' phase of the settlement of the West. About 60 percent of the Indians died of diseases, the rest had to be *removed*. That usually meant being relocated to reservations, where they would live in poverty and often starve. Those who didn't leave had to be eliminated—murdered."

"Betty, I've got to say something." Everyone turned to Doug. Will had been keeping an eye on him. His face was pale with flushed blotches on his cheeks. An oval of dried blood pasted one of his shirtsleeves to his forearm. Rather than scratching furiously and moving all the time as he had when they started, Doug had sat listlessly for the last hour. Will wanted to get him to the camp and Dr. Bright Eagle as fast as possible. He'd read that people could die detoxing cold turkey. Was Doug in danger?

"I know all this bad stuff happened and we need to know it, but I tried to tell you earlier—that isn't how things are now. We need to know that, too." Doug had railed against the Indians when they were doing the mock negotiation, talking about his summer experiences on some reservation. His arrogance put everyone off. But now, looking awful and sounding worse than Betty, they listened to him.

"Go ahead, Doug."

"I spent two summers working on a reservation when I was an undergraduate. I know some carpentry; I can fix things. I did it for my résumé, yeah, but I also cared about the Indians. It wasn't what I expected. They hated all of us from the get-go, even though we were with a charity, and even though we were fixing their toilets and roofs and making things better. Most of them sat around drunk all the time. They blamed us—white people—for everything that happened to them since we landed here. They wouldn't let their kids go to school, because the white man's education would ruin them. The kids were turned off by the time they were five. They stayed on the rez, raising the next generation of losers. After two summers, I quit. They didn't thank any of us for jack shit … and the reservation didn't look any better. They're probably still there, sitting in front of their shacks, hating us."

"Thank you, Doug." Betty tried to hustle him into silence.

"No, there's more." He appeared to be expending his last strength. "If you expect this Meeting to be all nicey, nicey, Oh, poor Indians, you're cruisin' for a bruisin'. Some of them hate us.

"And you haven't mentioned the casinos. When Proposition 5 passes next year—the *Indian Gaming Initiative*." He smiled cynically. "It should be called the 'Give the Indians a Monopoly on Gambling Initiative.' It will pass, too. The guilt vote will drive it over the top. Once the Indians can expand their casinos, California will become Nevada." Doug looked around the cabin.

"My folks have a house near Palm Springs. The Indians own the center of town. They already have a casino and hotel; give them the go-ahead to expand, and Palm Springs will look like the Las Vegas Strip. In ten years, the Indians will own half the state—we'll be begging them for jobs and they'll be driving around in Rolls-Royces, still feeling sorry for themselves. Everyone will hate them as much as ever, but for different reasons. You don't have to be a rocket scientist to see that coming."

Betty blustered, forming a response.

"Don't be so politically correct, Betty." Doug said. "You'll get hung out to dry."

Will pulled himself together hearing *politically correct*. He hated political correctness. People put blinders on themselves, trying to make the world nicer than it is. That was the way to go broke. "That's right. I don't want any PC bullshit. Tell it like it is, or don't tell it, Betty."

She ruffled through her binder. Betty knew the dangers of editing reality as much any of them. Her confusion told him she'd gotten the message. She was looking through her papers for the missed clue.

"They're trauma victims," Mark's voice came from the speakers. "What you say is true, Betty. During the 'Indian Wars', the atrocities on both sides were horrible, but the Indians definitely got the worst of it. And—what Doug says is also true. You see dispirited, dysfunctional people on the reservations today. The survivors. They're angry, they blame, and they don't know what to do or how to get out of the mess they're in—even with casino revenue.

"If you walked into a center where they treat rape victims and people who've survived abuse, you'd see the same thing. The ones where the trauma was fresh would be barely able to get through the day. Others, with more years on what happened, might be raging mad. Pissed, blaming the world. Some would have drug and alcohol problems—trying to self-medicate. They might be nuts, too—psychological symptoms are common in those who have been traumatized. Their symptoms are handy for the perpetrators, because if the guys who did it are ever called on what they did, they can say, 'Suzie? That drunk? She's been crazy since she was born. I didn't do anything to her. She's lying.'

"You see all of that in Indians, and other people who've been raped. They're trauma victims. And don't give me that *survivor* bullshit. Some of them are barely alive."

49

I'll try to say what needs to be said and not what's politically correct. Here's a question you may be able to answer, Mark. You're the psychologist. The guy who wrote this," Betty waved a book, "says that what happened resulted from the way we white people viewed Indians.

"He says that on the one hand, the Europeans thought the Indians were the noble and pure forerunners of European man. They were naturally peaceful and wouldn't hurt you unless they had a good reason." Betty looked around. "Like in *Dances with Wolves*." The group smiled nervously. Everyone loved *Dances with Wolves*.

"Europeans also had negative images of Indians. The early Pilgrims were Puritans in every way. Life was a battle for salvation; the devil lurked everywhere. I kept thinking of *The X-Files* when I was reading—you can imagine how the woodland Indians in feathers and paint would look to people who thought everything was the devil in disguise! They treated them like devils.

"I have a hard time believing that *thinking* could create a situation in which it was OK to wipe out millions of people. I just don't get it."

"It's called *projection*, Betty. It's a defense mechanism." Mark's voice was comforting now. He knew what they needed to know. "We all do it. Indians lend themselves to being its target—then and now. That author's talking about archetypes—the first man, the primal mold. We see Indians as archetypes, and they see us the same way."

Will barely heard Mark. Something was overtaking him, as Mark talked. "... Adolf Hitler felt angry and murderous ... It couldn't be *him* ... He blamed it on a group used as scapegoats for centuries, the Jews."

White sky. The towers hard against them. The cold. The chill. Will swallowed. He clutched the book that once had been his hope. What happened? He'd been so brave at first, so full of plans and dreams. He was on top of the world, and inspired.

He had the vision then, when he saw a world where capitalism created utopia. He saw a world where people *did* the things that they always said they wanted to do and never did. They cooperated, chose the high path, and were the best people they could be. He had that vision sitting in the first Numenon office late one night. His body sang as the images filled him. He'd never known such ecstasy, didn't know it could exist. He could still see that world, the world that he once intended to create. He could touch it and bring it back for Numenon conventions and rallies. He could pull himself together and shine like the early Will Duane. But he wasn't the same.

Something had deserted him. He'd have what he now knew was a kundalini experience just often enough to stay alive, but that was all. More and more, he felt that Old Mr. William, his father—the *real* William B. Duane— was winning. The bastard was sitting somewhere, watching him fall apart, saying, "I told you so." He could smell his father's cigars, and hear his rasping cough echoing through the stone palace he'd bought to show he'd *arrived*.

Will's chest ached. Marina's face appeared in his mind's eye. He watched her turn away from him and disappear. Why did he come on this trip? God, he felt like he was dying. And then he felt it, the presence that had marked him for years. The weaker he was, the stronger the stalker grew. Get it together, Will. He ran his hand through his short hair. He had to get it together. The stalker was watching them.

Get back to the discussion, Will. Concentrate. He grabbed onto his vision of the world of peace. Business people cooperating around the globe. Solving problems. Getting food to starving people. There was enough! There already was enough; we just had to distribute it. Glimmers of the way he felt when the vision came the first time returned. As long as he held onto that vision, the darkness was kept at bay. Will fought the murky currents that flowed within him. He came back to the room and Betty's voice.

"But Mark, listen to this," she glanced through her brief, looking for a citation. "You can understand the violence where the Indians fought back hard, but in California, where they didn't? How do you explain what happened in our state? People are aware of the famous massacres, such as the one at Wounded Knee. No one talks about what happened in California, but far more people died there than at Wounded Knee."

Reading from a number of pages, Betty described the '49ers driving Indians from their lands with no pretense of legal process. She reeled off examples of legally sanctioned murders. Hunting Indians was subsidized by the state of California. Bounties gave out-of-work ranchers and miners income. Hundreds of Indians were killed over the theft of a cow or horse. Hundreds were murdered at a religious festival, and babies—some still living—were thrown into a bonfire of ceremonial regalia. "In one area of Northern California, hunting parties went out several times a week, killing sixty or so Indians a day."

Will couldn't stay with the discussion. It was so horrible he retracted into himself, heedless of the danger his interior world posed. When did he lose himself? Life seemed to speed up when he entered college. He was already going fast when he founded Numenon. As he went faster, philosophy became less important and making money mattered more. Now, he went as fast as he could, skating a razor's edge, working to capacity and beyond.

How had he forgotten what he loved? Philosophy had bought him freedom from everything that happened when he was home. He made himself different from his father, as different as their worlds. As different as the corporations they'd built.

Numenon's headquarters on Page Mill Road appeared in his mind's eye. Brilliant architecture. Better than anything his father could conceive. *He* did that! Numenon was his personal philosophy, writ in land and structures, in business systems and strategy, in visionary thinking. In his blood.

Will never went home. He got his MBA at Stanford and started Numenon in California. He eventually inherited his father's business, but he was worth twice as much as the old man when he inherited it. His father's corporation was a minor profit center in Numenon, soon to be dissolved. Glee almost overtook him at that thought. He noticed Betty looking at him pointedly. He had better pay attention.

"It goes on and on. I couldn't believe that this happened in places I've been—on the way to Tahoe. North of Clear Lake. These are vacation spots now, but they were bloodbaths."

"The sexual area is most disgusting," Betty continued. "Slave hunters raided the Indian villages at will, stealing women and children for sale to miners and brothels. Some Indian agents and almost all the employees of certain reservations were personally involved. Husbands were forced to watch their wives and daughters prostituted before their eyes."

Melissa Weir bolted for the bathroom.

Will scarcely noticed her run past him; something evil was watching him. He'd never felt it so strongly. Will had only spoken of the stalker once, to that psychiatrist when he got sick. The son of a bitch doped him up so much that he couldn't make it to the john. He couldn't run Numenon like that. They'd crucify him. He threw out the drugs and the shrink with them. The idiot said he had paranoid delusions. If that two-bit phony lived in Numenon for a week and knew the threats from inside and out ...

Will knew he was *not* paranoid. He and his family had been stalked for years. His interest in security and surveillance systems came from that. His estate was so well protected that he knew if too many *leaves* were falling in his backyard. He knew if the *cat* had gained weight. And they were able to bug it, anyway. He shivered.

Betty was surprised at Melissa's sudden exit, and decided she had overdone it. She truncated her talk, omitting discussion of the thousands of Indians enslaved as agricultural workers. "Well, that gives you an idea of what happened. Saying it's from projection or myths doesn't seem to explain the level of hatred; how could decent people do this?"

"It's like trying to explain the Holocaust," Mark replied. "How could all those smart, technically inclined Germans do that? How could the rest of the world turn a blind eye? Projection—putting our inner monsters on someone else—is a very powerful mechanism.

"Indians are easy to make into archetypes," Mark went on. "Archetypes lie deep inside the human psyche. Tons of them exist: the savior, holy man, virgin mother; the devil; the angel, archangel. The virgin princess, the slut. The dark, romantic, primitive; the wicked, evil, primitive.

"We've all felt them. You're bopping around in life, doing fine. Happy, content—then whammo—you run into someone or something that grabs you. You're mesmerized—you have to have it—or destroy it. The power behind that overwhelming feeling is most likely an *archetype*.

"If you dump your wife and marry that eighteen-year-old, you can get in big trouble. But if *you* slip, it will just ruin a few lives. If you're a charismatic dictator like Hitler and you hit the right chord so society's sickos join you, you can wipe out millions.

"No one understood this back then—or almost no one. Other mechanisms were involved: social approval and social pressure. Once all that gets rolling, it's like a tide. The only thing to do is be watchful and stop it before it becomes a movement."

Betty asked, "How, Mark? How could the murder of the Indians have been stopped?"

Mark thought for a while. "I don't know. You read how people felt and wonder. How could they be so hateful? But then I hear about hate crimes now and see that some people *are* that hateful. Nothing has changed.

"The first thing to realize is that none of us are that different from those settlers. We fall in love with our desires and get blinded by greed. We tell ourselves that if we want something, it's OK to do anything to get it.

"Anytime you hear yourself or someone talking about us versus them—that's a sign of this process. If you hate someone or some group a lot, that's a red flag. That hatred is part of *you*.

"The bottom line is—the Indians got killed because they were in the way. The settlers wanted what they had. To justify taking it, they projected their shit on the Indians, making them into the scum of the earth. Then they could be killed with no guilt.

"Now, we can do a *Dances with Wolves* revision and make them into dead heroes so we can beat ourselves up, even though *we* didn't kill anyone. That's more bad mental health. Stereotypes never get to who the Indians actually were—or are. Hopefully, we'll get to know some real Indians this week."

Will sat slumped in his chair, pulled back to reality by Mark's words. He had no idea that he was so bright. Mark could explain how genocide might be controlled. But they wouldn't need that on this trip, would they?

50

Oh, God, not here! Melissa thought. She started out listening to Betty with interest. She thought only her own people had been treated so badly. What happened to the Indians was much worse. When Betty got to the rapes, her brain stopped; the others seemed far away. She started breathing quicker and her hands grew cold; she could feel her heart pounding hard in her chest. Her heart couldn't beat that fast. It would explode.

Melissa grabbed her purse and shot into the bathroom. She locked the door and turned her back to it, pressing against it. She put her purse on the sink counter and opened it with shaky hands. She found the plastic vial the second time that day. Thank God, she hadn't put both prescriptions in her medicine case. She'd have had to stop the caravan to get to her medication; people would have found out how crazy she was. Moving closer to the sink, she started to pour a pill into her hand. As she tipped the vial, the *Ashley* hit a bump. The pills flew all over the bathroom.

She scrambled frantically; she'd have to find them all—no one could know she took pills. She didn't take that many. Her doctor said she had no problem with overuse. Melissa had never taken psychoactive drugs before. No one in her family took drugs. When the thing with Doug happened, her life seemed to go haywire. She did everything she'd ever done to keep herself calm, to allow herself to sleep. When that didn't contain her fear, Melissa ran harder, worked out at the gym more often, and stayed at work until she fell asleep at her desk. She even went to a couple of the meditation groups dotting the Peninsula. Nothing helped.

Melissa woke up terrified every morning at three a.m., heart pounding, sweating and shaking, freaked out of her mind. No one was there, but she couldn't go back to sleep. Melissa was so glad when Will sent over his people and had her already state-of-the-art security system beefed up. She had a panic button by her bed, and added them in her kitchen, living room, and bathroom. She put another set of locks on the exterior doors and changed the existing locks. She continued to wake up hysterical. She bathed several times a day, and still felt dirty.

In desperation, she visited her doctor. "I'm working on a big project … Numenon is very tense. I've got lots of pressure."

The doctor listened to her watered-down description of her symptoms. "It sounds like you're having panic attacks. They often respond to medication, have you tried …" He rattled off about five possible drugs. She went numb. Half of Silicon Valley was on Prozac. How could she join those losers? *She* was a winner.

They settled on Klonopin. It worked; if she took one when she woke up scared stiff, she could go back to sleep in an hour or so. Even better, if she took two before going to bed, she'd sleep through. That way, her performance at work didn't suffer. As long as she was number one at the office, nothing was wrong. She rationed her pills, making sure she didn't take too many. It was only temporary. Her work was fine. She didn't have a problem.

She had been able to finagle two prescriptions from her pharmacist, claiming a long vacation would prevent her from getting a refill. She brought one hundred twenty tablets with her. She'd make it through the week; she could sit with other people until they arrived. She would be able to sleep in a motor home with two other women. She would be able to do it; all it took was a little pill. Except that earlier today, even two didn't work.

Melissa returned the tablets she'd recovered to the vial, then dropped to her knees to pick up those on the floor. Fortunately, they were bright orange and easy to spot. She thought she had them all, reaching behind the toilet one more time to be sure. She kneeled and counted the pills. The vial had held sixty. "Fifty-six, fifty-seven, fifty-eight." Except for the ones she'd taken, they were all there, thank God. She put number fifty-eight in her mouth and looked up before standing. One of the crystal lamps set in the mirrored wall was in Melissa's field of vision. Its bulb threw out rainbow halos, and light exploded into her eyes. Melissa gasped.

A curly ring of red hair with light emanating from behind it shocked her; a man's voice growled in her ears. Melissa froze. She couldn't scream. Melissa leaped to her feet and backed up against the bathroom wall. A voice in her head barked. Keep breathing! It's not real. It's your mind. Keep going. Look at it. It's not real. Melissa did breathe, and as she did so, was able to see the light fixture. No man was there. She stood up, shaken.

And then she remembered—the same thing had happened with Doug. Everything came back. She and Doug had been working on a presentation for a Southeast Asian government. They'd worked together for six weeks; they'd had fun, toward the end. Melissa began to change her opinion of Doug Saunders; he was almost a nice guy if you got him away from his buddies. Her hatred of him was turning to distant, if suspicious, interest.

They gave their presentation in the Palo Alto headquarters late one afternoon. It was a triumph! They were fantastic together. Will gave the Asian clients the star treatment, throwing a cocktail party after the presentation, and big sit-down dinner—the works.

She needed to be quiet for a while after a big presentation to calm down. She told Doug to go out to the reception, she'd meet him. They were going to sit together at dinner. Maybe she looked forward to sitting with him. Alone in the conference room, she sat quietly and meditated for a few minutes. As she was getting ready to join Doug, she knocked a bunch of papers off the table. She squatted down to pick them up. When she looked up, Doug was there in front of her. She hadn't heard him.

His form was dark against the ceiling lights. His disheveled hair stuck out, creating a ring around his head that looked reddish in the light. She was so scared she couldn't move. He took her hands and pulled her up. He reeked of alcohol. All she could see was the ring of curly red hair and a blank, black hole where Doug's face should be. He towered over her. He put his hands on her shoulders, then let them drop to her breasts.

"That's a good little Jew," he said to her, bending for a kiss.

Something in Melissa exploded. Her arms flew up and knocked Doug's hands away. She was enraged. With the movement of her hands, Doug shot across the conference room, slamming against the rear wall. Blood was everywhere. He moaned from the floor. Melissa could see what happened clearly for the first time. She stood by the conference table, while Doug thrashed on the floor like something was striking him. She screamed at him and kicked and waved her arms, but she never went near him. Doug recoiled as if being beaten.

"You monster! You're an animal! You're disgusting." She didn't know what she said, but she never touched him. His friends came in and she left, but didn't get very far. Someone had called security. They detained her. Will Duane went in to see Doug with the paramedics. When he came out, he didn't stop the police from taking her away. She'd never forget the look he gave her—disappointment, pain, and sorrow.

The cops took her to jail—she had to call her attorney to bail her out; Will didn't help her. The next day, he called her in for a "little talk" that she knew meant her job. She told him what she could remember, which included what Doug had said and done to her, but not much more. She knew he would interview Doug too when he could talk. Melissa felt awful when she found out what had happened to him. He'd broken his nose, his upper jaw, and a tooth. Cut his face. Broken ribs.

What he did to her didn't seem to warrant all that, and she didn't understand how he'd gotten hurt. She wasn't that strong, and there was no bloody baseball bat or anything—it would have taken that to hurt Doug that much. How could she do that much damage? Until now, Melissa didn't know what happened that night.

She did know what happened afterward. Doug was mad at her—and no wonder. He missed weeks of work. When he finally showed up, both eyes were bright red from the impact; they had wired his jaws shut; plus, he had scars on his upper lip and cheek and a funny-looking nose.

He retaliated by telling everyone that she was a bull dyke who decked him when he suggested a quickie. Melissa looked at herself in the *Ashley*'s mirror; she looked stricken. Everyone at Numenon thought she was a lesbian.

Will ended up believing part of her story—that she didn't mean to hurt Doug and didn't know what happened. The felony battery charges were dismissed when his initial sexual battery was established. She was defending herself after he grabbed her breasts. The legal hassle went away, but Doug's accusation didn't.

In Numenon's screwy world, being thought gay actually helped Melissa. All the top execs—led by Will Duane—were macho studs. The few women in the upper ranks were probably lesbians—"real women" were supposed to look and act like Sandy Sydney. The good part was that Will had stopped trying to set her up with creeps, but it also meant that he believed the rumors.

Melissa looked at the light fixture. It was only a light. Why had it looked so much like a head? Why did Doug's hair look red in the conference room lights? What was wrong with her?

What she'd remembered struck home. She didn't beat Doug up like everyone thought—she never touched him. But the blows that fell on him originated with her, she knew that absolutely. How could she hit him from across the room? It was impossible. Crazy.

She wasn't just an amnesiac; she was insane. She felt like falling apart again, but she couldn't. Everyone was just on the other side of the wall; they'd hear her. She pulled the vial out and slipped another pill in her mouth, then another. She'd never taken so many, but... she couldn't face the group or the truth.

She wasn't just an amnesiac or a criminal; she was crazy. Hallucinating. OK, she thought. When we get home, I'll go to a shrink. I'll get professional help. I'll figure it out. She just had to get through the retreat.

Melissa looked at her watch. In forty minutes, the Klonopin would work. She'd be able to sit with the others and not panic. Her eyes stung as tears filled them. Melissa wanted to know why Doug said that to her. She wasn't Jewish. She'd never had a bat mitzvah. She *wasn't* a Jew. Her parents were Jewish, not her. Why didn't people understand that?

She wiped her eyes, not bothering to replace her make up. She had decided to leave Numenon at the end of the week. Her talk with Betty back in the airport bathroom finally hit home. She couldn't be part of an organization that would do what Will wanted to do. As she touched the door handle, another face came to her.

Sandy Sydney's. Ever since the rumors started circulating about her being a lesbian, Sandy Sydney seemed to be smiling in her face. Melissa would have thought Sandy was gay, but for the Barbie dresses and the fact that she was fucking half the execs in the company. Melissa straightened her shoulders, a wry smile on her sad face.

How funny it would be if Numenon's studs and studettes knew the truth about her. Melissa Weir was thirty-one years old and a virgin. If that were known, it would total her career.

51

Doug watched Melissa dash to the bathroom. He was feeling a little better. He decided that he had the flu—the way he felt was like a virus. Chills and fever for a while, then feeling better. It was the flu, that's all, he thought. He'd be OK tomorrow. When Melissa ran by, he remembered why he was on the trip. He wanted to fix things with her. When Will told Doug what Melissa thought he said to her, Doug was appalled.

I never said anything about her being Jewish, he thought. Betty's voice droned on. He kept his eyes stuck to the bathroom door. God—he wished he could rewind the tape and do that night over. He remembered it so well. They'd prepared for weeks for a presentation for some Malaysian bigwigs. Weir was fun, once she got the stick out. More than that... OK, he said to himself. I was half in love with her.

He found out about Jennie getting married two days before the presentation. He was crazy. Really crazy. He felt like he'd never meet a classy woman again. And he was lonely. The presentation was a fantastic success—they worked like a world-class tag team. He'd forgotten how good it felt to work so closely with another person. Melissa wanted to be alone for a few minutes, so Doug went to the cocktail party.

He had a couple of drinks. That was true. He was pretty well lit. She didn't come out. He kept waiting... no Melissa. He kept drinking. Finally, he thought she might be waiting for him, being coy. Wanting him to come to her. He was getting horny. He recalled staggering back to the conference room. OK. OK. I'll admit it, he thought. I was *drunk*.

He had watched Melissa from the conference room door; she sat with her eyes closed. She looked so beautiful. He had wanted to kiss her. She opened her eyes, but didn't see him; then she dropped some papers and he walked over to her. He took her hands and pulled her to her feet. He ran his hands over her breasts and said, "I'll be good for you."

He went to kiss her and *wham!* He went flying through the air and hit the wall. Then Melissa started screaming at him. That was all he remembered, her shrieking at him. On and on. He was being kicked and hit, but he never saw who was doing it. He was bleeding and hurt with this crazy woman screaming. His friends came in when they heard her.

Then all the rest happened. The police report. The DA wanting to charge him. He found out that, in terms a crime being committed, where he put his hands made it *his* fault. She was defending herself, even if he was the one in the hospital.

He knew that what happened was a big deal for Will. Melissa was lucky to have her job, even if he was to blame. He had helped; he told Will that he was drunk and put his hands on her. Doug still didn't know what hit him.

He wished so badly that he could replay it. What he wanted more than anything that night was for the two of them to end up in bed. Not just once, either—he wanted to be her lover. He'd finally found someone who attracted him as much as Jennie. So what did he do? Slandered her all over the company.

Doug shifted uncomfortably. He didn't know how to act with a decent woman.

Melissa had a purity that Doug hadn't seen very much since joining Numenon. As tough as she was, she seemed innocent and untouched when you got inside her defenses. He had been in love with her.

The bathroom door opened and she walked out, taking her seat next to Gil again. Doug followed her with his eyes. He watched her sit down, catching a movement out of the corner of his eye. Sandy Sydney was also watching Melissa—with a look somewhere between a cobra watching a mouse and a kid picking out a candy.

He had no use for Sandy Sydney. One thing whoring with Will Duane had done was give Doug the ability to tell a pro from an amateur. If Sydney wasn't a pro, he was Santa Claus. His eyes narrowed; it wasn't the street-walkers who ended up with your pension plan and house, it was the ones who looked like Sydney. He'd seen something that he'd never forget the night before.

He had been outside Jake Neidermann's office, walking down the cor-ridor by himself after work. Jake's office was in the old building, built in the 1970s when open design and glass walls were cool. Then it was discovered that people worked better with more privacy. They'd installed miniblinds in the executive offices, but Doug could still see in. Jake was head of marketing for the US and was one of the guys screwing Sandy Sydney. Doug slowed when he saw them in Jake's glass-walled office. Jake was sitting at his desk, while Sydney stood next to him, looking at some papers. By the motion of both bodies, Doug could see Neidermann had his hand on Sydney's ass, rubbing away.

Doug blinked when he saw it. A heavy glass paperweight moved across Jake's desk by itself; the lovebirds kept smiling. The paperweight picked up speed and slammed off the edge of the desk, landing on Neidermann's foot. Hard, like it had been thrown. Neidermann yelled. Doug went in to help. Something inside him said, don't say anything about what you saw. He looked at Sandy Sydney, wide-eyed and innocent, and knew she did it. He found out from his driver that morning that Jake's foot was broken.

It was weird enough to see, but the discussion on the drive set off something in him. Mark and Jeff talked about energy and spiritual masters who could move things with their minds. He'd seen a special on PBS about some guy who could bend spoons with his mind. Doug didn't think that counted for much, but if you could bend a spoon, why not move a paper-weight? He felt creepy … and then it came together for him, what he'd been hearing for weeks.

Everyone at Numenon worked out at the company gym. The gym was the place to meet Will. He went every day, shaming everyone there with his stamina. If you wanted to make points with the boss and rise in Numenon, you worked out. Doug worked out. Everyone knew he'd partied with Will all over the world. Guys would come up to him—executives only, of course—and ask about problems they might be having in very personal realms. He was the expert, right?

Three guys had sidled up to him in the locker room over a period of weeks. Each told a story about a friend: "Doug, have you ever heard of this? One of my buddies said he got a crushing pain in his balls. It lasted a long time, and then it felt like pins sticking into him." When he expressed sympathy, they all said the same thing: "My doctor can't figure it out. There's nothing wrong with me, but man! It hurts." Doug couldn't imagine what would do that, but it sounded awful.

His biggest fear was AIDS. That was enough to knock him out of the fast lane with Will two years before. When Steve Pryor from international marketing came out positive, visions of Magic Johnson ran through Doug's head. But crushing pain in your balls and then pins and needles?

After Neidermann was shipped off to Stanford Hospital last night, Doug saw Sandy Sydney get into a car with one of the guys who'd approached him about pins and needles. Neidermann was another. It clicked. All of the men who'd talked to him were sleeping with Sydney.

She was the one who did it. It was that talk about spiritual masters that pulled the pieces together for him. Sandy Sydney was certainly not spiritual, but—Jesus—what was she?

Doug looked in her direction. She was staring back at him, her expression anything but her usual sweet pout. Her eyes caught his. Their brilliant blue captivated him. They were filled with murderous hatred. He couldn't look away, couldn't break the hold of her gaze. When she had demonstrated her power over him, Sandy let him go.

Doug turned away from her, shaken. What had happened? He wanted to yell to Will, call for help. But he couldn't move. She had paralyzed him. Sydney had so much hatred in her eyes, she could have been a demon from hell.

He had another burst of insight. The guys who had confided in him and the others he knew had been with Sydney were top execs. He could see their faces in the annual report. Sydney was fucking her way to the top of the Numenon org chart. She was some kind of industrial spy.

Sandy smiled at him. "Are you OK, Doug? Do you need anything?"

The baby face promised him satisfaction, however he might want it. But he knew she wanted to kill him. Who was she? *What* was she? She continued to look at him, but not sweetly. She knew that he knew.

52

The shades were still down, so the cabin's automatic lighting kept the room bright. Mark didn't think any of the professionals had noticed their problem. He was trying to drive straight and figure out how to tell his boss that the walls of the canyon were almost brushing the *Ashley's* side mirrors. And that the canyon might dead end, or if it wasn't a dead end, those storm clouds up there might create a flash flood that would kill them. He glanced into the rearview mirror.

Mr. Duane stood abruptly, looking at the windshield with panic on his face. He reached for the cabinets, heading toward the driver's seat in the moving vehicle. Mark turned back to the windshield.

"Oh shit! Hold on!" Mark shouted, jamming on the brakes. The *Ashley* jolted to a stop. Will flew across the cabin, landing in Sandy Sydney's arms. Instinctively, she spread her legs and ensured that every inch of her body touched him. Will leaped off her, bouncing back like a bungee jumper hitting the end of the line. It would have been comical but for the revolted expression on his face. He was almost knocked flat again when the vehicle behind them hit the *Ashley's* rear. Two more nudges marked the following vehicles coming to a stop against their predecessors.

"Oh, Mr. Duane—I'm so sorry! It was just *there*—I didn't see it."

The entire party looked out of the windshield. A ledge of rock protruded into the canyon and blocked their way. If they'd traveled a couple inches more, it would have shattered the glass. The canyon walls pressed up against the *Ashley* with barely enough room to open the door and walk between the rock and the vehicle. Mark expected Will to chew him out and fire him. He didn't. He got out with Mark, looked at the damage and said, "Nothing serious. It'll run. Is everyone OK?"

They were; some vehicles had bumps and dents, but that's all. They just couldn't go anywhere but back, in reverse.

Mark watched Will. He handled it so well, nothing like "The Prince of Darkness." He was all over the place—out in front of the *Ashley* looking up into the sky. He seemed to be sniffing the air as he had done when he checked out the canyon openings. This time, Mark would follow Mr. Duane's intuition and not any map. "I'm sorry, Mr. Duane," he whispered. "I kept expecting it to widen out ..."

"I saw it too, Mark. I should have made you stop. I thought it was OK too. There's no fault here." Will examined the ledge protruding into the canyon. About four feet off the ground, the rock abutment jutted three feet into the canyon. It wasn't large enough to block a small car or truck, but plenty big enough to block the motor homes.

"Too bad we don't have a jackhammer," Will said.

"We have some shovels and pickaxes." Mark never thought that the ridiculous assortment of junk Jon Walker insisted they bring would come in handy. Jon had included the picks and shovels in case they had a luau.

"Wild pigs are very common in the desert. All those Indians are sure to catch one, and we'll have to show them how to prepare it properly. Hawaiian style is the only way," Jon had pontificated. "It's easy to dig a pit in nice topsoil like they have in Atherton, but if they have that Woodside bedrock in the desert, you'll need pickaxes. In fact, you'll need a jackhammer." Jon was trying to get Mark to bring one when he rebelled.

I should have let him bring it, Mark lamented silently.

Will nodded, looking around, taking in everything. The group of drivers and most of the others stood in front of the *Ashley*. Mark felt reassured with Will there. He understood everything in a glance. They'd have to back up for hours to get out if they couldn't get through the canyon; they were exposed to any sort of attack, a flash flood could kill them instantly. Everyone could hear thunder in the distance. But he wasn't angry or looking for anyone to blame; Will just understood their situation and moved to handle it.

"I'm going to run ahead for a while and scout. Start taking down this rock," Will pointed to the projection. "Use anything we've got to knock it down; have people work in shifts. Let's get out of these monkey suits." Will indicated his suit. The shirt was tear-stained.

A few minutes later, Will stood in front of the *Ashley* in jogging shorts and a T-shirt. The rest clustered around him, wearing jeans and tennies. Will was so wired he could barely stand still; he *had* to run. "I'm going to see what's out there. The rest of you see what you can do to that ledge."

"Mr. Duane, I don't think that's wise. That rock just was *there*. It came out of nowhere. And the instruments have been acting weird. I think someone should go with you," Mark objected. The others nodded, but no one volunteered.

"Will, take someone with you. There might be wild animals." Betty radiated anxiety. Fear washed over all of them as they realized their predicament.

Will would not be dissuaded. His maximum capacity to stay in one place had been exceeded. The rock was the last straw—he would run, or explode. "I've got my cell phone, Betty. I'll call if there's any problem." And he was off, jogging up the canyon on the other side of the boulder with the strength of a marathon runner.

"Will!" Betty called. "Cell phones don't work here …" If he heard her warning, he gave no sign.

"I'll follow him," Doug said. He was also dressed in jogging clothes. Doug was a more powerful runner than Will, if that was possible. "If we're not back in an hour, Gil—come and get us."

"But Doug …" Everyone had seen what a mess he was.

"I'm OK now. It's the flu—I'm sick for an hour and a half and then I'm fine. I'll go slow. He *shouldn't* be alone …"

Everyone agreed with that; they let them go. They needed to work on the rock—they had to get out of there. The shovels and picks were laid out in a pile in front of the *Ashley*. Mark and the others milled around with no idea what to do with them.

"OK, we should work in shifts," Mark attempted to lead them. He lifted a pick in a way that indicated he'd never touched one before.

"College kids—don't know one end of a pick from th' other," Delroy West muttered as he walked to the front of the group. "This is how y'all hold a pick," he said, hefting the shank correctly. His previous life taught him all about picks and shovels. He never wanted to break up anything harder than topsoil again. He'd learned that lesson in a place he wouldn't admit he'd been and never wanted to revisit. "We'll work in two-man shifts ..." Delroy got them going efficiently. His expert use of a pick, and the thunder, kept them at it.

"Tape y'alls' hands if they blister. Ya' got any tape?" Delroy's voice exposed his Southern roots the more he swung.

For once, Jon didn't jump out with rolls of adhesive tape. No one had seen him since he entered his motor home.

Betty appeared carrying the *Ashley*'s first aid kit. "Is this the right kind of tape?"

53

Will bolted up the canyon. He sprinted like the jutting rock was chasing *him*. Aside from the tension produced by the morning's events, Will had lived alone in a fifteen thousand square foot house for twenty-three years. He could deal with people being close to him in business situations, but he had his limits. The ride in the *Ashley* was far beyond his tolerance.

Will's watch flashed weirdly. He tapped it and it stopped. That was the last time he looked at it—he flat-out ran from then on. Will had run as long as he could remember. The only sound was the crunching of his running shoes on the desert floor. It was dust-covered rock with pebbles here and there. An easy run. The pounding of the picks receded into the distance. Then, all he could hear was his own breathing. If anyone was following him, Will never knew.

He knew what would happen when he ran. Three miles it took. Three miles to oblivion. Will ran and the sound of Betty's weeping filled his ears; he could feel her in his arms. He'd never held her in all these years. He'd wanted to many times, but he knew. If he took her to bed once, that would be the end of their relationship. He loved her too much for it to end that way. He knew what was going on with her in the *Ashley*, what she wasn't saying in her silent fugue. He knew what happened back then.

For him it started earlier. Kathryn and he were married in 1960. She drank bourbon, Southern belle style. It was perfectly acceptable in her fine Savannah home. Kathryn drank. After Ashley was born, she never stopped. The more successful he got, the harder he had to work, and the more she drank. It was a circle. Did his success drive her to drink? Or did he stay away because she was drunk?

The images were always there, hundreds of them ready to pop up the instant he felt weak. He saw a dark red stain spread across the floor, its outline a ragged crescent. The stain was claret red, a half circle unfolding across the floor. It had stopped expanding by the time he got home. It looked like cloyed wine spilled on the marble checkerboard floor of their 1970s kitchen.

Will ran faster. His breath lengthened with his stride. He was running down the canyon, not noticing that it widened out, not noticing that it was brighter ahead where the canyon emptied into the plain. Not noticing anything but the fact that he had to run until that image went away, he had to run hard enough for the pain he felt when he saw it disappear. At three miles, it would disappear. It wasn't three miles yet, that was all.

The red crescent came back, and more. Her arm lay extended by her head. Her face was porcelain white, like all of her blood had spilled on the floor. Nothing else was stained; her white silk robe wasn't stained. He could see her profile, dark red lipstick against the white skin. Eyelids so fine that blue veins colored them like shadow. The white arm, white robe. She had fallen and hit her head on one of the iron barstools.

"Kathryn!" He jumped when he saw her on the floor; he took her in his arms. She didn't stir. Her hair was matted with blood. He could smell the acrid sourness of alcohol on her breath. "Oh, thank God! She's alive!" He wept.

The ambulance took her to the hospital. Their family doctor came out at two a.m. to see her. "I'll admit her tomorrow, Will. We'll get a hold of it." He didn't say, "This time it will work." He didn't mention the three other times at Sequoia, the time they'd sent her to Arizona, the stints in Florida and Colorado. He said, "We'll get it under control."

For how long? Will had thought. For six weeks? For three months, six months? How long? He was one of the most powerful men in the world, and he could not keep his wife from drinking. He had no power over his wife's disease.

Will went home that night and fired everyone on the staff. At four a.m., he called the afternoon nurse and fired her. He woke up the nurse who was supposed to be on duty that night and fired her; he fired the butler and the maids when they arrived the next day; he fired the fucking gardeners. He talked to the neighbors, though it almost killed him. They were very understanding. She hadn't gotten it from them and they'd keep an eye out.

Kathryn was drinking again in four months. Where she got it, Will never knew.

He kept Kathryn a prisoner on their estate. He bought her horses and dogs and whatever she wanted. He kept her a prisoner because he couldn't stand to see her destroy herself, anymore than he could stop what she was doing—or what he was doing. Finally, he gave up and let her go.

She went to Spain and Carlo Piretti. A groan escaped Will's lips. His chest heaved as his legs pumped. It had to be three miles; it had to be three miles. The euphoria should come and all he'd have was the wonderful high of running. The red stain would leave his mind.

It did, replaced by something else. He could see the white linen of her straight skirt flapping as she walked to the car the last time he saw her. She wove as she walked, staggering slightly at eight in the morning. She wore red high heels. The white linen dress bagged and flapped over her shrunken buttocks as she made her way to the limousine.

Her caretaker, the Spanish woman, Confidencia, who Kathryn had brought back from her first trip to Spain, looked at him with compassionate eyes. "We will take good care of her, Señor," she said. "She will come back to you better, you will see." Confidencia stepped closer and ran her hand down the front of his pants. "Everything will be better soon, you'll see." The door closed. That was the last time he saw his wife.

Gasps escaped Will. "I was screwing my wife's maid!" He was the reason she drank. Will felt like running into the canyon walls, over a cliff. He forced himself to go forward, faster. He shouldn't feel this bad, the high should be on its way. He didn't know how long he had run.

Finally, he burst out of the canyon and onto the plain like a growing stalk leaping from the dark earth into sunshine. He ran for a while longer, feeling the joy he had hoped for. The air was so clear! The morass of his mind was gone. He felt like jumping and shouting for joy. The red crescent had disappeared.

Will looked out into the desert before him, seeing it for the first time. He stood still and looked in every direction. "It's beautiful," he whispered. The desert floor spread out for miles. All around it, mountains jutted up like candy boxes. Different colors, striated. Cacti grew, looking fuzzy if you didn't get too close. The colors were wonderful. Overhead, two hawks circled round his head. Looking more carefully, he could see they were enormous.

"They must be eagles," Will said out loud. He never thought of eagles back in Palo Alto. He never considered that they might be alive and flying around somewhere. The birds seemed messages of regeneration and hope. Wild joy burst from him. The eagles were not all dead. Some were up there, circling over him. Will laughed like a madman and waved at them.

He looked around him, knowing exactly what direction they should go to get to the camp; it was easy from now on. The map was wrong, but that didn't matter. Will turned around, smiling. Near the mouth of the canyon on the way back, Will spied something very interesting. He slowed and then stopped ten feet away.

"Well, aren't you a funny old guy," he said, thrilled. An old coyote stood silently watching him. "You look worse than I do." The coyote's fur was scruffy and matted, one ear was half gone, the other notched. He had scars all over him, including a long one below his left eye. One front leg was crooked, Will saw as he cautiously approached. "Well, you're something, aren't you? Not afraid of anything," Will wished he had some bread, although nothing about this animal suggested that he ate bread. When the coyote was within three feet, Will dropped to one knee. Nothing inside him said, "This is unusual behavior, Will. This animal may be rabid. Be careful."

The coyote was very close to him. Its yellow eyes were mesmerizing, deep yellow gold with darker lines in them. The yellow of the eyes melted out over the animal so that all Will saw was the muted gold, filling his universe. The sienna of the canyon walls was gone; all the shades of rose around him, gone. Nothing existed but those entrancing yellow eyes and the coyote. Will extended his hand. The coyote sniffed it and explored it with his nose. He licked Will's hand softly, looking into his eyes. It was a sensuous experience. Will couldn't stop it. He knew that the coyote wished him well and would not hurt him. Will's heart leaped from his chest. As it did, the coyote bit him. Not hard. A light bite on his fingers; a piercing bite, not enough to break the skin. Just enough to break Will's heart.

He cried out—looking at his hand in disbelief. The coyote was gone. Will pulled his hand to his chest, falling forward on his face on the canyon floor; the pain was excruciating. He clutched his heart, crying, "Marina! I'm sorry; please take me back. I'll do whatever you want, just take me back." He writhed on the ground, telling the truth.

The coyote withdrew a bit, watching and listening. The corners of his mouth turned up in a canine smile when his visitor revealed his real reason for being where he was.

The coyote trotted back to Will Duane and nudged him with his nose. Will recoiled in fear, but not as hysterically as he might have; the yellow eyes stopped him. The coyote rubbed against him and poked him with his nose again. It had a calming effect. Will lay down on the ground, and the coyote lay down next to him, listening like a friend. He put his arm around the coyote as if it was a stuffed toy animal and he was a tiny boy.

A child's voice came from Will Duane's mouth. "Will she come back if I'm good?" The coyote nudged him. "If I do a good job this week, will she come back?" The coyote rubbed Will Duane with its body. "Did she love me, coyote?" said the child's voice. The coyote licked him. A huge sigh escaped Will. "I knowed that," the little voice said, "but I'm still going to do a good job in case she watches." Will looked at the coyote, "Will you stay with me, coyote? I have a big house."

The eagles above tipped their wings and the coyote laughed in his way.

The animal waited with Will until he became a man again. Will stood up and brushed himself off. He watched the coyote trot away, remembering nothing.

He sniffed the air once more, and looked at the thunderclouds gathering not very far away. He looked into the canyon. The desert floor formed a funnel, directing run-off into the gorge; the map had pointed them into a deathtrap. He looked over his shoulder at the clouds, then headed back to the caravan as fast as he could. They might have time.

54

Doug followed Will, trying to catch him. He needed to catch him. He had to tell him about Sandy Sydney and a few other things. Time to level with his boss—share his feelings, like they said in touchy-feely. He lumbered up the canyon, muscles aching, legs heavy as stones. How had he forgotten how bad he felt? It was like a flu—sometimes he ached and itched, then it went away. Once he started running, all the pain came back. Sound echoed in the canyon. Even though he never saw Will, he could hear his explosive breathing up ahead. He kept going, trying to catch up. He went pretty far, given how bad he felt.

Doug found himself struggling as Will's gasping filled his ears. Nausea overcame him. He stopped running and moved to the side of the canyon, one hand on the canyon wall, retching. He'd heard Will breathing like that before. When he first came to Numenon seven years before, he'd regarded Will Duane as the finest man on the planet. The billionaire was Doug's idol, his mentor, his *alter ego*. Will seemed equally taken by him. Doug forced himself back to the center of the canyon, plodding dully.

Over time, he and Will developed a close relationship based on what-ever Will wanted. Doug Saunders did Will's dirty work. No job was too rough for faithful Doug, or too illegal. He could go to jail until he was an old, old man if what he'd done for Will came to light. He couldn't blame anyone. Will didn't force him to do it. He jumped at the chance. He'd do anything to see him smile. He'd do anything to please him. And he had done anything and everything.

The first time he heard Will breathing hard like that was when he'd split up with Jennie. They'd lived together for three years, in love. Doug's brand of love, Numenon love. He cheated on her. Screwing around was a way of life at Numenon and part of working for Will.

Jennie didn't leave Doug because of his cheating. She left him because she never saw him. Doug didn't know how many hours a week he worked. Sixty was obligatory for anyone who wanted to stay at the company; way more than that was necessary if you wanted to rise to the top. That's how it was all over Silicon Valley, but Numenon's pace was insane. As usual, Will led the way. His drive propelled Numenon from a start-up to the huge international conglomerate it was. Will Duane was first at work and last to leave for forty years.

When Doug and Jennie split, Will picked up on—not that it was hard—how depressed he was. Will's solution was an all-night double date. The two of them and two of San Francisco's finest in one of the corporate condos in the City. When he saw the women, Doug would have never known they were pros. They looked like the classiest socialites. Designer clothes, real jewelry, beautiful faces. And their bodies!

It was the biggest turn-on in the world the first time when he heard Will in the next bedroom with his "lady." Doug remembered thinking, I've really made it—that's Will Duane! They were *that* close. He'd never known what *exotic sex* meant until Will's gals showed him. He liked it—boy, did he *like* it. For the next two years, Doug and Will "double dated" constantly, in San Francisco and wherever they were working. Will even took him on a couple of three-day "business trips" and a week's vacation in Italy. The trips were orgies. Pros, pretty women they picked up in bars, parties, by the pool, anywhere. Married, single, they screwed 'em all. He and Will never did it in the same room, but they were close enough so that each of them knew exactly what the other was doing. Doug knew the sound of Will's hard breathing very well.

When Steve Pryor tested HIV positive two years ago, that was the end of it. Doug's shaking increased. They had been with the same women. Did he get it? AIDS was a death sentence. Nothing like STDs—Doug didn't worry so much about anything you could treat.

He'd had himself tested every six months, and last week for this Meeting. Would those fucking Indians and their fucking Dr. Bright Eagle be the ones to tell him?

Steve Pryor was still alive. New medications could prolong his life, but who cared? The end was the same. Doug felt dizzy, imaging his face covered with sores. He couldn't even think about Jon Walker. He'd be next, for sure. Jon wasn't HIV positive, was he? Doug wouldn't touch anything cooked by someone with HIV. Nah, he couldn't be positive—Will would fire him.

His nausea rose and fell as he recalled the other reason he broke off with Will. He rubbed his chest, feeling dirty. Why the open doors? Why did Will need him to know what he was doing? It was almost like they were in the same room.

He'd always felt that people who criticized Will Duane were little people who couldn't keep up. He thought Will's ex-wife was a weak broad who couldn't take the heat, but he now realized what it must have been like for her.

It was like a disease. He gave up partying with Will two years ago, but he couldn't stop living the life. He wore a rubber now—that was the only difference. Doug liked the chase, the rush of adrenaline; and he liked fucking women he didn't need or want. Since that magazine named him "Bachelor of the Year," he didn't even have to try.

He knew what happened to Will two months ago and why he was so screwed up—Marina Selene dumped him.

Would he end up like Will Duane, sixty-three years old and pining over a whore? Doug staggered over to a boulder and sat heavily and care-lessly. He didn't check to see if he was sitting on a scorpion or if a rattlesnake was hiding in the rock's shade. He curled into a ball and wrapped his arms around himself. One thing Melissa Weir had done by decking him—she stopped him running around. He hadn't had anyone since, and he didn't want anyone. Doug shivered, unaware of anything but his pain.

55

andy Sydney was alone in the *Ashley*. Everyone had changed into jeans and tennies and clustered in front of the vehicle. The guys took turns with the pickaxes and shovels while Betty and Melissa watched and talked. The men had their shirts off; Sandy liked watching them through the windshield. They were making progress on the rock that blocked their way, but it still was taking time. Will Duane was long gone. She looked up the canyon after him. The way he jumped up off her so fast hurt her feelings. I'm not a whore, she thought. Sandy's eyes and feelings smarted.

I'm a courtesan, she said to herself, straightening her beautiful posture. She peered out through the windshield again. As before, no one noticed her. Betty was talking to Melissa in an animated fashion, a change from how she'd been minutes ago. This was how it always was for Sandy. She watched others having fun on the other side of an invisible wall. She went back to the banquette. Betty was the only person who believed in her. That old bugaboo, wanting to go straight, came up again when Sandy was around Betty. She wanted people to like her the way Betty did—for herself.

That morning, Sandy's moods changed like shadows of clouds. She lay back on the banquette, looking at the lounge chair where Will Duane had been, mindless of the fact that she had wanted to kill him earlier. The image of the two of them living in his glowing house haunted her. She could see them smiling at each other in the pale bedroom with its tall ceilings and silk draperies.

Sandy didn't *have* to go back to her benefactor. If she got a real offer, an offer to marry Will Duane, for instance, Carlo wouldn't mind. He loved her, he'd told her that many times. He would release her from her obligation to him. Maybe Will would fall for her this week. He would tell her what Carlo wanted to know, she'd pass it on, and they could be happy together. She could visualize the Indian holy man as though he stood before her. He was a sacred creature who wanted the best for her, as did her benefactor. Sandy Sydney was no whore. She was a human being. She would do right this week and keep all the rules. No sex, no making a little money on the side. No finding things out, except with Will.

The pain returned. She gasped, holding her side. The pain came so often, she could barely work. Sometimes it came as aching all over her body, like a horrible flu. Other times the pain stabbed, and she felt like something was slicing her up inside. She told Carlo about it, and he sounded alarmed. "You must come home, my darling. Finish your work and come home."

His reaction scared her. "Should I come home now?"

"No, finish your work first. You will be fine. You picked up a little something. One shot when you're back here, and you'll be OK."

Her benefactor had liberated her from thinking herself as worthless or ruined. He found her in Paris when she worked at Kris and Max's gallery. She was a lost soul when he took her to his villa. Sandy could remember what her stepfather did to her when she was little, but it always seemed distant, as if it had happened to someone else. When the memories came up full force in Spain, Carlo told her it happened to many girls; it wasn't her fault. She was safe now and could let her feelings out. Once he said that, the memories exploded as if they'd been waiting to let go. Sandy rocked and retched and cried for weeks. Carlo rescued her, becoming her Benefactor, her savior.

Sandy's story seemed normal to her. She was orphaned at age two in her native Oklahoma. An enchanting blonde, Sandy was adopted by an apparently respectable couple from Las Vegas, Nevada. They weren't respectable. Her Bible-quoting mother beat her and her adopted father started molesting her within a week. By the time she was eleven, Sandy Sydney had done every-thing sexual a female can do.

Papa Ralph gave her to all his friends and the men in his lodge. He took her to town to earn gambling money when she was thirteen. Tears filled Sandy's eyes. I was so happy when he died, she thought, recalling Papa Ralph's car being pulled from the river. Her mama died two weeks later, choking on a steak. Sandy was sixteen, a high school senior with straight As. She'd always known her grades were her ticket to somewhere else.

What she did after her parents' deaths didn't surprise her, but her anger did. In a rage, she sold their house and everything in it. She sold their car. She smashed her mama's favorite vase and sent everything she couldn't sell to the dump. She was going to start a new life as far from Vegas as she could get; she was going to buy a house of her own and a new car.

Papa Ralph's gambling debts took care of that dream. She knew the men he owed money to, and she knew better than to argue with them. When they came to collect, she gave them what they wanted. She ended up with enough for a bus ticket to Chicago, a tiny apartment, and tuition for secretarial school. Not much of a new life, but she went as far as she could with it.

Sandy's resume was totally accurate. She worked her way through sec-retarial school in Chicago. Sandy was determined to prove that she wasn't what everyone in her hometown said she was. She always *wanted* to go straight; it's just that she had such bad luck. She landed a secretarial job in a construction firm. The owner seemed so nice. She discovered very quickly that he had mob connections. She was banging him in two weeks, the rest of the "family" in four. Those were "the family friends" who paid for Wellesley. I wonder what Betty would say if she knew, Sandy thought.

She broke away from her mob connections after Wellesley, a true miracle. She found a rich, fat old hump with factories and businesses everywhere—the father of one of her Wellesley friends—to pay her way to France. He paid for the Sorbonne and everything else. All she had to do was spend holidays and summers with him. She paid off her "family" obligations by informing on Fat Freddy's business activities. They blackmailed him, and Sandy became an industrial spy. Her Chicago friends thought their investment in her was money well spent. She found her way to Kris and Max's gallery in Paris. Free at last! Kris and Max showed her how to dress and how to make it with sophisticated Europeans. Most wonderfully, they introduced her to their Benefactor. That's what many of his people called him—the Benefactor, with a capital B, like he was God.

He took her home. Sandy told him the horrible things that happened to her at her adopted father's hands. Her Benefactor would hold her and love her through it, touching her and calming her in the nicest way. His hands mesmerized her, tranquilized her. They turned her on. He would hear her terrible story and then touch her, slowly, talking to her, pushing her limits.

Whatever she confessed to him, he always ended by doing to her himself, but it was good with him. When she described the gang rapes, he did the same thing. He would listen quietly and sweetly, touching her and almost sending her to sleep, then he would take her first, then the members of the staff would come in and do what he told them, acting out what had been done to her before. Sandy loved it. He said that it was a kind of therapy he invented, going back and experiencing what happened again without it being traumatic, learning to integrate it. When he began to give her to his friends, Sandy felt like a queen.

He taught her to think of herself as a courtesan, a beautiful, ultradesirable, sexual gift available only for the highest and best. Expensive beyond belief, she was a woman worth dying for. She was so pleased that he trusted her enough to send her on this mission. She lived with him the last few weeks so he could give her skills and powers. Then, the staff party he hosted for her the night before she left ... Sandy rubbed her knees together. She would never forget it.

The pain grabbed her so hard she could barely think. She called out to Carlo. The pain eased a bit. She realized how much she loved him and what she owed him. Moaning, she lay back on the sofa. What was this pain? What were the other changes she saw in herself? Sandy had gotten back at people who hurt her before but not viciously, the way she did now. These days, she reveled in doing bad things. The pleasure she felt wasn't natural. Sex always felt good, but not like it did now. She could see things at a distance, on the other side of the world. She knew what others were saying and even thinking; it scared her.

Something was wrong. She didn't understand the accidents that followed her—how did that paperweight fall and break Jake's foot? They were saying she'd hurt the men she'd been with. She never hurt people (well, just in play, if they wanted it, but not really). She'd awakened twice in the last two weeks with men she didn't know—they weren't even from Numenon. And all those awful e-mails from Native Americans. What they said to her! Sandy was scared. She'd get the information Carlo wanted and get back to Spain. The pain ceased ... Almost immediately, Sandy's head drooped and she slept.

She awakened minutes later to the sound of pickaxes. For a moment, she forgot where she was. The pain was gone, but she felt terribly nervous and lonely. Something awful was going to happen, she knew it. Sandy sat up and looked out the windshield. No one was paying any attention to her. She wanted to unzip her jeans and play with herself, the way she did when she felt nervous, but someone might come in. Her mind went to food. The refrigerator held six sandwiches and a cake. And all those delicious juices.

She struggled with herself. She'd had to diet for more than a year after her parents died to look the way she did. The only thing she'd found that stopped Papa Ralph was eighty pounds of fat. She ate and he left her alone. Her last year of high school, he never bothered her once. Until she met her Benefactor, Sandy had loved food more than sex. You'll have to starve again, she said to herself. You can't go back to him looking like a pig. He'll only want you if you're beautiful.

Rocking back and forth, Sandy couldn't take her mind off the refrigerator. *Jon Walker* sandwiches and cake were in there, not just ordinary food. One sandwich wouldn't hurt. She crept around the peninsula that formed the back of the banquette where she and Betty sat. She only took one sandwich. Still five left. She was allowed to have a *snack*.

Mmm. So good. Sandy curled up on the banquette, nibbling a bite at a time. Her anxiety didn't go away. Strange things kept happening, like those e-mails. She had posted a few perfectly respectable requests for e-mail pals on major Indian Web sites, doing the research that Betty wanted her to do for her presentation. She and Betty discovered that Native Americans have a thriving Internet life, just like everyone else. Betty wanted her to chat with some to learn about their culture.

Soon, a few Indians answered her request to correspond about their culture. Then they wanted a picture of her, which she sent, a photo that Carlo had taken at his villa. She was seated on the terrace in a blue dress with miles of sky in the background. She couldn't understand the way they responded; it was as though she'd sent a porn photo. That was impossible. Carlo had all of those. Then she started getting really nasty e-mails from all over.

Sandy ran to the refrigerator and got another sandwich, ducking so no one could see her. This time she didn't nibble it. How did that happen? Indians were calling her names, bad names. That couldn't have been a trick picture, could it? Carlo wouldn't do that to her, would he?

She knew that he had supernatural powers. He knew what people were saying and doing around the villa or at any of his homes. And he could do things that she could barely comprehend. Sometimes she felt like he was in the room, even though she knew he was thousands of miles away. He was a master, a great master. That talk that Mark and Jeff gave excited her. She wanted to tell them, "Yes! Masters exist! They can do all sorts of things—reach across space, and know what you're thinking."

She wanted to shout, "They do things that ordinary people call *bad*. But they are things that we, the people who belong to them, know are *good*." Masters could use their power for whatever they wanted, not just for "*good*." They could destroy things for the fun of it. They could take things that belonged to others. They could inflict terrible pain. She knew all that because she'd seen Carlo do it. Jeff and Mark were wrong, the way Mark was wrong saying the highest pleasures of sex would come only if you were faithful and in love. Those were pathetic lies that the weak believed. Good and evil didn't exist—only what the master wanted mattered.

She wasn't weak. She was one of Carlo's people. She belonged to Carlo, all of her belonged to him. She began to feel dizzy, and knew why. She'd thought about the Benefactor too much. He could feel it. He had told them not to think about him if other people were near. If they had powers, they might feel his presence. Thinking about Carlo could betray him.

He *knew* she'd been thinking of him … Oh, no! She would be punished … "Don't hurt me, *please* don't hurt me," she whispered.

Sandy's eyes rolled back and her eyelids fluttered. She found herself in Carlo's palatial home. The steel-banded door to the great chamber beneath the villa swung open. They dragged her down the stairs. She clawed at them, struggling to escape. It didn't make any difference; it happened anyway. Her heart pounded as she struggled to make out her surroundings in the hushed darkness.

Dimly lit figures walked in a circle, moving around the table in the center of the room. Around *her*. She was on her back on the table, unable to move. Carlo stood behind her, muscles bulging in his white flesh. He raised his hands above his head. The blade flashed and the others leaped at her. Teeth glinted and she heard noises of sucking and tearing. Her screams made no sound.

Sandy sat up, clutching her shirt with both hands. She looked out the windshield, terrified. They were still pounding at the rock outside. What had happened to her? Something bad, but she didn't know what.

Mark Kenna stuck his head in the door and said. "Sandy, can you get some food and drinks together for the guys? Everybody's hot and starving."

"Yes, certainly." Sandy looked at the mess around her, quickly stuffing the sandwich wrappers under the seat cushion.

56

oug clutched his ribs. He leaned over and gagged, but nothing came out. As bad as his nausea was, guilt battered him harder. Guilt, revulsion, and shame over what he'd done with and without Will. Doug knew he couldn't blame Will for everything—he had been operating solo for two years.

He twined his arms around his head, rocking from side to side. The canyon walls and floor were red rock, but they seemed too bright. Sunlight crashed into the ravine. He squinted, trying to block the assault of light. Why was everything so bright? The light was so intense that color of the red stone seemed to bleach out. His head throbbed.

He remembered something. Jennie got migraines. When she had one, she reacted to light like he was, and she got sick to her stomach, too. He must have a migraine. He couldn't imagine being this sick. How would he make it back to the caravan? He looked back at the trail toward the *Ashley* and then huddled up with his eyes closed.

His eyes shot open; something told him to open them. He saw her instantly, lying in the middle of the path. Her heavy, sinuous form and heart-shaped head were clearly defined against the stone. Her tongue darted toward him. He froze. Any other day, he would have called her a rattlesnake, a *huge* rattler, but not today. He knew what she was without thinking, just as he knew she was female. She came toward him in slow loops, her rattle held aloft. He couldn't move. He knew what she really was. She was every bad thing he'd ever done coming for him. She was Will Duane and Numenon and his career and all those women. She was drugs. She was *sin*.

As she undulated toward him, she seemed to grow larger. Her red mottled scales were distinct, slipping and flowing as she moved. The sunlight was relentless, bombarding him. He could hardly focus because of its brilliance. He watched her, knowing that snakes didn't act like this, coming out in the sun. Approaching people. Stalking them. She had come for him. Now he would get what he deserved.

She kept getting bigger as her long curves edged closer. The serpent was relentless. When she touched his leg, he started to cry. "I'm sorry. I'm so sorry. I didn't mean ..."

But he *had* meant it, when he did what he did; he meant every bit of it. He simply didn't expect to get caught. He was caught. The heavy body and soft, dusty scales rose from the ground, pressing against his calf.

Sweat covered him and ran down his brow. The light became so bright that all color disappeared. The world tilted; he didn't know if what was happening was real. Everything was strange and out of proportion, too big, too small. She seemed far larger than he was; he was like a toy next to her. Did she make the world change, or did his wrongdoing make him small?

Doug sat still, barely breathing. He felt her rise up his shin. Her head poked over his knee, and she looked at him with bright eyes, her forked tongue shooting out. Her body followed her head, rising inexorably into his lap.

She wrapped around him like the slim-bodied women he had known with Will. He could feel her ribs inching across his body; her scales rubbing against him. She was like fire, like those lithe girls. As she coiled around him, the light blinded him. She glistened, eyes sparkling, the outlines of her scales all that remained in the glow. She was like a paper lantern, a radiant shell, stronger and more vital than anything he had known.

Doug couldn't resist. Her coils pinned his legs to the boulder while she wound around him again and again. She spiraled up his torso, moving like

Will's slender girls, swelling and surging, promising. Poisoning. She was there to kill him.

When her body wrapped his shoulders, she pulled away and faced him, staring into his eyes. Her head was twice as wide as his. She swayed from side to side, entrancing. Her tongue forked out, tasting the sweat on his forehead, lazily surveying his face. He raised his lips and let her explore him. She raised herself as high as she could and pulled away from him, preparing to strike. She hissed, her open mouth revealing white fangs and scarlet flesh.

He squeezed his eyes shut, the only thing he could do. She would strike him in the face or neck and he would die in minutes. He already felt dead. He wasn't afraid.

She struck his thigh. He felt four punctures like driven spikes, pulsing venom, and then he was flying. She raised him off the boulder with her jaws, swinging and snapping him in the air. Whipping him side to side in frenzied joy. When she tired of playing, she threw him down.

He slammed against the ground, landing on the side of his head and shoulder. Something snapped. His body moved convulsively, legs flailing in a circle, muscles twitching from her venom. He would have no easy, quick death. Doug shuddered in a white world, ears buzzing. He could feel her watching, amused in her way. She dissolved into the whiteness, disappearing the way she had come.

He was alone with the pain, his body dancing as the venom worked through him. His movement slowed; the pain lessened. He became numb. He could feel his breath traveling in and out. He could hear the beating of his heart. As his paralysis deepened, the interval between heartbeats lengthened. The movement of his breath became barely perceptible. Soon, it would cease.

57

Certainly, Mark." Sandy went to the refrigerator after Mark stuck his head into the *Ashley*. Only fruit juice, a couple of sandwiches, and half the cake remained. Sandy couldn't figure out what happened. She knew six sandwiches had been in the refrigerator, as well as a small cake. She had no idea who ate them. She put the remaining sandwiches on a plate and cut them in pieces, rimming the platter with small slices of cake. It looked like more than it was.

"Here you go," she said passing the tray around outside. She didn't say a word about the missing food, and no one asked. She passed out the juices and fruit, and some crackers she found in one of the cabinets.

They didn't seem to notice her presence, having measured the opening after reducing the projection from the cliff wall as well as they could. "We've got about six inches of clearance for the *Ashley*, twice that for the smaller vehicles. We'll get through," Mark said. "All we have to do is wait for Will and Doug to get back." He looked at the thunderclouds, visible even in the canyon. The rest of them followed his glance with their eyes.

Sandy suddenly felt queasy. "This is the best I can do. I'm going to go back inside. I don't feel very well." No one paid any attention to her.

Sandy's stomach churned. She bolted for the bathroom. She barely made it to the toilet before she threw up, and threw up some more. When she finally stopped, she stood, pale and shaken. She looked in the toilet. As she suspected, *she* was the one who ate the sandwiches and cake. She flushed and watched the evidence of her gorging disappear in profound sadness.

For some time, Sandy had known something was wrong. She woke up to find things had happened that she didn't remember. She might have new clothes or furniture, or she might be with someone she didn't know. She must have had something to do with those things, because who else could have? No one else was there.

Who ate the sandwiches? How could she throw them up if she hadn't eaten them? She remembered eating *one*. She wondered about what she might have done, and how. Sometimes, she felt like she might have had something to do with her parents' deaths. But how? She didn't remember anything. And what about all those e-mails—*did* she send a bad picture? Tears drifted down Sandy's cheeks and her shoulders slumped.

She wasn't sad about this latest proof of her suspicions; she was sad because she was beaten. The battle was over. She had tried so hard to pull herself above the life that had been handed her. She seemed cursed. After her parents died, she ran from Vegas to Chicago and secretarial school—the straightest career she could imagine. What happened? Her first legitimate job turned out to be a Mafia front. What were the odds of that?

No one could know how hard it was for Sandy to graduate from Wellesley. Getting rid of the Mob was another impossibility; going to the Sorbonne, the same. None of this could happen to a girl like her, but Sandy did it. In Paris, she met Kris and Max and got a straight job in their gallery. What do they do— introduce her to the Benefactor. She gave him her heart—and her soul.

Why did all that happen to her? She worked so hard to pull herself out of the sewer. Every time a new door opened, a monster was behind it. The last time was worst. She went through the door in Spain and walked into the Devil. She had been seduced by Carlo's looks, his lovemaking, and his wealth. Not anymore. The pain in her belly had awakened her; knowing what she did when time disappeared awakened her. Sandy finally admitted what she had known in the far corners of her mind for ages. Her Benefactor was the Devil himself.

That didn't matter now, because she had lost. He had placed something inside her, something so terrible she couldn't fathom it. She was carrying his child. No rising from the ashes this time. Sandy looked at herself in the bathroom's mirrored walls, seeing the beauty that she'd worked so hard to achieve. Tears ran down her cheeks. She had loved her Benefactor, and he made her worse than a whore and used her to bear his child. That's what the pain was—his baby was killing her. He must have known it would. She clutched her flat stomach. The baby was in there, visible or not.

Sandy imagined that having a baby inside would be like having a cute little seal in your tummy. It would move around and play and you could talk to it. The thing in her belly wasn't like that. It moved with sharp claws that tore her insides. It gnawed on her ceaselessly, a termite with razor teeth getting bigger and stronger, poisoning her day by day.

The baby was ready to be born. She moaned. It moved, positioning itself to emerge, shredding her. She was hemorrhaging; she grabbed the edge of the vanity and held on, pale and dizzy. She heard a *splat!* like a water balloon breaking on concrete—the waters had broken. She spread her legs and looked at her feet. All she saw were her trim ankles in their white tennies. There was no blood, no water. She looked at her face. She should have been deathly pale, bled white, and she wasn't. She looked lovely, with her fine skin and coloring, absolutely normal, like nothing was happening.

It hurt so badly. The beast was taking her over, killing her soul, taking her body. Sandy panted and held on to the vanity. She could see herself in her mind's eye. An empty shell, a crystal skin separating the maelstrom of hatred inside from the outer world. She had to stop it—but she couldn't. The ripping continued. Blood trickled into her transparent form; her feet were filled with opaque red. The liquid rose quickly, lapping at her ankles, then her calves. Sandy knew when it reached to top of her head, she would be gone. What would be left? She looked in the mirror. She looked the same as always. Pain swept over her again. Sandy cried silently.

She staggered back, reeling against the wall. She would not end this way. She would not die in a bathroom with no one knowing who she was or what happened or how hard she'd tried. Sandy summoned her last strength, the strength she'd used to break free so many times. She staggered into the *Ashley's* bedroom. She could hear Betty's voice from the cabin.

Betty… Tears filled her eyes. Betty was the only one who'd ever treated her like a lady, who ever believed in her. She wanted to say good-bye to Betty. She cast around the room. Sandy was fading. The bed beckoned to her.

58

Trotting back toward the *Ashley*, Will felt renewed. The canyon seemed bright and cheery, and he knew they only had an hour's drive once clear of the ravine. No shadows haunted him. He rounded a slight bend in the canyon and stopped.

Doug lay in the middle of the path, arms pulled up like claws, dried foam all over his mouth. His head was pulled back, spine pulled backward like a crescent. "Doug! Doug!" Will shook him and called his name. He was rigid, as if he were long dead. Will felt his neck and found a faint pulse. He jumped up, frantic. How far from the caravan were they? A mile, at least. He couldn't carry Doug.

Will pulled out his cell phone, ignoring the fact that cell phones didn't work in the canyon. He faced in the direction of the others and squeezed a button with both hands. Nothing happened. He did it again. Silence. It didn't work this far out … But the tech people *said* it would! He pushed the button again.

The *Ashley* erupted with sound. They jumped and covered their ears, scattering without thought. It made so much noise that rocks fell down the canyon walls from the vibration. The racket continued as the satellite on the roof opened and the dish appeared, ready to pick up signals and broadcast.

"It's *Will!* His cell phone has an alarm. There's something wrong with Will. We've got to save him!" Betty cried.

Mark ran into the *Ashley* and punched some buttons on the dashboard, remembering his security training. The alarm stopped its shrieking. "Mr. Duane, we're coming," he spoke into the mike. No answer.

They piled into the vehicles and took off. Slowly. Mark had a six-inch clearance. He didn't know if he could pilot a motor home bigger than a city bus through an opening with a six-inch clearance. He started out inching along. He was about halfway through when he jiggled his hand or breathed wrong. The *Ashley* tied up on the right side. He couldn't even open a door to see what was happening. Sweat burst out on his forehead.

"Mark, keep going!" Betty shouted. With a horrible screeching of metal on rock, the *Ashley* ripped free. "Drive, Mark! We've got to save Will." Betty stood behind Mark, urging him on.

Jolting down the gully, they hoped they would be in time. The alarm was now speaking in a computerized voice, "Medical emergency. Severe injury. Alert medical staff. Danger. Danger. Danger. Alert paramedics. Life-threatening injury."

Will tried pushing down on Doug's chest with both hands, trying to get a rhythm going the way they did on the television emergency shows. He would have tried artificial respiration, but the foam around Doug's mouth scared him. He'd seen the puncture marks. It looked like a snake bit him on the thigh. Twin punctures marked the top of his thigh, with a smaller set on the back.

It must have been a huge snake—the fang marks were almost four inches apart. What snake could have a bite that wide? Doug had thrashed around, kicking in a circle, Will could see. The pain must have been intense. And now this paralysis. He gave no indication of being alive, other than the faint pulse at his neck. Could rigor mortis set in so fast? Will had no first aid training. Did anyone on the *Ashley?* What was taking them so long? Were they still stuck?

He sat next to Doug, talking to him earnestly. "I'm sorry son. I knew it was wrong—I just … Hang on. We'll save you." He felt like he was losing a son—more than that, he'd been responsible for a son's desecration. He paid little attention at first, but then couldn't help noticing that the canyon's colors seemed to bleach. Everything became too bright. He felt a horrible sense of danger. The stalker! Will jumped to his feet. He had no weapons, just his keys and cell phone. He lay the cell on the ground and spoke into it, not even sure it was working.

"This is Will. I don't know if you'll get this. Something's happened to Doug—a snakebite, it looks like. We need antivenom. I don't know what else. He's barely alive." Will choked up, but kept talking. "Whatever it was is still around here. I can feel it. Contact the Indians. We need help …" He began to circle around Doug, keeping his back to his fallen friend. The stalker was *there*, no ambiguity. He made his stand and bellowed a challenge.

"OK you son of a bitch. I know you're here. You want me? Come and get me! What are you waiting for? …"

Something knocked him off his feet. He rolled and got up. It happened again. He got up more slowly. He couldn't see anything. "Coward! Let me see you. *Coward!*" He was down again. Looking up, he could make out the outlines of a face in the clouds. A handsome man was watching him, smiling with delight. Something struck him on the side of the head. His vision blurred. He tasted blood. Will struggled to his feet.

"Get me! If you want me, come and get me!"

Whatever it was played him like a mouse, maiming him before the kill.

"Something's killing him!" Betty cried. Will's cell phone picked up everything Will said and the sounds of his fight; and the *Ashley's* speakers broadcast it all. "They're killing him. Hurry, Mark!"

Mark jammed down the accelerator, rattling along. "Jeff, someone," he spoke into the speaker. "Call the Indians on the shortwave again. We need help."

Melissa picked up the receiver and shouted into it, "Mayday, Mayday. It's the Numenon people. We need help. Will Duane is being attacked. Doug may be dead. Mayday. Over and out … Roger." They looked at her. Melissa was so tense, she looked like she might shatter. "I've never used a shortwave before. Isn't that how you talk? Oh, they killed him."

Will was silent; sounds of blows came over the system, thuds and "woofs." Then nothing.

Everyone crowded behind Mark, holding on to anything they could to stay standing, looking out the windshield for any sign of Will or Doug. They almost bounced off their feet as Mark hit rocks and ruts.

Will lay on the ground, battered and bloody. His eyes never left those of the face in the sky. It had changed from a handsome man to some kind of animal. As it transformed, its cheery savoir faire had transformed to sadistic pleasure. Will couldn't say anything; his jaw was broken and his tongue too swollen to form words. He looked up and glared. Kill me. Go ahead, you've wanted to all these years. Fuck you. Blows fell on him. He could see the monster flicking its fingers as though he were playing with an insect. Every flick broke more bones. If Will couldn't fight, he'd hate. He'd hate until he died.

The monster smiled. Will's pain increased and increased. He moved spasmodically, the pain increasing again. He saw the outline of something moving along the ground, something huge. A serpent. Its tongue darted and it moved closer. Will tried to wiggle away, but he couldn't move.

"Wait, my darling," the monster in the sky said. "They must give themselves to me before they die. Especially this one… He must give himself to me." The voice spoke to Will, "Don't worry. I'll bring you back to life. You'll have everything you ever wanted. Immortality, more women than you can count. More money than you can imagine. You'll have Numenon forever—and you'll do exactly what *I* say."

The Benefactor's finger stretched across time and space to hover over Will's body. He would have enjoyed this kill, except that his victim refused to surrender. "Just give in, you bastard. Tell me you love me. *Now!*"

Something pushed Will into the ground, crushing the air from him, crushing his bones. No pain could be like that. Will refused to give in… would never give in… refused. Everything turned white.

59

B ud pulled up the pinto mare, listening. He could hear a high-pitched noise, an alarm. He looked at the others. Neither Willy nor Paul seemed to hear anything. It was coming from the ribbon canyon on the other side of the butte in front of them. He saw turbulence in the air over the canyon. A struggle. "Do you see that?" he asked the others.

They shook their heads, glad for the chance to stop.

"Don't you think we should have found them by now, Bud? If they went this way?" Willy rubbed his fanny. "I've never ridden this far. It hurts where I landed."

"Why would they be over here, Bud?" Paul said sourly. "I sent them the directions. I clearly stated where they should go on a map." Dust and sun had eroded his uncertainty as to what he had given the Numenon people. "I'm sure they're over by the main entrance with everyone else."

"They're over there," Bud said grimly. A battle was going on in the canyon, a deadly battle with grave implications. "Let's go." He forced the mare to move out. She seemed better able to perceive the danger than his human companions, snorting loudly. He petted the back of her neck and said, "Come on, girl, I need you." She moved forward, trembling. "Paul, come up here with your horse. She needs him for confidence."

The dun stud trotted out, then broke into a rolling lope, heading into the danger. The mare followed him. Willy's mule lumbered behind them, Willy bouncing out of the saddle at each stride.

"Stop! Please! I can't go anymore," Willy cried. Bud and Paul could sit their horses' gaits, but Willy couldn't. He jolted with each step. "It hurts too much!" Exasperation and pain filled his eyes.

Bud pulled up. "Willy, go back to the Bowl. Get Grandfather. Something has happened to the Numenon people. There's something terrible out there. We need him, and lots of warriors. Tell him to come. Go—ride as fast as you can!"

Willy turned around, both horrified at what was happening and happy to end the long ride. He hurried back to the Bowl, going as fast as he could stand. The mule cooperated.

Bud turned to the Badlands before him, "Ride, Paul. We have to get there in time."

In time for what? Paul urged the stallion on, trying to overcome his own reluctance to go forward. Something terrible had happened? Something dangerous was out there? He hadn't been told about danger. Grandfather told him to find the Numenon people, not that there'd be danger.

60

Grandfather was down by the horse corrals when he saw the turbulence over the ribbon canyon. None of his warriors seemed to notice. They came up to him, wanting to show him something they'd brought or tell him about something that had happened during the year. No. Not now.

He motioned to Carl Redstone and thought, Get a golf cart. Carl loped off to get one. Grandfather watched his massive form recede. A great warrior. The turbulence grabbed his attention. He found himself sinking, disappearing into the world of the Great One. The world of Spirit. Drums and voices came to him. A fight to the death raged. He bent over, a hunter. A warrior, seeking his enemy. The Enemy. Grandfather knew the stalker intimately; he'd known him all his life. Now he could see him, over there, beyond a vast sea, and behind rock walls. Far away, but not far enough away to be safe from the ancestors.

His singing filled the air, filled the area around the stables. The Power was upon him. The new people gathered around, craning their necks in curiosity. They were invisible to him; he had only the faintest awareness of the physical world. Grandfather danced, crouching down, the soul the warrior. A tiny man, an ancient fragment. Turning and looking. Seeking.

The other warriors took up his song, looking at each other with uncertain expressions, but ready to aid their leader. Carl arrived in a golf cart. To the martial arts field, Grandfather thought to him, so deep in the trance that he barely registered the outer world. Carl drove the mile or so to the place where the spirit warriors did their demonstrations and practiced every year. The field was level, but the Badlands behind the Bowl created a slight rise, a perfect stadium seating for as many spectators as cared to watch.

"Grandfather's giving a demonstration!" they shouted. People swarmed to the rise, staking out seats. "Wow. This is early. He doesn't usually do anything so soon."

Grandfather didn't react to the crowd pouring down from the Bowl for the unscheduled demonstration.

He listened, bent over, feet moving, ready to strike.

Carl Redstone stood ten feet away, waiting for his teacher to tell him what he needed. Carl was pulled into the vortex, the Power. He could see Grandfather forging ahead; he could see a monster's lair and feel the underworld, the land of darkness.

A spear! Get me a spear! Lots of spears! Grandfather commanded him wordlessly. Carl bounced back to the external world, running to one of the equipment sheds. He picked up as many lances as he could carry, lying them close to Grandfather's feet.

Snatching a spear, the old man held it to his chest, looking for the enemy. Carl could see him searching high and low, in this world and that. Finding. Feeling currents. Waiting for just the right moment. Keeping out of sight, hiding behind the delusion of Darkness, its arrogance and pride. Carl was right behind him, and knew his thoughts. The Dark Lord would never think that he could be attacked in his own home. Never.

The shaman whirled and parried with the lance, doing an elaborate dance. A subtle dance that bore little sense to those watching. Carl kept his eyes and senses glued to him, feeling the movement of the earth and planets, the exact position of each thing to each other thing. Knowing the time was soon.

"What's he doing?" said one newcomer to another. "Is that like karate? That's what it looks like. Is it some kind of exercise? Does he give classes?"

"I don't know. This is my second Meeting. He didn't do anything like this last year. But he's hard to figure out. Strange."

"Yeah, I'd say."

After a while, most of them became restless. Grandfather was perfectly still. He seemed to be waiting. "What's he doing?" someone whispered.

Whirling, spinning, faster than the eye, Grandfather threw the lance. It shot forward, then halted in midair as though it had pierced something. It plowed into the earth, burying half its length into the clay.

Grandfather came out of his trance and watched its haft shudder. He stepped back, giving a cry of jubilation and victory. Carl joined him, followed by the rest of the spirit warriors.

"Was *that* the end of the demonstration?" one of the newcomers said as Carl drove off with Grandfather in the cart. "That was *it*? What did he do? I thought he had all these *powers* … What did he do?"

"I'll tell you what he did, threw that spear damned hard." The other kicked at the dirt around the shaft. "This dirt is like cement. How did he get it that deep?"

The beginners gathered around the spear. Now they had something to ponder. The old man must be much stronger than he looked.

Grandfather heard what the new person said as he and Carl pulled away. So many people went through life as though it were a demonstration, he thought. They never realized that *this is it*. He chuckled, seeing in his mind's eye what his dance had wrought half a globe away. It had taken him a lifetime to do what he just did. How many knew what it was?

He looked back at the crowd, feeling its bewilderment. He couldn't leave his students like that, even if they were beginners. Even if he'd never see them again after this week. "Stop the cart, Carl. Back up."

61

J on sat on a bench in the cabin of his motor home, blinking and trying to wake up. He had slept for hours, awakening in the rosy state he'd known after his best nights with 'Rique. What he'd experienced seemed so real; 'Rique seemed so real. He looked up and swore he saw a shadow move. "'Rique? Is that you?"

Sí, querido. I will stay with you thees week, he heard in his mind.

Having a ghost with him at the retreat was spooky, but Jon felt so sleepy and happy, he couldn't get too perturbed.

On the other hand, where was everyone? He went out into the cabin. The motor home was parked and Rich Salles was gone. He could see the vehicle ahead of them though the windshield; it too was stopped. He looked out the side windows. Red rock walls rose a foot or so away from the vehicle's sides. A person could get out, but just barely. Where were they? What had happened?

He was tying his shoelaces to go looking when a blast of sirens and horns erupted from the front of the caravan. The noise was so powerful that the seat vibrated it from it. "Will!" he exclaimed, knowing immediately who was in jeopardy. And Doug. They both were … not dead. They couldn't be dead.

Swinging out the door, he almost ran into Rich Salles, who was crab-walking sideways along the wall as fast as he could. "It's Will!" he said.

"I know. What happened?"

"The alarms went off. Will's in trouble. And Doug."

"I know. Why are we stopped, and why are there rock walls on each side of us so we can't turn around?"

Rich started up the vehicle, telling Jon what happened in semicoherent sentences.

"But why didn't someone notice that we were driving into a deathtrap? Anything could trap us. A landslide ..."

"I don't know, man. I was just driving along, feeling like shit, remembering every rotten thing in my life, and then I almost ran into Hector when he stopped in front of me. This trip is the pits, man. We were all saying that when we were taking down that boulder." Rich ran his hand through his hair, his chauffeur's cap long gone.

Jon nodded in agreement.

"Mr. Duane's really hurt," Rich continued. "The sound system in the *Ashley* broadcast everything. He was fighting something *huge*. Man ..." Rich's voice broke. He drove as hard as he could, tailing the motor home in front of him. Both vehicles bounced furiously. Rich struggled to speak. "Hey, man, I'm sorry."

"For what?" Their current predicament had replaced Rich's previous behavior in Jon's mind.

"For being such a jerk when we started out. I've been having problems lately. I don't know why I acted like that."

"Oh, it's easy. You didn't want to drive with the only gay person on the trip. Five hours with me could stigmatize you for life. If it didn't kill you— I mean, 'Rique died of AIDS. I'll probably get it, too. Who knows, you might get it, just sitting with me." The words erupted from his mouth. Something inside him wouldn't let him pussyfoot around.

Rich stiffened and faced straight ahead, shoulders shaking. The vehicle swerved, touching one side of the ravine, then the other.

"What's the matter with you? Are you trying to kill us?"

"No, what you said was true. I thought *all* of that. I'm sorry, really. I've been thinking about it while you slept. I understand why you were crying. I know what it's like to watch someone die."

Jon thought for a moment that Rich was gay. Maybe he was in the closet and was losing someone to AIDS. Was that it? He walked to the front of the motor home, needing to see Rich's face to understand what was going on. To his surprise, tears streamed down the driver's cheeks. "I'm sorry, I didn't know." Jon's compassion spoke from every pore.

One dab of kindness and Rich lost it totally. The motor home veered wildly, banging off the canyon walls. Jon grabbed the wheel. "Watch it!" Jon wondered if this was what 'Rique meant when he said, "We'll be together soon?" He didn't think dying in a runaway motor home was what he was talking about.

"I know what it's like to lose someone you love," Rich blurted, "Damn it! Damn it to hell!" He banged a fist on the steering wheel, fighting for control of his feelings.

"Stop!" Rich did, and Jon took over. "Let me drive."

"You don't have a license to drive this thing.'

"You think the cops are gonna bust us out here? Let me drive before you kill us." Jon took the wheel, and the motor home moved along easily. "I've driven 'Rique's big delivery trucks. You wouldn't believe what I can do. I won't tell anyone about this, so settle down." Rich did. "You don't have to, but you might want to talk to me about it. I'm a good listener and I won't tell if you're gay and not out."

"No, it's not that." Rich pulled out his wallet. He handed Jon a photo. Jon glanced at it, one eye on the windshield ahead of him. The picture's subject was an ethereally beautiful woman. She was in a wheelchair with an oxygen tube in her nose. She appeared to be completely paralyzed.

"She's lovely," he said, not knowing what else to say. Rich gazed tenderly at the photograph.

"Her name is Carrie. We've lived together for three years." Rich said softly. "I don't talk about her much. I usually go home right after work. I work at home, painting, so I can be there for her. We stay close to home because of Stanford hospital. We need it sometimes." His chest heaved. "Especially this year. Her diaphragm started going."

Jon looked at the picture again.

"It happened when she was twelve. Skiing at Tahoe. Paralyzed from the neck down. Well, she can move her arm a little."

Rich looked like he wanted to continue, but the intercom crackled. Mark Kenna's voice barked, "We see them … They're right up ahead of us. They aren't moving."

Jon jammed on the brakes, speaking into the mike. *"Don't touch them!* I have stretchers, and splints. Everything." Turning to Rich, he said, "Get the big first aid kit. It's there," he pointed to the bathroom. Back to the mike, "I've got stretchers in the middle vehicle. I need you to get them out …"

And he was out the door.

Jon thought he'd seen the worst with 'Rique, but he hadn't. The worst was seeing Will and Doug lying on the ground. They seemed devoid of blood, both a ghostly pale color. Doug was normally very tan, but he looked blue, lying stiff and contorted in the dust. His spine was arched back and his hands held up like claws.

Will was squashed, that's the only way Jon could describe him. It wasn't a cartoon thing, like he'd been rolled over by a steamroller. His body and head were simply flatter than they could possibly be. He had blood all over him, and his arms and legs were twisted the wrong way. His head lay at a ninety-degree angle from his body, his neck broken. The clothes left on him were ripped and bloody. But the sight of his crushed form eclipsed the horror of the rest. Face mashed, everything compressed.

The group circled around them, stunned. Betty bent down to touch Will.

"Don't touch him!" Jon commanded. "I've had CPR and first aid classes. Let me do it." Everyone yielded; no one else had any first aid training. Jon approached carefully, walking around them. The wounds on his leg indicated a huge snake, or *something*, had bitten Doug. "No one touch that foam on his face, it's probably poisonous." Jon found a faint pulse on both of their necks. "They're alive," he said. Sobs of relief resounded. "I don't know how long they'll stay alive unless we get them out of here."

Rich approached with a first aid kit.

"There's nothing I can do with that," Jon said. He wanted to blame Mark Kenna in the worst way. He'd told him to bring a doctor, but Mark had said, "The Indians have *seven*, Jon, not including Elizabeth Bright Eagle. Nothing's going to happen between the airport and the campgrounds." Well, see what he knew. They needed a full-fledged trauma center. Jon searched for Mark in the group. He was standing, bent at the waist, in shock.

"OK. Let's get out of here. The Indians are over there," Jon pointed, not surprised that he knew exactly where to go. "I've got stretchers—we'll put them on the bed in the *Ashley*. Mark, is the shortwave working?"

"I can't tell. I don't get any response."

"Well, get back inside and send a message to every channel you can." Jeff and Delroy came up with the stretchers. "OK, let's load them on." He had neck braces, but their futility was obvious. What more damage could be done? "Just hold them as flat as you can and we'll put them in the bed in the *Ashley*."

They lifted the unconscious forms into the vehicle, maneuvering carefully. Jeff backed into the cabin, holding the stretcher bearing Will. Delroy held its other two handles, stepping up the stairs facing forward. He saw it first.

"What's that?" He pointed to something on the kitchen counter. Something red draped over a cabinet edge.

"It's the red phone they installed before we left." Betty pushed her way in. The phone was melted and hanging over the edge like something in a surrealist painting. It must have happened when they were outside. Every one of them knew the phone was something the government had required; Will wouldn't have brought it otherwise. Those not carrying stretchers huddled around the phone and gawked.

"What could do that?" Betty said for all of them. "It didn't go off when it melted, or the feds would be all over by now." The silence said what they all knew. They were stranded. No one knew where they were. They couldn't call for help. Two of their members were near death.

"What should we do?" Betty's voice had a tinge of hysteria.

Jon took over. "Look, we haven't been able to call out for ages. Don't worry about it. We need to get out of here. Let's go." He gestured to the stretcher-bearers.

"All right, you men, put Will and Doug in here," he led to the *Ashley*'s bedroom. Sandy Sydney was asleep on the bed. He jiggled her. "Sandy, you'll have to finish your nap somewhere else. We need the bed." He couldn't stand the hussy. *She's been sleeping all this time?* Jon thought with irritation. *It figures, the only way she could get in Will's bed was if he was unconscious.* "Shoo! Shoo! Go! We need the space."

She looked at him balefully, and then oozed out the door like the snake she was.

As Delroy and Hector were about to lay Will on his bed, Jon pulled off the raw silk bedspread. If they got out of this alive, Will would kill him if the spread was ruined. Jon folded it and put it in a cabinet while they put Doug next to Will. Doug's back arched, making it hard to lay him on the bed. They left him lying in a semicircle, taking up most of the space. Neither had moved or even moaned.

"OK, let's get out of here!" Jon commanded and headed for the door of the motor home.

"You're not going to leave us, are you, Jon?" Betty pleaded. "Stay with us."

He looked into her eyes. "Betty, there's nothing I can do. You stay here with the others. I'll ride with Rich. We have to go now, if we're going to save them."

"Oh, yes. Let's go, then!"

Jon galloped sideways down the row of vehicles. He hadn't wanted to tell Betty that Rich needed him. He was incapacitated by grief and couldn't drive. And then he was behind the wheel, and they were roaring down the canyon. As he expected, Rich Salles sat in a corner, consumed by sadness and shock.

"How did you do it?" Rich said when he could. "You just took control. All of us were … I mean, you saw them. They were …" He covered his face. "And you just *handled* it."

Jon thought about what had happened. He'd never thought of his last year with 'Rique as an apprenticeship, but it was. "I've been through hell, Rich, a little more is just a little more hell. Now what were you telling me about your girlfriend?" He wanted to distract Rich, and himself.

Rich took out her picture and looked at it. "We met at a coffee house in Palo Alto. She was funny, and smart. I started seeing her, coffee dates. Chess dates. She's good at computer chess." Rich's face looked wistful. "She can't do much else, though.

"We got together because her attendant screwed up. Disabled people have so little money, they have to hire the dregs. Carrie's attendants have not shown up to feed her. They've threatened her for money. Do you believe it? She can't *move.*" Rich shook his head. "She didn't show up for a date one night. So I went to her place. The door was unlocked. Carrie was in her room, terrified. Her waste bags hadn't been emptied. She was scared that she was damaged internally. She couldn't call for help. She was so upset that I spent the night. The rest is history." He looked at Jon with a challenge in his eye. "I don't tell people about her. I don't want them to think I'm a pervert."

Jon's eyes widened. "You had *sex* with her?"

"Yeah. As often as I could. For years. Do you have a problem with that?" Rich looked at Jon belligerently, then glanced at the picture again. "Her doctor said it was fine if I was careful." Rich seemed like he'd deflated. Jon understood. Rich had just come out; he'd told someone the truth about himself. And Jon didn't condemn him. "That's over now. Carrie is too weak.

"Now that her diaphragm's going, it's a matter of time. They can put her in an iron lung; she'll last for years. But neither of us wants that. She can't be at home with me if she's in a lung." Rich's voice broke. "…She wants me to help her. I can't." He stopped talking.

"*Help* her?"

Rich nodded, haggard, "I can't. I love her too much; I can't *help her* leave me."

Then Jon understood. He also understood why they were riding together; he knew exactly what Rich was feeling. They had both lost their lovers, inch by inch. Breath by breath. They were the only ones in the group who'd felt that pain. Sadness welled up inside him, along with gratitude. He'd met someone who understood. Perhaps something right was happening on this rotten trip.

Then he thought of his boss and Doug, all but dead. Why they weren't dead, he didn't know. "Rich, do you know anything about this intercom? Can you see if you can call someone? We really need help. I wish I knew where those Indians were."

62

Bud knew he was pushing the mare too hard; her fine bones and tendons wouldn't stand the stress, but he had to get around the loaflike mesa in front of them. The Numenon people were on the other side, emerging from the canyon. He couldn't get to them any other way but by going around the rock mass, and then dodging through the complicated rock formations beyond them. Hoodoos, they called the twisted stone sculptures formed by wind and water. Squirrelly Girl had to last for him to get there …

"That's a girl, you can make it," he bent down over her wet neck, putting a hand on its crest. He could feel energy flowing from him the way it had when he healed Abbie. The voices of his ancestors sang in his ears; he could feel them all around him He whispered their song, "They are riding, they are riding, warriors like the old days. Great warriors …"

Feeling the energy, the mare leaped forward showing *spirit,* not craziness or fear. Her breathing was strong and her legs reached out, pulling the terrain under her. Paul was slightly behind him, the dun stallion covering ground with ease. Something happened to Bud. The ancestors covered him like a blanket, making him see with their eyes. They were there; Grandfather was there, riding with him and inside him. Grandfather, Great-grandfather, and all those who came before, all riding with him into battle. Spirits swarmed around him.

Bud's mind stopped its questioning. What was going on? What had happened to their guests? What could he do to help them? He didn't know anything. He was riding toward them, that was all.

The corporate caravan burst out of the red rock embankment as they cleared a group of hoodoos. Bud charged straight at it.

Paul Running Bird slowed at the sight of the convoy. The vehicles took his breath away. They were everything he thought Numenon would be. The caravan was imperial. Five perfectly matched vehicles and the trailer, all bearing tasteful graphics and the beautiful Numenon logo—with the majestic *Ashley* leading. The fleet was a hymn to a world-class organization. Paul had read all the books on Numenon, books describing the story of Will's incredible rise to domination of the corporate world, his intuition and brilliance. He worshiped Will Duane.

"*The Ashley III*," whispered Paul. He'd bought the *Architectural Digest* featuring the aerodynamic motor home, but there she was, right before him! Maybe he'd get the chance to go inside her this week. He wanted to gallop forward and greet Will Duane and his party to let them know they were safe.

Something stopped him. Some would call it fear, but he preferred to think of it as intelligent self-preservation. Bud's horse moved ahead of him as he recalled a horrible possibility. What if he had guided them into the trap? He couldn't remember. Paul slowed the stallion to a collected lope. The idiot animal wanted to charge ahead. To what? Condemnation for a mistake?

But what if he *saved* them? What if he made such a great impression that they overlooked what he had inadvertently, possibly, done? Would he make a great impression, galloping up? He looked ahead at Bud, paunchy fool that he was. He looked magnificent on the mare. How could he outdo *that* on the crowbait he was riding?

He yanked the stallion to a halt, not caring about his mouth. He needed to take control. He needed to show himself the leader! Paul wiped his brow, thinking about how to make an impact. Thank God Bud sent Willy Fish packing. That cretin would ruin his grand entrance. And that stupid mule—hee-hawing!

Loosening the reins, he slammed the stallion in the sides with his heels. "Aiiiiiyah!" he shrieked, the only war cry he'd ever made. The stud took off, sturdy legs whirring, easily catching the mare. Bud didn't seem to notice him as they galloped along, side by side. Paul screamed again. The mare shied and Paul took the lead, covering the last few hundred yards with ease. He would save them!

The shock hit them like dynamite. Both men doubled over in the saddle, grabbing their genitals. The dun stallion staggered as though he might go down. When Bud lurched in the saddle, Squirrel Brains leaped to the side and dumped him. He managed to hold onto one rein, but almost lost it groveling on the ground in agony. He eventually rose to his feet.

"Did you feel that?" he shouted at Paul, who had managed to stay in the saddle. He was doubled over, moaning.

"Oh, what was it?" Paul made some incoherent noises. The stallion was prancing around, picking up its hind feet and turning his head to look at himself. Paul turned the horse away from Bud, his shoulders shaking. Bud didn't know what had happened. Something grabbed his balls and almost crushed them. Then it felt as if thousands of needles had jabbed him. What could do that? He looked around, trying to see what did it.

When he could, Bud swung back into the saddle and sat down gingerly. He looked at the caravan aghast. The *Ashley* had veered off to the left and was careening across the desert out of control. The other vehicles had swerved in all directions. Only the last one seemed unaffected—it steered straight and then stopped. The *Ashley* slammed into a boulder. Bud kicked the mare forward, heading for the *Ashley* as fast as he could.

He could hear screaming as he approached. The other vehicles stopped raggedly. Their drivers fell out one by one, holding themselves and looking agonized. Bud galloped around the front of the *Ashley* as the main door on the left side flew open. A dark-haired man staggered out. Not noticing Bud, he stumbled toward the mare. She spun and tried to bolt, but Bud held her. He jumped off, holding the reins, and grabbed the man's shoulders. He reacted by trying to run.

"Easy. Easy," Bud said. "You're OK. I won't hurt you." Bud's touch was calming. Mark relaxed a bit. "What happened?"

"I don't know! We were driving as fast as we could, and all of a sudden..." Mark shook his head, tears glistening in his eyes. "It hurt so much. I don't know what happened—for a moment, I thought you'd attacked us." He looked into Bud's kind eyes.

"No, I got a touch of whatever it was myself. Enough to fall off this horse." He indicated the mare. She stood rigidly, staring at the *Ashley*. She was able to hear the screaming inside as well as anyone. She was about to get out of Dodge by her body language. "Here, you hold her. I'll go inside." Mark took the reins like he knew something about horses. "Go slow and easy with her. She's crazy."

63

Sandy Sydney was horrified. How could she screw up like that? She awakened that afternoon feeling fantastic. Better than fantastic. She felt reborn, stronger than she'd ever been. Than *anyone* had ever been, tuned and toned like an Olympic athlete. She had no chance to test her physical prowess, but she felt as though she could do anything but fly. Mentally, she was just as good. She remembered tiny twinges of doubt about her Carlo before her nap and a feeling that she was dying. What stupid nonsense!

After Jon woke her up, she made her way across the cabin to her place on the banquette. The fact that she had had to give up her bed because they needed to stash her all but dead boss and his main man didn't bother her at all. No one noticed that her walk was less the indolent goddess than the assured predator. Completely unself-conscious, she stretched her arms over her head and said, "Boy, did I have a great nap."

She was wide awake, fully on, and ready for anything. Did she get any action? No, she had to listen to Betty's caterwauling about Will and Doug. Who the fuck cared? They got what they deserved. From the way they looked, she would swear that her Benefactor had a hand in what happened. But it couldn't have been him; they'd be dead if he had done it. She wondered what else was out there in the desert, waiting for her.

Betty kept blubbering, and Gil put his arms around her, saying, "It's OK, Betty. We'll get them to the camp. Grandfather will save them. Remember, you told us all about him. He can do anything."

"But this is so *bad*, Gil. How can he possibly help them? Oh, why don't the Indians answer? They must be able to hear us now. Where are they?"

Mark Kenna had been making himself hoarse calling for help on the shortwave. Sandy thought they were all stupid.

"Oh, did you *see* them? It was horrible." Melissa's anguish was delicious to see. She sniffled, succeeding in mostly controlling herself, and then went into the bathroom. Taking pills, Sandy knew. Lovely habit. And she *had* seen their bodies. The sight of her former boss and Dopey Doug's twisted and bloody forms thrilled her. Their mangled flesh aroused her more than sex, more than making money. More than stealing or spying. Trills of pleasure arose from deep within her body. What might happen next?

Her mind began to wander. It wandered to Melissa Weir's now-drowsy form lolling on the banquette. Whatever pills she'd taken worked fast, or worked fast when added to what she'd taken earlier. She looked like she'd be snoring again soon. What a beauty! Sandy had noticed Melissa the minute she got to Numenon. What a fine bitch she was. Sandy's senses were a million times as keen as they had been. She could turn any of them to the delicious Melissa and explore her as fully as if they were alone.

Extending her psyche, she imbibed Melissa's skin textures, projecting her touches under Melissa's clothes. She sniffed the MBA's personal perfume, savoring the essence of her body's folds. Her eyes caressed the delicate colors of Melissa's skin, the shadows of her eyes and lips. Sandy could hardly restrain herself from crossing the cabin and parting Melissa's legs.

Her Benefactor had led her to her true identity; he'd realized instantly that had Sandy's sexuality been allowed to develop naturally, she would have preferred her own sex. She'd been distorted terribly by the mistreatment she'd received. Now, she'd go with anyone. A useful trait, given her profession, but not her true nature. Oh, yes. She'd noticed Melissa right away.

Sandy decided that she would not go back to Spain without Melissa Weir. The little thing was too yummy. She and her Benefactor would share her. She pursed her lips and thought of the poor, traumatized Ms. Weir. It's not true what they say, is it, sweetie? You're not a lesbian, are you? But I am.

And you'll be mine by the end of the week. Wonderful images of the two of them entertained Sandy for some time.

She wasn't sure how it happened. Betty kept yapping about poor Will. The fantastic atmosphere of the desert was getting to Sandy. She began to feel reckless and intoxicated by the land around them. They were getting closer to the Bowl. She could feel the people there. Beautiful people, psychic people; women like her. She wanted to shout, "Shut up, you old bag! No one cares!" But Betty kept going on, and the rest sniveled and sniffed.

Bored, Sandy began to play. She found she could do things with her mind so easily now. Before, she wasn't conscious of what she did with her Powers. She turned her attention to the *Ashley*'s instrument panel, fooling around. She could feel Mark going nuts as the fuel went from almost full to almost empty and back. Recalling the bloody bodies in the bedroom, Sandy wanted more. More pain, more agony. She remembered what she did to her lovers at Numenon: little squeeze … followed by pins and needles. She always did it where they couldn't see her, but she could see them. So much fun.

One little thought, and *wham!* All the men were bent over, screaming. Sandy realized she'd done it. She didn't touch Betty, boring hag that she was. Sandy had something special for the delicious Melissa Weir. Using her mind, she felt Melissa up. The bitch should have been coming from what Sandy was doing to her. To keep suspicion away, Sandy doubled over and screamed like she was in pain. Watching Melissa every minute, she kept the sensations going deep inside her. Sandy wanted the bitch to come in front of everyone.

But Melissa didn't. She'd been dozing again. When she felt something touching her, Melissa's eyes shot wide open. She jumped up and started clawing at herself, trying to stop the sensations. Sandy thought that was hilarious and did it harder. Melissa leaped up, howling and trying to push away unseen hands. She fell and, screaming louder, dragged herself over to the corner, where she remained, wailing hysterically.

This was the most exciting reaction Sandy had ever seen. She realized that Melissa had been sexually abused, and knew that she'd make a perfect lover. Sandy had also been abused, and look how well she turned out. This was a job for the Benefactor.

Everything would have been all right had she not zapped the driver. Well, anyone could make a mistake. She hoped the *Ashley* could be driven after running into the boulder, but if it couldn't she'd figure a way to escape with Melissa. And maybe have some more fun doing it.

The door flew open and a fat Indian jumped into the cabin. Sandy started screaming again, so he'd think she was hurt.

64

Bud bounded into the *Ashley*. A blond woman was bent over, shrieking. An older woman sat next to her, horrified but silent. A black-haired young guy doubled over in pain was pulling himself across the cabin to a young woman on the floor. She was keening with such anguish that everyone's eyes were riveted to her.

"Don't hurt me! *Please* don't hurt me!" She clawed at herself, trying to get free of something. She didn't seem to know where she was. She kicked and scratched, pushing herself across the cabin into the wall on the other side.

The black-haired guy reached her. "It's OK, Melissa. It's Gil. I'm here." She fought him like the devil, screaming. The scene was so wild, Bud went into shock himself for a moment—who to help first?

Then everything Grandfather taught him came back. He headed straight for the girl on the floor. She needed him the most. "Excuse me," he said to the guy. "Let me help her."

The minute Bud touched her, Melissa went limp. "Is there a place where I can look at her?" Gil opened the door to the bedroom, which was right behind Melissa.

"*They're* in there," the guy said. He was Chinese or something.

Two bodies lay on the bed. Bud didn't react. First things first. He put the girl on the closest side of big bed. She was so tiny that the men's bodies left plenty of room for her. Bud kneeled next to Melissa and put his hand on her head. He'd only worked on horses before, but Bert said he was great with the backaches she got from being pregnant.

He took a breath and looked into her mind. He saw everything that had happened to her. It took a while to collect himself enough to comprehend it. He didn't understand how people could do things like that to other people. He couldn't heal this—it was something Grandfather would have to handle. Bud left his hand on Melissa's forehead. Her breathing lengthened and soon they could tell she was sound asleep. Then he turned to the man. "Are *you* all right?"

Gil was trembling. "Yeah. There was something like an explosion. I put my hands out to protect myself." He shrugged. "It worked some, but it still hurt like crazy."

Bud put his hands on Gil's shoulders and he seemed to deflate. "How do you feel now?"

"Better." His eyes swam with tears.

Bud left his hands on the other man's shoulders. "I know how much it hurt. I felt it way up in the rocks. I couldn't stay on my horse. You were right where it happened. That's got to be scary."

Gil shook his head. "No. That's not it. I'm worried about my wife. She's home alone. She just had a baby … I should be there … What if I get killed out here?"

Bud was appalled. He *should* be home.

"You won't get killed if we can help it. I've been to all the Meetings but the first one. No one's died yet." Gil seemed to be melting under Bud's hand. He could feel the tension go out of him. "How do you feel now?"

"Much better. Thank you. Can you help Will and Doug?" he begged.

"I'll try." Before beginning, Bud checked the others. "Are you OK, ma'am?"

Betty nodded. "But Sandy's really hurt," she pointed to the tear-drenched blonde next to her.

He was about to put his hands on Sandy Sydney's shoulders when every alarm in his soul went off. Something very powerful inside said, *"Don't touch her!"*

Bud backed off. This woman was responsible for whatever happened. *She* was the soulless monster he'd felt when he followed the caravan, the most dangerous thing in the desert by a long shot. She was far more powerful now than when he first became aware of her. When he originally detected her, he knew she was in a process of transformation. Now the process was almost complete. Soon she would become what she really was.

He looked into Sandy's baby-blue eyes and blinked in surprise. For an instant, Bud thought the pupils of her eyes turned into vertical slits, like a cat's. He blinked and the wide eyes were normal. Had he seen what he thought? A monster in the form of a beautiful blonde? His ancestors stirred in him. Remember this, Bud, they said. Many of us were fooled the same way.

Sandy stared at Bud. He could tell that she realized that he knew about her. She fake-sobbed a bit, crocodile tears streaming down her face. "It hurt so bad," she sniffed.

Bud nodded. She was lying; she was twice as strong as he was mentally and maybe physically too; they were at her mercy. Bud hoped Grandfather was getting all this. He was certainly sending out mental pleas for help as hard as he could.

Sandy regarded Bud coolly. OK. She'd lost control, but she could save the situation. No one but this fat slob knew she did it. She'd say *he* did it; they'd believe her. Everyone believed the pretty blonde.

She stared at Bud Creeman, feeling his friends joining him in the *Ashley.* Spirits. The old man, Grandfather, and the even older shaman, his teacher. All the rest of them. The ancients had come to protect this lard butt. They filled the cabin invisibly, swamping her powers. She'd missed her chance. She could have gotten him when he first entered, but now it was too late. She'd have to be a nice girl, waiting for a chance to escape.

She lisped a reply: *"I'll* be OK. It's Mr. Duane that needs help. And Doug. *Please* help them."

Bud went out to his horse. Mark Kenna held her by the reins. It was hard to say if horse or man looked more afraid of the other. He laid a hand on the mare and felt that energy coming from him again, soothing and calming the horse. She needed his help, too. She'd strained ligaments all over during their dash. Taking the pack Grandfather had given him off the saddle, he said, "Later, darlin'. I'll take care of you." Her head was down and she appeared to sleep after his touch. He took the fringed pouch Grandfather had given him, appreciative of its weight. It must have a lot of medicine in it. Good.

"This is a nice mare—treat her good," he said to Mark before reentering the *Ashley*. "She's a little crazy, but she ain't killed nobody yet, so you can relax. Breathin' once in a while won't hurt you, either."

Inside the bedroom, Bud leaned back against the door, surveying the human wreckage before him. He took a deep breath and held the pouch to his chest. Grandfather said he would know what to do with it when the time came.

Damned if he did. A lump stuck in his throat and his eyes burned. What was he supposed to *do?*

65

Bud was breathing so fast that he began to feel dizzy. He stared at the figures on the bed. The bluish skin and twisted limbs. The blood and dirt. That guy's body curved backward. He began to shake.

"I *can't* do it," he whispered. "I can't help them." The thoughts that always came when he had to do something difficult flooded his mind. You stupid bum... Worthless, no-good... You stinking drunk... Failure! He leaned against a wall of built-in furniture, clutching the medicine bag to his chest. Why had Grandfather sent *him*? Wesley could handle this in a snap, or Elizabeth. So could Leroy or Tyler. Grandfather could have healed them without trying. Why did he send *him*, his worst warrior?

Bud began to panic. "They're going to die." A scream arose within him. "Please... I *can't*..." Something struck him across the face. He felt his cheek redden and tasted blood in his mouth. He couldn't see anyone else in the room. Tears stung behind his eyes and words poured out. "I can't do what you want. I'm not good enough. I will *never* be good..." The next blow threw him to his knees. He dropped the bag and put his face in his hands, ears ringing.

Quiet! he heard a voice say. It was a silent voice, Grandfather's, that he had been hearing all day. The voice went on, I know what you can do better than you do. You will be silent and listen. Bud bowed his head. Grandfather had never been angry with him before. He picked up the medicine bag and held it to his chest.

"I'm sorry," he whispered. "I never saw nothing like this."

Neither have I, my son, but do you think that matters? Do you think I will desert you because something is new? Do you think the Great One will go away because of two blue bodies? Will *they?*

Bud looked up and noticed that the air seemed to be rippling, like clear water in a stream. The room was full of moving energy, boiling with it. Look! said Grandfather's silent voice. The ancestors crowded into the room, countless numbers of them from all the Nations. They had come from Spirit World to help him. They pushed against him, holding him up.

I will never leave you alone, and neither will your People. We will fight a great battle now, and save these men. You will listen and do as you are told.

Bud held the pouch and stood still, waiting for orders. He heard nothing. What was he supposed to do? An image came to him—a field of spirit warriors training with Grandfather. Bud remembered something. The shaman never sent a warrior into battle unprepared. People who didn't think they could do what Grandfather asked *did* when they tried. He was on the training field now, given his orders. But what orders? What was he supposed to do? The voices were silent. He thought hard.

What had Carl told him back at the Bowl? He said that Grandfather told him that when he saw what was in the pouch, he'd know how to use it. With trembling fingers, Bud loosened the medicine bag's ties and looked inside. It contained smaller deerskin packets and a bunch of other things: a feather fan, whistles, and rattles. Sage, cedar, and sweet grass to burn for purification. He pulled the largest deerskin packet out and sniffed it.

The Power was upon him before he could blink. The spirits in the room roiled, focusing on him, willing him to feel their support. Bud looked at the big packet, taking in its essence. He looked at Doug's contorted form. This was for him, and he needed it fast. He was worse off than the other man. The venom was destroying his body beyond repair. He held the packet to his heart, chanting a prayer. OK, OK. Something was telling him what to do. But how? He looked around the room. He couldn't see anything he could use to do it. He heard someone crying in the main cabin. He opened the door and leaned out, holding the package up.

"This is for the venom. I need to get this mixed with water real fast. It has to be clean water and blended real good. And I need some way of getting it into him slow." All at once would kill him, but he didn't tell them that. The blonde batted her eyes, posturing helplessness. The Chinese guy had been comforting the older woman. She looked up, face wet.

"Jon!" she and the Chinese guy said at once. "Jon Walker, the chef. He'll know how to do that. He's got everything ..."

Jon barged into the motor home as she spoke. "Do you need me? Oh, God, I had this terrible feeling ..."

"They'll be all right if we can move fast enough." Bud explained what he needed and handed Jon the pouch. Jon leaped out the door, heading for the last motor home, where he had all his cooking gear.

Bud looked into Betty's eyes, saying, "They'll be all right," before disappearing into the bedroom. She collapsed against Gil without a sound.

Bud faced the three people on the bed. The sleeping Melissa would be OK until Grandfather saw her. The other two ... he didn't know. Listen, he said to himself to ward off panic. Listen for what you're supposed to do. Bud let his body guide him; he did whatever it wanted to do. He found himself by the side of the bed where Mr. Duane lay. He put his hands over him, not quite touching the flesh. Eyes closed, deep inside himself, he prayed. The ancestors moved through him, sending energy out his hands. Bud could feel his patient relax, and feel his pain lessen. He'd be OK for a while.

Doug was harder to reach. Bud bent over his contorted frame, careful not to touch the venom-filled form. Something was telling him what to do all the time now. It was like being a funnel. Do this, do that. Chant. Point your hands at him. He said things in a way he never would, and began to sing in a language no one taught him. "Relax, bent man, relax ..." he sang to Doug. "Poison, leave him alone. Let go of him now. Let go of this man ..."

Doug was a little softer when there was a knock at the door. Bud went to the door. Jon was outside with a big kettle full of stuff. "I went through the motor home and grabbed everything I thought might work. Can I come in?" Bud let him in, not knowing if it was a good idea. If he freaked out the way he did at first, what would this man do?

"I'll set these over here." Jon said. The wall of cabinets had a low area like a desk with a mirror over it. Jon set the pot on it and pulled out a blender full of greenish liquid. "Don't worry. I used distilled water. It's very well blended." He set the container on the flat surface. "I brought everything I could think of to get that stuff in him slowly." Jon began pulling things out of the pot. "A French coffee press. A sieve and coffee filters. A baster… I brought this bottle of olive oil. You always can use that. I don't know. You look."

Bud went through the container, discarding almost everything. Jon kept talking, "I knew I should have brought an IV set up. I wanted to. I wanted to bring one, and a doctor, but Mark wouldn't let me. I told him we'd need them and he said I was crazy." Jon seemed a little tipsy. "What is that stuff, anyway? It looked like green dirt, but I sniffed the container while I was blending it. Whoa. What a wallop. I wanted to stick a finger in and taste…"

"*Never* do that with Grandfather's herbs! Not unless they're for you."

"I know. I heard this voice in my head say, '*No! Not for you!*' I *believed* it."

Bud looked at the chef. He was loaded. Many of Grandfather's herb blends gave people visions and ecstasies—it was the Spirit they called out that made them intoxicated, not any physical substance. Still, some of those blends could have you flying. Like this guy was.

Great. All he needed. He was ready to shove Jon out the door when something said, Let him stay. Bud turned to the job at hand, going through the big pot. "No, no, no," Bud discarded everything except an object in a cardboard box. He took it out of the box, nodding. "Perfect."

He unscrewed the plastic thing and threw it away, adjusting the regulator. "Pour some of that in here," He said. Jon did. Bud adjusted the flow so it was barely a trickle. "Let it out this fast, see. No faster."

"What do you mean?" Jon managed to say as he caught the runoff in the tureen. "Watch it! The carpet!"

"You'll be putting this into him while I work on Mr. Duane."

"I can't do that… I'm a *chef*."

"You're my assistant now. Get that oil over here." Bud dipped the end of the tube into the bottle of olive oil and crawled up on the bed between Doug and Melissa. "Follow me."

Jon crawled behind him holding the herb mixture in the blender. Bud heard Jon gasp when he saw Doug's body. It was soft and relaxed now, but it was still blue and dead looking. They had to get to work. Bud put his hand on Doug's jaw, muttering and jiggling it back and forth. "OK, jaw. Open now. I need you to open." It did. Bud had never done what he was going to do to a human, but he'd done it to horses many times.

What he was about to do was not part of a rancher's repertoire of healing tricks. This was something a rancher would call a vet to do. Tubing a horse was trickier than pulling a stuck calf out of its mother with chains or stitching up a barbed wire cut. When a vet tubed a horse, the first thing he did was sedate the animal. When the horse was so zonked it could barely stand, the vet would take a length of soft rubber tubing and lubricate it well, slipping it into the horse's nostril. He would thread the tube carefully past the juncture of the windpipe and food pipe, directly into the animal's stomach. That part done, the vet would funnel about a quart of mineral oil down the tube.

Vets tubed horses when they colicked—got bellyaches. They got stomachaches for all sorts of reasons, most having to do with the unnatural life styles humans imposed upon them. If the colic was due to a blocked intestine, it could be deadly. Mineral oil lubricated the gut so the obstruction could slip right out.

Most reservation horses didn't colic; they lived in a natural way with lots of grass and room to move. When Bud went to work for the Bayneses, he found that their show horses, with their box stalls and daily rations of grain, colicked regularly. He'd watched the vet tube many horses. When one of the champions was throwing himself on the ground because of the pain and the vet couldn't get there, Bud tubed him. The horse came right out of it. After that, Bud tubed whatever horse needed it.

So he didn't feel too nervous getting ready to do the job on Doug. The energy in the room closed in on him. All he was doing was what he was told. Grandfather and the ancestors, all of them, kept up that chant inside him. He looked at the man before him, considering. He would have slipped the tube in a horse's nostril and then down to his stomach, but Doug's nose seemed too small. He decided to insert down his throat. It would be OK if he didn't gag or bite. If his jaws stayed relaxed. He heard himself talking in that foreign way.

"OK, jaws and tongue, you need to relax and stay that way. You need to let this down there and not bite or nothin'." More of the energy came out of his hands. He began to thread the oiled tube down Doug's throat. The tricky part was the juncture of the windpipe and the food pipe. If he dumped that blender full of Grandfather's herbs into Doug's lungs, that would kill him.

"OK, windpipe, you just close up right now. Let this tube go down." And it did, so Bud threaded the rubber tube into Doug's stomach. He knew exactly where it was by fine changes in pressure he felt and because he just knew. His hands knew, all of him knew. He could see like he had X-ray eyes and fingers, too.

"You can pour that in here now, right to the top," he said to Jon. Jon slowly poured the contents of the blender into the container. "OK, I'll open the regulator the way we had it before. I want you to get where I am, and hold that up until it all drips in. I gotta work on this other guy."

Jon crawled along the bed, taking the sack from Bud and holding it up while he balanced on his knees. Bud crawled across Doug and Will until he was standing on the other side of the bed. Jon wanted to watch Bud, but his shoulders started hurting from holding up all that liquid. He looked at Doug, who was still blue but seemed to be breathing easier. Jon's arms hurt too much to remain the way he was. He wiggled up onto his knees, holding the loop with his thumbs and maneuvering to his feet. He stood on the bed with his back to the wall and one foot between Doug and Melissa, the other between Doug and Will. He could hold up the bag and watch that way.

Fumes were coming out of the sack. He could see them sort of bubble over the top and down his arms. A grin spread across his face, and he began to feel silly. What was that stuff? He'd never done any drugs that made him feel like *that*. He wanted to jump up and down on the bed and laugh. This was wild! This was like that party where he and 'Rique met. Remember, 'Rique?

The minute he thought of 'Rique, he stopped feeling high. He felt jelled, caught in wax. His eyes closed and his attention was yanked inside. A rippling feeling started at his feet; it was just the finest tremble. He could feel the inside of his body, everything about himself. He could hear Bud chanting in some language and saying things, but it was far away. The world outside him disappeared.

The tingling became a flood; something filled him and flowed upward from the bottoms of his feet, to his ankles, then knees. It was a fine substance, nothing he could name, and nothing he'd felt before. It flowed upward, jiggling and tingling. His head turned to the right without him willing it; his eyes closed. Whatever was moving up him was intense and unstoppable. It was light, brilliant light. Jon wanted to run, but he couldn't. Whatever had him was too powerful to resist, and too pleasurable.

His breath deepened. The explosive flow rose through his butt and belly, rising higher. Until it stopped, midgut. He could see it inside—a golden flood ramming against an obstruction. A huge, black mass. It was like a river hitting a giant boulder. Part of the flood went around while the rest pushed against the darkness inside him. Jon's ribs heaved. He wasn't high anymore. He heard himself sobbing. "Oh, 'Rique. You left me. You're never coming back." The river kept ramming against that.

He could see what it was doing. It was like he had a magnifying glass and could see what was happening inside himself. That light slammed against his grief and broke it up. He had seen something like it on the gardening channel on the TV in Will's kitchen. Little microscopic tendrils of roots covered a boulder and emitted *acid.* They just burnt up that boulder. First they made little cracks and then found other openings, eating and pushing through. The next thing, the boulder—the solid granite boulder—was in pieces and then chunks, and finally, flowers were growing on it.

He could feel this happening to *him,* to Jon the disgusting fairy who wasn't worthy of having anything turn out right or keeping the one he loved. Something was talking to him, something *huge.* He stood on the bed holding the bag, while something gigantic spoke. He could see his grief, that huge mass that no therapy would ever be able to erase, being broken into pieces by the subtlest force...

The tiny golden tentacles worked their way through and his sorrow broke up into chunks and grains and particles and flew upward into the air like confetti. Chest heaving, ribs moving like a bellows, Jon watched his convulsive breath blow his grief away.

He gasped when he realized what had happened. His depression was gone, along with his grief. In their place, he felt the most amazing thing—good. No shadows, no doubt, no guilt. No pain. Feeling good was almost more than he could handle.

The force wasn't gone. It kept moving, flowing all the way up his torso, through his neck, and out the top of his head. Boom! It was like the top of his skull blew off. Light everywhere. He was dancing, flying, everything was ... wonderful. Wonderful.

Abruptly, Jon came back to the room, to the present. His eyes snapped open. He knew that whatever was happening wasn't about getting high, it was about doing a job. He glanced up and saw that most of the liquid had dripped into Doug. He looked down at his patient. Doug was normal-colored and breathing easily. He looked over at Will.

One of Bud's hands was thrust inside Will's skull, while the other gently cupped it from underneath. Bud's eyes were closed, and he was talking to Will's body. The scene seemed perfectly normal. Jon blinked and watched.

"OK, you bone, you pop out now. Don't you be pushing on his brain. That's right. You go back to shape. OK, brain. Stop swelling. You don't need to do that. You stop swelling and feel good. Be just like you were, you're fine. You feel that bliss, bone? That belongs to the Great One, and it's healing you!" Bud put his hands on, and in, Will Duane's skull, moving its crushed plates, sculpting it, calling to it to return to its previous form.

"Let's move on down here." Bud probed Will's body, eyes closed. Jon could see the air around him ripple. He shivered. Bud spoke in an ancient language, opening his eyes and conferring with something Jon couldn't see. Then he focused on Will again and said, "Oh, this ain't right. You backbones, you have to get straight now. You have to stop this mess. This fractured mess. Just stop now."

His hands sunk into Will Duane's flesh, moving into the shattered bones of his neck, fixing them, cleaning up the splinters. "OK, you good cells, you go about your business. You just feel that Power and know that It's the boss. You understand? You know that, and know that you are healed!"

He moved down Will's torso into the ruined disaster of his internal organs. Jon watched as Bud's arms sunk up to his elbows in Will's flesh, fixing his ripped tissues and shattered skeleton. The mending bones made little noises as they slipped into place, crunches sometimes, and little slippery sounds. Bud's hands moved inside Will's body, reaching everywhere. Healing. He hummed as golden light filled in the room, moving and billowing like clouds of grace.

Jon watched Mr. Duane go from a flattened mass of human muck that was living for some reason into a normal human being.

"OK, flesh, you just puff up now. Get big again, now. That's the way. Blood, you keep moving, go on in there, you can do it! Yes! You can heal!" Bud's words were infectiously positive; Jon began to smile. When he did, the soupy but transparent thickness of the air in the room got to him. It was moving, simmering like broth before it came to a full boil. Sounds rang in his ears, bells, and voices singing. It sounded like the Gay Men's Choir in San Francisco, though Jon didn't think all of them could possibly fit in the *Ashley*.

He felt dizzy and happy. Like singing. Whatever had snapped him into the present and out of ecstasy a while before seemed to be loosening up. That energy began erupting again; his body began moving in a rhythmic roll from his feet to his head. He couldn't stop it; it was all he could do to hold onto Doug's medicine and not spill what was left. Jon realized, I'm healed! It healed *me*! Waves of pleasure passed through his body, which banged against the wall in time to its own beat. He felt like dancing, but didn't want to step on any of the unconscious people at his feet.

"Yes! Yes! Yes!" he hollered. "Yes! It's true!" He didn't know what was true, just that it was. The simmer in the room had become a full boil. Jon felt his heart—pop!—burst open and flood the *Ashley* with joy. He laughed uncontrollably. Bud looked at him. He was piecing Will's lower leg bones together. Something was coming out of his hands that acted like invisible Krazy Glue. Jon could see the bones coming together, knitting seamlessly, not even with residual cracks like you could see in the X-rays of Jon's arm that he broke when he was eight. He'd seen them a few years ago; he had had his arm X-rayed when he fell down the stairs after that other party with 'Rique. His arm was healed but not mended. What Bud was doing *mended* like nothing had happened.

"Yes!" yelled Jon. "Oh, yes! Oh, Bud! Do it!" Bud put the bones back in Will's flesh and molded it around them perfectly. Waves of bliss passed over Jon once more. He and his friends used to do drugs, trying to feel what he was feeling. He knew now that all they had to do was go out in the desert and get attacked by monsters. And then be healed by a native shaman. "Oh, God, I'm so happy! I can't believe it!"

"Is everything OK?" Gil stuck his head in the door, responding to Jon's shouts. "Betty's getting upset." Gil stopped dead, staring. Bud's hands were plunged into Will's abdomen. He had his eyes closed and sang, "OK, gut. Don't you cramp up now; this man has had enough pain. You do your job, now. Let him heal." Gil wanted to run, but he couldn't move; the air seemed thick, like it was a fishbowl with invisible fish swimming in it.

He looked at Jon. He stood on the bed, holding an old-fashioned rubber douche bag in both hands. He thrashed and banged against the wall like electric shocks were running through him, an enraptured grin on his face. The empty bag's hose disappeared into Doug's mouth. Doug looked relaxed and his skin was a normal tone. He looked like he was sleeping and perfectly fine, except for the puncture wounds in his thigh.

Gil heard a voice talking to him. It commanded, "Go tell Betty everything is all right, then get back in here." He didn't see anyone say that, but he went out and told Betty, "They're going to be fine, Betty. Don't worry. I'm going back in to help. Sandy will take care of you."

When the bedroom door closed behind him, the voice kept talking, "Get that medicine pouch. Take the stuff that looks like mud and put it in the holes in his legs. Just get it in there. And do the back of his leg, too."

Gil found a ceramic jar in the fringed bag Bud had brought on the horse. Sure enough, it was filled with some kind of guck that looked like mud. He packed Doug's puncture wounds, shoving in as much as he could. The back of his thigh was harder, but the stuff was sticky and held. "Get those leaves," the voice said. "Put them on top of the mud. Put the big leaves over that, and tie them with the leather." Gil did as he was told, finding a couple of types of leaves that made good dressings and binding Doug's leg with soft leather strips. He looked at his friend with the hose disappearing down his gullet and wanted to cry.

"Burn the sage! Burn the sweet grass! Burn the cedar. Do it! Fan the smoke to the four directions! Fan the smoke in the corners! Fan it out the window. Get rid of that poison!" Gil had no idea how he was supposed to burn sweet grass, cedar, and sage. Bud and Jon were very busy; he'd have to figure it out himself. He remembered the priest waving incense at Mass when he was a kid. But he didn't have an incense holder on a chain to hold the burning herbs. He decided to use the big kettle. He was able to determine which objects in the medicine bag were the sage, sweet grass, and cedar. Something in the air goaded him, "Hurry! Hurry!" He knew this was important.

He tossed all the vegetation in the pot and lit it with a barbecue lighter he found in a pile of stuff on the desk. Flames and smoke shot into the air. He wondered if he should open the window. Would the smoke alarm go off? "Wave it, wave it!" the voice commanded. It was a bunch of voices, really. Lots of voices in the room. He could almost see figures of bonneted Indian warriors. His heart beat hard, beating along with a drum. He couldn't stop; he had to wave the smoking kettle. But he couldn't touch its handles—they were very hot. The flames had charred the cabinets and the smoke blackened the mirror.

"Help me!" he breathed. "I don't know what to do." He found potholders by the kettle. Grabbing the pot's handles with them, Gil waved the pot in every direction in the universe. He knew he was supposed to say something. He hadn't prayed much in recent years. "Please help them, and us. Thank you very much." As he spoke, the smoke dissipated, grinding down to the output of maybe four priests on a good day. "Please don't let the smoke alarm go off ..." He waved the tureen toward the window and recited the Lord's Prayer. That worked.

"Dance! Dance now!" The voice was very clear. Gil had never been a very good dancer. He put the tureen on the scorched desk. It continued to smoke. "Shake the rattles! Wave the smoke with the fan." He knew he had to do it. "Dance! Do it! Take the rattle in the bag! Take the shaker! Wave the fan! Dance and sing! Do it now!"

Gil realized that this was an important part of the healing. He grabbed the rattle and fan and stood by the bed fanning and shaking as hard as he could. He was beginning to feel a little woozy. The "clear fish" he thought were in the room began to reveal themselves. He could see his grandfather in the corner, his ammunition belts across his chest. All around him were

Filipino guerrillas, armed and ready to kill. His grandfather looked at him and raised a hand. He could see the others there; warriors from all the Indian Nations were protecting them. Legions surrounded them. Healing them. Saving them. His heart swelled and Gil began to sing.

"Oh, when the saints go marching in, oh, when the saints go marching in; Lord, I want to be in that number, when the saints go marching in." The song just came to him. He rattled and shook and stomped and sang the song, until Bud Creeman patted him on the shoulder.

"You can stop now. They're fine."

Doug was propped up in bed, awake. He smiled wanly. "Hey, buddy. I didn't know you could dance."

Jon climbed off the bed, being careful not to step on Melissa, who was still asleep somehow. "It's never been used," he said defensively, picking up the douche bag lying next to Doug. "I *knew* we would need it."

"You sure were right," Bud said, grinning. "We couldn't have done it without it." He spoke to Doug, "I'm going to give you one minute to rest, then we need to take everything you touched when you were hurt—your clothes, the sheets, and everything on the bed—and burn them."

He looked around the room for things that they'd touched. Will was sleeping peacefully; none of them paid any attention to him as they gathered the bedding and clothes.

"Hey!" Bud exclaimed as Will leaped off the bed and shot across the room. He threw open the door and stormed into the cabin wearing the bloody shreds of his jogging clothes. The others followed him, astonished.

66

You're through, Sydney!" Will shouted. Betty let out a yip when she saw him. Mark jumped. They thought he was near death, but the blood-stained man confronting Sandy was not only alive and healthy, he also was enraged. His voice wasn't loud enough to disturb Melissa's slumber, but it carried an impact that could stop an avalanche. "You're done here!"

"What do you mean?" Sandy stuck to her baby doll routine. "I don't know why you're mad at *me*."

Will looked like he wanted to launch himself on her physically. "Nice lying, Sandy. If I didn't know you, I'd almost believe it."

Sandy batted her eyes, staring back through tears.

"I have been on to you from the minute I saw you," continued Will. "I can spot a whore anywhere." Sandy's face spoke murder when she heard that word. "You don't like hearing what you are? You're a *whore*, Sydney. That's all you are. And not a very smart one. I know what you've been doing. I know the name of every jerk you've screwed."

He turned to face Betty and Mark. "People act like I have to be pro-tected. 'Keep it from *Will*. Don't let *Will* know.' I *made* Numenon. I know *everything* that happens there." He turned back to Sandy. "Your johns were idiots. Sniffing around my office, asking questions. I'd have to be a fool not to know what they were after and who wanted it. I *gave* it to them, Sandy. I left stuff on my desk. On my computer screen. Left files open. I leaked my secrets everywhere!" Will strutted in front of her—laughing at her.

"I knew why you were at Numenon, Sandy. You wanted *me*, didn't you?" Will taunted her, his body rigid. "You will never, never get what you want from me. You will never have *me* or anything of mine. Never."

He stuck his face in Sandy's. Bud had come in from the bedroom. He closed his eyes, fearing what would happen. He opened them when no explosion followed. Mr. Duane could handle her. Sandy sat, squirming, hands at her sides. Will laughed.

"I let you stay on because I wanted to find out who sent you. I figured I'd get his name this week; that's why you're with us. But I figured it out myself—Carlo Piretti."

Sandy gasped, a dead giveaway belying all her training.

Will grinned viciously. "When we get there, I'm sending you to a special place I have. You'll never see your friend Carlo again."

"That's not right, Mr. Duane. It's *illegal*." Sandy's face projected indignant sweetness.

"Don't worry about the police, Sandy. The police won't matter where I'm going to put you. No one will know where you are, and you'll never get loose, either. We'll talk about Carlo when I get back, just you and me." His expression was murderous.

"Do you think he'll mind the bad information I fed your guys? Will your boss mind that every single word you gave him was *wrong?*"

Sandy's head flew back and her eyelids fluttered. A door in her mind opened. She was four years old. Her adopted father shoved her down the darkened hallway, into the bedroom; he pulled off his belt. "Pull down your panties..." First there was the belt, then there was the other. Always. Fear swept over her. Her eyelids fluttered and she heard a voice in her mind say, "*He will kill me.*" Whatever her feelings about Carlo, Sandy knew that he would never forgive her for giving him bad information. His people were probably after her already.

Sandy's old life was over; she couldn't go back to her Benefactor. She looked at Will Duane, not hiding her feelings. She would kill him. But first she had to escape. Strong as she was now, she couldn't attack Will Duane. Why not? Sandy looked at the fat Indian—something about him and Will together—she lost power. She couldn't even do what she'd done earlier.

Sandy breathed hard, wanting to kill. She had matured on this trip, but she hadn't come to her full strength. She had realized her purpose in life. She was put here to kill, any way she could. She looked at Will. Her life had been ruined by this asshole; she would kill him, destroy everyone at the Meeting, and take that sweet bitch Melissa with her. First, she had to escape.

"I don't know what you're talking about, Mr. Duane," the petulant little-girl voice whispered. "I've never done anything but my best for you and Numenon."

Will laughed at her, standing straight and tall, as powerful as he'd ever been. "Right, Sandy. Get in the bathroom."

She bristled and hung back, almost hissing. Her menace and hidden strength were obvious.

"Gil, go in that tall cabinet in my bedroom. Bring me a couple of shot-guns." Firearms were verboten under the Rules, but Gil did as he was told, finding the guns and bringing them out. He wasn't surprised that his boss would defy Grandfather. He handed one to Will.

"Do you know how to use that, Gil?"

"Yes, sir. I've shot plenty."

"Then go stand in the bedroom and aim that at the bathroom door. If she tries to come out, shoot her. OK, Sandy, into the bathroom." He herded her through the door between the cabin and bath. "Stay in there." He shut the door and turned to Betty. "Are you all right?"

"Shook up, Will, but I'll survive."

"Can you keep this pointed at the door for a minute? I want to check on Doug and Melissa."

"Fine, Will."

Bud followed Mr. Duane into the bedroom, looking at the open gun cabinet. The only thing that bothered him was the fact that he hadn't detected it and sent the information to Grandfather. In the Mogollon Bowl, bullets couldn't do anything that the Great One didn't want. And the small arsenal packed into the little steel-lined closet was nothing compared with what

Elizabeth Bright Eagle would bring. *Those* were guns. It just bothered him that he hadn't been able to sense these.

Inside the bathroom, Sandy listened to Will's orders with glee. *Betty* was guarding her? That old bag ate out of her hand. She would do anything Sandy said. She began to sniffle, softly, then louder. "Betty?" she whispered through the door. "Please, talk to me. I'm scared. I never did anything..."

"Shut up, Sandy," her mentor replied. "I've believed in you for so long, despite all I've heard about you. But the last few minutes have shown me exactly what you are."

"What do you mean, Betty? What did I do?" Sandy was furious, but her voice was babyish as always.

"I was really hurting while they were healing Doug and Will. Gil told you to take care of me. You turned from me like I was garbage. The look on your face... You showed me who you are better than anyone could.

"If you try to come out, I'll shoot you. You've made a fool of me. I don't like it." Betty didn't sound like the woman Sandy knew.

She was dismayed. Everyone knew that Will's top staff took "commando lessons" from Hannah Hehrmann. Shooting her with a shotgun at that range wouldn't take any talent at all. While she felt supercharged and strong, Sandy doubted she could survive a point-blank shotgun blast.

She was furious. She had no idea she'd done anything wrong when she was with Betty. She'd ignored the blubbering old hag; so what? And yet she knew Betty. She was as steadfast an enemy as a friend.

Sandy stopped talking and looked for another way out.

67

S he spun and looked for an escape route. Sandy almost laughed, it was so easy. The wall over the Jacuzzi was a picture window. It usually had a metal screen over it that probably would stop a rocket. For some reason, the screen was retracted into the ceiling. Stepping into the tub, she ran her eyes around the window frame to see if it opened. Quickly finding and unlatching the catches on the bottom, she pushed on the frame. The window's lower edge tilted outward, leaving an opening a horse could fit through.

Before exiting, she quietly locked the bathroom doors and turned their dead bolts. Everything was going right—even Will Duane's paranoia was on her side. How many motor homes had impregnable dead bolts in the bathroom? Only her crazy boss's. A wide smile replaced her frown.

Sitting on the edge of the window, she pushed off and found herself standing on the desert floor, her back to the motor home.

Paul Running Bird cautiously approached the caravan, staying hidden behind rocks as much as possible. The screams had died down some time before, replaced by songs and cries of joy. He could see a group of men in front of the *Ashley*, examining the damage done by the boulder. Bud came out and started a bonfire. Dense black smoke rose in a column.

Paul rode his horse forward from the rear of the caravan on its left side, where no one could see him. Whatever had assaulted him and Bud was horrendous, and he wanted to make sure that the danger was gone before exposing himself.

As he approached the *Ashley* from the rear, he was surprised to see a window move. In moments, the whole thing rotated outward. Legs emerged. A little jump and a gorgeous woman stood on the ground, looking around cautiously. Her blond hair blew in the breeze; she raised a slender hand to push it behind her ear. Paul had never seen such a beautiful woman. When she saw him, she smiled alluringly. She must be Will Duane's mistress. He'd heard about Will's sexual appetite.

She looked at him as though wondering whether he were a friend or an enemy. He smiled and waved to reassure her. Realizing she had nothing to fear, the woman put her finger to her lips and walked toward him. As she approached, Paul's sensible horse snorted as if it smelled a dozen mountain lions. Paul got the horse under control and faced the blond goddess. Seeing her close up thrilled him. Her pink and white checked shirt was pulled tight over lush breasts, and the rest of her was jammed into tight jeans. Paul wanted to roll with her in the worst way.

She smiled, wiggling her fingers at him. He heard a sweet voice in his mind. I'm playing a game with Will. We do it all the time. Don't tell him you saw me, OK? Her smile was blinding. Paul swore he could feel her hands in his crotch. Don't tell, OK? That voice in his head again, just like some people heard around Grandfather. When he nodded, the voice said, Later in the week, we can meet … If you like … Paul's eyes bulged. The voice cooed, I'll find you when it's time. She blew a kiss at him and stole away. Paul thought he was going to faint.

The blond apparition covered the distance between the caravan and the bluff so fast that Paul couldn't believe it. She dodged from rock to rock, as he had, and was lost in the bluffs in less than a minute.

He rode toward the front of the *Ashley*, careful not to be seen. Paul heard Bud's voice from the other side of the motor home, talking to someone, "Why are you way over here? It's a straight shot from the pass to the campground."

Another voice replied, "Someone faxed Betty a map that said we were supposed to take …" the voice paused like its owner was pointing at something,

"... that pass back there. Mr. Duane didn't want to go that way, but the map said we should, so we did."

A new voice burst out, "Some asshole named Paul Running Bird faxed us a bad map. We could have gotten killed. Who is this guy? I'm going to wring his neck when I find him."

After a pause, Bud said, "He was with me a minute ago, Mr. Duane."

The thunder of hooves announced Paul's departure. They looked out and saw a rider shooting across the desert. "Uh... his horse must have run away with him," Bud said lamely.

Gil Canao cut speculation short, shouting from the doorway, "Will! Will! Do you have a key for the bathroom door? Sandy doesn't answer when I knock and I can't get in. The doors are bolted shut."

68

Grandfather carefully alighted from the golf cart and spoke to the group of bewildered newcomers at the martial arts field. "How many of you know what I did a few minutes ago?" He scanned the faces, mostly new to him. "Speak up. Tell me what you saw." He pointed at one.

"It was a dance, a hunter's dance. But also an exercise, like tai chi." A thin young fellow spoke. He was very intense, a spiritual seeker for some time, Grandfather saw.

"How do you know that?" Grandfather decided to test him.

"I've studied with a tai chi master for years. He moves the same way you did. Tai chi is the inner form of the martial arts." A hint of pride was discernable in his voice.

"Ah. And where do you study with this master? What is your work?"

"In Silicon Valley. I'm a computer programmer."

"Ah. A smart person who has studied with a master for years. And you think I was doing an *exercise*?" He walked a few steps along the edge of the crowd, then turned back suddenly and faced the young man. His eyes were piercing. "It wasn't an exercise. It was real."

He scanned the group, looking for someone. He saw several candidates, but not the one he felt in his heart. And then he saw him, just down the line. Skinny and not much to look at. Tattered clothes. The man's eyes followed Grandfather as though they were attached to him.

"You! What was I doing?"

The young man jumped at being addressed, but spoke easily. "You killed something." He thought. "No, you wounded it. It is far away, but I think I can hear it screaming." He ducked his head. "That's impossible."

Grandfather beamed. He made a motion of his head to Carl, and Carl looked at a couple of the men and women standing by. Spirit warriors. They moved closer to the scrawny man.

"Yes, I struck something. Do you know what it was doing?"

The man turned to the west, where the battle had occurred. "He was killing someone, over there." He began to tremble violently.

"Yes, that was what was happening. I stopped a murder." Grandfather looked at Carl again, and he motioned the warriors to move closer to the man who had spoken. "Very good. You see with eyes that are in the present, not tied to ideas that you have been taught. You see what is there. And you have seen as much as you should, given the knowledge you possess. Be calm now."

Carl went to him and put a hand on his shoulder. The man let out a moan and collapsed. Carl caught him, and the spirit warriors gathered around and held him up. Carl went back to Grandfather, who had his eyes closed.

The shaman sang a few lines in a language none of them knew, and then opened his eyes. "I am to teach you. This is the last Meeting, so I will teach you everything." He nodded at the tattered man, now shaking and surrounded by warriors.

"Why is he upset and you are not? Because he saw the truth. The truth can be terrifying. You must train to see the truth. Carl has been my student for many years. He was with me when I did what I did. Carl, come here." Grandfather put his hand on Carl's shoulder, reaching up to do so. Carl immediately went into a trance state. "He is back with me where I was, stalking," he explained.

Some of the people in the crowd looked carefully at Carl and began to whisper to each other, repeating a name. A huge man, almost seven feet tall, Carl was a giant in all ways. His black T-shirt bulged with muscles that rippled down his arms and up his neck to his head. Muscles filled his jeans; his thighs bulged with them. Even his booted feet looked formidable. Tattoos rolled down his arms and up his neck, apparently covering all of him but his face. These were not polite eagles and names of girls. Carl's tattoos were tribal images, primitive and laden with power. Carl's face looked like a scoreboard for the fights he'd been in. His nose was mashed and he had scars across his forehead and down his jaw. He looked young, but his gray-streaked ponytail indicated his age.

"The Slasher/Rapist!" The words darted around the crowd. Carl stirred, coming out of his trance. *"The Slasher/Rapist!"*

"Stay where you are, my son. I will handle this," Grandfather said, hand remaining on Carl's shoulder. "Yes, this is the one who was branded with that name by the newspapers and television crews, by the people who bring us the *truth* in this world. He will carry that name forever, wherever he goes. Carl is branded and condemned for crimes he didn't commit. Who is the Slasher/Rapist?" he pointed at the man who studied tai chi.

"He's the guy next to you. But he was innocent. They proved that in court with DNA and new witnesses. He was turned loose."

"Good! You remember what happened, not just the name they gave Carl. How long did he serve for the terrible crimes he didn't do?"

"Nine years, I think..."

"Yes, he suffered for many years. And I found him when I visited his prison. I visit prisons, did you know that?" He chuckled. "I don't spend all year waiting for the Meeting. I work. Carl's prison is a hard place. None of you would survive there. But Carl did, and he came to me because he wanted to be free. I helped him, the Great One helped him, and he is free in the outside world now, as well as the inside.

"I have him with me because he is a great warrior. He has suffered more than most could bear and still he loves the Great One more than most of you can imagine. He came to me to be free.

"He is *not* my 'muscle'." He laughed, not a pleasant laugh. "I don't *need* muscle!" The old man seemed to grow and swell as he spoke until he hovered over them, terrible and terrifying. "The Great One gives me all the muscle I need. I like Carl. He is my friend. He helps me when I need help. Most of all, he doesn't talk too much.

"Talk, talk, that's all people do these days. And play on the *Internet*." His laugh bit. The crowd shifted uncomfortably. Some of them looked like they'd like to leave, but no one did. They didn't whisper among themselves, either. All eyes were on the old man. "I like Carl because he has been tested enough to go where I go and see what I see. Would you like to know what I just did from the eyes of someone who was *there?*"

A ripple of nods.

Grandfather left his hand where it was. "Tell them, Carl. What you saw and where we went."

Carl spoke slowly, his voice deep. "I followed you into the other world, where the Power lives. There, I could see him, the Evil One, bigger than the earth. He sat on top of the planet, looking down. He was like a dark shadow on a beautiful ball. He put his hand out, with his finger pointed. He stuck it over there." Carl's eyes were closed. His head nodded in the direction of the ribbon canyon.

"What was he doing?"

"Killing someone. The snake was already there ..."

"The serpent. What is she?"

"She is his wife, his favorite wife, and as evil as he is. The Evil One sent her there to kill, but changed his mind and butted in. He wanted to do it."

"And where was he, really?"

"In his ... It's like a castle. A huge house made of stone. He has a window that he can look out and see everything all over the world. He sat there and stuck out his hand ..."

"He was so big that he could sit on top of the earth and reach out and kill someone ... and he was small, just like a normal person, sitting in his house."

"Yes. Both at once. And everything changed. When I followed you, it was like moving through a forest, with trees everywhere, but the trees weren't trees, they were ..." Carl stopped, trying to describe what he saw. "Like universes, all smashed together so that just the edge of one showed. Like blades of knives. We danced through them."

"Yes, my son, that is right. So many universes exist that we cannot count them. One for each creature, one for each possibility, one for each moment in time. We moved through them like eels, swimming through the true reality. What then?"

"You reached his room, where he lives. Where he plots and thinks. He sat in a big chair, with a table in front of him. The canyon was on the table, and he was flicking someone with his finger. I could hear bones break. He was silent, enjoying his game. The snake was in the canyon, waiting to kill when he told her to." Carl put a hand to his face, covering his eyes. "The man looked like a man, but he wasn't … He was the …"

"He was the Evil One. Don't look at him, my Carl. You cannot yet. You must be trained, as I was, to do that. And then what happened?"

"You snuck in, I don't know how, and threw the spear. It went through his hand. He started screaming, and cursing. What he really looked like came out." Carl cried out. "He's a *monster!*" The group recoiled, feeling what Carl did.

"That is enough, Carl. Come out now!" Grandfather shook him, and then stood in front of him, reaching up to stroke his cheeks. "Carl, Carl. Come out!"

Carl looked groggy and weak. Grandfather called some of the warriors around him, directing them to put Carl in a golf cart and take him to the healing cave. "I will be there as soon as I finish with my new students."

He looked at their solemn faces. "Looking at the Evil One is dangerous. A look, and he can steal your soul. My brave Carl went with me to that place, and he guarded my back, fighting off the others so we could escape. He didn't tell you that. The Evil One has many allies. He has as many allies as the sun has rays. But his is a dark sun.

"Who has experienced evil? Raise your hands." Almost all of the hands went up. "Yes, we have all experienced evil. You …" He pointed to the tai chi guy. "Tell me how you experienced evil."

"Well, the founders of my company cooked the books. They got caught and the company went bankrupt. I lost my job. I got depressed and my wife took off with someone else. She hired a shark of a lawyer and took everything that was left …"

"That is a very sad story. Evil was definitely there. Do I have another? How about you?" He pointed at the scrawny man. The warriors stepped close to him. "What evil have you experienced?"

He looked down, and didn't speak.

"You can talk. No one will repeat it, will you?" Grandfather looked at the crowd. "In this sacred Bowl, everyone does what his soul needs, everyone says what he must. And no one repeats it or uses it for ill."

The skinny guy spoke slowly and softly. "I lost my wife and little girl ... I lost my job ... But I deserved it." The warriors pulled closer. Not a sound could be heard as the man struggled to speak. "I drank. I only did it once a month, but when I did, I got in fights. I wrecked our place ... I beat my wife." Sweat covered his forehead. *"I did that. Evil is in me!"* He hit his chest, shaking so much he looked like he might fall.

"There! There is a warrior!" Grandfather strode toward him, finger pointing. "Evil is in *me*! That is the mark of the warrior! It's not what others did; it's not *their* fault. It's what lies in each of us. Look at me!" He commanded the distraught man.

He looked deeply into Grandfather's eyes and then grabbed his own. "Oh, what did you do? It hurts!"

Grandfather held him, stroking his head. He whispered, "Don't worry. The pain lasts only a little while. Now you are going to become who you really are."

"I saw an eagle! Its claws came into my eyes ..." The thin man looked up at he shaman. "Oh, you're real. You are what they say. Oh, it's beautiful. I can see the eagle!" He looked amazed. "Thank you." He began to weep. Grandfather directed the warriors to take him to a quiet place.

To the group he said, "People wonder how they can become a spirit warrior. They don't have to do anything—they already are when they come here—or they are not. That man spoke the truth. He knew that evil lived in him, and that he did evil. That is the most important thing to know. Saying someone else did it is easy. Blaming is easy. Everyone feels sorry for you. They will feel sorry for you, but never respect you. You will never become a warrior that way.

"Saying that *you* did evil, *you* were the one responsible, that is very hard, especially if it wasn't pretty ... That man is a warrior. I knew it from the minute I saw him. What he just did proved it ... He doesn't drink anymore, I know that. He lives like a warrior now. I could see it without talking to him.

"I'm telling you this because you need to know it to become warriors. Only warriors will survive this week. This is not going to be a Meeting like the others. This will be a dangerous Meeting. I am going to talk about evil, because you need to know about it.

"We all have evil parts. We will cheat and lie and make ourselves look big and others small. We will steal and destroy—our evil manifests in many ways. I could name them all day, and the evil inside would think of new ways to come out.

"What is the foundation of evil? The foundation of evil is a hole in the person that should be filled with the Great One and with the glorious, powerful love that Creator is. People have all sorts of names for the One, so that even those who say they don't believe in God can know God very well. Just don't tell them that what they're feeling is God, and they'll be fine." The group tittered. "And those who say that they love God, they live for God, and they are filled with God often don't have the faintest idea of the living One that is in us and all the world.

"But this is complicated. Evil is not. We all have evil inside. Only if the Great One has come to you and burned it away can the good flower. The One burns evil up—and that is what it feels like. Like *burning, hacking, tearing* ... at our souls.

"That's because we love our evil. We don't say, 'Oh, I love to kill and destroy.' We say it like this, 'I'm a man of principle ... they can't do *that*, it's illegal ...' When *that* means saving their lives by crossing a border. Or we say, 'God told me that *my* religion is right. I can make war, drop bombs, and do whatever I want, because I'm on *God's* side.' This is how we do evil, by making it sound like good. We *think* we are good and don't see our evil.

"You need to be charred in the flame of the One to see the truth. To do that you need to study with someone like my teacher, someone so filled with Creator that there's no room for anything else. And you need to study holy books and work very hard.

"But there are other questions. Why does evil exist? What does evil want?" He looked around. Everyone was silent, staring at him. "Evil wants to destroy. That's all—it wants to destroy the world and everything in it. And mostly, it wants to destroy *you. You, you, you, and you.* All of you." He pointed at people in the crowd. "And me. That's what evil exists to do.

"Does evil want to kill our bodies and take our belongings? Yes. But it wants more than that. Evil wants the essence of what you are—your soul. It wants to destroy that. But your soul is immortal—you do know that, don't you? You live forever, this body is just a ... rest stop. Like beside the highway.

"Evil wants to *own* your soul, to bend it to its will. It wants you to kill, plunder, rape, destroy, and make more evil. It wants you to live like demons and be demons after you die. It wants to own you forever."

He smiled. "You know, our People didn't really have demons until the Europeans came. The creation stories of most of our Nations and our religions didn't have demons. The Thunderbeings are huge and powerful, but not evil. And our friend Coyote lives to teach us. He plays tricks on us, but not evil tricks. The Europeans came with their Devil and demons that wanted to destroy us if we didn't do what the conquerors wanted.

"Do you think that I am saying that we didn't have evil until the Europeans came?" Many in the crowd nodded. "No. Our *legends* didn't have it, not *us*. Were all of us holy men and women before the Europeans came? Did all of us serve the People with no regard for themselves? Were all of us like my teacher, the holiest man I have ever known? No. We had evil. It exists in these." He indicated his body, his head and his heart. "It comes 'hard-wired in,' as the young people say. Our 'operating systems' have it." He laughed. "You don't think I know such talk? I know *plenty*.

"We didn't have so many demons to start. The idea came with the Europeans. But the Europeans are not the only ones who have a Devil and demons. You need to read history. Not just from the West but from all over the world.

"In India, and China, and other places in the East, they know all about demons and devils. They have *big* demons in their writings. Read the sacred texts of all cultures. You must if you want to understand the Great One and evil. You have to read history too, not just philosophy and theology.

"Read the history of our People. Read the history of any conquered people. The conquerors become beasts. Demons. In India, there is a great holy text called the Mahabharata. It's about a war where the good brothers, true princes, have lost their kingdom. They fight a war to get it back. It is a just war. What happens? One by one, the good brothers and all their followers turn into beasts, just like those on the other side. Wars create monsters. It's written in holy books all over the world—and we see it in our lives.

"We become demons in war and whenever our evil parts are allowed out. Where many people do the same evil, it becomes like a monster that moves and kills. Hatred is the mother of this monster, but it comes from same place as all evil. From not having the Great One fill your soul to bursting.

"Is there a monster in addition to this kind of monster that is created by people? Is there a real monster somewhere, plotting to take over our souls and our world? A Devil?" He looked from face to face with a questioning look.

"Yes. I've seen the Devil. I studied with a person who could take me to worlds you cannot imagine. Great-grandfather took me everywhere as he trained me, to places that poets write about, the world of light and the world of greatest darkness." He smiled. "I think poets have been to that place too. They had to go there to write about it.

"Some people say, 'There's no Devil, just human evil. That accounts for what you see in the world.' That may be true. It may also be that whenever we join as one to do evil, a little bit is shaved off of our individual evil and goes into a pot. A big pot of evil is created. And that pot of evil begins to plot to destroy us. It is the Devil, but our evil causes it and feeds it. That could be true.

"Others say that the Devil is a fallen angel, separated from God because of spite and jealousy. That's one view. Then others say that Evil is simply the opposite of Good and they'll exist forever, fighting each other. And others say that God set the whole thing up as a game and what appears as evil is simply God's play. God is *playing* as a demon. It's all a play ... a rough, dark play.

"All these ideas. I know what I saw with Great-grandfather, and I know what I just saw with Carl. An evil power exists and wants to take over our world.

"What's the best way to do this? Hmm? Come on. How could evil take over the world?" He looked around. No one said a thing.

"Come on ... You talked just fine before you found out I wasn't a nice old man who was going to make you feel good this week. Talk to me now, now that you can see what I am." The faces looking back at him registered disbelief, shock, and awe.

"Yes, you see who I really am, and what we are about here. This will be a hard week, my friends. Hard lessons for brave men and women.

"How would an evil power take over the world?" He stared at them, waiting.

The tai chi guy finally spoke. "To take over the world, you'd take over the most powerful thing in the world."

"Yes. And what is that?"

He thought. "Numenon."

"Yes. People tell me that Numenon is the most powerful thing in the world, mightier than governments."

"So the Devil will go after Numenon?"

"Yes. How?"

"Uh ..." tai chi thought for a while. "By taking over its stock ... Or— by capturing Will Duane and controlling him." His mouth dropped open and his eyes widened in surprise.

"Yes. Evil would do anything to make him a slave."

"But they're coming here, to the Meeting this week. Will Duane and his most important people. It said so on the Internet."

Grandfather's teeth ground at the word. "Yes. They are on their way. The Evil One will do anything to stop them. What will it do?"

"Try to capture them. Brainwash them. Brainwash those around them. Attack them ..."

"Yes. And kill them, bringing them back to life as slaves."

"It can do that?"

"Of course. They won't be themselves, but they'll look like they did before they died. They'll be demons." He spoke very seriously. "This will be a Meeting like no other. You are in danger if you stay. The evil within you will rise this week, hearing the call of its master. Your minds will scream that you *must* do this or that, that you *must* disobey the Rules. Forbidden things will offer themselves to you, and you will want them like life itself.

"We are being stalked this week, my friends. The Evil One wants us to serve him, too. Who else is as powerful as Will Duane and Numenon? What else can stand up to Evil?"

"You!" someone shouted. The crowd gasped.

"Yes. And *you*—my students. The Evil One wants those who carry Spirit, because they are more powerful than the others. It wants to use your power to carry out its desires."

"But what can we do? *Oh, my God* ..." A moan rose from the group.

"Oh, my God is what we can do. The Great One is our rod and salvation, our protection in this and everything. We will pray, we will chant, we
will offer our souls and flesh to the One. And we will triumph—if we follow
the Rules and do what the ancestors and the One tell us."

"Are you saying that the Devil will attack us this week?"

"Yes." In the silence that followed, Grandfather looked at them with
great compassion. "You can leave the Meeting if you wish, but you should
know that the battle will go on in your souls whether you leave or stay."

He drove off in a cart, leaving them stunned. Might as well tell them
the truth, he thought. Truth was the most powerful weapon. What he had
said would spread throughout the Bowl and those who weren't supposed to
be there would leave. Good.

As he drove, Grandfather could see the stalker in his lair. Far away,
beyond a mighty ocean. He writhed in pain, his hand pierced by an invisible
lance. His stinking blood flowed on the floor. The old man chuckled. The
Evil One thought he was free from danger in his own house.

The shaman laughed. As long as good existed, as long as the ancestors
and Great One gave him life and breath, he would fight evil wherever he
found it. He looked at the people on the paths around him. Evil was here
as well. Here and everywhere.

But the Great One had arsenals that only angels knew. And love was
most powerful weapon of them all. He should have told those people that.
He should have told them that the Great One was everywhere, permeating
everything. No place existed that did not first host the Great One.

The Great One was the ground of *being*, the warp and weft of existence. The One existed prior to any thing or essence. In the darkest, most
evil place, the lair of the Devil himself, Great One was already there. Evil
existed only because the Great One allowed it.

Grandfather had been able to penetrate the lair of evil, moving on
waves of bliss and power, of consciousness and being, because the Great
One was already there. Moving on the body of the Creator, he was invisible
as he traveled on the foundation of existence. The One that he loved with
all his soul gave him all Powers. The old man understood that. He hoped
his students could comprehend it.

They stood around after Grandfather left, looking at each other. "He's not exactly what they said on the 'net," someone said.

"No. He's not a cute old guy. And this isn't a vacation, either."

The tai chi guy's teeth were chattering. He felt like Grandfather had dissected him. Inside, embarrassment alternated with elation and terror. "Was what he said true?" he heard himself saying. "We're going to be attacked by the *Devil*?"

"We'll find out." Another guy grinned as he spoke. He was one of the spirit warriors, tai chi could tell. He wasn't afraid at all.

"Are you going to leave?" tai chi asked.

"Nah. This is the safest place to be. Grandfather's here."

69

She climbed out the window?" Betty couldn't believe it, even looking at the gaping opening. "Sandy ran away?" The closeness of the cabin weighed on her. This *impossibility* after Doug and Will—her Sandy had betrayed her. Betty looked at her boss in his bloody shorts. The room began to sway.

"Grab the gun!" Will said, catching Betty and laying her on the banquette.

She looked at him blankly. "Will, you were …" The image of his still form and broken body came to her. "I thought you were …" Betty's eyes rolled back.

"Take care of her, Gil," Will said after sitting with her a few moments. "I'm going to clean up." His appearance was upsetting to all of them.

The bathroom smelled like a wild animal had been in it. Worse than that, like something evil had been there. He shooed the vileness out the window with his hands, unconsciously doing what Bud or Grandfather would have done. In the shower, Will took stock. What had happened? He couldn't remember clearly. Something had attacked him. The blue eyes and malevolence. The stalker. He'd seen him clearly. Then he didn't remember anything, except that he had to get Sandy Sydney. He flew at her without knowing what had happened.

Will examined himself in the shower. Once he washed the dirt off, nothing was wrong with him, not a scrape or scratch. Even his old scars were gone. Except for his dirty clothes and the sense of surviving something, it was as though nothing happened.

When he walked into the cabin cleaned up and in fresh clothes, Betty was still unstrung. She examined his face and hands, his unmarked neck. "I can't believe it."

"I'm all right, Betty. I'm fine."

"He did it—Bud, the Indian. He *fixed* you."

"Where is he now?"

"He's taking care of his horse. He burned the bedding and everything that touched you and Doug." She clutched his hands. "You're really all right?"

"I'm fine. And so is Doug. He's sleeping." Will blinked. What had happened to Doug? Something about a snakebite. He lay in the bedroom under a quilt. Doug looked like a baby as he slept next to Melissa. Will had smiled when he saw them. They *were* his kids. To Betty, he said, "Will you be OK if I go out and thank the guy who saved us? I think I need to burn these, too." He indicated the towel he had wrapped around his shredded shorts.

Bud squatted next to his mare, shaking his head. Squirrelly had really messed up her legs. He couldn't fix them. The power that had swept over him in the motor home was gone. Well, he could ease her pain enough to lead her back to camp, but her days as a riding horse were over unless Grandfather could do something.

Why could he heal at one moment, and not another? When he was healing, it was like being an extension of Grandfather and Great-grandfather and all the ancestors. Now, the drums pounded faintly in his ears, and that was it. A spooky unreality cloaked that interval. Whatever he did took less than an hour. He shivered. The Great One scared him. Its Power scared him.

Something else came to him: Sandy Sydney was running loose. And a greater evil existed and was after them; he felt it as clearly as Grandfather's presence.

"Is your horse going to be OK?" Jon asked for the assembled men.

"If Grandfather gets to her. Do you have any cold packs and bandages? I should wrap her legs before leading her in."

"I have Ace bandages, all sizes, and lots of cold packs." Jon ran to get them.

The drivers stepped back when Will Duane emerged from the *Ashley* in chinos and a starched, ironed shirt. He looked like he'd come from a spa. Will tossed the towel he'd wrapped around his shorts on the fire and turned to Bud.

"I'd like to thank you for what you did." Will held out his hand. Squirrelly pulled away, snorting.

"Oh, it was nothing, Mr. Duane." Bud touched the mare's neck. She calmed instantly and dropped her head. "Don't mind her, she's a little flighty. She's a good ol' gal, though." He took the other man's hand. "Glad I could help."

"Can she be ridden?" Will said.

"No. I rode her harder than she could handle. I'll have to walk her in. Can I leave my saddle in one of your motor homes? That will make it easier for her."

"Certainly."

Bud was getting nervous. They needed to get out of there.

Will seemed to be aware of their danger. "Can you tie her to a bumper or something?"

"Not this horse, sir. You'll see when you fire up them things," Bud indicated the vehicles. "But I can walk her in. It's only six miles."

"Six miles!"

"I can do it. Done it before."

Will nodded and took over, waving to the drivers to go back to their posts. "I can't leave you in harm's way. Are you sure you can't load her in the trailer at the end of the caravan?"

"No. She won't load."

Will pulled out his cell phone and saw that he still didn't have a signal.

Bud pointed. "After that ridge, you'll be in the open. Your phones might work."

"This is what we'll do," Will said. "You'll walk the horse out of the canyon. Jon and Rich will stay close to you. We'll keep you in sight, and call the camp when we get past the rocks. They'll send someone for you."

About twenty minutes after they started, Bud thought that was the best idea anyone ever had. Hadn't seemed like it at first. The caravan moved out and the last vehicle stopped by him. Jon jumped out, arms full of bandages and boxes. "You just rub these together and they get cold. Like this," he put the boxes at Bud's feet and gave a demo with one. In short order, Squirrelly's legs were cold and wrapped and her saddle was stowed in the motor home.

As he got ready to start walking, Bud took a good look at Jon. His bright red hair was cut very short around the sides and back. A spiky fore-lock fell forward, giving him the look of a stylish woodpecker. He was the most beautiful man Bud had ever seen. A wentke—gay—no doubt. Bud was glad that Grandfather held the traditional view that people were created perfect. Prejudice against homosexuals was unknown in many tribes before the Europeans came. Grandfather taught his students the old way. Many of the spirit warriors were gay. No one had any problem with that—Grandfa-ther's rules were the same for everyone.

"Thanks for helpin' me."

"Oh, you were the one who was fantastic! Will and Doug would be dead without you!"

Bud shook his head disparagingly. "It weren't nothin'. Grandfather did all the work." That's when he got the scare. He looked at Jon and could see the translucent image of another man's face next to him. He was bigger than Jon and heavier, with curly hair and sparkling eyes. Bud could see the motor home right through him.

A ghost! Bud wouldn't say he was afraid of ghosts; he just didn't like to be around them or anywhere they'd been, or around dead bodies. Oh, Lordy. Spirit guides were with him already. He was a spirit warrior for sure.

Bud had known Jon was a spirit warrior from the start, from the way he handled that douche bag, for one thing. He'd never see one of those things again without remembering Jon bouncing on that bed. He smiled, trying not to laugh.

When he heard how far he had to walk, Jon ran back inside and emerged with a backpack. "For the trail. A snack. And a surprise." Bud could feel a Thermos and lunch box inside.

He wasn't able to go very far before he needed to investigate the con-tents of the lunch box. The food seemed to call to him; his interest often ran to food. One bite, and it was over. How could a sandwich taste so good? What was that buttery stuff? He didn't mean to, but he gobbled all three

sandwiches down. Bert was a good cook, but this was beyond that. Squirrelly Girl turned to him, begging. He gave her a crust of bread. The food
made him feel better. Safer.

He drifted back from the motor home as he ate. Then he found the surprise—a piece of chocolate cake. The cake erased all memory of Jon's ghost
friend and the events of the day. Bud had to sit down on a boulder to eat it.
Nothing could describe the softness of the frosting, the firm texture of the
cake. Nothing was that good.

The mare looked at him, nostrils picking out the cake's aroma. She
nickered. He gave her a bite, all he would spare. Squirrelly looked at him
brightly, then lifted her upper lip in the distinctive flehmen response that
says, "Hey, that's good," in horse.

"You're right, girl," Bud said. "He sure can cook."

Everything seemed wonderful after the cake. He rubbed her neck.
"You aren't such a bad old girl are you?" She looked at the napkin in which
the cake had been wrapped hopefully. "Maybe he'll give us some more at
camp," Bud said, putting his arm over the mare's withers.

They walked along, talking about chocolate and life and all that mattered. He didn't notice the motor home drifting out of sight. Sandy Sydney
never crossed Bud's mind. Man and horse were lost in chocolate, oblivious
to the possibility that the monster that put Bud and the rest of the men in
terrible pain was very close—and watching them.

70

When he heard Will Duane say he would wring his neck, Paul Running Bird panicked. He couldn't let anyone know that *he* had steered the Buckwheat crew wrong. He'd have to keep away from the Numenon people the rest of the Meeting. He wouldn't be able to chat with the richest man in the world or see inside the beautiful *Ashley III*. Oh, man! Did that mean he wouldn't be able to have that blonde, either? "I'll find you," she said. How could she find him if he was hiding with his People—the great unwashed?

No one ever let him explain that he made a mistake in haste. Paul wouldn't put the richest man in the world in danger—he wouldn't jeopardize all that he and Grandfather worked to achieve. He'd had a very painful insight when he was passed over for the promotion and sued Microsoft. His bosses' depositions made him realize that sometimes he *did* put the group's success in jeopardy. But—he'd been very careful since then, except for this. What vengeful God would make him keep suffering? If God loved him, why should his life be destroyed?

As the dun horse loped along, Paul thought about his miserable future. Stuck in Seattle with his fat, whiny wife and kids. Stuck in a third-rate job in a third-rate city while Will Duane fucked that blonde in the sunshine.

"It was a mistake!" he shouted, with the result that the horse jumped forward. "I didn't mean it! It isn't fair!" The horse went faster with every word. Paul was so upset that he began to pray, "Please, please ..." The gross injustice of what had occurred had jolted his shaky faith in what Grandfather preached, namely that a Great One permeated the universe for the good of all. Instead, he prayed as hard as he could to whatever would listen.

"Please, please—let me get what I deserve, and not get passed over because of stupid mistakes that I didn't mean. You know how I really am."

He felt easier after praying, like something heard his anguish. For the first time, he noticed how easily the dun stallion covered the rocky terrain. He was like a cat, dodging ruts, boulders, and cacti like they weren't there. "Yah!" Paul yelled. "Yah! Yah!" The animal seemed to have no limit to his speed. Something took over in him, an energy he knew well. He wanted to spur the horse, feel him jump, but he had no spurs. He kicked instead, and the horse responded in a flash. Paul wanted more than that. He wanted the horse to run in terror and pain. The ends of the snaffle bridle's reins were too short to hit him with, so he took off his hat and fanned it by the animal's right flank. The dun took off like he'd used a cattle prod. Paul kept fanning the hat, and the horse galloped faster and harder.

71

Will tried to sit quietly in the cabin but he couldn't. He was out of focus somehow, not in the real world. Betty was distraught, dabbing at her eyes. He wanted to bolster her confidence. He couldn't do that either. Something terrifying was on its way. He didn't feel fear as a result of what happened to him. He could scarcely remember what happened. He went for a run. Doug was lying in the middle of the canyon— even the horror of seeing him was dimmed. Shock, he assumed. They told him he'd been badly hurt, that they thought he was dead. What he remembered was singing and eagles' wings beating.

He got up and walked toward the windshield, holding on to the back of Mark's chair and peering out. He could see a cloud of dust rising from a point in front of them, and many vehicles to their left. They'd finally found the Mogollon Bowl and the Meeting. Will knew that Grandfather was coming toward them. His jaws clattered. Why was he afraid? What had he done wrong? Everything. He knew that. He marched in place for a while, biting his lips. He looked around the cabin. Only four of them in it now: Mark, himself, Gil, and Betty. Gil was withdrawn, looking worried.

Will wanted to get out and run, but he knew that would upset Betty more than anything. His anxiety grew. Finally, he couldn't control it. He sat next to Betty and touched her shoulder. He wasn't ready to meet Grandfather.

"Betty, Grandfather's coming—I can feel him. Help me. What didn't you cover in your brief? Tell me what I need to know." Will gazed out the windshield, increasingly agitated.

"What you need to know?" Betty said as though she were dazed.

"What I need to know to succeed with Grandfather."

Gathering her thoughts took a moment. She replied deliberately, "Well, you always tell us to open our eyes during a negotiation—to see what's there. You might notice that you're *alive*, Will. A couple of hours ago, you looked *dead*. You were blue. And smashed. Now you're alive, sitting here, perfectly fine." Her voice caught. She turned to face him. "You certainly should notice *that*."

And then her anger erupted, replacing her earlier confusion. "We thought you and Doug were *dead*. You're both alive. It's impossible—you should have seen yourselves. That wasn't any *snake* that bit him. And what attacked you?"

She stared at him until he blurted, "I don't know. I never saw it."

"Doesn't that strike you as odd? That much damage without any evidence? You should notice that, Will. We're heading into something that all the briefs in the world can't explain. You're always talking about thinking out of the box—we *are* out of the box! We're so far out of the box I don't even know *what* we're in." Her voice rose. "Don't you know that? So much has happened on the way here, I can't even *guess* what will happen once we're in that Bowl. You can't do *business as usual* in a situation that's absolutely *not* usual.

"Are you listening to me?" She almost shouted. "Will! Give up your crazy mine! What you want to do is terrible—*mine* their holy lands. How could you even think of it?" Her disgust showed on her face. "It's even crazier with what's happened.

"Mark and Jeff talked about spiritual masters who can blow things up and … *do* things at long distances. We don't need stories to prove what Grandfather can do. We have you and Doug. I could feel Grandfather and all his ancestors in there healing you. And see them here in the cabin. Do you think that Bud healed you? Do you think it was *possible* for anyone to heal you?" Betty glared at him, breathing hard, lips slightly parted.

"Do you want to get us killed? Aside from all this supernatural stuff— and that's what it is, whether you or I or anyone says it or believes in it.

Supernatural. We're in a supernatural place with supernatural things happening. Aside from all that—Sandy Sydney ran off. I would have trusted her like a daughter this morning, and she betrayed me. Who knows what the rest of us might do by the end of the week? Who knows what we're capable of? Who's the next *Sandy?*

"We've harbored a traitor and stalkers have tried to kill us—we're in big trouble, Will. We need allies, not enemies." She shook her head. "Even without the supernatural stuff, even without Sandy—look at the numbers. There are four *thousand* of them and *ten* of us. They could tear us apart in an instant. And they will, if they find out what you want to do." She kept attacking him.

"You're right, I haven't told you what you need to know yet. Read my brief or spend ten minutes on the 'net—you'll find out that many Indians live history like it was happening now. The atrocities I talked about are real to them. Some of the people at the Meeting will *hate our guts.* All they'll need is to find out about your plan and we'll be dead."

She looked at the melted red phone on the countertop. "We're out here, by ourselves, with a holy man who is the real thing, and God knows what else. Drop the mine, *please.*"

Will cleared his throat. He'd heard what she said, but it seemed distant from him. He felt like he was in a fog. What she said was true, all of it, but… "OK, Betty. Don't worry about it. Everyone, forget about the mine. We're here to do the retreat. We'll stay the week, do our thing, and go home, period."

He didn't lie to her. He meant what he said, looking at her with his little-boy eyes and guileless face. She had reached him. At a level deeper than words, he had no intention of giving up the mine. He wanted it. The mine wasn't his main reason for being there, but it was a good one. Its financials were terrific, and he'd sunk a ton of money into the project. He didn't lose money.

"Trust me, Betty. The mine deal is dead. OK?" He spoke earnestly, totally unaware of his hidden plan. "Really." He turned to the others, "It's over. Forget I brought it up. I apologize for my bad judgment." They looked at him blankly. Will smiled his irresistible smile. Deeper than that, deeper than his own thoughts, he knew he'd speak to Grandfather about the mine privately. This was between them. At the right moment, he'd act.

Betty looked at him, eyes narrowed and arms crossed over her chest. "OK. I'll believe you." She didn't look like she believed him. She looked like she was thinking, I've heard that before. "Don't get us killed, Will. I don't want to die for your latest *whim*." Betty sat silently, rigid and white faced.

Finally, she said, "I'd like to propose that we do something positive this week since we're here. Why can't we do something that really helps them? We're the most effective organization in the world. Why can't we do something good while we're here?"

Will nodded, looking like an earnest little boy. "I'd like to do that, Betty. I'd like us to do something that *really* helps. Something that works all the way around. I'd like to make *that* our purpose this week; that, and becoming a team."

He spoke softly. The vehicle was silent. Not a breath stirred the air.

Mark could feel the atmosphere in the cabin. They were hanging on the edge of something. He'd been listening to the conversation, as stunned as the others. The only difference between him and the others was that he'd been in and led a dozen therapy groups and had an MA in counseling. He saw things even Will didn't see. He'd felt this moment before, right before a person's ego cracked, allowing real change to occur.

"Yeah," Will said. "Let's help people."

Mark wanted to jump up and shout, "Betty, you're a genius!" Mark remembered how bad he felt when Will outlined his plan for the mine and then put on the mock negotiation with Doug and Sandy. Everything had changed since. Betty had won on every score. He knew congratulating her would spoil it, and he couldn't say that anyone had done anything, really. Betty simply told her truth as events played out.

Will got up and stood near the door, looking out the windshield. He seemed to be looking for something. Mark couldn't see anything, just the desert and the cars and trucks to their left. Plus lots of dust.

72

Lisa Cheewa had tears in her eyes as she saddled the second horse. When she left the stable area behind the Mogollon Bowl, she looked back over her shoulder at the dun stallion tied to the hitch rack. They'd done what they could for him. The horse was back on his feet after he collapsed. The guys were taking care of him. They'd found a blanket in the tack shed and put it over him while he cooled out. They walked him carefully, then pulled the blanket off. He could hardly move, his legs were so destroyed. Lisa fashioned ice boots for the stallion with ice from her chest and some shipping boots. That's all she could do. She had never seen a horse in the condition in which Paul Running Bird had returned this one.

"Would someone put this horse away for me?" he had said, tossing the reins over the hitching rail. "I've got to get up to the camp."

She tried every healing trick she knew, but the horse's spirit was damaged as much as its legs and lungs. They ran to get Grandfather, but he was healing someone and said to get Bud. When Bud didn't return with Paul, Lisa knew what happened. That idiot mare he was on had broken down and he was walking her in. Leading a spare mount, she set out to find him in a horse-saving trot; she'd walk the pinto mare back while Bud rode the extra horse back faster.

She made good time, stopping at the Numenon caravan and asking if they'd seen Bud. "He's leading a horse after the last vehicle," they said. She stopped when she reached it and they said, "He's right back there." They were surprised that Bud and the mare had drifted so far back. "He's got to be back there. We'll wait until we see him."

She urged the horses faster and found him walking along, talking to the pinto mare like everything was wonderful. He looked up. His expression changed when he saw how upset she was.

"Oh, am I glad I found you! You won't believe what Paul did to that stallion…" She told him that the horse collapsed at the hitching rack after Paul walked away. That he never even tried to help. She started crying and didn't try to stop.

Bud looked at her, concerned. If Lisa was crying, it must have been bad. She was a wrangler at one of the big Arizona dude ranches, a team roper, and a seasoned hand with any horse. This was her third Meeting, her second as a Spirit Warrior.

She choked out, "I did what I could to help him, but it wasn't any use."

Bud handed Squirrelly Girl's lead rope to Lisa and mounted the spare horse. Rage welled up inside him. Grandfather's People didn't abuse animals. "Walk that mare in slow," he said to Lisa. "She's not a bad ol' thing."

Bud took off at an easy lope. His hands weren't tied this time, and he would see that Paul Running Bird got what he deserved. He was so agitated that he didn't think to tell Lisa that a blonde who was capable of anything had run off from the Buckwheat group. He waved at Jon and Rich as he loped by. They waved back and fired up that big box of a machine, taking off to catch up with the others.

Lisa led the mare slowly, looking around at the desert as she rode her horse. The area around the Mogollon Bowl was more beautiful than anywhere else. The desert's immensity surrounded her and the two horses. The young woman sighed, feeling safe and peaceful. She loved being alone.

73

Will stood by the door, looking out the windshield and hanging on. The *Ashley* continued her bumpy progress across the plain. He could feel Grandfather coming. He shook his head and shoulders, trying to loosen up. He couldn't. Everything Betty had said all day swirled in his mind. He tried to put together a crisp opening statement and establish a sympathetic position for his initial meeting with the holy man. He wanted to demonstrate his empathy and ability to help them. A lifetime of experience leaned into the process. He was the man who could negotiate anything.

"I'm so sorry about what happened to your People." Inadequate. An understatement. And what if something had happened to *him* too? "I'd like to do something to help *you* and your People." But not get stuck financing their entire economic recovery. The Feds were the ones who botched it, not he. If he had managed the mess, the Indians would be perfectly organized and on their feet. Profit centers all over the country. No. Wrong approach... Remember everything Betty said. The worst, most appalling parts. What they'd been forbidden from doing.

"If you ever need to hire lawyers, I've got the best on the planet. You can use my lawyers any time. And management consultants, too. I have great management consultants. I can send them out, do some seminars."

This was all wrong. Something was coming; he could feel it. Will experienced the universe churning. Everything was coming, absolute good and evil were converging from all over, from places he couldn't see. The Mogollon Bowl was the center, the place everything would collide in the next week. He knew that, and was thrown into the altered state he had during his spells. He couldn't stop what was coming. Nothing could stop it.

He knew that Grandfather was just over that rise, heading toward them quickly. Something else was approaching with him, something he couldn't see. Huge, powerful, more vast than his mind or thoughts or feelings, it filled the desert—and everything else, stretching across the horizon, filling the sky. He didn't see any angels or images, any old man floating above them. He didn't even see a color, or billowing clouds. He looked out the windshield and saw an ordinary desert scene, cars rushing toward the Bowl on their left and heat rippling along the horizon. Heat rippling and something magnificent revealing itself. He shivered.

His legs shook involuntarily and he didn't bother to see if anyone noticed. His eyes were fixed on a spot on the rise going into the Bowl. Grandfather would emerge there, in the exact heart of whatever he could feel coming toward them. As he thought of it, he realized that the thing, the power, was already around them. It was everywhere, permeating everything, vast beyond his comprehension. He'd seen the stalker's face, but this had no face.

His introductory speech was gone, swept away. Nothing to say, nothing to do. Grandfather already knew. This thing already knew everything about him. No subterfuge, no finely tuned strategy could win it over. As the old man grew closer, the power he felt grew stronger. It reached in every direction, nameless.

He wanted to bow down. Words formed in his mouth, strange words he couldn't decipher. Some language. Nothing to say but the truth. "I've done terrible things," he whispered to that vast intelligence. It was intelligence itself, life itself, the root of existence. This was what he'd sought his entire life. He began to choke; something vile was coming out of him. I've done terrible things. A panoply of images, contracts, and shady deals flooded his mind. I've done terrible things, he thought. I've cheated and lied. His wife's eyes. He felt ill. Women. Places. I can't stop doing terrible things. Doug

Saunders' face. Will groaned. That was the worst thing I've ever done. For-give me, please. Help me. I can't stop.

Mark looked at Will. He was groaning and looked sick. Maybe that miracle cure Bud worked was wearing off. He started to say, "Are you OK?" when he saw a spot appear on the horizon. "Look! That must be Grand-father!" A vehicle cleared the rim of the Mogollon Bowl in front of them. "Looks like a golf cart! It must be him, look!"

The cars heading for the rim stopped, turned around, and followed the golf cart. It looked like someone must have waved them off, because they returned to their original courses—into the Bowl. The cart was headed straight at them.

He could see two dots in it, dots that became people as the cart approached. A tall person was driving, and someone tiny sat next to him. They seemed to be going very fast, faster than the *Ashley*. Dust flew up around the cart. It must have blown toward them, because Mark choked up, like he could barely breathe. The air seemed to thicken. His mind stopped, Mark found himself staring out the window mindlessly.

He was surprised when he discovered they were stopped. The *Ashley* rested a few yards in front of the cart. How did it get there? He had lost track of time.

Will opened the door and staggered out, heading for the cart. Or for Grandfather. Mark watched a tiny, ancient man carefully step down and stand, waiting. Will struggled toward him, oblivious to the other person present. Mark's eyes bulged. The driver was the biggest, toughest-looking Indian he had ever seen. Grandfather's muscle, he thought. What had they gotten into? What if you weren't supposed to get that close to the shaman? Mark couldn't move to stop his boss.

Gil and Betty ran to the front of the cabin to see what was hap-pening, peering out the windshield. Was Will OK? No one attempted to help him.

Will made his way to Grandfather. He had to get to him; he had to say something. His eyes registered the old man's appearance, but something much larger drew him. He felt like he was crossing a desert, crossing mountains, ramming his way to the center of the earth. He heard himself panting as he struggled. The old man smiled softly, waiting.

When he finally stood only a few paces away, he stopped. All that time, the old man's eyes held his. They had been benevolent and kind. Now that changed. The eyes became hard and brilliant, piercing. Will felt something shoot from them into his own eyes, and a rending, a shredding. It was like fighting the adversary in the canyon, but not. This destruction sought to liberate, not destroy, him. It offered no escape and didn't stop until it reached his heart. Will grabbed his chest and kept going.

They were face to face. Everything fled, his clever strategizing, even the list of his sins. Eyes locked on the shaman's, his hands seeking the other man's. Will stood silently, then whispered what he needed to say.

"*I didn't give in …*" When he met the stalker, his will had held.

"I know, my son." Will had heard that voice before. He'd always known that voice. "You did not give in because you could not. You are a warrior. A warrior never gives in."

At those words, Will slumped, falling to his knees. He pressed his face to the shaman's belly, arms clutching his waist. Grandfather stroked his head and back, saying, "Good boy, good boy." Will broke, his shoulders shaking as he released the pain and terror that had been impressed upon his flesh and soul. "I didn't break." He felt like he'd known the other man all his life, before that, perhaps. He didn't need to talk to him; he already knew. But he needed to tell him everything, his whole life. He had been looking for this man forever. They were supposed to do something together. Will raised his eyes and asked, "What are you?"

"I am an old man who listens and does what he's told."

"Can you feel them?" Will whispered. He could feel forces circling them, congregating around the Mogollon Bowl. Evil forces that had attacked him and Doug—the stalker and more.

"Oh, yes, my son. They are always there, and this week, they will all be *here*." He indicated the desert around them.

"What are they? Who?"

"Phantoms, my son. Phantoms created of their own impotence, trying to pretend they exist. They are nothing."

"But they're huge. And so many. And they're powerful. They almost killed Doug and me."

"Oh, yes. They are coming. But so are they," He swept his hand across the sky and Will saw riders, countless riders galloping toward them. "They are much mightier, my son. But you won't believe that until you see what they do."

Will shivered. He was exposed, as insecure as he had ever been, yet he felt secure next to this man. *They* were coming, all that he feared, more than he could imagine to fear. And more was coming, that he couldn't imagine at all.

"Don't worry, my son. All is as it should be. You have found me. That is the hardest part. Now we can begin."

Will wanted to talk about the battle he knew was coming. The shaman raised his hand.

"The battle is always being waged. In the week that comes, we will do what's next. But not alone. Do you hear them, my son? The warriors singing? Do you feel the Power? Do you see the Great One all around us, protecting us? Raising us to Its height? Loving us as Its own?"

And Will did see at that moment. He saw warriors singing from beyond time and space. Something nameless everywhere. Glory. What he had felt when Bud's hands were in his body healing him. Grace. Splendor. Love. The One.

"What we will do is the only thing we can do. We will be what we were meant to be. And we will never give in."

In the *Ashley,* they watched the giant Indian lift Will up and steady him. He pointed him back toward them. Will looked like his mind had been erased. He climbed into the vehicle. They clustered around him.

"What did he say?" Betty was beside herself.

"He said that we've found him and it's time to begin."

GRANDFATHER & COMPANY:
EXECUTIVE SUMMARY

To do:

- Introduce the summary—"Will asked me to prepare this summary so we have key information at our fingertips."
- Hand out motor home assignments.
- Give Mark latest directions and map.
- Call John. Home. Office. ???

Prepared by Betty Fogarty
Chief of Executive Support Services
Office of William B. Duane
March 21, 1997

I included info about our team because it contains some surprises.
We're more talented than I realized! B.F.

THE NUMENON TEAM

WILLIAM B. DUANE (Will) Founder & CEO of Numenon, Inc. BA, Stanford University, Summa Cum Laude; MBA, Graduate School of Business, Stanford University, ranked #1 in his class ('54). No need to say more; we all know what Will's achieved.

ROBERTA FOGARTY (Betty) Chief of Will's Support Services since 1975, with Numenon since 1972. BA, San Jose State; Regency Secretarial School, San Jose. Who's Who in American Women.

DOUGLAS SAUNDERS (Doug) Office of Will Duane. BA, Stanford University, Summa Cum Laude; MBA, Graduate School of Business, Stanford University, ranked #1 in his class. Who's Who, etc. *These MBAs are the Dream Team.*

MELISSA WEIR (Melissa) Office of Will Duane. BA, Carleton College, Summa Cum Laude; MBA, Graduate School of Business, Harvard University, ranked #1 in her class.

GILBERT CANAO (Gil) Office of Will Duane. BA, University of the Philippines, Manila, Summa Cum Laude; MBA, Graduate School of Business, Stanford University, ranked #1 in his class.

SANDRA SYDNEY (Sandy) Assistant to Betty Fogarty. Chicago Secretarial Academy; BA, Wellesley College; MFA, the *Sorbonne*, Paris; Executive Secretary, *Gallerie Nautili DorO*, Paris.

SUPPORT STAFF: OUR CHEF & DRIVERS

JON WALKER BA, Culinary Arts, The Culinary Institute, NYC; Instructor, *Le Cordon Bleu*, Paris; Executive Chef, *Ao Punto*, San Francisco; *L'Ambien*, Paris, etc. Will says, "He's the best chef in the world." *Will's right!*

MARK KENNA BA, UC Santa Cruz; MA, Transpersonal Psychology, UC Santa Cruz. Chief of logistics for our trip. *Mark leads a band, the Counter Continuum!*

JEFFRY BLOCK (Jeff) BA, Philosophy, UC Santa Cruz; MA, Religious Studies, UC Santa Barbara. *Jeff plays in Mark's band!*

HECTOR CARRILLO (Hector) BA, Latin American Studies, San Jose State Univ. Hector's family came here from Peru in the 1970s. *That's where he gets that charming accent!*

DELROY WEST (Delroy or Del) Del worked for Executive Limousine in Florida until Numenon acquired it. *Worked his way up into Will's favorite drivers!*

RICHARD SALLES (Rich) BA, Art History, UCLA; MFA, Studio Art & Painting, UCLA. *Rich has exhibited in Los Angeles and San Francisco!*

Aren't we a talented bunch! B.F.

These people do not advertise their affiliation with Grandfather. They don't know that we have bios on them— including GRANDFATHER! Closed lips, team!

GRANDFATHER'S PEOPLE

GRANDFATHER. leader of the Meeting, the retreat we're attending. **Do not refer to him as "the Greatest Native American Shaman ever born." He hates being called that.** Surprise: He has two degrees from the All Faiths Theological Seminary in Oakland, CA.

ELIZABETH BRIGHT EAGLE (Elizabeth) BA, Stanford University; MD, School of Medicine, Stanford University; MPH, UC Berkeley. Private practice in Palo Alto. Philanthropist. *People Magazine's* Woman of the Year 1996, on *Oprah* and all the talk shows. One of the Meeting's Founders. *Impressive woman!*

TYLER BRAND (Dr. Brand) PhD, Religious Studies, UC Santa Barbara. Full professor at UC Santa Barbara and author of eleven books on Native and Eastern religions. Called "tough and scary" on student web page. A Founder of the Meeting

LEONA BRAND (Leona) MA, University of North Carolina, Chapel Hill. Member of the Board of Supervisors of Santa Barbara County, she's expected to run for Congress in 2000—and win. Wife of Tyler Brand. A Founder.

PAUL RUNNING BIRD (Paul) MBA, The Wharton School, University of Pennsylvania. Executive at Microsoft. Founder of the Meeting and its primary organizer. Our liaison. Provided us with maps and advice. *charming on the phone!*

JESSE CREED (Jesse) PhD English, University of Colorado, Boulder. Full Professor, St. Cloud College, St. Cloud MN. Author of three award-winning books of poetry; he's expected to win the Pulitzer Prize with his forthcoming book. May not attend the Meeting due to publication deadlines. *"The most soulful man in America."*

OTHERS: FOUR THOUSAND PEOPLE ARE EXPECTED AT THE MEETING. We have bios on *six*. Expect surprises, everyone.

OUR LOCATION & THINGS TO REMEMBER

THE MOGOLLON BOWL, our destination, was formed by a meteor. It has strange effects on the mind *and* laws of physics. Expect to feel unbalanced, overemotional. Our liaison says the Bowl is harmless.

THE RULES: THE RULES ARE: NO NUTHIN' DON'T DO ANYTHING EVEN SLIGHTLY OUT OF BOUNDS. Grandfather enforces the Rules: He kicks people out. Don't think he won't kick us out!

SPIRIT WARRIORS: Grandfather's elite force. Their role isn't clear: Is it purely spiritual or more militant?

You will not get into trouble with the Indians if you follow the Rules! B.F.

READ THESE BOOKS! To "Know our enemy" we must be prepared. You are required to at least skim these books. We have copies in the Ashley. Don't make mistakes out of ignorance.

READING LIST

NATIVE AMERICAN MYSTICISM. Will always says, "Get it from the horse's mouth." I've tried to list books by true mystics. These books should give us a hint of Grandfather's reality.

- Black Elk, *Black Elk Speaks: Being the Life Story of a Holy Man of the Ogalala Sioux* (as told to John G. Neihardt)
- John (Fire) Lame Deer and Richard Erdoes, *Lame Deer, Seeker of Visions*
- Chief Archie Fire Lame Deer and Richard Erdoes. *Gift of Power: The Life and Teachings of a Lakota Medicine Man*

NATIVE AMERICAN LITERATURE. I listed just a few books, starting with Dr. Jesse Creed's, since he's Grandfather's follower.

- Creed, Jesse, PhD, *Last Man In*

    _____,*Craven Truth*

    _____, *Heartstroke*
- Alexie, Sherman, *The Business of Fancydancing: Stories and Poems*
- Erdrich, Louise, *Tracks*
- Momaday, N. Scott, *House Made of Dawn*
- Power, Susan, *The Grass Dancer*
- Silko, Leslie Marmon, *Ceremony*

INDIAN/U.S. RELATIONS AND MYTHS ABOUT INDIANS. Will says, "A good negotiation is one where no one is happy with the result." This book is like that: Neither whites or Indians come out looking wonderful. Very well researched.

- Bordewich, Fergus M., *Killing The White Man's Indian; The Reinvention of Native Americans at the End of the 20th Century*

That's it, team! This is a working retreat!
Do your homework. B.F.

Want to know what happens next?

COMING SOON

MOGOLLON

Book Two of The Bloodsong Series
by Sandy Nathan

The Numenon team members reach their destination, the fabled Mogollon Bowl. They've been attacked, waylaid, deceived, and nearly killed. What else could happen?

Everything. The Meeting explodes as Grandfather's prophecies come true. The Shaman knows that Will Duane and his friends can make his vision of world peace a reality. Working together, his People and the most powerful corporation on earth can break down centuries of mistrust and treachery. The transformation can spread all over the globe.

The world where love is king can come to be.

Grandfather also knows that what they are doing at the Meeting is so important that all the forces of evil may arise to stop it.

And they do.

Which will prevail—cooperation and harmony or unrelenting strife? Is peace on earth something we can achieve? Or will our darkest nightmares rule?

Get ready for the next episode of Sandy Nathan's world of intrigue and mysticism.

MOGOLLON
(THE BLOODSONG SERIES II)

Trade Paperback ISBN 10: 0-9762809-7-3
Trade Paperback ISBN 13: 978-0-9762809-7-2

www.vilasapress.com
See sandynathan.com for more about author Sandy Nathan.

An excerpt from *Mogollon*, the sequel to Numenon

MOGOLLON
THE BLOODSONG SERIES II

1

She soared and dipped high over his head, an explosion of light from one wing tip to the other. He could make out her head: It was a bend in the arc punctuated by a curved beak and the bright points of her eyes. Will stood in a field, watching her sport in the dark sky above him. Bursts of light shot from the place where her body met the atmosphere: She seemed to be breaking a barrier as she flew. Delighted, he stretched his arms toward her and laughed.

She pivoted suddenly and pulled in her wings. Plummeting, she dove straight at him. Talons appeared. Her beak opened and she released a wild cry. Will dropped his hands to his sides. He wanted to run, but couldn't move. Her claws entered his eyes. He screamed as the talons tore their way to his heart. The eagle's eyes turned into those of the old Indian shaman. His face filled Will's mind as the claws dug deeper.

He was wandering among dozens of totems, craning his neck to see their tops. Carvings of whales, dolphins, wolves, and creatures that he couldn't recognize covered the massive poles. He carefully laid his hands on their ancient wood, the way he might have touched objects on an altar. Dark green, black, red, and white. Their colors were grayed with age, but their power remained undimmed. A shudder rippled across his shoulders.

Then he was inside the lodge. He and the shaman were to do a sweat ceremony together at the retreat. The lodge that would house their sweat was a magnificent log structure soaring high over his head and extending hundreds of feet. The totem poles guarded its entrance. The structure's beams and walls were covered with painted carvings. The shaman's warriors prepared for the sweat, piling logs in a fire pit below an opening in the ceiling.

Will and the old man sat by the fire, discussing politics and philosophy. The sweat was like being in the sauna at his club in San Francisco: a good place to unwind and talk about what mattered. Attendants came and went, bringing whatever they needed—ice water, clean towels. He and Grandfather discussed the problems of the people they served, getting to know each other and bonding.

He felt himself rise above that scene so that he was both in it and above it, watching. Manipulating. A smile lit his face as he prepared to do what he did best. After a sufficient interval, maybe twenty minutes, he told the old man about the mine. He—or his corporation, Numenon—had optioned the land just outside the reservation for the mine. Its mineral riches were barely conceivable. The feds required him to get the tribe's permission to mine the land, even though it was off the reservation. The shaman's approval was the only way to get the tribe to go along.

Will knew exactly how to sell the old man on the deal.

He had figured an angle that anyone would go for: cut the Indians in for a share. Of the profits from the completed project—the new nanotechnology computer chips—not just the ore. That was *major* cash flow. They'd make more in a year than all the Indians in the country did with their casinos. What they could do to improve their economic position with that wealth was staggering. He'd point out the benefits of the mine ... and the few problems.

But problems existed to be solved. They'd figure out a way to make the tailings look better. Flatten them out; maybe make a monument, a pyramid or something. Plant some trees. With their earnings, the Indians could turn the slag heap into Mount Rushmore. They'd forget the fact that the mine had destroyed their ancient burial grounds the minute the checks started rolling in.

He'd make them *rich*. No one could resist that.

Will had pondered various percentages to give them. He'd start with half a percent, but he'd go all the way to five if he had to. He could throw in some Numenon stock, put the whole tribe on the corporate health plan. The feds couldn't give them anything like that. Maybe he'd set up an employment training program. He'd even toss in management training. His trainers would whip them into shape pronto.

The shaman listened gravely, puffing on a pipe. He understood the benefits of the deal and wanted to go for it, but was a worthy opponent. He bargained all the way up to a 5 percent share before agreeing.

Will pulled out a contract. He'd be out of the sweat lodge and heading home in no time.

The old man leaned over to sign. Just before his pen touched paper, he looked at Will. Something shot from his eye. Will flew over backward, tumbling through space.

He was riding the eagle. Light burst from her head and wings as they flew. The world was as dark before, but different, as different as a clear stream of water was from a polluted river. Will gagged as they flew through toxic vapors and clung to the eagle. He could feel the strength in her body as she flew. She fought her way across the turgid gloom. Will began to feel dizzy and nauseous. Something terrible lay ahead. The night was permeated with … Will gasped as he realized it: the stalker. The evil that had hounded him all his life waited for them.

And he was riding against it, at last. Will felt no fear; he began to shout, urging the eagle to fly faster. When he shouted, a roar arose from behind him. He turned and saw an army of warriors covering the horizon, filling the sky. The warriors were mounted on eagles and horses and elephants, all manner of creatures. From all of history, they rose to fight the Evil One.

Before him, he could see nothing but darkness, feel nothing but malevolence. He heard the sound of leather wings flapping close by. Too late, he saw the shadow of a dark wing and its claw, the outline of a toothed beak. The teeth snapped.

Will was falling, dropping through space. The monster dropped faster, gaining on him. It would catch him …

Something touched his arm. He struck at it.

"Will. Will. Wake up." He struggled to awaken. Betty. It was Betty, his secretary for so many years. His friend. He opened his eyes, confused.

Betty's blue eyes looked into his. "Will. You were dreaming. I couldn't wake you."

He sat up in his command chair, coming into himself. He was in the *Ashley III*. His motor home. He could see Mark Kenna, the driver, peering out the windshield. He'd agreed to attend a Native American spiritual retreat; the others were accompanying him. They'd been traveling for hours, lost in the desert.

"Are we there, Mark?"

"Yes, sir. The Mogollon Bowl is right up ahead."

Will nodded, still not totally awake. What had happened? They had left the Bay Area at one a.m. Flew to Tucson and then traveled by motor home. They got lost. Images darted through his mind. Something had happened, but he couldn't remember properly. Something attacked him. He fought. Pain and then darkness. The memories were flashes, disappearing as fast as they came.

He bent forward, peering at the melee in front of the *Ashley* through the windshield. The desert looked just as it had since the sun rose on the caravan that morning: dusty, dirty, full of cacti and rocks, undoubtedly teeming with scorpions and snakes. But this was worse—look at those people.

At the entrance to the Bowl, their fellow retreat attendees surrounded them. The mélange of vehicles looked like a traffic jam from the 1970s. Not a single car was new; none were even from the 1990s. The junkers flowed over the incline ahead of them with camping stuff sticking out the windows and trunks. Other vehicles drove out of the Bowl, empty.

Will shook his head to clear it. The Mogollon Bowl they'd worked so hard to reach was just over that knoll. Betty gave a presentation as they drove. She said it was a supernatural site. The Bowl caused strange psychological changes. Will could feel them: His mind operated oddly, blurring the edge between what was real and what he wanted. And bringing those bizarre dreams.

"We're almost there," he said, smiling broadly. He was the man who mastered every challenge. "It's been a long trip, but it will be worth it. You'll see."

They pulled over the bank and got their first glimpse of their destination. Mark stopped the vehicle abruptly. Will jumped up and grabbed the back of the driver's chair, eyes widening and jaw going slack.

"What is it, Will?" Betty asked. She moved forward, straining for a look at the place where they would spend the next week.

"Oh, my God," she said.

The others were speechless.

What if the world was ending tomorrow morning at 7:35? And what if it was a thousand years later than you thought?

SANDY NATHAN CREATES A NEW REALITY IN...

THE ANGEL
& THE BROWN-EYED BOY

A NEW BOOK COMING SOON

An Excerpt

1

The girl appeared on the sidewalk. When she first showed up, the outlines of her body and clothing were fuzzy, as if all of her hadn't arrived She looked up and down the street, the way a person would if she'd forgotten an address or lost her way. Had anyone noticed her, they would have seen that everything about her was off-kilter. Her hair was frizzed and matted, sticking out akimbo. She was thin, had a dirty face, and wore a scratchy coat that was far too big. Its sleeves were rounded little capes and her arms stuck out of them like chopsticks protruding from under a napkin. The coat slipped off her shoulders, first to one side, then the other. She hitched it up and kept walking. When she walked, the coat opened to reveal her feet and lower legs.

Her thin socks, trimmed with grayed lace, were pulled up to make a ruffle below her knees. Pink satin laces held up the socks, their Xs snaking up her shins from her shoes. She looked pretty much like everyone in that neighborhood of disenchanted souls, except for the shoes. Long, pink ballet slippers stuck out from beneath her coat, as improbable as roses spouting from the cement.

She stopped and raised one foot, turning it gracefully and resting it easily on the other knee. She flicked the shoe with her finger, listening. A trill of clear notes deep within her brought the hint of a smile. She held the coat closed and stood still. She was where she was supposed to be. It had begun.

She fingered the piece of paper in her pocket. Her map. Beneath it, in the pocket's depths, was the notebook. What was written on it would get her where she needed to go. It was sufficient to ensure her success. She had all she needed; she knew that. She had been given enough.

Others walked along the hard, treeless path. To her left, gray, inert structures rose high in the sky, blocking the sun. Their lower levels, next to the path where she walked, had panels she could see through. She touched the see-through parts, looking at the lifeless people inside. Everything was cold. In the street, engines spewed poisons. No one noticed her—all were absorbed in frantic rushing. Her people had told her it would be like this. She choked when a very large carrier with many people inside passed, spewing smoke. She couldn't stay here. Better get on with her purpose. She didn't have much time.

Searching the faces streaming past, she tried to find the right one. A man with a round stomach and a gray hat walked with many others out of an opening in the ground. He walked like he had a mission. His coat was the same scratchy stuff as hers, but it was buttoned up and looked new. *He* looked new—his face was ruddy and clean. His shoes reflected the pale sunlight. The trill of notes resounded in her mind once again.

He was the one! She stood in front of him, making him stop. She hoped he could comprehend her speech.

"Will you help me?" she said, working to form the strange words.

He bent down to look at her. A homeless waif, dirty and lost. She didn't smell, thank God. But look at her. His eyes took her in, repelled. Then he saw her shoes. "You take ballet? My daughter takes ballet. Those are *pointe* shoes. You shouldn't be walking in those. They're just for dancing."

She listened intently, forming his words with her mouth. "Dance," she said with a tiny smile. She looked beautiful when she smiled. Something about her touched him.

He pulled a five-dollar bill out of his wallet. He never gave money to street people, but this was a new one: a bedraggled ballet dancer out begging. Probably her mother got the shoes at Goodwill and put her up to it.

He looked at her again and knew that she didn't have a mother, Not a mother on this earth, anyway.

"Take this," he said, handing her the bill. He wanted to get rid of her. The first race was starting soon. He had bets to place.

She looked at what he'd given her as if she'd never seen a fiver before, then up at him with wonder in her face. She pointed at the image of the Lincoln Memorial on the bill and whispered, "Temple." He could barely make out what she was saying, her foreign accent was so strong.

He tossed her another five. She had a good act, if it was an act. Yet everything about her told him it wasn't an act. She wasn't from anywhere near here. She was so foreign that he couldn't even realize how foreign she was. She'd never seen money, and she acted very strange. But she was wonderful, too. He felt wonderful being around her. He wanted to help her. He took a deep breath. She looked at the money and tried to give it back.

"It's for food." He pointed at his mouth. "Food. You know what that is, don't you? I gotta go." She didn't know what food was, he could see. She wanted him to do something. He looked around frantically. He always took the subway down here so his wife would see his car in the office parking lot when she checked up on him. He took two subway lines and a short cab ride to get to the track. She never knew he wasn't slaving away all day.

He was the boss. He could take an afternoon off once in a while. He could imagine the horses parading in the paddock area, ready to head onto the track. Overhead, flags would be flapping. All the guys would be there. "Hey, long time no see. The little lady keeping you on a short chain?" They'd drink beer and, for an entire afternoon, life would be what it should be.

"Sayonara, ballet princess. I gotta go." He tried to step around her, but couldn't.

"I gotta go," she whispered without moving. He couldn't move. Something about her was breathtaking. He knew he had to help her.

"Where do you want to go?"

"School." She looked at him with huge, solemn eyes.

"Well, go. I'm not stopping you."

"Where? Where is school?" She pulled a piece of paper out of her pocket. The name and address of a high school was written on it. The Hermitage Academy. Everyone had heard of it, it was famous. Kid actors and dancers and artists went there. "Dance school," she whispered, looking at him hopefully.

He got it: Some of those hippie artist kids looked like her. The ones on stage and such. He'd seen them on ads for plays like *Grunge* and *Road Dirt*. Maybe she fell out of her mommy's Rolls and ended up down here.

But she wasn't rich and she hadn't fallen off anything, except maybe another planet. "It's uptown, a long way." He tried to grab the paper and draw a map but she pulled it away, alarmed.

"Honey, I gotta go. I got people waiting. Take this, and hail one of those cabs. The yellow cars? That's a cab. Wave one down and go to school. Use the money I gave you. Here's some more." He gave her a twenty and then a demonstration of waving down a cab. None of them stopped for him.

They stopped for her. She walked into the traffic, looking into the eyes of a cabbie. Horns screamed and brakes shrieked.

"Whatsa matter with you? You crazy?" the cabbie bellowed. "You tryin' to get killed?"

The man scooped her into the cab and sat next to her. "The Hermitage Academy. That art school in Manhattan. The famous one. Take us there."

His hand shook when he placed his arm around her shoulder. Such a close call. He had to protect her. Light radiated from her, light and something good. She was here to do something important. Something good. He had to get her to the school, and then he could play the ponies.

The school looked like a prison, a stone-fronted hulk rimmed by chain link fencing with rolls of razor wire on top. The playground was concrete. All of it was unmarked by graffiti, which he took as a sign of its esteemed position in the world.

She looked at it, eyes wide. "School?"

"What's the matter? You haven't seen it before? That's your school. Right at the address you showed me. Go. I'm not taking you any further."

She fumbled with the door handle. He could see she had no clue how to get the door open.

"Jesus, do I have to do everything?" She looked at him with those clear eyes and he knew that he had done exactly the right thing. He got out and walked around the car, opening the door. He took her hand and set her on the curb. Her hand was as tiny as a little elf's. White and cold. "You button up that coat. Just walk across the street to that guard station. They'll let you in and see you get home."

She looked at him solemnly, digging into her pocket. She brought up a ragged notebook and opened it. Light blasted out of it. She showed him a page.

His eyes bulged. Letters blazed off of the paper. He couldn't believe what they said. He'd been working the numbers all week and knew every horse and its odds. This was amazing. He tried to take the book from her. "You even got their *weights* down. Where did you get this?"

She pulled away and said. "Write. This is for you. They are wins."

"How did you know that?"

"This for you. You help me."

He pulled out a pen and scribbled what was on the page. "Damn right it's good." How could anyone not believe tips that came from magical letters in a fairy's notebook? Just the same, he asked, "You sure this is right?"

"They are always right." Her wide gray eyes couldn't lie.

And they were right. Every horse on that list won by what she said it would. He won all day. He maxed out his credit cards—and he won and won. He wished he had more to bet. He'd bet the house if he could. His buddies were freaking out. Rich said, "Hey, let me bet with you. We can split the money."

Something inside him said no. What was in that little girl's notebook was only for him. If he tried to share it, it would all backfire.

He had to go through security when he left with his bags of money. Two men in black suits took him to an office under the track. It had filing cabinets, a desk, and a window covered with a grille high on the wall. He didn't mind. He already had eaten the paper on which he had written the tips. They couldn't nail him on anything.

They frisked him and questioned him. They had a file open on the desk. He started when he saw his pictures stapled in it. They had a file on him! One photo must have been taken at the window when he had made a bet. It had bars up and down; his face looked expectant. The other one showed him and his buddies sitting in the stands laughing. "A low-bet regular," it said under his photo. He was insulted.

"Hey guys, a little angel came to earth and sat on my shoulder." He grinned. They let him go; there was no reason for them to hold him. When he went back to that school and found that little girl, he'd come back. Tomorrow, they'd call him something else. They'd change the caption on his file to "All-time winner."

He stopped short. The girl. He had to get that girl. He was nothing without her.

www.sandynathan.com